Praise f

"Naked, noble, and i
of Sally MacKenzie's h
Times bestselling author

"Providing plenty of heat and hilarity, MacKenzie has great fun shepherding this boisterous party toward its happy ending; readers will be glad they RSVPed."
—*Publishers Weekly*

"The latest in MacKenzie's delectably sensual "Naked" historical Regencies series has plenty of sexy sizzle and charming wit."—*Booklist*

"MacKenzie continues her delightfully humorous, sexy series with a nice and naughty naked hero who matches wits and wiles with an equally irresistible heroine in the author's typically touching style."—*Romantic Times*

"With a hero and heroine every reader will fall in love with and secondary characters who love to meddle in their lives, you have the recipe for a romance you won't be able to put down."—A Romance Review

"If you're looking for a fun and sexy romp, sit back and prepare to enjoy yourself."—BooksForABuck.com

Praise for *The Naked Marquis*

"*The Naked Marquis* is an endearing confection of sweetness and sensuality, the romance equivalent of chocolate cake . . . every page is an irresistible delight!"
—Lisa Kleypas, *New York Times* bestselling author

"With a delightfully quirky cast of characters and heated bedroom encounters, MacKenzie's latest Naked novel delivers a humorous, sprightly romance."
—*Romantic Times*

"A pure delight . . . filled with very loveable characters, and perhaps the sexiest hero I've read in a long, long time."—Rakehell

"Charming . . . funny . . . full of delightful characters . . . *The Naked Marquis* merits a place on the keeper shelves of readers of the traditional Regency and the spicier Regency-set historical romances alike."—Romance Reviews Today

"A highly enchanting and thoroughly polished novel . . . you will not want to let the characters out of your sight. Their lives are your life, their discoveries are your discoveries, and their passions become your desires."—The Road to Romance

Praise for *The Naked Duke*

"MacKenzie sets a merry dance in motion in this enjoyable Regency romp."—*Booklist*

"This is a funny, delightful debut by a talented writer who knows how to blend passion, humor and the essence of the Regency period into a satisfying tale."
—*Romantic Times*

"A well-written and enjoyable first novel. Ms. MacKenzie has a wonderful voice."—The Romance Readers Connection

"Debut author Sally MacKenzie has penned a marvelously witty novel . . . Readers who enjoy a large dose of humor will love *The Naked Duke*. The characters are charming, and the pace is quick. It is the perfect book for a cozy winter retreat."—A Romance Review

"Sally MacKenzie's first novel, *The Naked Duke*, runs a range of emotions that will have you laughing out loud and then biting your nails in anticipation . . . The characters were realistic, the story was fast paced and the love story of an American girl returning to her father's homeland to find love and happiness is straight out of a fairy tale."—Fallen Angel Reviews

HIS KISS

Meg contented herself with the fiercest glare she could manage. "At the risk of repeating myself, Mr. Parker-Roth—*go away!*"

"And at the risk of repeating myself, Miss Peterson, no. I am not leaving you alone in this garden."

She really, really would like to kick him.

"Sir, you are not my keeper—"

"Bloody hell, woman." Mr. Parker-Roth transferred his grip to her shoulders. "Someone needs to be your damn keeper and I don't see a blasted queue forming for that honor."

"I do not need a kee—mpht."

The annoying man had covered her mouth with his own.

The Naked Gentleman

SALLY MACKENZIE

ZEBRA BOOKS

Kensington Publishing Corp.

www.kensingtonbooks.com

ZEBRA BOOKS are published by

Kensington Publishing Corp.
850 Third Avenue
New York, NY 10022

All Kensington titles, imprints, and distributed lines are available at special quantity discounts for bulk purchases for sales promotion, premiums, fund-raising, educational, or institutional use.

Special book excerpts or customized printings can also be created to fit specific needs. For details, write or phone the office of the Kensington Special Sales Manager: Attn. Special Sales Department. Kensington Publishing Corp., 850 Third Avenue, New York, NY 10022. Phone: 1-800-221-2647.

Zebra and the Z logo Reg. U.S. Pat. & TM Off.

ISBN-13: 978-0-8217-8076-3
ISBN-10: 0-8217-8076-X

First Printing: April 2008
10 9 8 7 6 5 4 3 2 1

Printed in the United States of America

For Dad; for Ruth; and, as always, for Kevin and the boys.

Chapter 1

Viscount Bennington was a terrible kisser.

Meg repressed a sigh. What a pity. She had been willing to overlook his receding hairline, large nose, and frequent petulance, but this was too much. How could she wed a man whose lips felt like two fat slugs? They were trailing wetly over her cheek toward her right ear at the moment.

She should strike him from her list of potential suitors.

Still, he did have one of the largest plant collections in England. She would dearly love to have daily access to all that botanical wealth.

The slugs had diverted to her jaw.

How important could kissing be? Only a small portion of one's married life was devoted to the amatory arts, after all. Chances were Viscount Bennington had a mistress or two. He'd only look to her for an heir. Once that task was accomplished, he would leave her alone.

She could do it. More than one woman had suffered through the activities of the marriage bed by lying still and thinking of England. She'd spend the time mentally cataloguing Bennington's vast gardens.

His lips wandered to a spot behind her ear. She would need a handkerchief to dry her face when he was finished slobbering over her.

She drew in a deep breath, but stopped when her lungs were only half full.

He smelled. The odor was quite pronounced at these close quarters. Thankfully he was only a few inches taller than she, so she did not have her nose squashed against his waistcoat.

And he should have a word with his valet about the state of his linen. There was a thin line of dirt on his collar and cravat.

Eww! He'd stuck his tongue in her ear.

That did it. He could own the Garden of Eden and she would still have to eliminate him from her list of possible husbands.

"My lord!" She shoved against his thin chest.

"Hmm?" His mouth moved down to the base of her neck and fastened there, just like a leech.

"Lord Bennington, please." She shoved again. None of the other men she'd taken into the shrubbery had been this bold. "You must stop . . . eep!"

His hands had slid down to her hips. He pulled her tight against him. She felt an ominous bulge in his pantaloons.

She shoved harder. She might as well be pushing against a stone wall. Who would have guessed such a short, scraggy man would be so immoveable?

"My lord, you are making me uncomfortable."

He pressed his bulge more tightly against her. "And *you* are making *me* uncomfortable, sweetings." His voice was oddly thick. His mouth returned to her skin. He nipped her shoulder.

"Ouch! Stop that."

The man was a viscount. A gentleman. Surely he would not do anything untoward in Lord Palmerson's garden, just yards away from a crowded ballroom?

He was not stopping. Now he was licking the place he had bitten. Disgusting.

"My lord, return me to Lady Beatrice this instant!"

He grunted and returned his mouth to her throat.

Should she scream? Would anyone hear her over the music? If she waited for the quiet between sets . . . Perhaps another couple had chosen to stroll in the cool night air and would come to her assistance.

Lord Bennington nuzzled her ear. "Don't be alarmed, Miss Peterson. My intentions are completely honorable."

"Honorable? I—" Meg paused. "Honorable as in marriage honorable?"

"Of course. What did you think?"

What *did* she think? Yes, he was somewhat revolting, but should a little dirt and slobber really eliminate him from matrimonial consideration? This was her goal, to be wed or engaged before the Season ended. The Season was barely a month under way and here she was already on the verge of a respectable—no, a brilliant— offer. A vicar's daughter nabbing a viscount? The society gossips would have their tongues working overtime to spread the news.

He did have all those lovely plants. A greenhouse and garden in London and acres of vegetation in Devon.

Really, how many times would she have to put up with his attentions if she married him? Papa and Harriet were extremely attached to each other, and her sister and her friend Lizzie spent a great deal of time with their husbands, but most married couples of the *ton* barely saw each other. If she were lucky, she would conceive quickly, maybe even on her wedding night. Then she and Bennington could go their separate ways.

She could endure a few moments of inconvenience to get the key to his greenhouse, couldn't she? There was no one else who had such a wealth of plants. Well, no one but Parks—Mr. Parker-Roth—and *he* clearly wasn't interested in marrying her.

She moistened her lips. Could she say yes? It was past time she wed. She wanted a home of her own. A garden. Children.

Children with Lord Bennington's overwhelming nose?

"My lord, I don't . . ."

"Come, Miss Peterson. You won't get another offer. Surely you know that."

"Lord Bennington!" He might be a viscount, but that did not give him license to be insulting.

"The other men haven't mentioned marriage, have they?"

"The other men?" Had he noticed her excursions into the shrubbery? Surely not. She'd been very discreet. "I'm not certain what you mean. I thought since we share an interest in horticulture, touring Lord Palmerson's garden with you would be stimulating."

He chuckled and flexed his hips. His annoying bulge dug into her. "Very stimulating."

Something was definitely stimulated. Who would have thought such a short man would have such a large, um . . .

"My lord . . ."

"At this rate, you are more apt to lose your reputation than win a husband, Miss Peterson. Men talk, you know."

It was a very good thing the garden was dark. Meg felt her cheeks burning. Surely he didn't think . . . ?

"Lord Bennington, I assure you—"

"Oh, I know you haven't done anything but exchange a few kisses. Lord Farley said you were quite untutored. Thought he might have been your first. Was he?"

"Lord Bennington! Please. I would like to return to the ballroom *now*."

"I imagine at your advanced age you are a little curious." He laughed. "Probably a little desperate, too."

"My lord, I am only twenty-one."

"Right. Well past the age when you might expect to grab a husband, hmm?"

"Not at all."

"Come now, Margaret. I may call you Margaret, mayn't I? I believe we're sufficiently acquainted to dispense with the proprieties."

His left hand landed on her bodice.

She grabbed his wrist. Somehow he had managed to shed his gloves. "No, we are definitely not sufficiently acquainted."

"You are just suffering from maidenly fears, sweetings." His fingers brushed across the tops of her breasts.

"Lord Bennington!"

"Call me 'Bennie.' All my intimates do."

"I couldn't possibly. Remove your hand this instant."

He moved it to her shoulder.

"I'm thirty-six. It's time I thought of getting an heir. Your family is respectable. Your father is connected to the Earl of Landsdowne, isn't he?"

"He is Lord Landsdowne's uncle, but the earl doesn't concern himself with us." She looked through the leaves toward the beckoning light. Did she see movement in the shadows? She hoped someone was nearby to assist her if necessary.

The viscount's fingers stroked her skin. She clenched her teeth.

"But your sister is the Marchioness of Knightsdale. I'm certain she concerns herself with you. Didn't she raise you after your mother died?"

"Yes. The ballroom, my lord. It is past time we returned." His palm was unpleasantly damp.

"And the Countess of Westbrooke is your good friend."

"Yes, yes." Had the man made a study of all her connections? "The ballroom, Lord Bennington. Please escort me back to the ballroom. If you wish to discuss my family further, we can do so there."

"And both the earl and the marquis are close friends of the Duke of Alvord—in fact, the earl is the duchess's cousin."

"Lord Bennington . . ."

"I would like to be connected to all that power and wealth. Any one of those men could finance an expedition to the jungles of South America without a second thought."

"Jungles? South America?" Had the man lost his mind?

"I want to send my own men out to find exotic plants, Margaret."

"I see." She would like to do that, too, but it was clearly impossible. "An expedition such as you are describing is very expensive. Mr. Parker-Roth was telling me—"

Bennington's hand tightened on her shoulder.

"My lord, you are hurting me."

"You know Parker-Roth?"

"Slightly. I met him at a house party last year." Meg shifted position. "Please, Lord Bennington, you will leave a bruise."

He loosened his fingers. "My pardon. I just cannot abide the man. He's a neighbor of mine. Spends most of his time in the country."

"Ah." So that was why she hadn't seen him in Town—not that she'd been looking, of course.

"It's disgusting the way everyone fawns over him when he does attend a Horticultural Society meeting. *He* has plenty of money—he sends his brother all over the globe looking for plant specimens."

"I see." Lord Bennington's hold on her had slackened. Would he let her go now? "Shall we return to the ballroom, my lord?"

"But you haven't given me your answer."

"Answer?"

"Yes. Will you marry me or not?"

Lord Bennington was frowning at her, all signs of passion gone. She found it quite easy to make up her mind.

"I am very sorry, my lord. I am fully aware of the great honor you do me, but I believe we would not suit."

The frown deepened.

"What do you mean, we would not suit?"

"We would not . . . suit." What did the man want her to say? That she thought he was a hideous oaf and she had made a huge error in judgment even speaking to him?

"You brought me into this dark garden and yet you are turning down my offer?"

"I really did not expect an offer of marriage, my lord."

"What kind of an offer did you expect? Are you looking for a slip on the shoulder, then?"

"My lord! Of course not. I was not expecting an offer *now*. I mean, I was not expecting an offer of anything—

any offer at all. I just wished to take a turn about the garden."

"Miss Peterson, I was not born yesterday. You lured me into this darkened corner for a reason. Was it just to steal a kiss? Are you that starved for amorous activity?"

"Lord Bennington!" Had the man actually said "amorous" with regard to her?

"You are not going to use me to satisfy your urges."

Urges! Her only urge was to get back to the light and sanity of the ballroom.

The viscount was becoming markedly agitated. She really had not anticipated such a reaction. The other men had been completely amiable when she'd suggested they go back inside. Lord Bennington was almost hissing.

"You chose to come into the garden with me, so now you'll pay the price. When I'm finished with you, your wealthy relatives and friends will beg me to wed you."

"Lord Bennington, be reasonable. You are a gentleman."

"I am a man, Miss Peterson. Surely your sister has warned you it is highly unwise to be alone with a man in an isolated place."

Emma had warned her of many things—perhaps she should have listened to this particular lecture. At least she would be spared Emma's jobation this time—her sister was safely ensconced in Kent with her children. If she could just get away from Bennington, all would be well. She had learned her lesson. She would not be visiting any shadowy shrubbery again.

The viscount stuck his hands into her coiffure, sending pins flying everywhere. Her hair cascaded over her shoulders.

"Lord Bennington, stop immediately!"

He grunted. He had his hands on her bodice again. She jerked her knee up, but she missed her target.

"Playing that game, are you?"

"My lord, I will scream."

"Please do. The scandal will be delightful. How much do you suppose the marquis will pay to keep it quiet?"

"Nothing."

"Oh, Miss Peterson, you *are* naïve."

He mashed his mouth on hers, parting her lips. His tongue slithered between her teeth like a snake, threatening to choke her. She did the only thing she could think of.

She bit down hard.

John Parker-Roth—Parks to his friends and acquaintances—stepped out of the heat and noise of Lord Palmerson's ballroom into the cool quiet of the garden.

Thank God. He could still smell the stench of London, but at least he wasn't choking any longer on the foul mix of perfume, hair oil, stale breath, and sweat that permeated the air inside. Why his mother wanted to subject herself to that crush of humanity was beyond him.

He chose a path at random. Palmerson's garden was large for Town. If he could ignore the cacophony of music and conversation spilling out of the house and the general clamor from the street, he could almost imagine he was back in the country.

Almost. Damn. Had the plants Stephen sent arrived yet? He should be home to receive them. If they'd traveled all the way from South America to die waiting to be unpacked at the Priory . . . It didn't bear thinking of.

Would MacGill follow his instructions exactly? He'd

written them down in detail and gone over each point
with the man, but the pigheaded Scot always thought
he knew best. All right, usually he did. MacGill was a
bloody fine head gardener, but still, these plants required careful handling.

He wanted to be there himself. Why had his mother
insisted on dragging him to Town now?

He blew out a pent up breath. He knew why—the
blasted Season. She said it was to get more painting supplies and to catch up with her artist friends, but she
didn't fool him. She wanted him wed.

He'd heard Palmerson had a good specimen of *Mag-
nolia grandiflora.* He'd see if he could find it. With luck
it would be in the farthest, darkest corner of the
garden. He wouldn't put it past his mother to come out
here looking for him, dragging her latest candidate for
his hand behind her.

Why the hell couldn't she accept the fact he did not
want to marry? He'd told her time after time. Was it
such a hard message to understand?

Apparently it was. He grimaced. Now she sighed and
got that worried frown every time she looked at him.

He batted aside a drooping vine. The fact of the
matter was there was no need for him to marry. He
didn't have a title to pass on. The Priory could go to
Stephen or Nicholas, if Father didn't outlive them all.
He was very happy with his life. He had his work—his
plants and his gardens. He had an accommodating
widow in the village, not that he visited her much any
more. Frankly, he'd rather be working in his rose beds
than Cat's bed. The roses were less trouble.

No, a wife would just be an annoyance.

Damn it, was that rustling in the shrubbery? That
would make this evening complete—stumbling over

some amorous couple in the bushes. He veered away from the suspect vegetation.

The problem was Mother firmly believed marriage was necessary for male contentment. He took a deep breath and let it out slowly. God give him patience. Didn't she ever open her eyes and look around the bloody ballrooms she'd been dragging him to? *She* might be happily married, and Father might be content, but most husbands and wives were not.

He had no interest in stepping into parson's mousetrap. Maybe if Grace had—

No. He would not entertain such a ridiculous notion. He'd decided that years ago. Grace had made her choice, and she was happy. Last he'd heard, she had two children. She'd been in the ballroom just now. He'd seen her laughing up at her husband at the end of the last set.

The noise from the bushes was getting louder. Wonderful. Were the lovers having a spat? That was the last thing he wanted to witness. He would just—

"You *bitch*!"

Good God, that was Bennington's voice. The man had the devil's own temper. Surely he wouldn't—

"My lord, please." The girl's voice held a thread of fear. "You are hurting me."

He strode forward without another thought.

She must not panic. Bennington was a gentleman.

He looked like a monster. He stared at her through narrowed eyes, nostrils flaring, jaw hardened. His hands gripped her upper arms. She was certain his fingers would leave bruises.

"You *bitch*!"

"My lord, please." She moistened her lips. Fear made

it hard to get her breath. He was so much stronger than she, and the garden was so dark.

He was a viscount, a peer, a gentleman. He wouldn't really harm her, would he?

She had never seen a man so angry.

"You are hurting me."

"Hurting you? Ha! I'll show you hurting."

He shook her so her head flopped on her neck like a rag doll's, then he yanked her bodice down, tearing the fabric. He grabbed her breast and squeezed. The pain was excruciating.

"Bite me, will you? How would you like me to bite your—"

A well-tailored forearm appeared at his throat.

He made a gagging sound, releasing her to claw at the black silk sleeve cutting across his neck.

"You bastard." Mr. Parker-Roth jerked Lord Bennington back, spun the viscount around, and slammed his fist into the man's jaw, sending him backward into a holly bush. Meg would have cheered if she hadn't been trying so hard not to cry. She pulled up her bodice and crossed her arms over her chest.

"Parker-Roth." Bennington spat out the name along with some blood as he extracted himself from the prickly vegetation. "What the hell is the matter with you? The lady invited me into the garden."

"I'm certain she didn't invite you to maul her."

"A woman who goes off alone with a man . . ."

". . . is not asking to be raped, Bennington."

The viscount opened his mouth, then closed it abruptly. His jaw was beginning to swell and he had blood on his cravat. "I wasn't going to . . . I wouldn't, of course . . . I merely lost my temper." He glanced at Meg. "My humble apologies, Miss Peterson. I will do the proper thing, of course, and speak to your brother-in-law in the morning, then travel down to Kent to see your father."

"No!" She swallowed and took a deep breath. She spoke slowly and distinctly, "I will not marry you. I would not marry you even if you were the last man in England—no, the last man in all the world."

"Now, Margaret—"

"You heard Miss Peterson, Bennington. I believe she was quite clear as to her sentiments. Now do the *proper* thing and take yourself off."

"But—"

"I will be happy to assist you in finding the back gate—in fact I would be delighted to kick your miserable arse out into the alley."

"Margaret . . . Miss Peterson."

"Please, Lord Bennington, I assure you there is nothing you can say to persuade me to entertain your suit."

"You are merely overset. I was too impassioned, perhaps."

"*Perhaps?*" She pressed her lips together. She would not have a fit of the vapors here in Lord Palmerson's garden.

He frowned at her, and then sketched a small bow. "Very well, I will leave since you insist." He turned, then paused. "I do apologize most sincerely."

Meg nodded. He did sound contrite, but she just wanted him gone. She closed her eyes, listening to his steps fade away. She could not bear to look at the man still standing beside her.

Why had *Parks* been the one to find her in such an embarrassing situation? What must he think of her?

Perhaps he would just go away and let her expire in solitude.

She felt a gentle touch on her cheek.

"Miss Peterson, are you all right?"

She shook her head.

"I'm so sorry you had to endure Bennington's attentions. You shouldn't have . . . Well, he is not the sort of man you should . . . He has a terrible temper."

That was supremely evident.

"You can't go back to the ballroom like this. Who is your chaperone?"

She forced herself to speak. "Lady Beatrice."

"I shall fetch her. Will you be all right alone?"

"Y-yes." She bit her lip. She would not cry—well, not until he left.

He made an odd noise, a short exhalation that sounded both annoyed and resigned.

"Oh, for God's sake, come here."

His hands touched her shoulders, urging her gently toward him. She resisted for only a heartbeat.

The first sob escaped as her face touched his waistcoat. She felt his arms, warm and secure, come around her, felt his hand lightly touch her hair. A tight knot in her chest loosened.

She sobbed harder.

Parks repressed a sigh. The girl was Miss Margaret Peterson—Meg, Westbrooke had called her. He'd met her at Tynweith's house party last spring. He'd liked her. She'd seemed quite levelheaded—very knowledgeable about garden design and plants in general. He'd enjoyed talking to her.

And looking at her.

All right, he *had* enjoyed looking at her. She was very attractive. Slim, but with generous curves in all the right places. Warm brown eyes with flecks of gold and green. Silky brown hair.

He tangled his fingers in that hair, massaging the back of her head. She felt very nice in his arms. It had been too long since he'd held a woman.

Much too long, if he was feeling amorous urges toward a lady who was blubbering all over his cravat. He would pay Cat a visit as soon as he got back to the Priory, right after he checked on that plant shipment.

He patted her shoulder. Her skin was so smooth, soft . . .

He dropped his hand to the safety of her corseted back.

What had she been thinking, coming out into Palmerson's dark garden with a man of Bennington's stamp? Was she no better regarded than she should be? She *had* been a guest at Tynweith's scandalous house party.

And had behaved perfectly properly there. She had gone into the garden with him, but always in the daylight and always to discuss a particular planting.

She made a peculiar little sound, a cross between a sniff and a hiccup.

"Are you all right, Miss Peterson?"

She nodded, keeping her head down.

"Here—take my handkerchief."

"Thank you."

She still would not meet his eyes.

He studied her. There was enough light to see one slender white shoulder was completely exposed, as was the lovely curve of her breast . . .

He moved his hips back to save her the shock of his sudden attraction.

Damn, he had *definitely* been too long without a woman.

"I'm sorry to be such a watering pot. I've thoroughly soaked your clothing."

"You've had an upsetting experience." He cleared his throat. "You do know you shouldn't be alone with a man in the darkened shrubbery, don't you?"

"Yes, of course." She stepped a little away from him. "None of the others so forgot themselves."

"Others? There have been others?"

Meg flushed. Parks looked so shocked.

"I'm not a debutante."

"No, but you are young and unmarried."

"Not so young. I'm twenty-one."

Parks lifted an eyebrow. Meg felt a spurt of annoyance. Was the man criticizing her?

"Lady Beatrice has not commented on my behavior."

He lifted the eyebrow higher. Suddenly she wanted to grab his spectacles and grind them under her slipper. She was so tired of people looking at her in just that way.

"Ohh, you are as bad as the rest of the priggish, nasty beasts in that ballroom."

She spun on her heel, took a step—and caught her foot on a root.

"Aaa!" She was falling face first toward the holly bush Bennington had recently vacated.

Strong hands grabbed her and hauled her up against a rock hard chest. She shivered. The cool night air raised goose bumps on her arms and . . .

She looked down. Her breasts had fallen completely out of her dress.

"Ack!"

"What's the matter?"

"Close your eyes!"

"What?"

Oh, lud, was that the crunch of shoes on gravel? Someone was coming this way! She had to hide.

There was no place to hide. She twisted around and plastered herself up against Parks. Perhaps God would work a miracle and make her invisible.

The Almighty was not interested in assisting her this evening.

"Halooo! Mr. Parker-Roth . . . is that you? I didn't know you were in Town."

"Ooo." Meg muffled her moan in Parks's cravat. It couldn't be . . . Please, not Lady Dunlee, London's biggest gossip!

She felt Parks's arms tighten around her. His response rumbled under her cheek.

"I've recently arrived, Lady Dunlee. Good evening, my lord."

"Good evening, Parker-Roth. We were just taking a turn in the garden, but, um . . ." Lord Dunlee cleared his throat. "I, um, believe it's time we returned to the ballroom."

"Just a minute." Lady Dunlee's voice was sharp. "Who's that with you in the shrubbery, sir? I can't see."

"My dear, I think we interrupt the gentleman."

Lady Dunlee snorted. "Obviously. The question is, what exactly are we interrupting?"

Meg closed her eyes. She was going to die of embarrassment.

"That's Miss Peterson, isn't it? My word, I had no idea you two were quite so . . . friendly."

Chapter 2

It looked as if his mother was going to get her wish.

Parks crossed his arms and stood in a corner of the small parlor where Lady Palmerson had deposited them. She'd given Miss Peterson a shawl and him a contemptuous look before leaving to find Lady Beatrice. She must have assumed Miss Peterson's reputation was as shredded as her gown—or that he had exhausted his animal instincts—since she closed the door behind her when she left.

Damn, damn, damn. He looked up and met the accusatory scowl of some long dead Palmerson ancestor.

I'm innocent, God damn it. I'm the hero of this tale, not the villain.

The painted peer was not impressed.

What the hell was he going to do? He felt society's noose tightening around his neck as surely as if he were off to dance the Tyburn jig.

Miss Peterson sat on the settee, staring down at her slippers, worrying the fringe on her borrowed shawl.

He should have left her to Bennington. If the man was to be believed, it was the girl's own fault she found herself in the bushes with an over-amorous male.

No. He wouldn't wish Bennington on any woman. And Miss Peterson had looked completely terrified when he'd come upon them. She must not have known what the man was capable of.

Why *had* she asked Bennington to stroll in the shrubbery?

Well, it really didn't matter now. There was no way in hell they were going to keep their interesting little garden scene a secret. He'd wager his latest plant shipment that Lady Dunlee was already spreading the shocking news as fast as her short little legs would carry her around the ballroom.

Only an act of God would save him now, and it appeared the Almighty was in league with Mother. Would she approve of Miss Peterson?

He watched the woman twist the shawl's fringe. "If you aren't careful, you will ruin that."

"What?" She finally looked up at him.

"The fringe. You are in danger of pulling it out."

"Oh." She smoothed the colored silk and sighed. "I am very sorry to have gotten you into this mess."

He grunted. He didn't trust himself to say more.

"I'll explain everything, of course. You don't have to worry that there will be any repercussions."

He snorted. "Miss Peterson, if you think I'll escape unscathed from this evening's little contretemps, you have windmills in your head."

She frowned up at him. "What do you mean?"

Good God, she could not be that dense, could she? If she were, it didn't bode well for the intelligence of his future offspring.

Future offspring. His traitorous body leapt at the thought.

Damn. He had most definitely been too long without a woman.

But that was going to change, wasn't it? He studied Miss Peterson. If he had to marry, he could do far worse. Her hair was lovely, spread out over her borrowed shawl, the candlelight picking out golden strands among the warm brown mass. It was straight, smooth. Silky. His fingers twitched at the memory. And her skin was creamy, tinged pink at the moment. Her mouth . . . her full lower lip begged to be kissed. The tip of her tongue peeked out to moisten it . . .

He had a sudden vision of her stretched naked on his bed.

He turned away abruptly.

"What's the matter?"

"Nothing." He adjusted the fall of his pantaloons. *Think about soil composition. Watering schedules. The new plant shipment.*

"Why were you looking at me like that?"

He cleared his throat. "Like what?"

"You were staring at my hair."

Anger was a good antidote to desire, wasn't it? And he certainly had plenty to be angry about. He turned back to face Miss Peterson.

Bloody hell! She had let the shawl slip. He could see her lovely rose-colored nipple blooming from the snow white of her breast.

She followed his gaze.

"Eek!"

The beautiful skin disappeared under the fabric.

Anger. He was supposed to feel anger, not this maddening desire—maddeningly obvious desire. He hadn't had such an uncontrolled physical response to a woman in years, not since he was little more than a boy.

He couldn't turn away again, so he stepped behind a splendidly ugly upholstered high-backed chair.

Was it possible to die of embarrassment, Meg wondered? Apparently not or she'd have cocked up her toes already.

Mr. Parker-Roth had seen her br—

She'd fan her cheeks if she didn't have both hands fully occupied clutching this shawl.

He was obviously appalled by the situation. He was hopping around as if he could barely contain his annoyance. And now he was hiding behind that hideous red chair. Did he think she was going to attack him?

This evening had been a disaster. Who would have thought Lord Bennington would behave in such an outrageous fashion? And then to have Parks come along. Meg closed her eyes and bit her lips on a moan. Of all the men in England, why did it have to be him? Wouldn't Lord Dunlee have done as well?

Parks *had* dispatched the viscount decisively—it was unlikely Lord Dunlee was so handy with his fives. And when he'd caught her from falling . . . Well, she had admired the depth of his botanical understanding during Lord Tynweith's house party, but she had not fully appreciated all his other attributes.

She flushed. All right, she had dreamt of his dark brown hair, green eyes, and slow smile more than once. Several times. Almost every night. But if she'd known he had rock-hard muscles, she would never have gotten any sleep.

How could she have guessed? He looked like a scholar with his spectacles. He'd sounded like a scholar when he'd discussed Repton's *Fragments on the Theory and Practice of Landscape Gardening* with her at the house party. He'd been so intent, so passionate. She'd been captivated by his mind.

It was a very good thing she'd not been aware of exactly how captivating his body was. She examined what wasn't hidden by the chair. Hmm. What would he look like without all that muffling cloth?

It really was uncomfortably warm in this room. She would benefit from a fan and an unencumbered hand with which to wield it.

"We should talk before Lady Palmerson returns with your chaperone and my mother."

"Your mother?" Lud! She was sure her eyes were starting from her head.

Parks had a mother? Well, of course he did. Most people had a mother tucked away somewhere. Except her. Her mother had died not long after she was born. But gentlemen's mothers were supposed to stay conveniently absent in the country, unless they had a daughter to put on the Marriage Mart.

"Your mother is here?" Had she squeaked? She swallowed. She had to get her voice under control. "Is your sister out this year?"

He frowned. "No. Jane is already married, and Juliana and Lucy are too young."

"Oh. Yes, of course." She'd met his sister Jane at some society function last year. "I haven't seen Lady Motton this Season, have I?"

"No, fortunately for you." He smiled slightly. "Poor Jane is not the most pleasant companion at the moment. She is increasing—well, she has already increased significantly at this point—and is not terribly comfortable. And when Jane is uncomfortable, everyone else is as well."

Meg understood completely. "Emma was the same way, especially at the end. You must not consider upon it too much. Is the baby due soon?"

"Not for a month or so." He cleared his throat. "But that is beside the point."

It certainly was. Meg felt another spurt of panic. Parks's mother was going to see her with her hair down and her dress torn. She couldn't do anything about her dress, but could she fix her hair? Impossible. Even if she had any pins, which she didn't, she couldn't let go of her shawl long enough to manage the task.

"What am I going to do?"

"I don't believe you have any choice, Miss Peterson."

The man was right. The hair would have to stay as it was, unless . . . ? He was looking at it again. Well, not *looking* precisely. Darting glances, really. What was the matter with him?

"I don't suppose you know how to braid hair, do you?"

"Braid hair?" Now he was staring at her as if she were completely addled.

"Yes. You do have sisters. I thought perhaps you'd know how."

"God give me strength! Why are you talking about your hair?"

"Because your mother will be here at any minute and I don't want to look like a scarecrow."

Parks grabbed the back of the chair so hard his knuckles showed white. "Believe me, Miss Peterson, my mother will not be concerned about your hair."

"I wouldn't be so certain about that. I look a complete hoyden." She grabbed the shawl with one hand and tried to gather her hair with the other. She felt cool air—and Parks's gaze—on her chest. She flushed, dropping her arm. Apparently the shawl was not quite large enough.

"I assure you, Miss Peterson, my mother will not remark upon your hair. She will have much more interesting things to occupy her mind."

"She will?" If she knotted the shawl in front, would it stay in place when she lifted her arms? She would feel much better if her hair was properly restrained. "What else could possibly concern her? This really is not the time to play guessing games, sir."

Was that his teeth she heard grinding?

"I am not playing guessing games!"

"There is no need to shout. My hearing is perfectly adequate."

"Your hearing may be, but your understanding is sadly lacking."

"Mr. Parker-Roth!"

"Miss Peterson! You do understand that we will be compelled to marry?"

Her jaw dropped. The man's tone was beyond insulting. He might just have said they'd be compelled to crawl naked through a bramble bush. Well, she knew she was not a diamond of the first water but she was not precisely an antidote, either.

She shot to her feet, tugging the shawl securely around her. "I'm so delighted the prospect of wedding me sends you into such raptures."

Parks frowned. He was eyeing the shawl. "I did not come to this blasted ball with the expectation that I'd leave an engaged man."

"And you won't. I *told* you I would explain everything."

Did the man roll his eyes? She stepped closer. Her hands went to her hips—until she felt a slight breeze and his gaze on her skin again. Damnation. She knotted one hand securely in the ends of the shawl, sidestepped the chair he was hiding behind, and poked him in the chest with her finger.

"Don't condescend to me, Mr. Parker-Roth. I will make it very clear to your mother and Lady Beatrice that you are not the villain of this piece."

He trapped her hand against his body. "And will you also make it very clear to the rest of the *ton*? Will you hurry off to the ballroom, dressed as you are—or rather, *not* dressed as you are—and make an announcement?"

"Of course not! Don't be ridiculous." She pulled back, but he wouldn't release her.

"Then how are you going to stop the news from flying through society? Come, Miss Peterson, surely you know Lady Dunlee is flitting through the ballroom right now, like a bee in a flower bed, spreading every detail she noted."

"No one will care what we were doing." She was only a vicar's daughter after all—and a marquis's sister-in-law. She tried to ignore the dread growing in her stomach.

Parks snorted. "How long have you been in society, Miss Peterson?"

"This is my second Season—"

"Then you know everyone cares what we were doing."

"Well—"

"*And* you know you can't stop the gossip just by addressing the crowd in Palmerson's ballroom. I'm certain several people have already hurried off to their next engagement hoping they'll be the first to entertain their acquaintances with Lady Dunlee's delightful report. No, you'll have to take out space in all the papers to stop this story—and, of course, that won't work either, will it?"

"You are absurd."

"I am correct. Admit it, Miss Peterson. You are as surely caught as I." One of his obnoxious eyebrows flew up. "But perhaps that is what you wanted. Why *did* you invite Bennington into the garden?"

She dropped her gaze to study his cravat. It was sadly limp. Cravats were not designed to be cried on.

"Miss Peterson?"

She did not want to lie to him, but she most definitely did not want to tell him the truth, that she was auditioning potential husbands.

A sharp note entered his voice and his grip on her hand tightened. "Did you hope to catch a viscount? Is that what this was all about? You were angling for a title?"

"No, of course not."

"Speak up, Miss Peterson. My waistcoat cannot hear you."

She raised her chin to meet his gaze. "I was not interested in Lord Bennington's title, sir."

The right corner of his mouth crooked up, but he did not look amused.

"No? What *were* you interested in then? I do not presume to know the female mind, but I would not have supposed Bennington had much else to recommend him."

Parks had a very nice mouth. Surely *his* lips wouldn't feel like slugs on her skin.

"The viscount has extensive horticultural holdings."

The lips turned up into a sneer.

"Miss Peterson, you cannot go to bed with his begonias."

She sucked in her breath. "You are insulting, sirrah!"

She jerked back again. His hold on her was unbreakable. Not that his fingers were hurting hers—they weren't. Neither did they appear to exert any effort to keep her in place.

Somehow he had managed to shed his gloves between the garden and this small room, but his hands were not hot and damp like Bennington's. They were warm, strong, tanned from his hours working with his plants.

She wished she could remove her own gloves to better feel his touch. Her breasts tingled, as if they, too, would like to encounter his fingers.

What an idea! Heat flooded her—her face must be as red as a ripe tomato.

"How many men have you lured into a darkened corner?"

"Mr. Parker-Roth, I must insist that you release me." She certainly was not going to answer that question. Not that the number was so great. There had been only five before Bennington.

"Did they all maul you? Is that what you want, Miss Peterson? Are you that anxious for male attention?"

The man was insufferable. His words were beyond insulting. She opened her mouth to give him a set down and noticed a peculiar gleam in his eye. It was . . . hot. Quite at odds with his cold tone.

"Shall I kiss you, then? Is that what you would like?"

"Yes, indeed."

It wasn't until she saw the startled look in his eyes that she realized she had spoken aloud.

Good God! Parks blinked. Had he heard correctly? She wanted him to *kiss* her?

What was it about this woman? He did not make a habit of lusting after ladies of the *ton*. Of course, most society ladies did not appear in shredded bodices with their hair tumbled about their shoulders. When she had asked him if he could braid it for her, he'd thought he was going to explode. To have his fingers in all that warm silk again . . . And then she kept moving her arms so her lovely white breasts flickered in and out of view.

And now the girl had asked him to kiss her.

She was mad—and maddening. A proper young lady would be sitting demurely on that settee, sobbing quietly into her handkerchief, overset by the scene in the garden. Hopeful that she would get an engagement ring on her finger immediately. But when he'd stated the obvious, Miss Peterson had flown into the boughs. She'd put her hands on her hips—until she realized what a delightful view it afforded him—and had poked him in the chest. And now she'd asked him to kiss her.

He was a gentleman, first and foremost. He could never turn down a lady's request.

He smiled slightly. She was gaping up at him as if she had even shocked herself. How nice that her mouth was already ajar. He would perhaps discover just how much she'd learned from those other men.

He kept her hand cradled against his chest, but pulled her slightly closer. She came without protest. He bent slowly, giving her time to flee, but she stood still, like a startled deer.

His mouth touched hers. He half expected her to bolt then, just as a deer would when one approached too close, but she didn't. Her lips were soft and motionless under his.

He cupped her jaw with his free hand, stroking her cheek with his thumb. It was soft, like a rose petal. She smelled of roses, too—light, sweet.

She made a small inarticulate noise. Her other hand released its grip on the shawl to come up to rest on his waistcoat. Still her mouth was quiescent under his.

He smiled slightly, putting his arms around her, gently pulling her close. These were not the reactions of an experienced woman. Whatever Miss Peterson had been doing in the shrubbery with the men of the *ton*, she had not lost her air of innocence. It was proving incredibly seductive.

He ran a hand through her hair, lifting a heavy length away from her neck. He trailed kisses along her jaw line to a spot just below her ear. She tilted her head, giving him more room. Her breath came in little pants. Her hands slid up to his shoulders, and her shawl slipped to reveal more of her creamy skin.

Beautiful.

The line of her throat, her collar bone, the sweet curve of her breast. He gathered one breast into his hand. It was warm and heavy, filling his palm. He glanced at her face for any sign of alarm at his boldness, but her eyes were closed. Her small white teeth caught her lower lip.

He kissed each eyelid lightly while he stroked the treasure in his palm. Her body sagged into his.

When his thumb found her hard, stiff nipple, she inhaled—and he let his tongue follow into her moist heat.

His last coherent thought was a wish.

If only the door were locked and the settee bigger.

Embarrassment was definitely not fatal—she had proven that too many times to count tonight. Had she actually asked Parks to *kiss* her? Surely not. But then why had his eyes widened in just that fashion? And then they'd narrowed and assumed a very alert, intent gaze.

She should step back. He had her hand against his chest, but he would let her go if she wanted. He would not force her. There was no coercion in his hold.

She felt a slight pressure urging her closer, and she went. He was going to grant her request. She knew it.

She should move her head away from his descending lips.

She couldn't move. Like a field mouse faced with an adder, she stood perfectly still, but unlike the field mouse, she wanted to be caught.

She watched his mouth come closer. She closed her eyes.

His lips were cool and firm on hers. Gentle. Asking, not demanding. Inviting, promising, teasing.

His fingers cradled her jaw, his thumb brushed her cheek. His skin was slightly rough against hers, but his touch was light.

Her heart beat like the wings of a caged bird. Heat pooled low in her stomach. An odd throbbing started even lower, in the space between her legs. She felt dampness there.

What did it mean?

Her legs felt weak, as if they could no longer support her. She braced herself against his chest with both hands. She needed to feel his arms around her before her knees turned to water.

He must have read her mind. Thank God.

He brought her carefully against him. His strength surrounded her. She felt his heart beating under her palms. She breathed in his scent—a clean mix of soap and fresh linen and wine.

She felt his fingers tangle in her hair, felt him lift it, felt the cool air touch her skin.

She felt his mouth along her jaw.

Where Bennington's lips had oozed slug-like, disgusting and wet across her skin, Parks's mouth was like butterfly wings, brushing, teasing. Like sunlight, warm and warming. She tilted her head, stretching, hoping he would find the suddenly sensitive spot beneath her ear.

He did.

She felt a wave of weakness again. She needed to hold onto him. She moved her hands to his shoulders.

Her shawl slipped down. No matter. She was not chilled—she was warm. More than warm. Hot. So hot she was panting, and the low throbbing had turned to an ache.

She'd thought she'd learned a few things about kissing this Season, but she'd been wrong. She'd never experienced anything like this before. The other men had been rough and awkward and hurried. Or practiced and oily. This? This was perfect.

It suddenly got more perfect.

His hand touched her naked breast.

Her conscience whispered she should be shocked. Appalled. Mortified. She should scream for help.

She bit her lip to keep from screaming for pleasure. The warmth of his skin on hers was beyond anything she'd felt before.

And then his fingers moved.

She sagged into his body. She felt his lips brush her eyelids. He touched the hard little point of her nipple.

Heat shot through her. She inhaled—and his mouth covered hers. His tongue glided in.

She clung to him while he filled her, his tongue sweeping through her mouth. It should have been revolting, but it was wonderful.

She pressed herself against him, sliding her hands down to his waist, under his coat, around to his back. He had too much clothing on. *She* had too much clothing on. Her gloves, for example, were very much in the way.

His tongue was withdrawing. No! She wasn't ready for this to be over. She pressed closer and tried to copy his actions, thrusting her tongue into his much larger mouth. She was certain her efforts were extremely clumsy, but he seemed pleased. Enthusiastic even. His tongue encouraged hers. His hands cupped her head.

He grunted and pulled back.

"I think we'd do better sitting down."

"Huh?" She blinked up at him, then reached for his mouth again.

He laughed and picked her up. He sat in the ugly red chair and deposited her on his lap.

"Mmm, perhaps this *is* better." She loosened his cravat.

"Much better." He kissed her first on her mouth, then on her throat, then down to . . .

"Oh. Oh my."

Both of her breasts had escaped her corset. He wasn't going to . . . ? Surely that was highly improper . . . ?

"Mr. Parker-Roth . . ."

"John."

"What?" His mouth was hovering over her naked breasts. She put her hands on his head to pull him back from disaster. He looked at her—at her face.

"John. My name is John."

"Oh."

"Say it." He kissed the side of one breast.

"Eek." She tried to move his head away. He wouldn't budge.

"Say it." He kissed the other side.

"John. I'm sure you really shouldn't be . . ."

He swirled his tongue around her nipple, close but not quite touching the aching center.

"Oh. Oh, John. Ohh."

He flicked his tongue over the point, then latched on and sucked.

"John!"

Had she screamed? She was sure she'd wanted to, but had she actually done so? She—

"Good God." Parks abruptly pulled her up against him, but not before she'd caught a glimpse of the shocked-looking woman standing in the open doorway.

"Good evening, Mother."

Chapter 3

"Pardon me if I don't stand." Parks closed his eyes briefly. He was going to die. How had he gotten into this position? Stephen, now, he wouldn't be surprised if Stephen turned up at a society ball with a half-naked woman on his lap. His brother was very . . . adventurous. But he? He'd never done a scandalous thing in his life.

"Yes, I can see you have your . . . hands full." His mother pressed her lips together and stared at Miss Peterson's back—Miss Peterson's shockingly naked back with his bare hand plastered across it. He dropped his hold to her very rigid, perfectly proper, though improperly exposed, corset.

"Please tell me this is a nightmare," Miss Peterson whispered into his cravat, "and I'll wake up in a moment."

"I only wish," he muttered. He needed something to cover her with. "Are you sitting on Lady Palmerson's shawl, do you know?"

She shifted slightly. "No. I think maybe I dropped it when you, ah, when we, um . . . Maybe it fell on the floor when you picked me up."

He glanced over his shoulder. The shawl was indeed in a puddle on the floor. Unfortunately, it was well out of reach.

"Cecilia, what is going—oh." Lady Beatrice's substantial form joined his mother's in the doorway. Thankfully, Mother was in a blue and gray phase at the moment, because Lady Beatrice would have clashed with any other color scheme. Her green dress with its knots of purple and red ribbon and the array of yellow plumes swaying among her gray ringlets made her look like an overgrown mulberry bush with a canary nesting in its boughs.

"Meg, what are you doing sitting on Mr. Parker-Roth's lap?"

Miss Peterson moaned softly and pressed her face into his shoulder.

Lady Beatrice chuckled. "Ah, I see. Young love . . . or young lust, hmm? Well, it's spring. The birds and the bees and what have you. I believe there's a wedding to plan, don't you agree, Cecilia?"

Mother smiled slowly. "I believe you are correct, Bea. Let—"

"What is going on?"

Mother and Lady Beatrice turned to see who had spoken. In a moment, a short, plump woman with spectacles and wildly curly brown hair came into view. She scowled at Lady Beatrice.

"Lady Palmerson said Meg—" She glanced into the room. Her jaw dropped and her eyes widened in obvious shock.

"Oh, no." Miss Peterson twisted her head around to look at the new arrival. "What's Emma doing in London?"

"Emma as in your sister Emma, the Marchioness of Knightsdale?"

"Yes." She buried her face back in his shirt. "This has *got* to be a nightmare."

He had to agree. The woman pushing past Lady Beatrice looked like she wanted to carve off his balls with her hairpin.

"Get your hands off my sister, you blackguard!"

He put his hands on the chair arms, until Miss Peterson tried to turn to confront her sister. He grabbed her before she could move more than an inch.

"You are not exactly dressed for company," he whispered. He kept his eye on the marchioness. She wouldn't really come after him with her hairpin, would she? She *did* look like she might vault the settee at any moment to reach him.

"Didn't you hear me?" The marchioness stepped toward him.

"Just a minute!"

His mother had perfected that tone with six children. Miss Peterson's sister stopped immediately.

"That's my son you're calling a blackguard." Mother stepped up close to the marchioness. She was an inch or two taller than Miss Peterson's sister, but Lady Knightsdale was probably a stone heavier and twenty years younger. Still, Mother was not one to back down easily, especially if one of her children was threatened. If they went foot to foot, it would be a close call who'd come out the victor.

"And that's my sister your bounder of a son has his hands on."

"I have got to get that shawl," Miss Peterson muttered.

"Yes, I quite agree. Do you suppose you could ask your sister to fetch it for you?"

Miss Peterson glanced over her shoulder.

"She looks rather occupied at the moment. She won't hurt your mother, will she?"

"She's *your* sister. How would I know?" He frowned. "Should I be worried?"

Miss Peterson bit her lip. "Emma has gotten more, um, outspoken since Charlie and Henry were born."

"Wonderful." Now what was he to do? Dump Miss Peterson on the floor and leap the settee himself to separate the women?

Fortunately, the issue was not put to the test.

"Aunt Beatrice, what—" The Marquis of Knightsdale, a powerfully built man with a military bearing, stopped on the threshold. "Emma, what is the matter? Who is the woman you are glaring at?"

"I don't know her name. She is *that* man's mother." She pointed at Parks. The venom in her voice left everyone in the room with little doubt as to her sentiments.

The marquis looked at him and raised an eyebrow. "Isn't that your sister Meg sitting on his lap?"

"*Yes!*"

"This is ridiculous," Miss Peterson muttered. "If I get up carefully I should be able to reach that shawl."

"Wait, there are more people arriving." Parks wished someone would close the door. "Ah, perhaps help has come. Westbrooke and his countess are here."

"Good. See if you can get Lizzie to come over."

"Shall I shout across the room to her, Miss Peterson?"

She made an odd little sound. "Please call me Meg. I do feel our acquaintance has gone beyond the formal."

He smiled slightly. That was an understatement.

"Charles," Westbrooke said as Lady Westbrooke hurried over to Meg, "don't you think this room is getting somewhat crowded? I'll shut the door, shall I?"

"Please do, Robbie."

Westbrooke pushed on the door. Something was impeding its progress. He looked to see what the problem was.

"So sorry, Lady Dunlee. If you could just step back a little? Need to give the family some privacy, you know."

"Oh, but I don't think—"

The rest of Lady Dunlee's words were lost when Westbrooke shut the heavy wooden door in her face.

"Hallo, Parks. What are you doing here?" Robbie grinned. "Is there a particular reason you're entertaining a partially clad lady in this rather inappropriate location?"

"Robbie," Lady Knightsdale said, "that partially clad lady is Meg!"

"It is? Well, well." Westbrooke leaned against the door. There were still muffled noises coming from the other side. "It's about time."

About time? Parks was definitely not going to add anything to the conversation—he had a strong sense of self preservation—but what the hell did Westbrooke mean? Fortunately Meg was whispering to Lady Westbrooke and appeared to have missed the comment.

Lady Knightsdale had not. "*About time?* Did you know this was going on, Robbie?"

"Since I'm not certain what 'this' is, no I did not. But I'm not surprised to see Parks and Meg together." He coughed. "Well, perhaps I am a trifle startled so see them so, um, together in this particular venue."

"So you know the miscreant, Robbie? You would not counsel me to kill him?" Knightsdale smiled at his wife. "Much as Emma might like me to."

"Well, no, Parks—John Parker-Roth, that is—is actually a good fellow. I've known him since Eton." Westbrooke nodded at Mrs. Parker-Roth. "And I do suppose his mother might object to your dispatching her son to the hereafter."

"Indeed yes." Mrs. Parker-Roth glared at the marquis. "My apologies, ma'am. No insult intended."

Lady Knightsdale snorted.

"By me, at least," Knightsdale said. "Come, Emma, do try to be civil. If you do not care for the man's explanation, you may rend him limb from limb afterward."

"Yes, Emma." Lady Beatrice lowered her bulk to the settee. "I do think you should ask Mr. Parker-Roth and Meg to explain what happened before you fly too high into the boughs."

"Well, I would like to know what happened, too." Mrs. Parker-Roth turned to Parks. "John, would you care to explain?"

Lady Westbrooke had just handed Meg the wayward shawl.

"Of course, Mother. I—"

"No," Meg said, wrapping the shawl securely around her shoulders and standing. "This is all my fault. *I* shall explain."

What was Emma doing here? She was supposed to be home in Kent. Well, that was a question to be answered later. Now everyone was looking at her, waiting for her to speak.

Meg pulled the shawl a little tighter around her. She had never appeared so disheveled anywhere but her bedchamber. She opened her mouth.

What exactly was she going to say?

She glanced at Mrs. Parker-Roth. Instead of anger, she saw cautious curiosity in the older woman's moss green eyes, eyes that looked so much like Parks's.

"Go on, Meg." Emma's voice was sharp enough to draw blood. "You said you would explain."

"Give her a moment to gather her thoughts, my dear."

"That's not the only thing she should be gathering, Charles. Her dress, her hairpins . . ."

Meg felt Parks's hand on the small of her back and

took courage from his touch. She appreciated his letting her explain instead of trying to do it himself. Now if she only knew what to say . . .

She took a deep breath and let it out slowly. "First I should say that Mr. Parker-Roth is completely blameless."

Silence and stares of incredulity greeted this statement.

"It's true." Why did they look as if they did not believe her? "He had nothing to do with my, ah, current situation."

Lord Westbrooke turned a sudden laugh into a cough.

Meg glanced up at Parks. He appeared to be studying a large painting of a bewigged Palmerson ancestor.

"So, let me be certain I understand this," Lady Beatrice said. "Mr. Parker-Roth had nothing to do with your current dishabille?"

"That's correct. I was in the garden with—" Did she want to mention Bennington's name? Surely Emma wouldn't force her to wed that reprobate? "With another man. Mr. Parker-Roth happened upon us and rescued me."

"Who is this mysterious other man?" Emma was still glaring at Parks.

"I would rather not say." How could she have had the poor taste to consider the viscount for even a moment? She did not want Lizzie, Robbie, and Charles—let alone Emma—knowing how bacon-brained she'd been.

Emma snorted. "Because there was no other man."

"Now see here—"

Meg put a hand out to stop Parks. She felt as if she'd been kicked in the stomach, but Parks's intervention would not help matters. Emma's face had its mulish expression.

"Emma, you know I would not lie to you."

Emma simply glared in reply.

"Yes, my dear," Charles said. "You are letting your anger—"

Emma turned to glare at him.

"—your *understandable* anger cloud your judgment."

"*Look* at her, Charles."

Charles—and everyone—looked at her.

Meg bit her lip. She knew she looked terribly shocking. And it was clear Emma wouldn't rest until she had all the details. "Very well, it was Lord Bennington."

"Bennington? That lump?" Lizzie blushed and covered her mouth. "Pardon me. That just slipped out."

Lord Westbrooke grinned. "This will give old Bennie something else to hate you for, Parks."

"I am well aware of it."

Emma shook her head, clearly surprised. "I would not have expected such behavior from Viscount Bennington."

"Neither would I," Meg said. "You can be sure I would not have ventured outside with the man if I'd had the least inkling of it."

"You should not be venturing outside with any gentlemen!"

"Emma, I am twenty-one. I am not a child any more."

Charles put a hand on Emma's shoulder. "Perhaps we should wait until a more private time to have our family squabbles?"

Emma scowled. "Very well." She shot an expressive look at Meg. "We will continue this discussion in the carriage on our way home."

Meg held her tongue. She had come with Lady Beatrice and she intended to leave with her, but there was no need to tell Emma that now. In fact, if she played her cards carefully, she should be able to avoid having

Emma ring a peal over her altogether. She relaxed slightly. A mistake. She was only out of the frying pan and into the fire.

"However, I do wonder," Charles said, looking at her, "how you happened to be sitting on Mr. Parker-Roth's lap when we arrived."

"Um." No adequate answer presented itself.

"Excellent question, Charles. It's not as though the gentleman's lap was the only option. He might have stood to give you a place to sit." Lady Beatrice ran her hand over the dull red upholstery of the settee. "And while I grant you this seat is unattractive, I am quite comfortable."

"Well . . ."

"And why did you become separated from that shawl you are now clutching? It does not seem especially warm in here"—Charles focused on Parks, his voice becoming sharper—"unless perhaps you were engaged in some, ah, heat-producing activity?"

"I, um, well, you see . . ."

Parks cleared his throat. "I am happy to offer an explanation for Miss Peterson, my lord."

"No." She turned to search Parks's face. His expression was pleasant, polite, and totally opaque. "We discussed this. You rescued me from Bennington. You should not be punished for a good deed. I said I would explain."

Parks smiled slightly. "Would you care to explain what we were doing when my mother came in?"

Meg turned a bright shade of red. Her mouth opened and closed several times, but no words emerged.

"What *were* you doing, Parker-Roth?" The marquis's voice was soft and unpleasant.

"Let us just say that, regardless of what happened

in the garden, I believe it would be best if I wed Miss Peterson."

"Did you harm my sister, you . . . you . . ."

Knightsdale put a restraining hand on his wife. "*Have* you harmed my sister-in-law, Parker-Roth?" His tone was even colder. Parks knew he was a dead man if he answered yes, but he was not going to truckle to the marquis. He turned to Meg.

"Did I harm you, Miss Peterson?"

"No, of course not. Don't be absurd." Meg turned to look at her sister and brother-in-law. "You are all making too much of this. There is no need for me to marry Mr. Parker-Roth. Let's just pretend this evening did not happen."

"Let's just pretend Lady Dunlee is not the world's biggest gossip," Lady Beatrice said.

"Lady Beatrice—"

"You know she's right, Meg." Lady Westbrooke put her hand on Meg's shoulder. "Lady Dunlee will spread the story in a trice."

"No, she won't, Lizzie."

Westbrooke coughed. "Thing is, Meg, she already has. Two fellows mentioned it to me in the ballroom. Were surprised Parks was such a wild . . ." He coughed again. "Well, the truth is, the word is out—be all over Town by morning."

"And all over England by next week." The marchioness scowled at her sister. "You have no choice. You must marry Mr. Parker-Roth."

Meg's mouth was set in a straight line. She was beginning to look as mulish as her sister. "You are working yourself into a pother over nothing, Emma—as you always do."

Lady Knightsdale drew in an audible breath. Parks was certain her husband would have to hold her back from Meg. Surely this argument wouldn't degenerate into the hair-pulling sessions his youngest sisters too often engaged in? He glanced at his mother. She gave him an intense look.

It was definitely time to intervene.

"Perhaps it would help if Miss Peterson and I could have a few moments alone to discuss the situation, Lady Knightsdale?"

"There is nothing to discuss." Meg almost spat the words. Was she going to take her venom out on him?

He was shocked to realize he found the thought rather stimulating. In fact, a specific part of him was especially stimulated.

"Exactly. The decision is made." Lady Knightsdale turned her scowl on him. "And we've seen what happens when you two are alone together. Come, Meg. We are leaving."

"*We* are not leaving. I came with Lady Beatrice. I will leave with her."

"Meg—"

Knightsdale put his arm around his wife's shoulders. "I believe we can give you a few moments, Parker-Roth."

"But Charles—"

"You are understandably overset, Emma, but I think we can trust the man not to ravish Meg in the five or ten minutes we'll allow them alone. We'll wait right outside in the corridor in case Meg needs help, shall we?"

"Well . . ."

Mrs. Parker-Roth had obviously had enough. She was perfectly polite, but firm. "There is no need for concern, Lady Knightsdale. You can trust my son to behave as a gentleman. I did not raise a complete cad, you know."

The marchioness's brows snapped down and she opened her mouth as if to flay Parks's mother with her tongue, but stopped in time. She blushed. "No, of course not." Her tone was stiff. "I meant no insult, of course. As my husband says, I am slightly overset. Please excuse me."

Mrs. Parker-Roth smiled. "That is quite all right. Indeed, I know exactly how you feel. I had a similar experience with my eldest daughter."

"You did?"

"Indeed. You must remember the incident last Season involving Lord Motton?"

"Lord Motton . . ." Lady Knightsdale nodded. "Yes, I do remember the scan—I mean, story."

Mrs. Parker-Roth took the marchioness's arm and started toward the door. "Oh, it was indeed a scandal, and at first my husband and I—and John, too—were very angry. But once we saw how happy Jane was, well, we couldn't stay angry." She laughed and shook her head. "Even at the time I suspected Jane was an active participant in her seduction—she is not a namby-pamby sort of girl, you know—so I couldn't think too harshly of Edmund. And now we like him very well, especially as Jane is expecting our first grandchild."

"Really?"

"Yes. So, I'd say everything turned out well for my daughter, and I believe everything will turn out well for your sister."

Lady Knightsdale paused in the doorway to glare back at Parks. "I hope so."

The marquis was the last one to leave the room. "Ten minutes, Parker-Roth," he said as he pulled the door closed.

Meg exploded the moment they heard the latch click.

"Can you believe Emma? She's always tried to run my life, but since she married, she's become unbearable. I

thought once Charlie was born—and then Henry—
she'd be too busy to concern herself with my affairs any
longer, but I was wrong."

"She loves you." *As Mother loves me.*

He could certainly sympathize with Miss Peterson on
the subject of interfering family members.

What did Mother think of this evening's drama?
She'd dragged him to Town to find him a leg-shackle—
was she pleased with Miss Peterson?

Was he?

It made no difference. He had compromised the girl
past redemption. Lady Dunlee had seen to that—and
after the rather heated . . . exchange they'd had in this
room, he couldn't even consider himself an innocent
victim. What the hell had come over him?

The long and short of it was he had no choice. The
Marquis of Knightsdale was not letting him out of this
room an unengaged man—he just needed to convince
Miss Peterson of that fact.

She sighed and tucked a strand of hair behind her
ear. His fingers twitched to touch the silky length again.

He clasped his hands behind his back.

"I *know* Emma loves me. I know she only wants the
best for me, which makes me feel even worse, but I
can't let her dictate my decisions."

"No, of course not. I'm sure she doesn't wish to."

"Ha! You have no idea. She thinks I must be married
to be happy. She's been torturing me about it for the
last three years. You should have seen the men she was
throwing at my head. It was enough to drive me to
Town for the Season."

"Surely they couldn't have been *that* objectionable."

"They were ancient. Well into their dotage."

He laughed. He couldn't help it, her expression was
so horrified.

"I find it hard to believe your sister would think an old man a suitable match for you." Especially if the rumors about the marchioness's marriage were true. More than one wag had said the marquis and his wife didn't need a fire in the bedroom grate—they produced enough heat on their own. After seeing them together, he believed it.

"Well, the younger men were equally revolting. Cabbage heads, all of them—and that's insulting the cabbage."

"Miss Peterson—"

Meg waved her arm—and caught the shawl before it slipped far enough to reveal anything interesting.

"I don't live at Knightsdale—I live at the vicarage with my father and his wife, Harriet—so I'm not even underfoot. Well, not under Emma's feet at any rate. There is no need for her to worry about my future."

"Still, it is perfectly natural that she'd want to see you well settled. Surely your father has made a push in that direction as well?"

Meg shook her head. "No. He hasn't said a word about my marrying."

"So he's happy to have you spend your life with him?"

"Yes. No. Oh, botheration." She frowned at a garish red vase on the mantle. "Truth be told, I'm certain he and Harriet would enjoy the privacy my absence would give them." She sighed. "And I would like a home of my own. It's not marriage I object to, it's Emma's meddling." She turned and met his eyes. "If you must know, I came to London this Season with the express goal of finding a husband."

"Then you should be happy to have achieved your purpose so quickly." He could not keep an edge from his voice. Why did he feel this spurt of annoyance? She had been honest. And it was far from surprising. Lady

Palmerson's ballroom was filled with young ladies intent on exactly the same objective.

"Well, I . . ." She flushed. "I had thought to, um, spend more time looking."

So she was not happy with him as her bridegroom? He gripped his hands tightly together. What was it about him that failed to impress the ladies of the *ton*? Hell, Grace had been so unimpressed she'd left him standing at the altar.

It wasn't a mystery. He had no title. A mere mister could not hope to compete with a lord.

He should have left her to Viscount Bennington.

Parks was scowling. Of course he was. He obviously did not want to marry her. His tone of voice made that abundantly clear. Mauling her, though, that was another matter. Men must all be alike. They were happy to—oh.

She suddenly remembered exactly what she and Parks had been doing when Parks's mother had entered the room.

Dear God.

She covered her face and moaned.

"What must your mother think of me? We were . . . I was . . . I looked like a . . . well, I won't say what I looked like. It is too shocking. And Emma and I were squabbling like children." Had Emma actually shouted at Mrs. Parker-Roth? "My sister could hardly have been more insulting. I'm certain your mother must want nothing to do with me or my family."

"And I'm certain Mother understood completely. As she said, Jane got herself into a similar predicament last year. Mother was as upset then as your sister was just now."

"Still, she cannot want you to marry me."

"Miss Peterson, I hope you will not take it poorly, but

some days I think my mother would be delighted if I wed the lowest scullery maid just as long as I wed someone. You say your sister thinks you must be married to be happy? Well, my mother has the same notion. She firmly believes that a man cannot find contentment without a wife at his side, guiding him in the right direction."

Parks sounded extremely bitter.

"And you do not agree?"

"I do not!" He frowned, running his hand through his hair. "I do not wish to marry. Ever. My mother has been dragging me to Town for years, nagging me on the subject without mercy. Since I turned thirty, she has become relentless—and Westbrooke's marriage has only made matters worse. I don't doubt she is in ecstasy now that I've finally been tricked into parson's mousetrap."

"I did *not* trick you." Meg felt another spurt of anger. Yes, the situation was monstrously unfortunate; yes, Parks had not chosen his fate; yes, in some regards his predicament was her fault. But she had not planned for things to happen as they had. She was almost as much a victim as he.

Well, perhaps not. Some people would doubtless have said she'd gotten her just desserts if she'd been forced to marry Lord Bennington.

Apparently one of those people was Mr. Parker-Roth.

"No, you did not trick me. However, if you had not been so bold as to disregard society's rules—if you had not gone out into the garden with Bennington—" He tugged on his waistcoat and pressed his lips together. "Well, the least said about that, the better, I suppose."

She did not care for his tone of voice at all.

"You do not have to marry me, sir."

He looked exactly as if he'd eaten a lemon.

"Come, Miss Peterson, be sensible. You know as well

as I do that we have to marry. Your reputation can only be mended by wedding vows."

"No." She wanted to hit something—like Mr. Parker-Roth. She hated being forced to act because of someone else's rules. "There must be another way to solve this problem."

"There is not."

Yes, she would definitely like to hit the man. Perhaps a well placed punch in the chest would wipe that supercilious expression from his face.

"There are *always* alternatives."

"Not this time. Not this problem. Your sister—your brother-in-law, the marquis—will not allow me to leave this room without offering for you."

"Then offer. I just will not accept."

"Miss Peterson, you—"

"Just ask me, sir."

Parks clenched his teeth so hard his jaw flexed. He glared at her. She glared back.

"Oh, very well. Miss Peterson, will you do me the honor—*the very great honor*—of giving me your hand in marriage?"

Sarcasm did not become him. It was very easy to reply.

"No."

"You can't say no."

"I just have. Is your hearing defective? Do I need to repeat myself? No. There. It is not a difficult word to understand."

"Miss Peterson—"

The door swung open.

"So," Emma said, "when is the wedding?"

Chapter 4

"I cannot believe you refused Mr. Parker-Roth, Meg." Emma started in the moment the carriage door shut behind them. "Have you lost your mind? Do you want to put paid to any hopes of marrying?"

Meg arranged her skirts on the carriage seat. She definitely did not want to be here. If she could have accompanied Lady Beatrice, she would have, but Emma had latched onto her arm and virtually dragged her to the Knightsdale carriage.

"Mr. Parker-Roth was not to blame for the scene in the garden, Emma. He should not have to pay with his freedom for being a Good Samaritan."

"Bah! The garden has nothing to do with it. If what Mrs. Parker-Roth and Lady Beatrice hinted at is even close to the truth, it was not charity the man was practicing in Lady Palmerson's parlor. Lud, my own eyes told me that. You were sitting on his lap, Meg, in a state of undress."

Meg's cheeks felt as red as the fabric on that hideous chair where she and Parks had—

No, she could not think on it.

She looked out the window.

"I have to agree with your sister, Meg." Charles's voice was calm at least. "And I believe Parker-Roth does, too. He seemed perfectly willing to wed you, even without my insistence."

Meg shrugged. "Willing, perhaps, but not happy."

"Meg, for heaven's sake!" Emma was almost shouting. "The man hardly knows you. Of course he's not happy. No one—especially no man—likes to have his hand forced, even when it's his own actions doing the forcing. He'll get over it." She shrugged. "He'll have to."

Wonderful. What an exciting wedded life to look forward to—a husband who barely tolerated her. Not that such a marriage would be unusual, of course. Most males of the *ton* sought out their wives only to attend to the chore of producing an heir—and Parks didn't even have that compulsion. Perhaps they would live together like brother and sister.

She swallowed a sob.

"Did you say something, Meg?"

"No."

And, yes, she realized she'd been considering just such a marriage ever since she'd made marriage her goal. Certainly when she'd considered Bennington as a husband. But that was different.

She refused to consider exactly why it was different.

She rested her head against the window and watched a man stroll down the sidewalk. He was moving faster than their coach. If only she could get out and stretch her legs . . . if only she could get away from this conversation.

There was no escaping Emma until they reached Knightsdale House—*if* she could escape her then. She sighed. Emma would probably follow her to her room to continue her harangue.

Why was she going to Charles's townhouse anyway?

"All my things are at Lady Beatrice's, Emma. I do think it would be best if I returned there."

"No. Definitely not. And your belongings are no longer at Lady Beatrice's. I had Charles send a footman round to fetch them as soon as I arrived. Now that I am here, I will take over all chaperone duties."

Why *had* Emma come to Town? Her sister hated London, preferring to stay home in Kent even when Charles came up to attend the House of Lords.

"Why are you here, Emma? I thought you considered the country air much better for the boys."

"It is, but I couldn't very well sit home when I kept hearing such shocking reports of your behavior." Emma paused, obviously struggling with her temper. "I should have come up with you at the beginning of the Season and not delegated the job to Lady Beatrice. It was obviously asking too much of her."

Meg felt as if she'd swallowed a rock. "What do you mean? Has someone been spreading tales?"

"More than one someone, miss. I've gotten coy letters from Lady Oldston and an alarmed missive from Lady Farley who, by the by, did not think you were at all the thing for her son. I take it you've made something of a habit of disappearing into the shrubbery with men. How many gentlemen *have* you entertained in the bushes, Meg?"

"Um." Put that way, it did sound somewhat sordid. "It wasn't exactly . . . I mean—"

"I thought you liked Parker-Roth," Charles said. "Didn't we hear some mention of the man last year?"

"What?"

"Parker-Roth. Wasn't he at Tynweith's house party? I'm certain either you or Aunt Bea mentioned him favorably in one of your letters."

"I'm sure it was not I who wrote about him." She was

confident she'd been careful not to allude to Parks. Yes, she'd been taken with him, fool that she was. Well, it was not so odd. It wasn't every day she found a man who could discuss Repton's *Fragments on the Theory and Practice of Landscape Gardening* intelligently—or at all.

Stupidly she had hoped he'd show an interest in her when they'd returned to London. He hadn't. She pressed her lips together. He had definitely not shown any interest in her. He'd attended Robbie's and Lizzie's wedding and then vanished. She'd looked for him at every soiree, every ball, every Venetian breakfast. Finally after weeks of discreetly searching, she'd asked Robbie where he was. He'd told her Parks had gone back to his estate in Devon.

Clearly he had not been as impressed with her as she had with him.

"You're right, Charles. I do think Lady Beatrice mentioned Mr. Parker-Roth. I think she even said you favored him, Meg."

"Ack. Um. I mean, well—"

"After I got over the shock—and you do have to admit the scene in Lady Palmerson's parlor was shocking"—Emma eyed the shawl still wrapped around Meg's ruined gown—"I began to see the advantages of this match."

"Advantages?"

"Yes. You'll be married. Mr. Parker-Roth is relatively young—just a little over thirty, I believe—and can give you plenty of children. He has a number of brothers and sisters, you know."

"Oh?" Meg swallowed. Children? With Parks? The notion made her feel very . . . odd.

"Yes, indeed. And he likes plants. His mother says he has quite a few of them around the estate."

"Oh."

"I think he is perfect for you." Emma leaned back against the squabs. "His mother and I had a comfortable coze while we waited in the corridor. She's a lovely woman. You can be sure I apologized profusely for my rude behavior. She could not have been nicer—said she understood completely. I will quite like being connected to her."

"Emma, you are not going to be connected to Mrs. Parker-Roth. I am not going to marry her son. How many times must I say it?"

"As many times as you like—it makes no difference. You must marry the man or be ruined."

"I do not."

"Meg—"

"Ladies," Charles said, "it is time to call a halt to this battle. Neither of you is listening to the other."

"What do you mean, Charles? Of course I'm listening to Meg. She just is not being reasonable."

Charles draped his arm around Emma's shoulders and pulled her tight against his side. "I think you would both benefit from a good night's sleep. Sometimes problems look different in the morning."

"I don't know what's going to be different."

"Emma . . ."

"Oh, very well." Emma sat stiffly for a moment and then relaxed against Charles.

"That's better," he said. "Now tell me about Isabelle and Claire and the boys. What new tricks is Henry up to?"

Meg turned to look out the window again. Emma's voice droned on in the background, talking about nine-month old Henry and Charlie, who was almost three, and Isabelle and Claire, Charles's orphaned nieces; telling Charles all the boring, everyday details of their lives that he missed when he was away in London.

Meg pressed her forehead against the glass, but that didn't cure the sudden ache in her heart.

Would she ever have anyone with whom to share such mundane stories?

"This is splendid news, Pinky. I wish your father were with us. He'll be so pleased when we tell him."

"Mother, you promised not to use that ridiculous nickname any more." Parks opened the door to their rooms in the Pulteney Hotel. "And I cannot imagine Father would notice if I were married or not. Which I won't be. Married, that is. Didn't you hear Miss Peterson? She refused my offer."

Mother brushed by him. "Oh, pish! That is merely a temporary setback. You know as well as I do the girl has no choice. She must wed you."

"Who must wed whom?" Miss Agatha Witherspoon, Mother's friend and sometime companion, looked up as they entered the parlor. She put aside the tome she was reading, dropped her slippered feet from a low table, and sat up. "Never say Pinky's been getting under some chit's skirts?"

"Of course not. Well, not exactly." Mother sat next to Agatha on the settee.

Parks counted to ten. Twice. It did not help.

"Will you *please* not use that infernal nickname!"

"Pinky!"

He glared at his mother.

"Oh, very well—Johnny. But you must learn to keep your temper under control. It is most inappropriate to raise your voice."

Agatha was grinning like a bedlamite. "So, the dry old stick actually has some sap running through his veins?"

"Agatha, please. You are embarrassing Pinky."

"Mother!"

"I mean Johnny. And he is not old—he's just past thirty."

"Humph. He acts like he's as old as Methuselah." Agatha snorted. "Older. If Methuselah was like those other Old Testament fellows, he knew his way around a bed better than Pinky here."

"Now, Agatha, Pinky"—Mother looked at him—"um, Johnny has a nice widow in the village—"

"*Mother!*"

"Really, Pin-Johnny, what did I say about raising your voice?"

He was going to strangle her. He was going to strangle his mother and her elderly friend.

"I believe I could use some brandy," he said instead.

"Splendid. You may pour me a glass as well. Agatha, would you care for some brandy?"

"Certainly. Now tell me all, Cecilia. What has Pinky been up to?"

"John!" Parks said. "Or Parks. Or Mr. Parker-Roth. Not Pinky. Do you understand, Miss Witherspoon?"

Agatha shrugged. "Oh, very well, but I will tell you you have no sense of humor, sir. It is a distinct fault in your character."

He handed Agatha her brandy without spilling it down the front of the ridiculous red and gold men's banyan she was wearing, though he was sorely tempted to. "Thank you. I will certainly make note of your observation."

She rolled her eyes. "I do feel for the poor girl you've compromised, but perhaps she's as dour as you are."

He contented himself with baring his teeth in a formation that might pass for a smile and taking a seat in the chair farthest from the ladies.

"What are you doing awake anyway, Agatha?" Mother

asked. "I thought you were too tired to come out tonight. I expected to find you sound asleep."

Agatha took a healthy swallow of her brandy. "You know I only came up to Town with you to visit Ackermann's and the Royal Academy and perhaps go to the theater, Cecilia. I want no part of all the social torture. Can you see me standing in some stupid ballroom? I'd die of boredom listening to all those fat-pated frumps prose on and on about the other society nodcocks." She looked at Parks. "Though tonight might have proved an exception. Tell me, who's the young lady Pinky— I mean, *John*—has lured into misbehavior?"

"I did not lure the young lady into misbehavior."

"No? Why am I not surprised? So what did happen? Some argument over the flora turn ugly?"

"Stop, Agatha. You are as bad as Pin-Johnny. No, I believe the young lady did the luring—and it was not Johnny she lured, but Vis—some other man."

Thank God Mother had chosen discretion at the last moment. Agatha was obviously not one of society's gossips, but she also did not watch her tongue. She would think nothing of linking Miss Peterson's name with Bennington's. She probably would delight in it—she knew how much Bennington hated her.

"So why is John the one stuck making the offer?"

"He was the one caught in the, um, act."

"Mother, there was no 'act'!"

"Perhaps not that Lady Dunlee saw; however . . ." Mother raised a damn expressive eyebrow.

Agatha grunted. "Sounds like the chit's no better than she should be. Perhaps a little money judiciously applied will solve the problem. Who did you say she was, Cecilia?"

"I didn't, but it's no secret. Lady Dunlee was spreading the tale through the ballroom as quickly as her lips would move. It's Miss Margaret Peterson—and no, money is not the answer. The girl is good *ton*. Her sister is the Marchioness of Knightsdale."

"Knightsdale?" Agatha sat up a little straighter. "That's the Draysmith family. Lady Bea is a friend of mine."

"She was there. I believe she was acting as Miss Peterson's chaperone."

Agatha sprayed brandy over her banyan. "Lady Bea, a chaperone? That's rich. What cod's-head thought Bea would make a good duenna? She was never one to be overly concerned with propriety. Isn't Alton still her butler?"

"Yes, well, I don't believe anyone thought Lady Beatrice was ideal for the position, but necessity dictated the arrangement." Mother took a sip of brandy. "Lady Knightsdale intends to take charge now—though that's a bit like closing the barn door after the horse has bolted."

"Mother, no horse bolted. Nothing happened."

"Nothing?"

Damn it. Mother had only to raise her eyebrow just so and he felt like he was ten years old again and had just tracked mud over the entry hall. Not that Mother minded the mud so much, but it always sent Mrs. Charing, their old housekeeper, into a frenzy, and Mother did not like *that* at all.

"I'm going to bed."

"Very well, Johnny. Sleep well. We can discuss this further in the morning."

There was nothing to discuss, but he wasn't about to get into an argument, especially with Agatha Witherspoon sitting there, itching to join in the fray.

He couldn't force Miss Peterson to the altar. If she remained adamant, there was nothing he could do but go home to the Priory and get on with his life.

He was surprised the thought didn't give him more pleasure.

His valet was sitting by the fire, reading, when he came into the bedroom.

"You should have joined Agatha, Mac."

"Sure, and when did ye get the daft notion I'm an idiot, man?" The large Scotsman grinned. "Nor do I think the lady would be verra pleased to share a candle with me."

"Probably not. What's that you're reading?"

Mac's grin widened. He held up the pamphlet.

Parks squinted to read the cover. "*A Complete Guide to the Cyprians of Covent Garden Including Prices Charged, Places of Business, and Special Amatory Skills.* Good God. 'Special Amatory Skills'? What does that mean?"

"Do ye really want to know?"

"No!" The gleam in Mac's eyes warned him that he definitely did not want to hear any more.

"Yer sure? Ye don't want to hear about Red-haired Peg—it's not the hair on her head's that's red, by the by—who can, with her mouth—"

"Stop! I do not want to hear another word, I assure you. You have said too much already."

"And then there's Buxom Bess who has the largest—"

"Mac! Please. I have had a hellish evening. I do not need you adding to my headache."

"Ack, ye've got the headache again, do ye? I'll just be brewing ye some of my special tea, shall I?"

"No." He just wanted to get into bed, pull up the covers, and pretend the evening had never happened. That he'd wake in the morning a free man again.

But he *was* a free man. Miss Peterson had rejected his offer.

Why didn't he feel free?

"Just help me out of this blasted coat will you?"

"Yer sure ye wouldn't like to take a stroll over to Covent Garden and see if we can find one of these lassies?"

"Good God, no! What we'd find would be a case of the pox."

"I don't know, Johnny. The man who wrote this guide seems verra enthusiastic—of course, he did include an advertisement for Dr. Ballow's Special Pills, so I don't know if we can trust his recommendations completely. Still, it's not every day we get up to Town, ye know. Need to see the sights, as it were." Mac got him out of his coat and went to hang it up.

"Believe me, I don't want to see any more sights. I'd leave for the Priory tomorrow if I could."

Mac's voice was muffled by the wardrobe. "Ye aren't usually quite so anxious to go home, Johnny. What happened?"

"I may have gotten myself a wife."

"*What?*" Mac spun around and banged his head on the wardrobe door. "Bloody hell, now I've got a headache to match yers."

"Where's Miss Peterson, Bea?" Alton, Lady Beatrice's butler, glanced out into the night. "Surely you didn't misplace her?"

Lady Bea sighed and stepped past him into the entrance hall. "Not exactly."

"Not exactly? What do you mean?"

She handed him her cloak. "Let's go upstairs, Billy, and I'll tell you all about it."

He took her arm as they walked up to their bedroom.

"Lord, it's good to be home." Bea collapsed onto the

sofa. "I don't know how many more of these social gatherings I can take."

"That bad?" Alton poured them both a glass of brandy.

"Yes." She patted the seat beside her. "Come give me a hug."

Alton handed her the brandy and settled down next to her. She rested her head on his shoulder.

"Mrrow!" Queen Bess, Bea's large orange cat, leapt up and draped herself over Alton's pantaloons.

Bea laughed. "Did you miss me, Bess?"

"Her highness always misses you, Bea."

"That's what you say, but I know better. Bess is completely content to have you for company. See whose lap she prefers?"

"She's spent more time with me recently." He dug his fingers into the thick fur behind Bess's ears. Her highness closed her eyes and purred.

"That's because I've had to waste hours trotting from ballroom to drawing room." Bea rolled her eyes. "Have I told you how *idiotic* the *ton* is?"

"I believe you may have made that observation once or twice before."

"Become a dead bore on the subject, have I?"

Alton kissed the top of her head. "Bea, you could never be boring."

Bea snorted. "You must be the only one to think so."

Alton eyed her current colorful attire, but wisely held his tongue.

Bea stroked Queen Bess's ears. "Well, the good news is, I believe I've lost my chaperone duties."

"Hmm." Alton left Bess to Bea's ministrations and stroked one of Bea's curls instead. "You do seem to have lost your charge. Have the society tabbies torn

Miss Peterson into little pieces and scattered the bits over the ballroom floor?"

Bea laughed. "No, not quite, though she did manage to create a splendid scandal this evening. Mmm. Keep doing that."

"This?" Alton massaged the back of her neck. "Or this?" He leaned over and kissed the sensitive spot behind her ear.

Bess meowed and moved to Bea's lap.

"Both." Bea tilted her head to give him more room to roam. He did so for an enjoyable few minutes. When he reached her lips, he kissed her and sat back.

"So, where is Miss Peterson?"

Bea sighed. "Emma took her to Knightsdale House."

"Ah, yes. A footman did come round earlier for her things. But I thought the marchioness was in Kent."

"She was until she heard the rumors about Meg and her propensity to disappear into the shrubbery."

Alton nodded. "I knew Miss Peterson's actions would come to no good."

Bea sat up and glared at him. "Are you saying you told me so, Mr. Alton?"

He pulled her back down to him. "Of course I am. I'm a boring old man, remember? Anticipating disaster is one of the requirements of my position."

Bea chuckled. "True."

"So Emma was angry?"

"Very. It didn't help that she arrived just in time to hear Lady Dunlee telling everyone she'd seen Meg half naked with a man in the bushes."

"Hmm. I thought the girl was a bit more discreet than that."

"She is—or has been. It was one reason I allowed the behavior to continue. She *is* twenty-one, after all. It's expected she would be a little curious, much as Emma

would like to deny it." Bea grinned. "Meg hasn't had
the benefit of associating with an especially knowledgeable footman, you know."

"Now, Bea, you know you were the one who seduced
me. I was a naïve young man when you lured me into
your father's attic."

"You were, weren't you? Not that I knew any more
than you did—I just knew what I wanted." She kissed
his cheek. "I'd say we've done quite well together."

Alton grunted.

Bess meowed.

"Shh, your highness." Bess bumped her head against
Bea's hand. "Yes, yes. I'll scratch your ears, Bessie."

"So who was the man Miss Peterson was entertaining in the vegetation?"

Bea's hand paused—and Queen Bess complained.
Bea resumed her stroking.

"Bennington."

"*Bennington?*"

"Yes. I don't know what Meg was thinking. The man
is about as exciting—and as attractive—as leftover
mutton."

"He *does* have an extensive plant collection, however."

"Plants!"

"Mrrow!" Queen Bess protested Bea's strident
reaction.

"Shh, Bessie." Bea ran her hand from her highness's
ears to her tail and sighed. "I think you are right, Billy.
That must have been what attracted Meg." She frowned,
her hand moving methodically over Bess's back. "Well,
you can be sure if I'd seen her duck out with him, I'd
have been after her in a trice."

"Of course. So she's engaged to the viscount?"

"Oh, no, thank God. Parker-Roth stumbled upon
them. Dispatched Bennington before Lady Dunlee

came on the scene. Unfortunately for him, the woman assumed he'd been the man rearranging Meg's clothing and shared her observations with half the *ton.*"

"So Mr. Parker-Roth is angry that he needs pay for a good deed with his freedom?" Alton asked. "That's understandable. The man *was* innocent of any wrongdoing after all."

Bea snorted. Bess hissed, jumped down from Bea's lap, and retreated to a nearby chair.

"He may have been innocent in the garden. He was somewhat less than innocent in Lady Palmerson's parlor. *Much* less than innocent."

"Really? So he's not adverse to wedding Meg?" Alton began pulling the pins from Bea's hair.

"Oh, he's adverse all right. You know how men hate to be forced into anything."

"I have no idea what you mean."

Bea rolled her eyes and started untying his cravat. "And idiot Meg has declined his offer. She can also be extremely obstinate." She pulled his cravat free of his neck and dropped it on the floor. "I would love to see how this battle is waged—but not enough to stay in London."

Alton's hands froze. "You're planning to leave Town?"

"As soon as I can."

He sat back. "I will miss you." His face was as impassive as only an excellent butler can manage. "Where do you go?"

"To the Continent with you, you lobcock. We are finally getting married."

"Married?" Alton frowned. "Bea—"

"Shh." She put her finger on his lips. "I don't want to hear all your arguments. You've repeated them for years and I am still not impressed. You promised to wed me once Meg was settled. She is as near to settled as can be now. I'm no longer needed here—in fact, I've been relieved of my duties. I am, after all these years, free to follow my heart and I intend to do so."

"I still don't think—"

"Don't think. I am going to marry you, Mr. William Alton, so just get that through your thick skull."

"But—"

Bea covered his mouth with her own, ending one discussion, but beginning a much more interesting exchange.

"Charles, I'm worried about Meg."

"I know you are, sweetheart. I've been watching you pace the bedroom for the last five minutes."

Emma stopped by the fire and gazed into the flames. "What could have gotten into her? I never thought she'd do something so hare-brained as go off into the shrubbery with a man. She's not a debutante. She's twenty-one. This is her second Season. You'd think she'd have more sense."

Charles grunted.

Emma scowled at the hearth. "I should have come to Town earlier. I know I should have. I thought about it when I received Lady Oldston's letter, but Henry was getting a tooth, and you know how fussy he is when he's teething. He won't go to Nanny at all. I must have been up two straight nights with him."

Charles grunted again.

"To be truthful, I assumed Lady Oldston was just being a jealous old cat. But then I got the note from Lady Farley." She turned toward Charles. "Can you believe Lady Farley said Meg was no better than she should be? I was so furious, I wanted to come to Town just to wrap my hands around her scrawny, wrinkled neck." She blew out a short breath. "And then Sarah wrote. I knew I—"

Emma *really* looked at Charles. He was sitting in bed, propped up against the headboard, covers down to his waist. The candlelight flickered over a vast expanse of skin—strong neck, broad shoulders, muscled arms and chest, the light brown curls sprinkled down to his . . .

"Are you naked?"

He grinned and peered under the bedclothes. "It appears I am. Would you care to see for yourself?"

Suddenly, she would—very much. It had been almost two months since she'd felt his weight. Her body ached for him.

She took a deep breath. "You are trying to distract me."

"No, I am trying to seduce you—to lure you into my bed so I can kiss every inch of your body and bury myself in your heat."

She grabbed the back of a handy chair. Her knees threatened to give out.

She tried to concentrate on something other than her sensitive breasts and the throbbing between her legs.

"Why didn't you write me about Meg, Charles? If Sarah noticed, you must have—or at least, Sarah must have told James and he must have mentioned it to you."

"Well, he didn't." Charles shrugged. Emma watched his muscles shift.

Meg. Think about Meg.

"How could James not have said anything? How could *you* not have seen what was going on?"

"Because, Emma, I've not made a habit of going to balls and other social events. I don't want to hear the silly chatter that goes on there, and I certainly don't need to see the latest crop of young girls."

She straightened. "I should hope not." She did not like to think of Charles looking at other women—or of other women looking at Charles.

He smiled briefly. "I go to the House of Lords, to White's, to meetings with likeminded men. I come home and read—and miss you and the boys and Isabelle and Claire."

"Oh."

"And, as you say, Meg is not a debutante. She survived last Season with Aunt Bea. I didn't think there was cause for concern."

Emma sighed. "Neither did I, but obviously I was mistaken. What am I going to do?"

"Come to bed. You've fed Henry?"

"Yes. He should make it through the night now." She smiled. "He's a greedy little devil."

"Just like his father. I have missed you dreadfully, you know."

"As I've missed you."

She came over and climbed into bed. Charles stretched out his arm, and she laid her head on his shoulder, putting her hand on his chest. He held her close.

He was so big and solid. She got used to sleeping alone when he was in London, but she much preferred having his comforting body next to hers. She closed her eyes for a moment, inhaling his scent, soaking up his warmth and strength.

She wanted this for her sister—this connectedness. This love. Would Meg find it with Mr. Parker-Roth?

How could she? Scandal was not a very good matchmaker.

Charles started stroking her hip, reminding her of all the other reasons she missed him.

"I should have come to Town when I first received

Lady Olston's letter." She ran her fingers through the short, springy hair on his chest. "I should have been Meg's chaperone instead of Lady Beatrice."

Charles shifted to lean up on one elbow. He started unbuttoning her nightgown. "Emma, you had the children to care for. You know they are happier in the country."

"Hmm." His fingers felt so good brushing against her skin. She knew his mouth would feel even better. "Maybe I'm wrong. Maybe the children would do fine in London, and then we wouldn't be away from you so much."

He grinned down at her. "Well, I'd certainly like to have you here."

And she would like to be here, if she could spend all her time in bed with him. She ran her hands over his shoulders and chest. She felt his erection heavy against her leg, and her body came to life. Heat and dampness blossomed between her thighs. She remembered so clearly it was almost painful just what he felt like sliding deep inside her.

Need and a sharp emptiness expanded in her womb.

He kissed her eyelids. "But London is not a good place to raise children. It is much too dirty and noisy. And if you were going to all the society events with Meg, you'd be exhausted all the time."

"Yes, but—oh." Charles's hands were on her breasts now. She wanted his tongue and lips there.

"Meg is not a silly, young girl, Emma. She is twenty-one, in her second Season, independent, and strong willed. She is more than capable of making her own decisions."

"You don't understand—"

Charles put his finger on her lips.

"I do understand that you feel the need to take responsibility for too many people. Let Meg live her own life. You have Charlie and Henry and Isabelle and Claire and me to take care of. Isn't that enough?"

"Yes, but—"

"Part of loving is letting go, sweetheart. It's time to let Meg go. From what Robbie tells me, Parks is a good man. She could have done much worse. Would have done much worse if Bennington had been found with her."

Charles sounded so reasonable. "Perhaps you are right."

"Of course I am right. I'm always right."

She pushed on his chest. "No, you're not."

He covered her hand with his and grinned down at her. "No? Well, I think I'm right in saying it's time to stop talking about Meg."

"Well . . ." She sucked in her breath as his hand skimmed over her breasts again.

"And I am also right in my opinion that this nightgown is very much in the way. I want to have your beautiful body naked under mine."

He started to pull her nightgown up. She lifted her hips to assist him, and then sat up to yank the gown over her head. She sent it sailing off into the shadows.

"On that point at least, Lord Knightsdale, I will not argue."

Chapter 5

God, he had to piss.

Viscount Bennington pushed himself into a sitting position and paused. His head throbbed, his jaw ached, and he felt every damn scratch from his encounter with Palmerson's holly bush.

He was in Lord Needham's house. He felt like hell.

He cradled his poor head in his hands. How many bottles of port had they consumed last night—or was it this morning? His mouth felt like the bottom of a horse's stall.

He should have gone home after that scene in the shrubbery. He would have if he hadn't stepped out of the alley right into Claxton's path. Of course the man had wanted to know what had happened to him. He'd looked like he'd been set upon by brigands.

He had been. Damn Parker-Roth. The bounder had given him no warning, sneaking up behind him like that. He'd had no chance to defend himself.

But then what did he expect from horse dung like Parker-Roth?

Lord Peter emitted a loud snore from a nearby couch. Bennington considered stuffing his cravat in the man's mouth. The linen was beyond saving anyway, covered with blood as it was.

Really, the scene in the garden had all been Miss Peterson's fault. She had lured him into the bushes. Not that he hadn't known what she'd wanted, of course. It wasn't a secret. She'd been working her way through the men of the *ton.* At least he'd offered marriage.

He snorted. She was little better than a light-skirt. He was well quit of her.

Lord Peter must be the loudest snorer in Christendom. Bennington picked a snuff box off a nearby table and flung it at the man. It bounced off his shoulder. He didn't waken, but at least he turned over.

Blast. Would Miss Peterson tell Knightsdale what he had done? He didn't relish explaining to the marquis that his sister-in-law was Haymarket ware, but he would if he had to. He could only tell the truth, after all.

Damn, where was the bloody chamber pot? You'd think Needham would have several in evidence given the number of men scattered about the room.

He struggled to his feet. Perhaps Needham had a water closet, but he didn't have time to go searching for it and he sure as hell couldn't make it to the privy out back.

He couldn't abuse the potted palm . . . it would just have to be the hideous urn by the door. The way he felt, he could probably fill the damn thing to the brim.

Lady Felicity rested her head against the cool glass of the window and watched the sun struggle through the sooty London air. One ray of light managed to reach the garden, illuminating the tangled mass of greenery.

Once she had thought the garden exciting, a place for endless trysts. Now it merely looked untidy. Well, of course it did. The gardeners had all quit. They were tired of not being paid.

She closed her eyes and pressed her forehead harder against the glass, swallowing the panic that was becoming her constant companion. How long before the *ton* knew her father was teetering on the edge of penury?

She took a deep breath. Calm. She must remain calm.

Perhaps society would not find out for a few more months. She had not known until just a fortnight ago. The signs had been there, of course. She just had not seen them.

She took another breath. She needed to get out of this house before her father was completely disgraced. She needed to find a husband while she still could. She needed . . .

Damn. She dashed the stupid tears from her eyes. Crying never solved anything. What was the matter with her? It wasn't even the right time of the month for her to be all weepy.

She turned from the window, her eyes sliding over the empty spot on her bureau where the little china cat had stood. She winced. How could she have been so stupid? It had taken this to make her see the facts right under her nose.

The servants had been complaining and then leaving, but her father often didn't bother himself with paying wages on time. Certainly he would never pay a tradesman promptly. He still had his brothels, his gambling dens. He went out every night. How was she to know?

And then she'd come home from the Amberson soiree and found the china cat gone. She'd stared at the blank spot, the clear round circle surrounded by dust, and realized how many other empty circles she'd noticed recently. She'd gone directly to the earl.

At first he'd said the maid had broken it, but she'd heard the lie in his voice. His words had been just a little too smooth—and the maid had left the week before. Finally he'd told her the truth. He'd sold it.

She gripped her bedpost tightly. Why? It was just a trumpery piece of crockery. She'd only kept it because it had belonged to her mother. He couldn't have gotten more than a farthing or two for it.

When she'd asked, he'd shrugged and said he was sorry, but he was that desperate. He'd made one bad investment too many, that was all. He would come about shortly.

Once she heard he'd gone to the cent-per-centers, she knew there was little hope of that.

What was she going to do?

Marry. A husband would solve her problems. She'd been such a fool to waste four years of her life running after the Earl of Westbrooke.

Enough. She was like a dog chasing its tail. Her senseless pursuit of Westbrooke was in the past. She had to look to the future. Quickly. Surely she could find a man to marry before her father's financial situation became known. It could not be so obvious. The denizens of the *haut ton* never paid their bills on time, and the earl was still spending as if he had plenty of the ready.

She sighed. He'd had another of his parties last night. Why couldn't he entertain the riffraff of the *ton* at his brothels or gaming halls instead of his home?

At least this had been a male-only gathering. The men played cards and drank themselves into a stupor. Occasionally there was a fist fight, but the commotion was nothing compared to that which ensued when a few prostitutes were added. She'd taken to arming herself with a suitably long, sturdy pin if she had to venture into the corridors during one of those entertainments.

Well, the beaux and dandies should be waking up and taking themselves off in a few hours. She would just curl up with her book and read until they had vacated the premises. With luck, the detritus of their visit would not be too disgusting to clean up.

She looked on the table by her favorite chair for the novel she was reading. It wasn't there. She searched her sitting room. The book wasn't by her bed or on her bureau or desk. When had she last had it?

Ah, now she remembered. She'd been reading in the blue drawing room when her father had come in with four or five loud, tipsy men. He'd asked her to tell Cook to make up a late supper. She must have put the book down when she'd gotten up to hurry to the kitchen.

She rubbed her forehead. Cook had not been happy. She was certain the woman was going to quit at any moment. It didn't help that she, too, had not been paid recently.

She glanced at the clock on the mantel. It was not quite ten. The men would still be asleep. She should be able to fetch her book without having to deal with any unpleasant gentlemen.

She made her way downstairs, slowing as she approached the door to the blue drawing room. Long experience had taught her to be cautious.

She heard only snoring. Good. The men were still sleeping off the effects of their carousing. If she tread lightly, she should be able to retrieve her book with no one the wiser.

She stepped up to the door—and froze.

Oh, my.

Not all the men were asleep. Viscount Bennington

was standing not five feet from her, urinating into late, unlamented Great Aunt Hermione's favorite urn.

Damn. She was going to lose another servant over this. She opened her mouth to tell the man exactly what she thought of his action.

And then she looked at the action a little more closely.

Impressive—*very* impressive. She never would have guessed such a short, unimposing man could be so, so . . . imposing. Apparently the size of a man's nose did reveal the size of his other attributes.

Hmm. Lord Bennington might be an excellent matrimonial candidate. He certainly was well equipped to perform his marital duties.

"My lord—"

"What?!"

The viscount jerked toward her. Unfortunately he had not yet completed his previous activity. She dodged.

"Lady Felicity—ack!"

Bennington hit Mrs. Tadmon, this week's housekeeper, squarely in the bodice. He had quite a remarkable range.

She didn't need to hear the woman scream to know she'd soon be trying to fill that position, too.

"Lady Isabelle, Lady Claire, and Miss Peterson, my lady."

Meg stepped past Bentley, the Earl of Westbrooke's butler. She didn't want to be here, but when she'd received Lizzie's note this morning, she'd known there was no help for it. Lizzie was quite capable of hunting her down at some society affair to ferret out whatever information she wanted. Best to see her now, in the privacy of Westbrooke House. Hopefully the girls' presence would keep the conversation from becoming too uncomfortable.

Of course, if she were really engaged, she'd be dying to discuss the details with her best friend.

"Thank you, Bentley." Lizzie put down the letter she'd been reading. "I see you've brought the girls, Meg. How lovely."

Lizzie raised her brows, giving Meg a very pointed look. Meg tried not to flush. So, Lizzie had seen through her subterfuge. Well, she'd known it was a weak plan.

"Would you bring our guests tea and cakes, Bentley? I assume you'd like some refreshment, ladies?"

"Yes, please."

"No, thank you."

Claire skipped over to take a seat by Lizzie. "Don't pay any attention to Isabelle, Lady Westbrooke. She's practicing being perfect for her come-out."

"I am not. My come-out's not for four years, Claire."

"Well, you're worrying about it already. I can tell." Claire rolled her eyes. "You're always trying to be extra good and grown up. You're like a mouse with a cat staring at it, afraid to move."

"That's not true!" Isabelle's face turned red.

"Yes, it is." Claire smiled at Lizzie. "Cakes would be lovely, Lady Westbrooke. I 'specially like poppy cake. Do you suppose you have any in your kitchen?"

"Claire!" Isabelle said. "You have no manners at all. What would Emma say?"

"She'd say I was acting just as I should."

"She would not."

"Would, too."

"Girls!" Meg felt like rolling her own eyes. "Please do not argue."

"I'm sorry, Aunt Meg, Lady Westbrooke. It's just that

Claire—" Isabelle pressed her lips together, obviously holding back a few choice words.

"Sorry." Claire shrugged, then grinned at Lizzie. "I *would* like tea and cake, Lady Westbrooke, if it's not too much trouble. I do get *so* hungry, you know."

Lizzie laughed. "Yes, I can see that you do." She looked up at her butler. "Bentley, could you see if Cook has any poppy cake?"

"Certainly, my lady."

Bentley left to search out provisions. Claire tapped Lizzie on the knee.

"Where's your baby, Lady Westbrooke? I was hoping to see him."

"He's up in the nursery, Claire, sleeping. Nurse should be bringing him down in a little while, though, as it's almost time for his next feeding." Lizzie turned to Isabelle. "You've changed so much since last I saw you, Isabelle. You look very much like a young lady now."

"That's because she's grown breasts, Lady Westbrooke," Claire said. "It makes her shape all different."

Isabelle's face grew even redder, assuming the color of a very ripe apple.

"Claire! I would not have brought you if I'd realized you lacked any sense of decorum." Meg frowned. She felt a surge of sympathy for Emma. She knew her sister loved her nieces as much as her sons, but raising a thirteen-year-old girl and an eight-year-old had to be challenging. *She* certainly felt challenged at the moment.

Claire crossed her arms and pushed out her lower lip. "I don't see why you are in such a miff, Aunt Meg. It's just us ladies. I wouldn't have said it if Lord Westbrooke were here. Isabelle is quite proud of her breasts—she studies them in the mirror all the time."

Isabelle made a strangling sound.

"Claire," Meg said, "you are not making things better."

Lizzie bit her lip, her eyes dancing. "It is my fault for broaching the subject. I apologize, Isabelle. I do remember what it was like to be thirteen, though I didn't have the . . . joy . . . of having a sister."

"You were very lucky, Lady Westbrooke."

"You may be correct, Isabelle, but I did want a sister desperately." Lizzie smiled at Meg. "I made do with a good friend."

"Friends are *much* better than sisters." Isabelle glared at Claire.

Claire stuck out her tongue. "I don't know what you are so upset about, Isabelle. Most women like their breasts. *I'm* looking forward to having a pair."

"You are?" Meg had always thought Claire precocious, but surely she was much too young for such concerns.

"Of course. I want to have babies and feed them like Emma does Henry. I'll need breasts to do that, won't I?"

"Well, er, yes."

Fortunately Bentley returned just then. Claire grabbed a cake before the butler could set the tray on the table.

"Claire, Lady Westbrooke will think you are starving."

"I *am* starving, Aunt Meg," Claire said around a mouthful of cake. "It's been hours since breakfast. And Lady Westbrooke's Cook will be offended if we don't eat some of her treats." Claire popped the last of the cake into her mouth and reached for a biscuit.

"Would you care for something before your sister eats it all, Isabelle?" Lizzie asked. "Cook *is* a very good baker."

"No, thank you, Lady Westbrooke."

"A cup of tea, then? Meg?"

Claire licked her fingers. "I'd really like to see your new baby, you know, Lady Westbrooke. If Nurse doesn't bring him down soon, do you think we could go up to the nursery? After we finish the cakes, of course."

A mouthful of tea went down the wrong way. Meg coughed. "Claire!"

Lizzie laughed. "Once you've assuaged your hunger, Claire, we can—"

"Waaah!"

They turned to see the Earl of Westbrooke standing in the doorway holding a small, screaming bundle.

Meg felt a sudden, sharp pain around her heart. How would Parks handle a baby? Their baby.

What a ridiculous thought. She would not be having any babies with Mr. Parker-Roth.

"Sorry to interrupt," Robbie said, "but Lord Manders is hungry."

"So I hear." Lizzie held out her arms. "Why are *you* bringing him? Where's Nurse?"

The earl flushed slightly and handed the wailing viscount to his mother. "She's in the nursery. I just happened to stop by when the baby woke up."

"I see. Did you, perhaps, wake the baby?"

Robbie grinned sheepishly. "Perhaps. He was so quiet, I needed to be certain he was still alive. And Nurse said it was almost time for him to eat."

"Hmph." Lizzie adjusted her clothing and offered her son her breast. He stopped crying immediately.

"Ah," Robbie said. "Peace at last."

Lizzie smiled slightly. She was looking down at the viscount, stroking his tiny hand. She had a completely besotted expression on her face.

Meg felt another odd stab of pain. Tears pricked her eyes, but she blinked them away. What was the matter with her? She'd never felt maudlin when she'd watched Emma nurse Charlie or Henry.

She looked at Robbie instead, but that didn't help. His expression was even more besotted than Lizzie's. It was such a mix of love and joy, wonder and pride, it made her want to cry all the more.

Robbie had been forced to marry Lizzie. Perhaps if Parks—

No. Her situation was not the same at all. Robbie and Lizzie had known each other forever. No one had been able to understand why they hadn't wed years ago, when Lizzie'd made her come-out.

Parks barely knew her. He had no feelings for her at all.

She flushed, remembering with painful clarity their activities in Lady Palmerson's parlor.

Well, yes, he had *those* sorts of feelings, but they meant nothing. They weren't feelings, really—they were urges. Animal instincts. Appetites. He would feel the same . . . frenzy with any female.

She swallowed a sob.

Robbie tore his gaze away from his wife and son. "Did you say something, Meg?"

"Oh, no. A crumb got stuck in my throat." She took a sip of tea.

"Oh." He looked at her searchingly and then smiled at the girls. "Forgive me for not greeting you when I arrived, ladies, but as you saw—or heard—I had other issues to deal with."

"We understand completely, my lord," Isabelle said.

Robbie grinned. "Did you have a pleasant trip up to Town, Lady Isabelle?"

The girl's thin face flushed and she sat even straighter. "Yes, my lord. Very pleasant."

For once Claire didn't squeeze into the conversation.

She was still sitting by Lizzie, watching Viscount Manders.

"The weather has been unexceptional, don't you agree, my lord?"

Meg hid her smile. Bless Robbie. He didn't laugh at Isabelle's attempt at conversation. He was treating her as if she were indeed a society lady.

"Yes," he said. "I—"

"Bwaaap!"

Claire—and even Isabelle—giggled.

"My lord, your manners!" Robbie said. "Don't you know it is impolite to belch in the presence of ladies?"

Lord Manders gave his father a wide smile, dribbling a bit of milk down his chin, before returning to his meal.

"Did you know," Claire said, "that he has red hair?"

"By George! So he does!"

"Robbie . . ." Lizzie gave her husband an intense look. He grinned back at her.

"I guess it is no surprise, since many people say my hair is red."

"It is, my lord," Isabelle said seriously.

"Do you think so, Lady Isabelle? Then it must be true." The earl sat back, his smile growing broader. "But enough about me and mine—what do you think of Miss Peterson's approaching nuptials?"

Dead silence met this query.

"Oops," Robbie said.

"Aunt Meg is getting married?" Isabelle turned to Meg.

"When? Why didn't you tell us, Aunt Meg?" Claire demanded.

Meg felt her face flame. "Nothing is decided. I have not . . . I really don't think I'll . . . there's been no announcement."

She hoped. Oh dear. She hadn't thought to check the papers this morning. But surely Parks wouldn't put anything in print when she had clearly refused his suit.

"Robbie," Lizzie said, "why don't you take the girls out to the stables? I believe Bentley mentioned there's a new litter of kittens."

"Kittens?" Claire jumped up. "I love kittens."

"These are an especially splendid set, I'm sure." Robbie rose and offered Claire his arm, then turned to Isabelle. "Are you coming, Lady Isabelle?"

Isabelle flushed. She looked at Meg.

Meg repressed a sigh. It was clear Isabelle was dying to go. It wasn't fair to hide behind her—and Lizzie was completely capable of saying what she pleased even with Isabelle present.

"Go along. I'll stay and talk with Lady Westbrooke."

Isabelle treated Meg to her sweet, fleeting smile and took the earl's other arm.

"I think Isabelle may be forming a tendre for Robbie," Meg said once the voices and footsteps had faded down the corridor.

"It will do her good. He'll be careful of her feelings."

"I know he will."

Lizzie held Lord Manders on her shoulder. "I shouldn't speak ill of the dead, but it was a blessing in disguise when the former Lord and Lady Knightsdale were killed. The girls are much better off with Emma and Charles for parents." She patted the viscount on the back. He burped again.

"Ooo, what a *good* baby." She bussed his fat cheeks loudly. He giggled.

Meg tried not to roll her eyes. She certainly would not be such a ninny when she had a child.

If she had a child.

"So tell me about Parks," Lizzie said, putting the

viscount to her other breast. "What did he say when he proposed? When is the wedding? Are you excited?"

"Um. Well . . ."

"I knew you two would make a match of it when I saw you together at Tynweith's house party." Lizzie frowned. "I don't think I saw the notice in the paper this morning. Was it there?"

"Ah . . . no." So that question was answered. She shouldn't have worried. Why would Parks send something to the papers? He obviously did not want to tie the knot.

"Oh. Well, I expect it will be in tomorrow."

Meg avoided Lizzie's eyes. "I don't think so."

"Why not?"

"Because, well . . . I'm not engaged."

"*What?!* How can you not be engaged? You were sitting on Parks's lap, your dress—"

"Yes. I know. But it really wasn't Mr. Parker-Roth's fault—"

"*You* pulled your dress down?"

"No, of course not." Meg shifted in her chair. "One thing just led to another, if you know what I mean."

"I can't say that I do." Lizzie grinned. "Oh, I understand the bit about one thing leading to another, but usually that all leads to an engagement."

"Well, in this case it didn't."

"Why not?"

"Lizzie! I really don't want to discuss it." Meg cleared her throat. "I hope we didn't interrupt anything with our visit this morning. You were in the middle of reading a letter?"

Lizzie gave her a searching look. She was clearly not giving up on the topic. "Yes, I was. From Aunt Gladys." She laughed. "You may not be engaged, but Aunt Gladys is."

"Lady Gladys?" Lady Gladys would not see seventy again. She had been Lizzie's chaperone until she'd retired to Bath. She was much stricter than Lady Beatrice. If Lady Gladys had been in charge last year, they would never have gone to Tynweith's house party and Meg would never have met Mr. Parker-Roth—which would have been a very good thing.

If her first encounter with Parks had been in Lord Palmerson's garden last night, would she feel differently now? She was not a starry-eyed debutante. She hadn't expected to fall madly in love with a potential suitor. She'd been prepared to make an intelligent, rational choice without the discomfort of a pounding heart and heaving bosom.

Viewed dispassionately, Parks was a perfect matrimonial candidate. He was wealthy, male, and interested in horticulture. Perfect—except he'd not shown the slightest interest in her from the time he'd left Tynweith's estate until he'd rescued her in the garden. And his reaction in the parlor could hardly be called "interest." Animal lust, that was all it was.

She didn't need to be loved, but she didn't care to be ignored and then treated like a . . . whore.

She sniffed. She would not cry. How ridiculous. And she would not marry a man who could treat her with such a lack of respect.

An annoying little voice whispered in her conscience: *You weren't exactly pushing him away, were you?*

Heat rushed up her neck to her cheeks. Her heart pounded in her ears.

All right, perhaps she, too, had experienced lust. She would not have thought herself capable of such a feeling, but apparently she was. How embarrassing! Certainly Emma and Lizzie were not prone to such a base emotion. They must conduct their conjugal encounters in a much more dignified fashion.

"Are you finished eating, sweetums?" Lord Manders had twisted to look at Meg. Lizzie lifted him up, patting him on the back. "Is your little belly full?"

He answered with yet another hearty burp.

"Good, boy." She kissed him—and he grabbed a fistful of her hair.

"Ow!"

Lord Manders squealed and grabbed more hair.

Meg tried not to laugh. "Do you need help, Lizzie?"

"What does it look like? Of course I need help."

Meg wrapped her hands around the baby's sturdy middle while Lizzie worked to free herself. The viscount had gotten so much stronger since last she'd seen him. He was four months old now.

"Come, my lord. Let go of your poor mother."

He looked up and gave her a wide baby grin.

Lizzie curled his last finger open.

"There." She sat back quickly. "You take him, will you? I'll never be able to look at the letter if I've got him on my lap. He's turning into a regular octopus."

Meg sat down with Lord Manders in her arms. His solid little weight felt good. Emma's Henry was already nine months old, so holding him was more like a wrestling match—he always wanted to be off crawling into mischief. Viscount Manders was too young to squirm. She cuddled him closer.

She'd never been one of those girls who cooed over babies. She'd expected to have some, of course. It was her duty—an inconvenient but inevitable chore that would take time away from her horticultural pursuits. But now . . . well, perhaps having children would not be so dreadful. She just had to find the proper husband and father.

Resolutely, she banished Mr. Parker-Roth's image from her mind.

Lizzie squinted down at the letter she now held in her hand. "Yes, Lady Gladys is definitely engaged."

"To whom?"

"Lord Dearvon."

Meg frowned. Lord Dearvon . . . surely it couldn't be . . . "The elderly bald man with the hairy ears who's always talking about Waterloo?"

"Well, I believe Aunt Gladys refers to him as an old friend who shares her love for the theater, but yes, I think you have the correct gentleman."

Lady Gladys and Lord Dearvon. Together. Married. Doing things married people did . . .

No. It was not possible.

"Isn't Lady Gladys rather old for marriage?"

"One would certainly think so."

One would certainly hope so. "Perhaps she is looking for a companion to share her old age—though I thought she already had a companion."

Lizzie grinned. "You won't believe this either, but Lady Amanda is marrying as well—a Mr. Pedde-Wilt. I think, though I am not completely certain—Aunt Gladys, in a moment of false economy, crossed her lines so much I have trouble understanding her scribble— but I think they are having a joint ceremony. Soon. In May—unless Aunt Gladys was saying Lord Dearvon's gout *may* keep them from a wedding trip. It really is very hard to puzzle out."

The entire situation was very hard to puzzle out.

Lizzie put down the letter and leaned forward. "So about Parks—"

"Ack!"

Lord Manders looked up to see who had made that strange sound.

"I do not wish to discuss Mr. Parker-Roth."

"I don't care what you wish, Meg." Lizzie frowned at her. "You know, Robbie and I were getting very worried about you."

"Worried?" Meg tried to laugh. "Why would you worry about me?"

"You've been disappearing into the shrubbery at every social event."

Meg flushed. "I only stepped out with one or two—"

"Or five or six. If you thought you were being discreet, you were mistaken. Robbie told me men were starting to make wagers as to whom your next partner would be."

"No."

"Yes. Surely you noted the rakes beginning to cluster around you?"

"Um . . ." She *had* been slightly uncomfortable recently. She hadn't missed the men's odd pauses, significant glances, and muffled laughter, but she'd chosen to ignore them. Most of the men of the *ton* were coxcombs and jinglebrains—she didn't expect much rational behavior from them.

"You used to be very observant; I thought you must have noticed. And it's not just that—mothers are starting to shepherd their little debutantes away from you. In fact, all the marriageable misses are avoiding you as if you had the plague."

"No." Meg frowned. "I'm certain you must be mistaken." Perhaps she had noticed fewer women talking to her, but she'd been happy for it. She didn't like the London girls. They were silly, shallow, boring creatures capable of discussing only the weather and the most recent gossip.

"Robbie and I were delighted to see you with Parks

last night. I don't know why you refused his offer—he did offer, didn't he?"

"Yes."

"So why did you decline? You were quite taken with him at Tynweith's house party."

"I was not."

Lizzie just looked at her. Meg shifted in her chair.

"I enjoyed talking to the man. He is very knowledgeable about horticulture. It was nothing more than that."

Lizzie raised one eyebrow. "I seem to remember at least one luncheon you missed because of Mr. Parker-Roth."

"We were discussing garden design."

"Hmm."

"Don't look at me like that. It is perfectly permissible for a man and a woman with common interests to have a sensible conversation without the need to call the banns. My feelings for Mr. Parker-Roth are nothing more than respect for another horticulturist."

Lord Manders chose this moment to let out a very ominous noise. The sound did not emanate from his mouth.

Meg wrinkled her nose and looked down in horror at the smelly little creature sitting on one of her favorite dresses. The creature grinned back.

"Those are my sentiments exactly, Bobby," Lizzie said, picking up her son. "Auntie Meg is indeed full of . . ."

Lizzie rolled her eyes and went to change her baby.

Chapter 6

"Lady Knightsdale would like to speak with you, Miss Peterson. She's in the nursery with the Duchess of Alvord."

"Thank you, Blake."

"Did the duchess bring her children?" Claire asked.

"Yes, Lady Claire."

"Oh, good."

Claire ran ahead. Isabelle waited for Meg.

"Did you enjoy your visit with Lord and Lady Westbrooke, Isabelle? Claire was rattling on so in the carriage about the kittens, I don't believe you got a word in edgewise."

Isabelle smiled fleetingly. "Yes, Aunt Meg." She looked down, fiddling with her bonnet ribbons. "*Are* you getting married?"

Trust Isabelle to remember Robbie's comment.

"No, of course not."

Isabelle looked up, her eyes full of doubt and worry. "Then why did Lord Westbrooke think you were?"

"I don't know." Meg did not want to discuss last night's events. The entire business was best forgotten. "Let's go see the duchess, shall we?"

Isabelle frowned, then dropped her gaze back to the floor. "All right."

They started up the stairs. It was so quiet, Meg could hear the whisper of their slippers on the marble. Isabelle was not a chatterbox by any means, but she usually said *something*.

This silence was heavy, too full of unspoken words.

"Did you like the kittens, Isabelle?"

"Yes."

There was no enthusiasm in her voice. Meg glanced at her. Isabelle had grown. Her eyes were almost level with Meg's—if she would raise them from the stairs.

"Did you have a favorite?"

"No."

Meg felt like a chatterbox now. "Are you certain? Claire seemed very partial to the black one."

That made Isabelle look up. "Aunt Meg, I am thirteen. I am not a baby. I—" She bit her lip and looked back down at her slippers.

They climbed the last few steps in silence.

Isabelle was correct—she was not a baby. She had survived a cold, abusive mother and a selfish, self-centered father—and the shock of their murder when she was nine. Physically, too, she was almost a woman. Too soon she would take an interest in men—and they would take an interest in her. She deserved the truth. She needed it.

Meg stopped at the top of the stairs. "Isabelle, I was not completely honest just now. I do know why Lord Westbrooke thought I was getting married. Something happened last night at the Palmerson ball. Some people feel I've been compromised, but I do not agree."

"What happened?"

There was honesty—and then there was honesty.

"It's rather complicated. I made the mistake of going into the garden with a man."

"Aunt Emma said you'd gone into the garden with lots of men."

Meg felt herself flush, partly in anger. "It was not lots, Isabelle. I'm surprised Emma said such a thing to you."

"Oh, she didn't tell *me*. She was talking to your stepmother. She didn't know I was listening."

"Oh." Meg could believe that. Isabelle had perfected the skill of listening unobtrusively in the last year. "Well, I do agree that I made a definite mistake last night." She put a hand on Isabelle's shoulder and looked directly into her eyes. "Emma will give you many lectures on proper deportment—"

Isabelle smiled. "She already has."

"I'm sure." Sometimes, growing up, Meg had felt Emma spoke only in lectures. "Well, much as her . . . advice can be annoying, you should listen to it. Especially the part about not being alone with a man. You cannot always tell by looking at him whether a man is a blackguard or not."

Isabelle nodded. "I know."

Unfortunately, she probably did know—her father had been a prime example of a handsome blackguard.

They started up the next flight of stairs to the nursery.

"Who is the blackguard you have to marry, Aunt Meg?"

Meg stumbled, catching herself on the banister. "I do not have to marry the blackguard! I mean, the blackguard is not the man people think I have to marry— not that I need to marry anyone, of course."

Isabelle stared at Meg. "I don't understand."

Meg examined the banister rather than meet Isabelle's eyes. "I went into the garden with one gentleman. When he became too . . . amorous, another gentleman rescued me. Unfortunately, someone saw me with the second gentleman and assumed . . ." Meg cleared her throat. "This person took it upon herself to spread the story, telling everyone the second man had behaved inappropriately, which he had not."

At least not in the garden.

Meg repressed that thought.

Isabelle frowned. "That isn't fair." She sounded suitably incensed.

"No, it isn't."

"Who spread the story? Perhaps the woman did not tell that many people."

Meg continued up the stairs. "It was Lady Dunlee."

"Oh." Isabelle hesitated a moment before following her. "Then you *are* ruined."

"I am *not!*"

"Aunt Meg, even I know Lady Dunlee's the *ton's* biggest gossip."

They reached the nursery level just in time to hear a large crash. A baby started wailing.

"That sounds like Henry," Isabelle said. "He's probably pulled something over on himself again."

"Again?"

"Yes. He keeps trying to stand. He pulls up on things and they inevitably fall over. It is driving us all mad."

Sure enough, when they entered the room, Emma was holding Henry and a small chair was on its side.

"I swear I am going to bolt everything to the floor until he can walk," Emma said to the Duchess of Alvord.

Her Grace smiled. "David started walking just last month, so I know exactly how you feel."

"Thank God we left Prinny at home. A dog running around the nursery is the last thing we need."

"It would make things more difficult, to be sure." Her Grace smiled at Meg. "Miss Peterson. How are you?"

"Very well, Your Grace."

Emma spun around. "Meg! I've been waiting for you." She looked at Henry in her arms. "Oh, hush, you silly baby. I can't hear myself think." She followed this with a loud, wet kiss on Henry's cheek, turning his cries to belly laughs. Then he was squirming to be let down.

"Isabelle, can you watch Henry for me? Try to keep him from tipping over something else, will you?"

Isabelle smiled and followed Henry as he crawled across the nursery floor to where Claire was watching the duchess's second son, one-year-old Lord David, drop lead soldiers into a pot. The duke's heir, the Marquis of Walthingham, and Emma's oldest son, Charlie, Lord Lexington, were at the far end of the nursery, building a tower with blocks.

"Don't let Henry eat the soldiers, Isabelle."

"I won't."

Emma turned her attention back to Meg. "Meg, Mrs. Parker-Roth sent word round this morning. She asked if we might call on her this afternoon. Of course I said yes."

Meg felt her stomach knot. She did not want to see Parks's mother.

"I don't know if that's a good idea."

"Of course it is. You want to get to know your future mother-in-law, don't you?"

"She is not my future mother-in-law. I am not marrying Mr. Parker-Roth."

"Don't be a goosecap, Meg. Of course you are. You don't have a choice."

"Emma . . ."

"Perhaps it would be wise to lower your voices, ladies," the duchess said. She tilted her head toward where Isabelle and Claire were playing with Henry and David—and obviously eavesdropping.

Emma frowned, but said more softly, "Sarah, can you persuade Meg?"

"I doubt it. I refused to marry James just to suit your British notions of propriety, remember."

"I assure you that even in the United States Meg would have to marry Mr. Parker-Roth."

"Really?" The duchess looked at Meg. "So there's a chance of an interesting event in nine months' time?"

"No!"

Lord David dropped the infantryman he was about to put in his mouth. All the children turned to stare at Meg.

She took a deep breath and let it out slowly, speaking in little more than a whisper this time. "No, there is no chance of that whatsoever, Your Grace. It is completely impossible."

"Well, if nothing of that nature occurred . . . ?"

"Definitely not."

"Then I don't see why you must marry Mr. Parker-Roth if you don't wish to."

Emma made an annoyed sound. "Sarah, you don't comprehend the gravity of the situation. Meg was found in an extremely disheveled state by Lady Dunlee. There's no hope of containing the scandal. You might as well try to collect dandelion seeds after a strong wind."

"It can't be that bad. You and Charles will stand by her, Emma, as will Robbie and Lizzie and James and I. I've been among your society long enough to know the *ton* will not risk offending a duke, a marquis, and an earl."

"But, Sarah—"

The duchess put her hand on Emma's arm. "You are

understandably concerned. There may be—will be—a little talk this Season, but after a few months, when it is obvious there's nothing"—the duchess nodded at Meg's waist—"developing, people will move on to other scandals. It is certainly not worth Meg chaining herself for life to a reprobate."

Meg opened her mouth to protest the duchess calling Parks a reprobate, but Emma spoke first.

"There will be far more than a little talk!"

Sarah shrugged. "So Meg goes home for the rest of the Season. That's not a tragedy."

Emma was visibly struggling to contain her temper. "If she goes home now, everyone will assume the worst."

"Emma!"

The children looked at Meg again. She dropped her voice with effort. "Emma—"

"Meg, that is exactly what they will think. You would not be the first young lady to retreat from London because she is breeding."

"I am *not* breeding."

Emma put her hands on her hips. "And you won't ever be if you don't wed soon. You are twenty-one. You are not getting any younger."

The duchess laughed. "Emma, both you and I were well over twenty-one when we married."

"That was different. Neither of us had had the opportunity to meet an eligible party. And neither of us was darting into the shrubbery with any passing gentleman."

"I was not darting into the shrubbery with any passing gentleman."

Emma glared at Meg. "Your reputation is hanging by a thread, miss. Sarah has been giving me an earful."

"Your Grace." Meg had not expected the duchess to bear tales.

"It's true, Meg. I don't think you should wed Mr. Parker-Roth if you cannot care for him, but you *are* in danger of putting yourself beyond the pale.".

"I suppose you could go home and marry Mr. Cuttles," Emma said. "He's recently widowed. I believe he's in the market for a new wife."

Emma couldn't be serious. "I am not marrying Mr. Cuttles. He's at least fifty years old!"

"Oh, I don't believe he's much past forty-five. And he's in fine shape for a man his age."

"He could be in spectacular shape—I am not marrying him." Meg turned to the duchess. "And though I'm not marrying Mr. Parker-Roth either, he is *not* a reprobate."

"He's not?" The duchess frowned. "But he attacked you in the shrubbery, didn't he?"

"No, that was Lord Bennington. Mr. Parker-Roth rescued me."

"And attacked you in Lady Palmerson's parlor," Emma said.

Meg flushed. "He didn't precisely attack me—and, in any event, Lady Dunlee did not see that."

"Mrs. Parker-Roth did, though." Emma smiled for once. "She said it was completely out of character, that her son was usually a fusty old stick. I think she was rather pleased."

"I'm certain you are mistaken." Meg was certain if she got any redder, she'd burst into flame.

"Ah." The duchess looked like she was trying not to laugh. "And I assume you were struggling to escape Mr. Parker-Roth's attentions, Meg?"

"Um . . ." Meg looked away, down to where Lord Walthingham and Charlie were still building their tower. Lord David was just about to—

"Watch out!"

Too late. David laughed and grabbed for a block, sending the tower crashing to the ground.

The earl and the marquis wailed. David fell down and started crying. Henry, not to be left out, opened his mouth and howled.

Meg wished she could scream along with the children.

"Pinky, I've invited Miss Peterson and Lady Knightsdale to call this afternoon."

Parks put down his coffee and glared at his mother. "Do *not* call me 'Pinky.'"

Mother smiled briefly. "Sorry. I forgot."

"You did not forget. You did it on purpose to annoy me."

Mother looked at him reproachfully. Damn. Now he'd hurt her feelings.

"Your pardon. I'm a little peevish this morning. I did not sleep well."

Mother reached over and patted his hand.

"Of course you're a bit out of sorts. A lot has occurred in the last few hours. You'll feel better once you settle into your new role."

"My new role?"

"Of married man, of course."

"There is no 'of course' about it, Mother. I told you, Miss Peterson declined my offer. I am not getting married. In fact, I think it was extremely ill-advised of you to invite the ladies here."

"Oh, pish." Mother dipped her toast calmly into her tea. "Of course I invited them. I wish to become acquainted with your future wife." She took a bite of soggy toast. "Don't feel you need to be here, though."

"Mother." He took a deep breath. He would not bellow at her. He would speak slowly and distinctly.

With authority. "Miss Peterson . . . has . . . declined . . . my . . . offer. She will *not* be my wife."

Mother snorted. "Miss Peterson cannot decline your offer."

"Well, she has done so."

"Her family will persuade her to see reason. She'll meet you at the altar."

No one had persuaded Grace to see reason. She'd left him quite alone at the front of the church.

Damn, where had *that* thought come from?

"Mother, this is England. Women cannot be forced to marry. If Miss Peterson does not wish to wed me, there is no more to be said."

"Johnny, you are being purposely obtuse. I know what I saw in Lady Palmerson's parlor. No one was forcing Miss Peterson to hold your head while you—"

"Yes, well, um, enough said about that." He pulled at his cravat. It was damn hot in here. "That was a momentary aberration."

"Well, stage a few more aberrations. I'm sure you can get the girl so overcome with lust, she'll say yes to anything. Why, your father—"

Parks leapt up, spilling his coffee. He mopped at it with his napkin before it could cascade onto the floor. He most assuredly did not want to hear any sentence that began "your father" and followed a sentence containing the word "lust."

"Forgive me. I have just remembered an urgent appointment with my . . . banker. Yes, my banker." He checked his watch. "By Jove, I'm late already. I really must run. So sorry to have to interrupt our chat."

Mother snorted into her tea. He chose to ignore the sound.

"Mac will escort you and Agatha wherever you need to go. I will be out all day."

"Just be certain you are back in time to escort me to the Easthaven ball."

"Yes, yes. Don't worry. I'll be back in time."

He almost ran from the room.

"Hiding?"

Parks grunted. He'd thought he was safe in this remote corner of White's, half hidden by an undernourished ficus tree. He should have known better. Although Westbrooke was normally very easy-going, he could be as tenacious as a terrier if he thought the occasion warranted it.

This, apparently, was such an occasion.

The earl sprawled into the chair next to his, putting a bottle of brandy on the table between them.

"You did pick the perfect place to go to ground, though. White's won't let even the most determined woman through its portals." Westbrooke poured two glasses and handed one to Parks.

It was useless to protest the company—and he needed a drink. He took the amber liquid after only a moment's hesitation.

"Miss Peterson is not determined to find me, I assure you."

"I'm not so sure of that, but I wasn't talking about Meg. Emma is the one who will not let you escape." Westbrooke grinned. "If she chooses to go after you—*when* she chooses to go after you—you have no hope. If she can't locate you, she'll send Charles to find you, wherever you try to hide."

"Surely neither the marchioness nor the marquis want Miss Peterson cursed with an unwilling groom."

Westbrooke paused with his glass at his lips. "Eh? *Are* you unwilling?"

"Of course. You know I do not want to wed. I have no need to. Unlike you, I have no title to pass on."

"Hmm." Westbrooke gave him a long look.

Parks dropped his gaze to study his brandy. Surely the man would let sleeping dogs lie.

A vain hope.

"There are other reasons for marriage, Parks, than primogeniture."

He forced a laugh. "What? Having a female handy for bed play? A mistress can do that as well—better—than some frightened, frigid virgin."

The words came out more harshly than he'd intended. He glanced at Westbrooke. The earl was frowning at him.

"Well, there is that, though I wouldn't have put it quite so crudely."

He wouldn't have either, normally. Damn, his nerves were shot, and his head was pounding as if a blacksmith had set up shop inside it.

"My apologies. Headache, don't you know. I didn't mean any insult. Obviously, marriage is a fine institution. It is just not for me."

"Parks, just because Grace—"

Zeus! He could not go there. "Westbrooke, please. I'm certain you mean well. I just . . . I really do not wish to discuss the topic."

There was a long pause, and then the earl sighed. "Very well. I will change the subject."

"Thank God."

"After I have said just one more word."

Parks groaned. "Must you?"

Westbrooke grinned. "Hear me out and then I promise to leave off teasing you about it—at least for today."

Parks grunted. His teeth were clenched so tightly, he feared his jaw might shatter.

"I hate to see your life ruined because of an event that happened three years ago."

Four, but Parks wasn't counting. "I don't know what you're talking about."

"A little matter of being left at the altar on your wedding day."

"Oh, that." Parks tried to laugh, but the sound got caught in his throat. He turned it into a cough. "Please, Westbrooke, that's ancient history. I hardly give it a thought any more." If "hardly" meant less than ten times a day. "I'm on completely cordial terms with Lady Dawson and her husband."

"Have you spoken to her about it?"

Parks closed his eyes so they didn't start from his head. Talk to Grace about that mortifying morning? Was Westbrooke mad? He'd rather have all his finger and toenails pulled out slowly than talk to Grace about their failed wedding.

"I don't believe the subject has come up. I'm not in London often, you know, and Lady Dawson rarely visits her father."

"That's no surprise. The man's a petty tyrant. I'm certain you can lay the blame for your matrimonial disaster squarely on his doorstep. I wouldn't be surprised if he'd starved the girl to accept your suit. Certainly he must have threatened her in some fashion."

Splendid. That made him feel even better—he was such a sorry connubial candidate a woman had to be forced to wed him. And even coercion hadn't worked. Grace had still managed to flee.

"Why do you think Miss Peterson's family would urge her to accept my suit if another woman so loathed me she had to elope in the dead of night?"

"Lady Dawson didn't loathe you, Parks."

"You don't know that."

Westbrooke gave him an exasperated look. "All right, for the sake of argument, we'll assume she *did* loathe you. She is still only one woman."

"Miss Peterson is not clamoring to wed me, either, as you may have noticed."

"No?" Westbrooke smirked. "I didn't see her struggling to get off your lap in Lady Palmerson's parlor. And one does wonder how she happened to disarrange her dress so noticeably."

"You know she'd been attacked by that bounder, Bennington."

"Bennington wasn't the only one attacking that evening."

Certainly it was too dark in this corner of White's for Westbrooke to see him flush? And he wasn't blushing in any case. He was merely overly warm.

"The fact remains—Miss Peterson rejected my offer. There is nothing more to be said on the matter."

"Oh, I give up. You are impossible." Westbrooke stood abruptly. "Stay here and stew if you like. I will leave you the brandy so you can be well marinated. Just think on this—I almost let my past rule my future. If events hadn't fallen out as they did—if I hadn't been forced by scandal to wed Lizzie—I would never have known happiness. I'd hate to see you miss such pleasure because you also lack the courage to face your past."

"Now wait a minute—"

Westbrooke was already gone.

Bloody, bloody hell. Parks took a large swallow of brandy. It went down the wrong way, sending him into a coughing fit. A few denizens of White's peered around the sad ficus to see who was choking. He muffled his paroxysms with his handkerchief.

He couldn't muffle the galling thought—was Westbrooke right? *Was* he a coward?

Ridiculous. The earl had no idea what he felt. *He* had not been left standing before a church filled with friends, family, and the gossip-hungry *ton*. Westbrooke had not had to see pity in his parents' eyes or listen to the whispering.

Westbrooke had no bloody idea how much Grace's betrayal had hurt.

Damn. He pounded his fist on his knee. The pain felt good. Westbrooke was right about one thing. The disaster with Grace was in the past. It should stay there. It *would* stay there. As soon as Mother finished buying her blasted paints, they would go home to the Priory and he would see if MacGill had taken proper care of the latest shipment of exotic plants.

He would be delighted to leave London. Bloody delighted. He poured himself another large glass of brandy. God, how he hated Town. Once he'd shaken its dust from his feet, he'd feel much better. Everything would be back to normal.

He had a sudden image of Miss Peterson in Lady Palmerson's hideous red parlor, her hair spread over her shoulders. Her long, lovely hair, her white skin, her soft, white breasts. The lovely taste of—

Bloody hell.

He couldn't help it if his male instincts were inflamed by the sight of a half-naked female, could he? He frowned at the specific organ that was currently so inflamed it was almost painful. He shifted in his seat. He was a man, after all. Men were made with certain . . . needs. It was a purely physical, animal reaction.

He took another swallow of brandy.

The worst of it was he couldn't get a decent night's sleep. The damn woman had invaded his dreams. He'd woken twice—no, three times—last night in an extremely uncomfortable state.

He shifted position again. He needed to visit Cat as soon as he got home. A quick session in her bed would cure him of this malady, he was sure of it. It had to or he would go stark, raving mad.

Chapter 7

"Emma, this is most definitely a bad idea."

"Nonsense, Meg. You need to become acquainted with your future mother-in-law."

Meg was sorely tempted to drum her heels against the carriage floor. "Mrs. Parker-Roth is *not* my future mother-in-law. Do I need to take out an announcement in *The Morning Post* for you to understand that?"

"Hmm. Excellent point. Mr. Parker-Roth should place an announcement in the *Post* as soon as possible. I will hint about it to his mother, though I imagine she has already mentioned it to him. She struck me as a very capable woman."

"Emma!" Meg took a deep breath. Shouting never worked with Emma. The woman existed in her own little world, merrily planning away other people's lives. A mature, measured tone would be better.

"Emma." Yes, that sounded more the thing. Calm. Mature. "There. Is. No. Announcement." Excellent. Taking a breath after each word worked wonders. Relaxing her hands would also be a good idea. She was not going to engage in fisticuffs with her sister. "Do. You. Comprehend?"

Emma frowned at her. "What is the matter with you? You sound as queer as Dick's hatband. You didn't hit your head getting into the coach, did you?"

Fisticuffs sounded like an excellent notion. Or strangulation.

"I am *not* marrying Mr. Parker-Roth."

"Meg, please, lower your voice. Whatever would Mr. Parker-Roth's mother think of you?"

Meg tried another deep breath, but it wasn't working. Mature and measured had deserted her. Once Emma got the bit between her teeth, there was no stopping her. She was just like a runaway horse.

She only hoped Mrs. Parker-Roth was more rational.

The coach slowed. Emma looked out the window and nodded. Meg's stomach dropped to her slippers.

"Here we are. Come along, Meg. We don't want to keep our hostess waiting."

Emma was out of the carriage the moment the footman let down the steps. Meg paused and looked up at the impressive façade of the Pulteney, one of London's most fashionable hotels.

It looked like the gates of Hell.

Lud! What if Parks was with his mother? She hadn't considered that, but obviously he was staying here as well.

"Miss Peterson?" The footman extended his hand again to assist her down the steps.

She stared at his gloved fingers. They looked smaller than Parks's. Were they as unfashionably tanned as well? Not that she objected to sun-darkened skin . . . or strong fingers, slightly roughened, sliding over her, cupping her breast, touching her aching nipples—

She took a deep, shuddery breath.

She definitely did not want to see Mr. Parker-Roth, especially in the company of his mother and Emma.

"Are you all right, Miss Peterson?" The footman's voice held a note of worry.

Emma came back to the carriage. "Meg, what is the matter with you?" She glanced at the men and women walking by and leaned closer to hiss, "You are making a spectacle of yourself."

"I—" People *were* beginning to stop and gape at her. "I, um . . ."

"*Come on!*" Emma turned to nod at Mrs. Windham who'd chosen to examine them through her lorgnette. The old bat raised her eyebrow; Emma raised her nose and looked down it as if she were a . . . a . . . marchioness. Meg blinked. Emma *was* a marchioness, of course, and had been for almost four years, but she'd been simple Miss Peterson, the vicar's daughter, for twenty-six years before that. She'd always been somewhat bossy—at least toward Meg—but hardly imperious. Apparently now she'd mastered the trick of putting nasty old tabbies in their place.

Mrs. Windham flushed and nodded back, resuming her progress down Picadilly.

"Stop sitting there like a complete stock and come inside." Emma crossed to the Pulteney's front door where a doorman stood ready to throw open the portal.

Meg scrambled down the steps and grabbed Emma's wrist.

"I really don't think . . . that is, do we have to . . . ?" Meg struggled to breathe.

Emma scowled at her. "What is the matter? You are behaving like a bedlamite."

Meg looked at the doorman. He looked straight ahead as though he were just another Coade stone statue. He had probably seen any manner of minor dramas while at his post, but Meg did not want to add another tale to his collection. She lowered her voice.

"Emma, did Mrs. Parker-Roth happen to say if her son was going to be present?"

Emma grinned. "Anxious to see him again, are you?"

"No!" Just the thought threatened to send her luncheon ignominiously spilling over the walk. Her cheeks felt clammy and her fingers tingled.

God forbid! Was she going to faint?

Emma patted her hand. "Calm yourself. I'll wager Mr. Parker-Roth has taken himself off. He would be very much in the way, as I'm sure he knows."

"He would?" Meg eyed the Knightsdale coach. The footman hadn't put up the steps yet. If she made a dash for it, she could climb back in before it pulled away. "What exactly are we going to discuss?"

"This and that. His family, his interests, his estate."

"Emma . . ."

"Wedding plans—"

"*Emma!* I told you, I'm not marrying Mr. Parker-Roth."

"Don't be ridiculous. Of course you are marrying the man. You have no choice." Emma linked her arm through Meg's and nodded to the stoic doorman. "Come along. Mrs. Parker-Roth must be waiting for us."

A red-headed giant opened the door to the Parker-Roth apartment.

"Please tell your mistress that the Marchioness of Knightsdale and Miss Margaret Peterson are here," Emma said.

"Ack, is that so?" The giant turned to examine Meg from her bonnet to her slippers. "Is this the master's lassie, then?" He gave a low whistle. "I'm thinking Johnny will be a happy man afore he's much older."

Meg felt her cheeks flush. They must be as red as the giant's hair.

"Sir!" Emma said, "I don't believe we asked for your opinion."

The man grinned. "Then ye'll be thanking me fer giving it to ye so generously, won't ye?"

Emma drew in a sharp breath. "You are impertinent."

"Aye." His grin broadened. "I've been told that afore."

"MacGill!" Mrs. Parker-Roth's voice echoed from somewhere in the suite of rooms. "Stop toying with the ladies and show them in."

MacGill smirked. "If ye'll follow me?"

Emma leaned close as the giant set off down a short corridor and whispered, "The man is a very odd sort of butler. You must have a word with Mr. Parker-Roth after the wedding about his suitability."

"Emma," Meg whispered back, "how many times do I have to tell you that there will be no wedding?"

"And how many times do I have to tell you that you have no choice? You *will* marry Mr. Parker-Roth."

Emma spoke a little too loudly. MacGill snorted. Meg was certain he was going to make some comment, but instead he stepped aside for them to enter the parlor.

"Lady Knightsdale, Miss Peterson, welcome." Mrs. Parker-Roth came forward to take their hands. Her face creased into well-worn smile wrinkles, and her green eyes, so like her son's, twinkled at them. "I am so happy you could visit." She gestured to a woman on the settee. "Let me make known to you my traveling companion, Miss Agatha Witherspoon. Agatha, Lady Knightsdale and her sister, Miss Margaret Peterson."

Miss Witherspoon nodded at them. She looked to be on the shady side of sixty. Her hair was gray and wiry, cut so short she bore a striking resemblance to a hedgehog.

She wore an odd, reddish orange printed garment wrapped around her body.

"A sari," Meg muttered in surprise as Mrs. Parker-Roth conferred with MacGill. Father had spoken of these Hindu garments once, but she had never seen one.

"Don't be sorry," Emma said. "Just be sensible."

"What?"

"Didn't you just say you were sorry?"

"No."

"Yes, you did. I heard you quite distinctly."

Miss Witherspoon snorted. "I believe your sister was referring to my gown, Lady Knightsdale."

Emma frowned. "Meg would never make such an impolite observation, would you, Meg?"

"Emma—not *sorry*—sari!"

"I don't know why you need to talk in riddles. If you are not going to—"

Mrs. Parker-Roth turned as MacGill left the room. "Pardon me, Lady Knightsdale. *I* am sorry. I'm sure MacGill's behavior is not what you are used to."

"Definitely not."

Meg bit her tongue. Until Emma had married Charles, she had not been used to any servant behavior whatsoever.

Her sister was not usually so haughty. The strain of being in London—and of dealing with Meg's situation—must be testing her sorely.

"The man's Scottish, you know. Very independent. He's my son's valet, but he acts as our general manservant when we travel. His twin brother is Johnny's head gardener."

"I see. So your son thinks highly of him?"

"Oh, yes indeed. Johnny thinks both the MacGills are beyond reproach." She smiled. "MacGill will be bringing tea in just a few minutes. Please, take a seat."

Meg chose a straight-backed chair with sturdy wooden arms and a seat cushion that had all the give of a small boulder. Emma joined Miss Witherspoon on the settee. Her eyes widened as she finally focused on the woman's attire.

"That *is* quite an unusual frock you are wearing, Miss Witherspoon. I don't believe I've seen its like in Kent. Is it something new?"

"It's a *sari*, Lady Knightsdale," Miss Witherspoon said, speaking very distinctly. "Many of the native women in India wear them. They are quite comfortable."

"Ah. I . . . see."

Emma was obviously struggling to find a suitable rejoinder. Meg took pity on her.

"Have you been to India, Miss Witherspoon?"

"Oh, yes—several times. And to Africa and South America—all over the globe. We just returned from Siam a few weeks ago."

"We?" Meg glanced at Parks's mother. Miss Witherspoon followed her gaze and laughed.

"Oh, not Cecilia. I could never get her away from the Priory for so long a time, though I have tried. No, I travel with my very dear friend Prudence Doddington-Prinz."

Emma frowned. "Is that safe—two ladies traveling by themselves?"

"Well, we don't go alone, of course. Often we have an expedition leader. And Mr. Cox accompanies us as well. He's a former pugilist who can be quite intimidating when the need arises. Not that it does. We are experienced travelers. We do not take unnecessary risks."

Mrs. Parker-Roth snorted.

"Now, Cecilia, you cannot judge. This is the riskiest thing you do—travel to London occasionally." Miss Witherspoon rolled her eyes heavenward. "You lead such a sheltered—such a tame—existence. Frankly, I don't see how you bear it."

"There is nothing tame about my existence, Agatha. I have six children who often bring more excitement into my life than I quite care for."

"But how can you call yourself an artist when you've never visited Italy or Greece and seen the art of the Masters?"

Mrs. Parker-Roth's mouth thinned to a tight line. "Agatha—" She stopped, obviously getting hold of her temper, and then smiled at Meg and Emma. "Forgive me. This is a long-running argument, I'm afraid."

"Indeed it is." Miss Witherspoon leaned toward Meg. "Consider carefully, Miss Peterson. Do not make the same mistake Cecilia did and fall in love with a pair of broad shoulders."

Meg flushed, remembering exactly how being pressed up against a certain pair of broad shoulders—and broad chest and muscular arms—had felt.

"I did not make a mistake," Mrs. Parker-Roth said.

"You did, Cecilia. You could have been a great artist."

"Agatha—"

"Marriage and motherhood are all very well for some people. Obviously if we want the human race to continue, someone must produce the next generation. It just didn't have to be you, Cecilia, and you didn't have to produce so much of it. A little restraint would have been a good thing."

Mrs. Parker-Roth flushed. "Agatha—"

"It's not as though your husband has a title to pass on—and in any event, you took care of that concern, had it been one, promptly with Pinky and Stephen."

"Pinky?" Meg asked. A distraction seemed to be in order.

Mrs. Parker-Roth gave her a somewhat harried smile.

"We called Johnny 'Pinky' when he was little to differentiate him from his father. His middle name is Pinkerton. He doesn't care for the nickname now." She turned back to Miss Witherspoon. "Agatha, really, I don't think—"

"*That* is self evident," Miss Witherspoon said. "You didn't think. Once you met John Parker-Roth at your come-out ball, your brain ceded control of your behavior to your—"

"Agatha!"

"—to some other organ which led you into marriage and then motherhood. Still, if you'd stopped after Stephen, you could have been free years ago—though I grant you, Napoleon made continental travel extremely difficult, if not impossible, for some of that time. But that's neither here nor there. It wasn't the Corsican Monster keeping you chained to England, but your own brood of little demons."

Mrs. Parker-Roth gasped. "You go too far!"

Miss Witherspoon shrugged. "Yes, all right. I apologize. They are very well-behaved demons."

"They are . . . you called my children . . ."

Miss Witherspoon touched Mrs. Parker-Roth's arm. "You could have been such a fine artist, Cecilia."

Parks's mother finally mastered her breathing sufficiently to emit a short, exasperated noise. "I am persuaded I'm as fine an artist as I could ever have been, Agatha."

"I don't think so. Remember all those years ago when we met at Lady Baxter's soirée? You were such a fiery young woman. You said you were only tolerating a Season because it brought you to London and the Royal Academy of Arts. You swore you'd defy your father to pursue your muse."

"I was ridiculous."

"You were *passionate*." Miss Witherspoon sighed. "It is partly my fault, I suppose. I should not have put John in your way, but I never suspected you'd be tempted by a poet."

Meg glanced at Emma. Her sister looked distinctly uncomfortable, as if the conversation was galloping at breakneck speed toward a precipice and she had not an inkling how to rein it in.

"Agatha, why can't you understand? I don't need—or want—to go to Italy or Greece. I can see as well in England's light as I can anywhere. There is plenty of beauty in my own little corner of the world. And if the choice is between my painting or my children—well, there is no choice. Nothing—*nothing*—is as important to me as my family."

Miss Witherspoon clicked her tongue, throwing her hands in the air and sitting back on the settee.

"Oh, pish! That is what you have persuaded yourself to believe, Cecilia. It's what men want us to believe. We've been taught from our cradles that marriage is a woman's highest calling. Gammon!"

"Just because you've never wed—"

"Thank God! I have more sense than to sell my body to the highest bidder."

"Agatha!"

Meg looked down quickly and studied her hands. Miss Witherspoon on the Marriage Mart? The thought of anyone bidding for her stout, aging form was beyond ludicrous, but perhaps she had not resembled a hedgehog—an angry hedgehog—so markedly in her youth.

"Don't 'Agatha' me. It's too true that many women would be happier if they'd remained single. They say 'I do' once, and their husbands say 'you won't' ever after."

Emma was scowling. "You make marriage sound like prison."

"It is, Lady Knightsdale. Oh, you may be confined to a lovely estate and your warden might be rich and handsome, but you've still given up your freedom. You must serve his needs, letting him use you as he will, when he will, pawing you whenever the urge strikes, leaving you bulging with child over and over again—"

"Agatha!" Mrs. Parker-Roth almost shouted. "You exceed the bounds of propriety."

Miss Witherspoon's nose twitched. "My apologies if I've offended anyone's sensibilities. I merely wish to save Miss Peterson from disaster."

"Disaster? Are you equating marriage to my son with disaster?"

"I've nothing against Pinky, you understand, Cecilia. He's nice enough, for a male."

"Miss Witherspoon." Emma's tone was a touch strident. "Disaster will strike if my sister does not marry Mr. Parker-Roth. Her reputation will be in tatters."

"Balderdash." Miss Witherspoon waggled her finger at Emma. "A reputation is required only if one wishes to wed in the *ton*. If that is not of interest, then reputation, as society defines it at least, becomes irrelevant. Look at your husband's aunt, Lady Beatrice."

"I'm not certain we should look at Lady Beatrice."

Miss Witherspoon continued as if Emma had not spoken. "Bea chose to live her life to suit herself. The society tabbies whispered, but she ignored them all and eventually they had to accept her." She tapped Meg on the knee. "You can do the same, Miss Peterson. Ignore the old cats. Let them hiss among themselves—you turn a deaf ear. Follow your passions. You do have passions, don't you?"

"Uh." Passion. The word was becoming synonymous with Parks. With his hands, his mouth, his tongue . . . Heat flooded her. "Um, I'm very interested in plants."

"Agatha, Miss Peterson cannot expect society to treat her as it does Lady Beatrice," Mrs. Parker-Roth said. "Lady Beatrice is the daughter and sister of a marquis. Society is much more tolerant of women who have powerful families behind them."

"And Miss Peterson is a marquis's sister-in-law. Most of the tabbies will hesitate to give her the cut direct. They'd be afraid of alienating Knightsdale."

"As well they should be," Emma said. "Charles would eviscerate anyone who insulted Meg."

"Exactly. So you see, Miss Peterson, you don't have to wed Pinky."

"*Johnny*, Agatha."

"Johnny. You don't have to chain yourself to some man—"

"Johnny is not 'some man,' Agatha. He is an excellent, steady, loyal—"

"—boring—"

"He is not boring." Mrs. Parker-Roth paused, and then sighed. "Well, perhaps he is just a slight bit boring, but he is very reliable."

"Predictable."

"There is nothing the matter with being predictable, Agatha!"

Were these women talking about Mr. Parker-Roth? The man who'd appeared *deus ex machina* in Lord Palmerson's garden to save her from Bennington's evil attentions? Who'd felled the viscount with one blow? Who'd gathered her close and held her while she sobbed into his shirtfront?

The man who had put his tongue in her mouth and his mouth on her breasts and his hands . . . everywhere?

Meg shivered, the odd throbbing starting low in her belly again.

There had been absolutely nothing boring or predictable about Mr. Parker-Roth's actions in Lady Palmerson's parlor.

"Are you feeling quite the thing, Meg?" Emma frowned at her. "You look rather flushed."

"Um."

Fortunately, Mr. MacGill chose that moment to bring in the tea tray.

Chapter 8

"Domestic bliss becomes you." Felicity tried to keep her tone light and sarcastic, but the vaguely pitying look Charlotte gave her indicated she'd not been completely successful.

"It does." Charlotte's eyes drifted over Lord East-haven's ballroom, stopping when they reached a man of middle height with thinning hair and thickening waist. She smiled. "I've never been happier."

Of course Charlotte had never been happier. Her first husband—that old goat, the Duke of Hartford—had cocked up his toes just over a year ago. Well, if rumors were true, it was his cock, not his toes, which had been up at the end. But his last effort had apparently born fruit, and nine months after the duke's demise, Charlotte delivered a boy to her great relief and the previous heir's greater consternation. A year and a day after Hartford breathed his last, his poor widow wed Baron Tynweith.

Lord Tynweith concluded his conversation with Sir George Gaston and made his way toward his wife's side. Felicity frowned. One would think they were starry-eyed young lovers instead of mature, experienced adults. Their devotion was nauseating.

Her gut twisted. Nausea—that's what she felt. Not jealousy. Of course not. How ridiculous. "You have taken to motherhood much more enthusiastically than I would ever have guessed."

Charlotte kept her eyes on Tynweith, a slight smile playing over her lips. "I've surprised myself."

"And how fortunate the baron seems so content to be a step-papa. Not every man would welcome his predecessor's brat, even if the brat is a duke."

"Edward is wonderful."

Felicity kept herself from snorting. Tynweith's generosity was not hard to explain. She'd wager the baron, not the dearly departed duke, was the new Duke of Hartford's real father. She examined the man as he approached. He looked . . . boring. True, he'd been wild in his youth, but now he was no different from any other aging country squire.

Except he had climbed into Charlotte's bed and stolen her heart. There must be something special about him. Something that didn't show in his unremarkable façade.

Bennington's face with its prominent nose pushed its way into her thoughts. Hmm.

He was here tonight. She'd seen him talking to Lord Palmerson when she'd arrived. They were probably discussing horticulture. Bennington was quite partial to plants.

Would he take a turn in the garden with her? Charlotte had said he'd strolled through Palmerson's foliage with Miss Peterson.

Her stomach clenched. The clock was ticking. At any moment, her father's financial failures might come to light. She had no time to waste. She must lure *some* man into the bushes as soon as may be. Bennington might do.

"Do you hear from Lord Andrew? He's in Boston, isn't he?"

"Hmm?" But would he go? She'd always thought him a trifle staid. More than a trifle. As stuffy as a churchman. But if he'd been frolicking in the foliage with Miss Peterson . . . And surely no churchman would have been filling Aunt Hermione's urn . . .

He was a viscount. He needed an heir. He was heading rapidly toward forty.

Perhaps he, too, heard a clock ticking.

"Felicity."

"What?" She looked at Charlotte. What was she prosing on about? Where was Tynweith? Ah, he had stopped again to chat with Lady Dunlee. Now that he was a married man, he was a social pussycat.

"Felicity, you are not attending."

Perhaps she had been looking for the wrong type of man all along. Perhaps the less showy specimens were the most . . . rewarding.

"Felicity!"

"What?! There is no need to shout, Charlotte."

Charlotte looked heavenward for a moment. "I asked you if you ever hear from Lord Andrew. Really, it's a wonder Westbrooke and Alvord let him live, after what he did to Lady Westbrooke at the house party."

It *was* a wonder. What had he—and she—been thinking? "No. Andrew is not a correspondent." He had written once, asking for money. When she'd said she had none, he'd lost interest in her.

Andrew was showy. He was quite beautiful to behold, but his beauty was only skin deep. He was rather rotten on the inside. Bennington, however . . .

She definitely needed to take a stroll through Lord Easthaven's gardens with the viscount.

"I cannot believe not a single gentleman has requested you stand up with him this evening, Meg! If only Charlie did not have the earache and want his papa at his side. You can be sure if Charles were here, you would have plenty of partners."

"Hmm." Emma was probably correct, but somehow the thought of dancing with a man who had the social equivalent of a gun to his head was not especially appealing.

"Perhaps Mr. Symington is looking for a partner."

"Mr. Symington is always looking for a partner." He was looking for one now. Meg watched ladies duck behind pillars and potted palms as the short, balding, portly Mr. Symington—Simple Symington, the wags called him—walked past. Rumor had it his good wife had died of boredom during one of her husband's discourses.

Rumor also had it she'd died with a smile on her face.

Simple Symington was coming her way. Botheration! Was the man actually going to ask her to dance? It would be torture. Not only was he fat and boring, he reeked of garlic and onions. Still, beggars couldn't be choosers. Standing up with him would be better than—

Symington glanced at her, reddened, and scurried off in the other direction.

"Lady Dunlee must have beckoned to him," Emma said. "She is always looking for gentlemen to partner her silly daughter."

"Of course." Emma made perfect sense—except that the new Lord Frampton was already escorting Lady

Caroline, Lady Dunlee's daughter, to join a set, and Lady Dunlee was dragging her husband toward the garden door, probably to see what other scandals she could flush out of the bushes.

Tonight Meg had all the attraction of a fresh pile of horse-dung. The fastidious *ton* was stepping carefully around her.

She did not care. Miss Witherspoon had the right of it. She would not let society rule her. She would follow her passion.

Mr. Parker-Roth's strong face—his green eyes behind his spectacles, the brown lock of hair falling down over his forehead—flashed into her thoughts.

She flushed. No. *Plants.* Plants were her passion. Stamens and stigmas. Leaves and stems and habitats. Not hands and lips and tongues. Not broad shoulders or hard chests or a chin with the slightest cleft. Definitely not.

She did not need a husband. She could do very well on her own. Well, there was the small problem of funds. She didn't have a rich, eccentric aunt kind enough to pop off and leave her a fortune. She couldn't very well ask Charles to support her, even though he could afford to. She didn't want to be beholden to him.

Perhaps she would ask Miss Witherspoon if she could travel with her. The two older ladies might have use for a younger companion. She would like to see the world beyond England—dahlias in Mexico, roses in China, orchids in the West Indies. She could do some plant hunting of her own. She might even find a new species—*Rhododendron Petersonus* or *Fuschia Petersonia.*

The thought was not nearly as enticing as she'd expected.

"Oh, look," Emma said. "Mr. Parker-Roth has arrived."

"He has?" Surely she hadn't squeaked those words?

The look Emma sent her confirmed that she had. What was the matter with her? Her heart fluttered in her chest like a bird trapped in a net.

She was being foolish. She was not some silly debutante, sent into paroxysms of delight at the sight of a well formed male—though Mr. Parker-Roth was indeed well formed. Very well formed. Excellently formed.

He was standing in the doorway with his mother, greeting their hostess. His black coat stretched tight across his shoulders; his pantaloons hugged his powerful legs. He was not especially tall, but his presence dominated the room. Surely all the other women in attendance must have noticed his arrival.

They had—or if they hadn't, the women standing next to them alerted them to the fact. Whispers spread like wind through tall grass. All female eyes swiveled from Parks to her.

She wanted to puke.

"I believe I need to repair a tear in my gown, Emma."

"Nonsense. You can't—"

There was no time to debate the issue. Her stomach insisted she find the ladies' withdrawing room immediately.

He wanted to puke.

He nodded at Lady Easthaven and smiled. Why the hell had he allowed Mother to talk him into coming to this asinine ball? He should have stayed at White's. He should have refused to leave the Pulteney Hotel. He could have pleaded a headache. She knew he'd been plagued by the damn things since childhood. And it would have been true. His head had begun pounding at White's. Listening to Mother's discourse on marriage all the way over in the carriage hadn't helped matters a whit.

How many different ways could he say Miss Peterson had declined his offer? What did Mother not understand about that? Certainly she didn't expect him to abduct the girl? This was England, for God's sake, not some heathen country. Women could not be spirited away in the dark of night and forced into matrimony.

If Miss Peterson said no, there was no more to be said. And she *was* the Marquis of Knightsdale's sister-in-law. She would manage perfectly well without the protection of a mere mister such as himself.

Devil take it, he just wanted to go back to his room, drink a cup of MacGill's medicinal tea, snuff the candles, and lie down with a cold compress on his forehead.

He glanced around while his mother chatted with Lady Easthaven. Where was Miss Peterson? She must be here. Mother would not have dragged him to this blasted gathering if she hadn't been certain the girl would be attending. Surely Lady Knightsdale had shared her schedule when she'd visited this afternoon.

There. He saw Miss Peterson's hair, the warm brown of rich earth glinting gold with the candlelight. Back straight, head high, she was striding away from him to a door on the far side of the room, leaving her sister-in-law standing by a pillar. Where was she going?

"You've caused quite a stir, Mr. Parker-Roth. As you can hear, everyone is buzzing about your antics."

"Antics, Lady Easthaven? I don't know what you mean." There *was* a lot of whispering going on and far too many arch looks directed his way.

Lady Easthaven tapped his arm with her fan. "You know, sir." Blast, she was smirking. "They involve a certain lady." She winked at Mother. "Such a naughty boy you've raised, Cecilia."

Mother's jaw had dropped. She clearly could not gather the breath to reply to this affront.

He clenched his teeth. He had a reply, but he was quite certain it was not good form to whack one's hostess over the head with her own fan. Still, he was sorely tempted. "I believe you are misinformed, Lady Easthaven."

"Misinformed? I don't think so. Lady Dunlee—"

"Is the biggest gabble grinder in England. Surely you don't believe every tale she spins?"

"Well, I—"

Mother gathered her wits enough to retort. "Have you ever known John to engage in anything even remotely resembling an antic, Dorthea?"

Lady Easthaven frowned. "Well, no, not exactly."

"Not at all. John does not believe in antics, do you, John?"

Antics? He could tell them about antics. He had been the perpetrator of some very interesting antics in Lady Palmerson's parlor.

"Definitely not. Most improper." And he was feeling shockingly improper at the moment. Surely Miss Peterson wasn't looking for more sport in the garden?

"Mr. Parker-Roth." Lady Easthaven's voice sounded oddly gleeful. "Did you just growl?"

He glanced at the ladies. Eyes wide, they stared back at him like a pair of barn owls.

"No, of course not. I do not growl. Preposterous." He needed to speak to Miss Peterson. She had vanished through the blasted doorway. "If you'll excuse me?"

He didn't bother to wait for the ladies to murmur their permission.

Lady Easthaven could congratulate herself on a

shocking squeeze. He could barely inch around the edge of the room, damn it. Where the hell had Miss Peterson gone? One would think Lady Knightsdale would keep a closer eye on her sister. It was the girl's penchant for disappearing into the shrubbery that had propelled the marchioness out of the wilds of Kent and into London's ballrooms, after all.

Lady Knightsdale was proving to be as lax a chaperone as Lady Beatrice.

Surely Miss Peterson couldn't have gone into the garden, could she? She'd taken the wrong door if that were her destination—of course, she might be getting wilier. Perhaps she'd chosen a circuitous route to meet this evening's paramour.

"Parks, I see you managed to pour yourself out of White's. Are you taking my advice and pursuing Meg?"

Westbrooke had obviously gotten too friendly with the brandy bottle. "Will you keep your voice down?"

"Don't get into such a pother. No one can hear me in this din."

Parks glanced around. Plenty of ladies were staring at him, but none was obviously reacting to the earl's words. Perhaps Westbrooke was correct, but he didn't care to risk it. Besides, his goal was none of Westbrooke's damn business. He lowered his own voice in the hopes that the earl would follow suit. "Where is your lovely wife?"

The earl pointed with his chin—his hands were occupied with what looked to be two glasses of lemonade. "Lizzie's over there with the Duchess of Alvord." He raised his burdens. "I was sent to procure them drinks."

"I see. Well, you'd best hurry on, then. They look quite parched."

"Gammon. You're sneaking off somewhere, aren't you?" Westbrooke grinned. "I wager you *are* heading for the garden, hoping to find Meg out in the shrubbery again."

Westbrooke's appearance would be much improved by a liberal application of lemonade to his head.

"Of course not. I merely wish to inspect Lord Easthaven's plantings."

"Right." The earl grimaced. "I hope you're kidding, but I suspect you're not." He raised his lemonades again in mock toast. "Well then, enjoy the foliage—and any females you find lurking there."

There was no point in replying. Westbrooke found his own humor very entertaining—he did not care if the rest of the world shared his amusement.

Parks watched the earl walk off, and then slipped out into the cool night air. A few couples were chatting on the terrace. He avoided them and strode down the steps into the garden. In a moment he'd put the light and noise of the ballroom behind him.

He drew in a deep breath and released it slowly, letting the quiet and the comforting smells of dirt and vegetation calm him. He was losing perspective. He always grew tense in London, but this was much worse. He rubbed his forehead. He really needed a cup of MacGill's soothing tea.

He'd felt distinctly short-tempered with Westbrooke just now. That was not normal. He rarely lost his patience with his friends. What was the matter with him?

Miss Peterson's countenance flashed into his mind.

He took another deep breath. Of course he was thinking about her. He'd come out here to find her, hadn't he? To keep her from making more of a mess of things than she'd already done. To keep her from finding herself in exactly the situation she had been in the last time she'd ventured into a garden—tussling with a man in the bushes.

He clasped his hands behind his back. And why exactly was he involving himself? She had declined his offer. She was not his responsibility. She would not thank him for meddling in her affairs.

Affairs . . .

Bloody hell! He did not want Miss Margaret Peterson engaging in affairs with other men. He did not want other men doing to her what he had done to her in Lady Palmerson's parlor. He did not want another male touching . . . kissing . . .

Confound it! Insidious thoughts of milky white breasts and rose-tipped nipples belonged to his salad days. He was far too mature to allow lecherous musings to distract him.

He would visit Cat the moment he arrived at the Priory, perhaps even before he attended to the new plant shipment.

He paced deeper into the garden.

It was all a certain hoydenish female's fault. If she had behaved like a proper young lady, he would not be in his current predicament. Lady Easthaven would not have taken the slightest note of his arrival; Mother would not be prosing on and on so relentlessly about marriage; and, most importantly, he would not be tortured by shocking dreams that left him waking in a most uncomfortable state.

The entire situation was highly annoying.

And where the hell was Miss Peterson now? He eyed the surrounding vegetation. *Was* she engaged in some salacious behavior in the shrubbery? Had she lured some poor buck into the bushes?

There was plenty of leafage to hide any lascivious activities Miss Peterson might wish to engage in. Lord Easthaven had allowed his plantings to become sadly overgrown. Did the man have incompetent

gardeners or was he purposely encouraging his
guests to engage in wanton assignations? He should
have a word with the earl at the next Horticultural
Society meeting. The man was certainly not in evidence at this gathering.

He heard muffled giggling and a lower, male
murmur. Another giggle, a rustling of leaves, and
silence.

Damn it to hell, she *was* out here. Whom was she frolicking with now? Surely not Bennington? Devil take it,
she had no need to repeat herself. There was a long
line of peers who'd be more than happy to oblige her
in the bushes. It was none of his business. He was well
quit of her.

So why were his feet carrying him toward a panting
yew tree? He should turn around and go back to the
ballroom. Miss Peterson was not in need of rescuing
this time—from the sounds of it, she was enjoying herself immensely.

His feet refused to listen to reason. He charged
around a branch and drew breath to inform Miss Peterson exactly what he thought of her conduct.

He choked.

Good God.

He would die of embarrassment here in Lord Easthaven's very untidy garden.

Meg reached the ladies' withdrawing room without
disgracing herself—any more than she was already disgraced, that is. Lud! Thank God the room was empty.
She took a deep, sustaining breath and felt her stomach
begin to settle.

How could she ever go back out there and face the *ton*,

the sneering, whispering, sniggering *ton*? She covered her face with her hands.

She would stay here until it was time to leave. She—

"Hiding?"

"Eep!" Meg snapped her head up so quickly her neck hurt. Her stomach rebelled again. Lady Felicity Brookton stood in the doorway.

Could the evening get any worse?

"I'm not hiding."

Felicity snorted. "Liar."

"I assure you, I was just . . . that is, I wished to . . . I felt—" Oh, why bother to dissemble? It was patently clear Felicity did not believe a word she was saying. "All right, I suppose I *am* hiding."

"Couldn't take the old cats sharpening their claws on you, hmm? They do so like a tasty tidbit of gossip, and you've presented them with a plate full. Aging spinster, marquis's sister-in-law, disappearing into the bushes with a procession of men. Luring the reticent Mr. Parker-Roth into misbehavior." Felicity grinned. "Delicious."

"I—" Meg put her hand over her mouth. "I feel sick."

Felicity pushed a chamber pot toward her with her foot. "I cast up my accounts the first time, too. It gets easier."

"It does?" Meg sat down and drew in another deep breath. She avoided looking at the chamber pot. It was within easy reach if necessary.

Felicity took the chair next to her. "Yes. Of course, I was only ten the first—and only—time I let the *ton* upset me." She looked away, jiggling her foot, her mouth pulled tight.

Meg had a sudden urge to touch the other girl's knee in sympathy. "What happened?"

Felicity shrugged. "Nothing, really. I'd only been in

London two days. Before then, I'd been living in the country with my mother. But she died, so the servants shipped me up to the evil earl." She smiled briefly. "My father was rather appalled to see me standing on his doorstep."

"Would no one else take you in?" Meg tried to keep the horror out of her voice, but a ten-year-old girl in Needham's care . . . ?

"No. I suppose the earl could have sent me back to the country for the servants to mind, but he didn't. I think he forgot about me almost immediately. And it wasn't so bad, once I adjusted."

"Oh." Meg could not imagine it, but then, she had grown up with Papa. He might be forgetful, especially when he was deep in a Greek translation, but there was no question he loved her.

"Anyway," Felicity said, "the second day I was in London, I wandered over to the garden in the center of the square. I heard a girl laughing, and then I saw Lady Mary Cleveland playing by the fountain." She glanced at Meg. "I thought I'd found a friend—until her mother rushed up to save her from my evil influence."

"Lady Cleveland *is* a bit of a high stickler."

Felicity snorted. "*That* is an understatement. She looked at me as though I were the devil incarnate. She grabbed Lady Mary and pulled her away, all the while screaming at the nursemaid"—Felicity's voice took on a mocking tone— "*Didn't you know she was Needham's daughter?*"

"That's awful."

Lady Felicity shrugged again. "Actually it was an excellent introduction to the *ton*. I learned an important lesson that day which I will now share with you. The only way to survive in Town is to not give a damn what anyone thinks." She shook her head. "I did try to conform when

I made my come-out, but I soon realized it was hopeless. So now I do what I want. As long as I'm moderately discreet, I am received most places. Not by the Lady Clevelands of the *ton*, of course, but since I find them colossally boring, I don't mind having their doors shut in my face."

"I see." Meg swallowed. A ten year old subjected to such venom . . . Poor Felicity. But she was right. Meg straightened her shoulders. She had long thought the *ton* silly and vain, yet here she was, falling into the trap of caring about their judgment. She would not continue to do so.

"Well, I didn't follow you in here to give you advice," Felicity said.

"You followed me?"

"Yes. I have a question for you. Charlotte—Baroness Tynweith, the former Duchess of Hartford—said she saw you at Lady Palmerson's the night of the . . . incident with Mr. Parker-Roth."

Meg stiffened. She definitely did not wish to discuss that night.

Felicity leaned forward. "Charlotte said you went into the garden with Lord Bennington, not Mr. Parker-Roth. So why isn't the viscount's name the one being linked to yours?"

Meg cleared her throat. "It's slightly complicated."

"How complicated?"

"Really, Lady Felicity, I don't believe—"

Felicity held up her hand. "I'll make it simple for you. I don't need to—or care to—know the details. Just answer me this—do you have an interest in Lord Bennington?"

"No!" What a revolting thought. To be subjected to that man's mauling again . . . perhaps she *would* have need of that chamber pot. "Definitely not."

"Good." Felicity grinned. "I asked because I *do* have an interest in him."

"I see." Should she warn Felicity that Bennington's lips bore a close resemblance to slugs? Ridiculous. Felicity was quite capable of making her own judgment on that subject. "You are more than welcome to him."

"Thank you. Now, shall we return to the ballroom?"

The ballroom? Face the tittering, staring, gossiping *ton*?

"I'm not certain that would be a good idea." Meg's stomach twisted again. She might not care what society thought, but she certainly did not wish to subject herself to its nasty scrutiny.

"Well, you can't spend all evening lurking in here. Or did you come especially to admire Lady Easthaven's rather garish taste in furniture?"

Meg dropped her gaze to the gilded, winged sphinxes supporting her chair's arms, sphinxes with rather prominent breasts—

"No, of course not."

"Then come." Lady Felicity stood. "Show some courage."

Was Lady Felicity intimating she was a coward? Meg stood up quickly—and remembered the whispering she'd fled. Perhaps cowardice wasn't completely despicable. It was more . . . prudence. If she stayed here—

She heard giggling approaching. Oh, no. She closed her eyes briefly. Please let whoever was approaching be headed somewhere else—but where else could they be headed?

She heard the sharp intake of breath and looked to the doorway. Two little debutantes stood frozen on the threshold, identical looks of horror on their faces as they glanced from Meg to Felicity and back.

"Don't worry, girls," Felicity said. "We were just leaving."

She turned and offered her arm to Meg, a slight smile twisting her lips. "Coming, Miss Peterson?"

Meg hesitated for one heartbeat only.

"Yes, Lady Felicity, I am."

She linked arms with evil Lord Needham's daughter and swept past the cowering young girls.

Chapter 9

"My abject apologies. I mistook you for someone else." Parks would have withdrawn without comment if he could have, but Lord Dawson had seen him.

Grace turned in her husband's arms. It was too dark to see if her cheeks were the same shade as the hair that now tumbled over her shoulders.

"Did you?" Dawson grinned. "I wonder whom you were looking for?"

"I wasn't looking for anyone." A small mistruth. "I came out for the air—it is exceedingly stuffy inside. When I saw there was someone here, I assumed—" He was not going to say what he assumed. "Well, I have already apologized for intruding." Damn, *he* was blushing now. Thank God for the dim light. "I'll just be on my way. Please, carry on with what you were doing." Ack. He hadn't actually said that, had he? Dim light or no, if he kept on this way, his face would illuminate this entire section of London.

Dawson had the most annoyingly white, perfect teeth.

"Right. I'll be delighted to resume my activities. Where were we, love?"

"Oh, stop it, David." Grace adjusted her bodice and pushed a strand of hair behind her ear. "Your levity will be your undoing." She smiled. "How are you, John?"

"I'm well." He'd be better if he could escape this little scene. He got along fine with Grace and Dawson. There were no hard feelings on his part. Hell, the two had been wed for years now; he'd had more than enough time to come to terms with . . . things. But that still did not mean he wished to stand here chatting with them. Especially given what they had been doing—and were going to resume doing as soon as he left. He could tell Dawson was anxious to get back to making love to his wife.

Really, couldn't the man wait until they returned home? It was unfortunate that he'd stumbled upon them, but Dawson should have anticipated such an occurrence. It *was* a crowded social gathering.

"Were you touring Lord Easthaven's garden, John?" Grace sounded amused. She'd always thought his fascination with botany odd. It hadn't mattered. She'd been beautiful and charming and her father's land abutted his own. They'd known each other since childhood.

"Hardly. Easthaven has a most plebian selection of plantings, and his gardeners should be reprimanded for neglecting to take proper care of them. This yew, for example, is in serious need of pruning."

"Oh, I don't know," Dawson said, "I rather like its bushiness. It was serving as an admirable screen." He laughed. "Did you ever think Easthaven might wish to give his guests a variety of opportunities to enjoy themselves in the foliage?"

"David! I'm certain John does not know what you mean."

Not know what he meant? Did Grace think him a eunuch? True, he'd never tried to get her alone in the shrubbery, but that did not mean he wasn't completely aware of the possibilities overgrown vegetation afforded.

Dawson sent him a commiserating look. "If the rumors flying through the ballroom are true, Grace, Parker-Roth knows exactly what I mean."

Grace frowned. "I've been meaning to ask you about that, John. Who is this Miss Peterson?"

"She's the sister of the Marchioness of Knightsdale. Her father is a vicar, I believe." There was something stuck in his throat. He attempted to clear it. His mouth was infernally dry as well. "You really cannot listen to rumors, Lady Dawson."

"Really, John, you are being absurd. We grew up together, after all. If it hadn't been for that unfortunate misunderstanding—"

"Misunderstanding!" He bit his lip. He'd promised himself he would not discuss the matter with her. "Yes, right. The misunderstanding."

Grace put her hand on his arm. "I've tried to apologize. You know I have. It was all my fault. I should have stood up to Father sooner. And I did love you—I *do* love you—just more as a sister than a wife."

Good God. Could this evening get more embarrassing? "Yes, well, that really is neither here nor there. I mean, water over the dam, don't you know. Ancient history and all that. Say no more. Please."

"But I must, John."

Dawson put his arm around his wife's shoulders. "Grace, I think Parker-Roth would rather you spoke of something else." He laughed. "Actually I think the man would prefer you held your tongue and let him escape back to the ballroom."

"Well, I can't, David." Grace squeezed Parks's arm. "John, I want you to be happy. It has plagued me all these years that I caused you pain. It was not well done of me—not well done at all."

"Please, Lady Dawson—"

She shook his arm. "I should have come to church and stood in front of your family and all your friends and explained. I should never have left you to face them alone. I have wanted to beg your pardon ever since—I am begging it now."

"There's no need to apologize. It was—" It was the most painful moment of his life. But Grace was clearly contrite. And he—he just wanted to have this conversation over. "It was four years ago. Do not give it another thought."

"But it is not fair. I've been so happy." She leaned her head on Dawson's chest. "And I think you've not been."

"Lady Dawson, please." Damn. He'd thought he'd always feel unrequited love for Grace, but at the moment all he felt was annoyance. Couldn't she understand he truly did not wish to discuss this topic? He glanced at Dawson. The man smiled sympathetically and shrugged.

He didn't need sympathy, he needed action. Lord Dawson should haul Grace back inside—or back into the bushes. Anything to distract her from her current focus—him.

"Is this Miss Peterson someone who can make you happy, John?"

Parks looked hopefully into the sky. Perhaps a sudden storm would come up and put a period to this uncomfortable conversation. No, not conversation—monologue.

There was not a cloud in sight.

"You must not marry her if she will make your life miserable, John—and I'm afraid she may do just that. She does not have the best reputation. It's rumored she's been vanishing into the shrubbery with men all Season."

Anger surged in his gut.

"Lady Dawson, you must not speak ill of Miss Peterson." Damn, where had that come from? Well, any emotion was better than his current paralyzing embarrassment. He took a steadying breath. "I am sorry to say it, but I must ask you not to concern yourself with my affairs any longer."

With that, he retreated to the safety of the ballroom.

"Well." Grace blinked and watched John Parker-Roth walk away. The man had never spoken to her like that before. Not that she wouldn't have deserved it—her treatment of him had been unconscionable. She cringed at the memory. She hadn't meant . . . she hadn't realized . . . She blew out a short breath. Her intentions were immaterial. She had hurt John.

She wanted desperately to make amends.

"I'd say you've been put in your place, my dear."

"Yes." She pushed a length of hair off her face. "Maybe that's good. John has always been unfailingly polite to me in the past—when he can't avoid me—but I knew he must be angry. How could he not? I jilted him at the altar."

"You could not have avoided it."

"I *should* have avoided it." If only she could go back and do things differently. "I never actually agreed to marry him, you know. Father arranged everything."

"I know." David kissed her. "Parker-Roth is an idiot."

She laughed. "You are the idiot, David." She stretched to wrap her arms around his neck. "I did not exactly have a crowd of suitors clamoring for my hand. I am far too much of a Long Meg for most men of the *ton.*"

"And most men of the *ton* are pygmies."

She smiled. "No, they aren't. It's you who are a giant."

"And you love every inch of my muscled body."

Her smile broadened. "You know that I do." She ran her hands down to the front of his pantaloons. "*Every* inch."

David captured her mouth and resumed the delightful activities he'd been engaged in when John had interrupted them.

God, she loved him. Whenever she thought of how she had ruined John's life, she thought of how her own life would have been ruined if she had not wed the man who was now kissing her so thoroughly. She burned for him, even after four years of marriage and two children.

If she had gone to the church as her father had insisted and had said her vows to John, she'd be trapped now in a polite, tepid, boring marriage. It would be hell.

David's mouth had moved to a very sensitive spot on her neck.

"Let's go home, Grace." The words tickled her ears and sent shivers down her spine. "I have a sudden need to go to bed."

"What, are you sleepy, David?"

"*Hard*ly." He pressed his hips against hers. "I am very much awake."

She laughed. "I see that—or rather, I feel that."

"I would like to make you feel it even more."

"Later. We can't be dashing off like newlyweds."

"Why not?"

"Society would be scandalized."

"Good."

David put his hand on her breast. It felt wonderful. Perhaps they *could* slip out the back gate . . .

No. She wanted to observe Miss Peterson. True, John's matrimonial plans—or lack of plans—were really none of her concern, but she couldn't help herself. She needed to find out what type of woman Miss Peterson was. If the girl were a harpy, she would find some way to put a spoke in her wheel. John might not thank her, but she couldn't stand by and watch him suffer more. Too often men thought only with the organ concealed in their pantaloons.

David cupped her bottom and pulled her against that very organ—that very hard organ.

"Stop it."

"Must I?"

If she didn't speak firmly, they would be out here all night—not an unattractive prospect, but quite impossible.

"You must. I wish to see what Miss Peterson is up to."

"Parker-Roth told you to stay out of his business."

"Yes, I know. Unfortunately, I choose to ignore his request."

"Request? It sounded like an order to me."

"I don't take orders."

David chuckled. "How well I know that!"

"Oh, stop it. You are being absurd. Help me tidy up my appearance, will you? I'm sure I must look like I was dragged through a bush backward."

"Well, you do look very interestingly mussed, but I doubt anyone will blame the vegetation."

"Of course they won't—everyone must know what you are about. You drag me into the garden at every social event."

"I believe you dragged me out here this evening."

Grace shrugged. "Did you bring extra hairpins?"

"Of course."

After four years of marriage—and countless garden

excursions—Lord Dawson had become quite an
accomplished lady's maid.

Meg watched Parks slip into the ballroom from the
garden. What had he been up to? Not that it was any
business of hers, of course, but he looked guilty. His
face was so expressionless, he must be hiding something. What?

Had he been trysting with someone in the bushes?

She ducked behind a pillar when he looked her way.

He'd been lurking in Lord Palmerson's garden, too,
now that she considered the matter. She'd been so
happy to be rescued from the disgusting Lord Bennington she hadn't wondered about it at the time, but now
she did. Had Parks simply been admiring the foliage—
or had he been admiring something else? *Someone* else?

That was why men toured gardens during social
events, wasn't it? To steal a kiss . . . or more?

She glared at a sickly-looking potted palm that
shared her secluded location. To think she had been
feeling guilty that she had, completely inadvertently,
trapped poor Mr. Parker-Roth into offering for her.
She'd thought him an innocent passer-by, a selfless
Good Samaritan.

How naïve could she be? Yes, he had been perfectly
blameless in her situation, but had he been equally
blameless in another section of the garden?

He'd said he never wished to marry. Why would he
be so against matrimony? Because a wife would curtail
his amorous exploits, that's why.

He must have a mistress and any number of other accommodating females at his beck and call. He certainly
knew all there was to know about dalliance. If his actions in Lady Palmerson's parlor were any indication,

he was a master of seduction. Only a hardened rake would know to put his lips on . . . his tongue in . . .

She flushed. It would never have occurred to her to . . .

She would not think of their activities in Lady Palmerson's parlor.

The man was a confirmed rogue. A scoundrel. How had he had the *gall* to take her to task for her behavior? It was very much the pot calling the kettle black.

She wished she had a pot handy. She would use it to knock some manners into Mr. Holier-Than-Thou Parker-Roth. She peered around the pillar again. The bounder was talking to Lady Easthaven right now.

No one was treating *him* as if he had the social equivalent of the bubonic plague. Why were they treating her that way? It was not fair.

Well, she was not going to hide away like this pitiful palm. She examined the plant more closely. Someone should move it to a more congenial location. She touched its limp fronds. It might well be past saving.

But she was not. She was going to do exactly as Lady Felicity recommended and ignore the *ton*'s opinion. She would emulate Miss Witherspoon and Lady Bea. She'd be herself. The *ton* could either accept her or reject her, but they would not change her.

She would do as she pleased, and right now it pleased her to interview possible husbands in the garden. After all, one could not spend one's life waiting for a knight in shining armor to magically appear and carry one off into a fairy tale existence.

Mr. Parker-Roth's image intruded, but she pushed it firmly from her thoughts. She was not going to pine away her life, waiting for love. Emma had done that. Emma had loved Charles since childhood, but had done nothing to secure his affections. It was just luck— well, bad luck for Charles's brother but good luck for

Emma—that Charles had inherited the title, come home, and married her. If Charles's brother hadn't been murdered, Emma would still be a spinster, keeping house for Papa and driving them all mad.

She glanced around the ballroom again. Emma was talking to Mrs. Parker-Roth on the far side of the room, and Parks was now talking to Lord Featherstone. How appropriate. He was probably trying to get some advice from the old roué. Disgusting.

She stepped out from behind the pillar and surveyed her prospects, being careful to stay turned away from Emma. It would not do to let her sister catch her eye.

So, which man should she take into the bushes? Lord Locklear? Too young. Mr. Cashman? Too old. The Earl of Tattingdon? Too fat.

Lady Felicity had cornered Lord Bennington and was herding him toward the garden door. He was smiling slightly, his enormous nose overshadowing his sluglike lips. Ugh. Felicity was more than welcome to Lord Proboscis.

A tall woman and a taller man stepped through the door right after Felicity and Bennington exited. They looked slightly disheveled, as if they had been doing something more appropriate for a bedchamber. The man whispered in the woman's ear as he plucked a leaf from her hair. The woman laughed.

They must be married—*their* actions did not precipitate a storm of whispering.

It would be nice to have a marriage like that. Emma and Charles, Lizzie and Robbie, the Duchess and Duke of Alvord all had such marriages, but they were the exception rather than the rule. She could not set her sights so high.

Lord Frampton was standing alone. Hmm. She'd

barely glanced at him since she'd come to Town, but now that she looked at him . . .

He might do. He was not so ugly, really. He still had a large Adam's apple that bobbed rather distractingly whenever he swallowed, and his muddy brown hair was already thinning, but at least the pimples that had earned him the nickname "Spots" had faded. Now that he'd inherited the title, gossip said, he'd given up youthful folly. He no longer tried to introduce piglets into noblemen's drawing rooms.

He needed an heir, so he must be in the market for a wife, and it was unlikely women would be lining up to vie for the position. He was only a baron and not the richest or most attractive specimen. It would be an even trade—a home for her, her body for him.

Her stomach twisted. Put that way, the notion was rather unpalatable. Best not to think about it too closely. She could not be so nice in her requirements. She *was* only a vicar's daughter, even though she was the sister-in-law of a marquis. She would not be bringing much besides her body to the altar.

She watched Lord Frampton's Adam's apple jump as he took a swallow of champagne.

If only the man had an extensive garden like Lord Bennington, but, sadly, Frampton was interested in hunting, not horticulture. Foxes, not foxglove. Still, she must remain hopeful. Surely he had a plot of earth, no matter how small, that she could cultivate.

And surely Lord Frampton's lips would not be as slug-like as Bennington's. They were far too thin. She should be spared that unpleasantness, at least.

She made her way along the perimeter of the room. Being a pariah had its advantages. People moved briskly out of her path. It was almost pleasant, if she ignored the sneers and affronted looks.

She stepped past a cringing clump of debutantes. They erupted into a frenzy of whispers and giggling as soon as the back hem of her dress had passed them.

"Good evening, Lord Frampton."

The poor man almost jumped out of his skin.

"Miss Peterson. How, ah, good to see you." His Adam's apple bobbed furiously, as if it were trying to leap from his throat and flee her presence. He glanced at her; then looked away. Was he searching for someone to rescue him from her evil clutches? She'd never before provoked such obvious panic in a male breast.

"I believe the last time we spoke was at Knightsdale before my sister married the marquis. You attended a house party with your parents and sister."

"Uh, yes. I remember." The Adam's apple was still bouncing at an alarming rate.

"I have yet to extend my condolences on the death of your father last year. I am so sorry for his passing. Was he sick long?"

"No, not sick at all. Hunting accident, don't you know. Horse refused a fence. Pater went flying. Landed on his head. Broke his neck. Nothing to be done about it."

"What a tragedy. Hunting is such a dangerous sport."

"What?" Lord Frampton examined her as if she had suddenly sprouted a second head. "Not dangerous. Bad luck. He'd have been up on his horse in a trice if he hadn't been dead."

"Ah. Of course." She would never understand the attraction of hunting if she lived to be a hundred years old. Riding across the fields, ruining the plants—well, it was clear there was no benefit in arguing the point. If she married this lunatic—that is, this lord—she'd best keep her tongue between her teeth on that subject. She fanned her face. "It's rather stuffy in here. Would you like to stroll in the garden?"

She might as well have suggested a stroll through Sodom and Gomorrah.

"Garden?" His voice cracked. He cleared his throat. "I don't believe . . . I think . . . that is, I—"

"I understand Lord Easthaven has some extraordinary plantings." Extraordinarily dull, not that Lord Frampton would notice.

"I'm, um, not much interested in vegetation. Could all be weeds for all I know. Leave that sort of thing to the gardeners. Pay them enough."

She almost took pity on him, but there were no other gentlemen at hand.

"Still, it *is* a beautiful evening."

"A bit chill." He eyed her shoulders. "You'd catch your death. Best stay inside."

She tried to smile. Perhaps Lord Frampton was too much trouble. If she looked—

Lud! Parks was heading her way. He wasn't going to approach her in such a public location, was he?

He was. She could tell from the intent look on his face and his determined stride.

So could the *ton.* She could almost hear their collective inhalation of anticipation as they caught the scent of scandal in their supercilious nostrils. They were no different from Lord Frampton's hounds.

And she was the fox. She had to flee. She grabbed the baron's arm and pulled him toward the garden door. "My lord, I'm in need of air."

She must have looked as desperate as she felt, because the man followed her into the night without further protest.

* * *

This was by far the worst evening he had ever en-
dured. First he'd made that hideous error in the
garden. Then, when he'd come back inside, he'd been
pounced on by Lady Easthaven. He'd no sooner shaken
her and her pointed references to Miss Peterson than
he'd been cornered by Lord Featherstone. Parks struggled to keep his hands at his sides while his fingers
twitched to wrap themselves around the old reprobate's
scrawny neck. He'd thought—no, he'd hoped—the
man had been put to bed with a shovel years ago, but
unfortunately the dirty dish was still above ground.

"So, the chit was a disappointment, heh?" Featherstone leaned close, his stale breath spoiling the air.

Parks stepped back. "I have no idea what you mean."

"Miss Peterson. Everyone knows you sampled her
charms at the Palmerson ball. I take it they were not delicious enough to entice you into parson's mousetrap?" The
old man wheezed with laughter and punched Parks in the
shoulder. "Or perhaps you decided there's no need to pay
for what you can get free, hmm?"

He was going to strangle the cur here in the middle
of Easthaven's ballroom. "Lord Featherstone, you completely misconstrue the situation."

The man smirked and gestured with his head. "Perhaps you'd best tell Frampton. Looks like she's trying
to lure him into the garden now."

"What?" Damn, Miss Peterson was indeed standing by
the garden door, talking to the baron.

"Not that it's any of my concern, of course," Featherstone said, "but it does seem a shame. I've been watching
Lady Caroline hunt Frampton the last few Seasons, even
before he inherited. Thought she was finally close to
bringing him to bay. Doubt she'll care for Miss Peterson
getting her claws into him."

Parks grunted. Lady Caroline need not worry. He'd

see to it that Miss Peterson did not drag any more men into the shrubbery.

"Excuse me, my lord. I have a matter to attend to."

The old man chuckled. "Thought you might."

Parks did not bother to reply. He was saving his words for Miss Peterson.

Chapter 10

She felt like the hounds of hell were after her.

"Miss Peterson."

She needed to get away, get out of sight. She couldn't bear to have Mr. Parker-Roth confront her. Yes, her flight was cowardly. She *was* a coward. She readily admitted it. She would try being brave and standing up to the *ton* another day, when this particular member of the *ton* was not present.

"Miss Peterson."

She scrambled down the terrace steps. Lord Easthaven had a few lanterns hung on poles, but there were still plenty of shadows. Another ten yards and she'd be in blessed darkness.

"Miss Peterson!"

Someone tugged on her arm. She tugged back. She could not stop here. Parks must be right behind her.

"Miss Peterson, stop. The air is just as good on the terrace as elsewhere in the garden."

She looked over her shoulder. Parks had not yet appeared, but she knew it was too much to hope he would not do so very soon. She still had time to hide, if she could only get Lord Frampton to cooperate. She glanced up at him. He did not look at all cooperative.

"It is partly an agitation of the mind, Lord Frampton. Light exacerbates the condition. Complete darkness is what I need."

Lord Frampton crossed his arms. "Came on rather suddenly, didn't it?"

"Yes." She glanced back at the ballroom again. She must have only seconds before Parks appeared in the doorway. "I am certain a short turn about the darker portion of the garden will have me feeling much better."

Lord Frampton snorted.

"Excuse me?" She had not expected this reaction.

"No. Sorry for your indisposition, but I won't go any farther. Can't."

"Why can't you?"

"Reputation. Yours ain't great, you know. Don't want mine to suffer, too."

When had Lord Frampton turned into such a prude? Was this the man who'd been flinging bachelor's buttons at his friends just four years ago and who'd tried to introduce a piglet into Charles's drawing room?

He looked back at the ballroom this time. Relief washed over his features.

"Maybe Parker-Roth will take a turn about the grounds with you."

"What?" She followed Frampton's gaze. Parks had finally stepped onto the terrace. He did not look happy.

She picked up her skirts and ran.

"I don't know what to do about Meg." Emma pleated the fabric of her gown and then smoothed it flat. She'd asked Mrs. Parker-Roth to step into a deserted sitting room. She definitely did not want to discuss such a sensitive topic in the ballroom. Far too many nasty ears would be cocked to catch every whisper.

Mrs. Parker-Roth's hand appeared in Emma's line of sight and patted her knee. Emma looked up. How could the woman remain calm? Her own stomach was knotted so tightly even the sight of a lobster patty made her nauseous. The way the *ton* had treated Meg in the ballroom—

She sniffed back tears and reached for her handkerchief.

"I have made such a botch of this."

"No. How can you say so?"

Emma blew her nose. "You are just being kind. I should never have let Meg come up to Town with only Lady Bea to chaperone her."

"Lady Knightsdale—"

"Please, call me Emma." Her voice broke.

"Emma, then." Mrs. Parker-Roth took the hand that did not contain Emma's crumpled handkerchief. "Lady Beatrice is a rather eccentric character—"

"Rather? She is going to marry her butler."

"Yes, I know." Mrs. Parker-Roth smiled. "She does follow her own path, but you must not think she is a complete ninnyhammer. On the contrary, she is awake on every suit. I'm certain she knew exactly what your sister was doing."

"How could she have?" What sane woman would let her charge entertain men in the bushes? "Did she *want* Meg to ruin her reputation?"

"Of course not. But you know Lady Bea isn't especially concerned about reputations. Agatha was right on that score."

The knot in her stomach tightened, if that were possible. "A woman who cares nothing for reputations should not be a chaperone."

"I didn't say Bea cared nothing for reputations." Mrs. Parker-Roth's tone was reproachful. "She just cares about other things more. Meg's happiness, for example."

"Yes, but—" Emma closed her eyes. Everything was such an awful mess. How could she have told Charles's aunt that she was an incompetent chaperone? But she *was*. She'd let Meg run wild.

On the other hand, who could have imagined Meg running wild anywhere but through a field of unusual vegetation? If anyone had asked her before this infernal Season, Emma would have sworn the only reason Meg would drag a man into the shrubbery would be to secure his help in identifying a rare plant.

Who *was* this girl who was her sister?

"I just don't understand. Meg's always been, well, different, but not reckless. She's not a light-skirt."

"No one would think for a moment she was."

"How can you say that? Half or more of the *ton* in that ballroom think so—they are even saying so."

Mrs. Parker-Roth dismissed the ball goers with a wave of her hand. "Gossip only. They are enjoying today's scandal—they will enjoy tomorrow's scandal tomorrow. Do not worry."

"Not worry? The gossip will force Meg to come h-home and spend her d-days a s-spinster." Emma closed her lips firmly to repress the wail that threatened. "It's not that I don't want Meg home. I l-love her." She sniffed. "I want her to be h-happy."

She took off her spectacles and sobbed.

She felt an arm go around her shoulders, urging her close. She breathed in the scent of roses and linen, and rested her cheek against Mrs. Parker-Roth's warm, soft chest.

She had not felt a mother's touch in over twenty years. She cried harder. Mrs. Parker-Roth just held her.

"You've done a splendid job, Emma," Mrs. Parker-Roth rubbed her shoulder. "You took on so much responsibility at such a young age."

"No. I've made micefeet of everything."

"Nonsense. You are being foolish beyond permission."

"I'm not." Emma sat up and blew her nose. "Meg's reputation is in shambles and I've insulted Charles's aunt. I'm sure Lady Beatrice will never speak to me again."

"Of course Lady Bea will speak to you. You're Charles's wife and the mother of his sons. You are making him very happy." Mrs. Parker-Roth grinned. "Actually, Bea is probably thanking you right now."

"She couldn't be."

"Indeed she could. You know she has no patience with the *ton*. She hates society entertainments. She's always bored and desperate to escape when she has to attend them. I imagine it's the reason she drinks so much. It's imbibe or scream."

"Do you really think so?"

"Yes, I do. Bea would much rather be home with Mr. Alton. She does love him, you know."

Emma sighed. "I hope you are right."

Perhaps she should take Meg home to Knightsdale and come back next Season to start over. Some people would remember Meg's missteps, but many would have forgotten, their attention taken up with new scandals.

It was a good idea. The boys had more freedom in the country. The air was healthier. Perhaps Charlie would not have gotten an earache if they'd stayed home. And country society was much more congenial. In fact, perhaps it would be best not to come back to London at all. She could host a house party and fill

Knightsdale with eligible bachelors, much like Lady Beatrice had done with ladies when Charles inherited the title and was looking for a wife.

"I think we should go home."

"No, Emma, don't do that."

"Why not?"

"It is retreating." Mrs. Parker-Roth shook her head. "It is admitting defeat."

"Well, I *am* defeated!" Despair sat on her chest again like a lead weight. "If only . . ." If only Mother hadn't died. If Meg had had a real mother growing up, she probably would be happily married today—not dashing off into the vegetation with any stray man.

It was as if Mrs. Parker-Roth had read her mind. She put her hand on her arm. "Do not blame yourself for your sister's behavior."

"But—"

"No buts, Emma. You cannot live Meg's life for her, no matter how much you try." Mrs. Parker-Roth smiled slightly. "Believe me. I have six children, and I can assure you, no matter what I do, no matter how much I try to direct them, they all do exactly as they please. It can be exceedingly annoying, but ultimately it is what you want—to raise strong, independent people who know their own mind."

"But luring men into the shrubbery?"

"Is perfectly fine as long as it's the proper man who is lured." Mrs. Parker-Roth grinned. "I'm sincerely hoping Meg can lure my son into more misbehavior."

Lord Bennington's impressive nostrils flared with disdain. "I see Miss Peterson is still attempting to lure men into the shrubbery."

"Is she?" Lady Felicity turned and glanced over the

balustrade. Miss Peterson stood at the base of the terrace steps with Lord Frampton. The man was scowling, his arms crossed. "I doubt she'll be successful. The baron looks as if he does not intend to be lured anywhere."

"Wise man." The nostrils flared again. "Miss Peterson is not worth the trouble."

"Oh? And how do you know that?"

Bennington cleared his throat. "I, um"—he coughed and glanced away—"I may have once—"

"Lord Bennington, you've been trysting in the bushes! I never knew you were so wild."

The viscount looked so adorably embarrassed, Felicity wanted to kiss him. Well, kissing him—and other activities—had been her purpose in getting him out of the ballroom, but his current flustered state made him even more enticing. And was he preening just a bit as well? Did he think he was now a rake? She smiled to herself. Hardly. Unless she missed her guess, he was a rank neophyte in intimate relations.

However, she would be delighted to expand his experience. More delighted than she'd expected. She felt an odd warmth when she considered the issue. Excitement, yes, but something else. Something unfamiliar.

Bennington hunched a shoulder. "I may have taken a turn in the garden with the woman. As I say, it was not an activity I wish to repeat."

"Poor man." She patted his forearm. She would make certain that he *did* wish to repeat any activities they engaged in. "At least you did not get caught like Parker-Roth."

That was the wrong thing to say. Bennington's face froze. One would have thought someone had rammed a stick up his arse. He stepped back and turned toward the ballroom door.

"I don't wish to discuss it."

"Of course not." Damn. She knew in a vague sort of way that Bennington didn't admire Parker-Roth, but she'd had no idea such rancor existed between them, at least on Bennington's part. She could scream in frustration. She'd worked for the last half hour to get the man to herself. If he went back inside, all that effort would be wasted.

The odd warmth twisted in her chest. It must be the lobster patties hadn't agreed with her. She couldn't feel . . . sad at the thought of missing her planned seduction of Lord Bennington, could she?

No, it was just that she didn't have time to waste. Every morning she woke certain someone had discovered her father was floating down the River Tick. Once word was out that she was a pauper, she could put paid to any hope of catching a husband.

She wanted to grab Bennington's arm and dig in her heels. How could she keep him on the terrace?

She got help from an unexpected quarter.

"Blast!" Bennington muttered. He stopped short. Felicity bumped into his back. She had to stop herself from wrapping her arms around his nice, solid waist.

"What is it?" she whispered. She peered around him. Talk of the devil! Parker-Roth was standing on the terrace, blocking the door to the ballroom. He did not look happy.

They might have been invisible for all the notice Parker-Roth took of them. It was obvious what—whom—he was looking at. Felicity watched Miss Peterson pick up her skirts and dash into the darkness, leaving Lord Frampton a free man.

Parker-Roth strode across the terrace and descended the steps in record time.

"I say, Parker-Roth—"

"Later, Frampton." The man didn't bother to glance at the baron. He had his quarry in his sights. He went off into the greenery.

Frampton shook his head and climbed back to the terrace. "You'd think they'd be a bit more discreet, wouldn't you?"

"Definitely," Bennington said. "Miss Peterson will have no reputation left if she does not take care."

Frampton nodded. "Thought there would be an engagement announcement after the Palmerson affair, but apparently not. Wonder what the problem is." He shrugged. "Not my concern." He coughed. "I'll not spread the tale, of course. Wouldn't want to be the one responsible for earning her the cut direct." He paused, then frowned. "Though I might put the word in an ear or two. Warn an unsuspecting lady. Wouldn't want some well-mannered miss to be led astray."

"No, indeed." Felicity stepped out from Bennington's shadow. It was vastly amusing, watching Frampton's eyes widen. There was even sufficient light to see his face turn a dull red. "Thank you, my lord. I will consider myself suitably warned."

"Lady Felicity, I didn't mean y—I mean, I didn't *see* you there."

"No? And here I was certain your comments were addressed directly to me."

Frampton made an odd strangling noise which he quickly turned into a cough.

"Of course they were," Bennington said. "You should definitely stay clear of Miss Peterson, Lady Felicity. The girl is not the thing at all."

The warmth in her chest grew. Was Bennington trying to protect her?

She blinked. Her eyes were suddenly wet. No one

had ever tried to protect her before. Certainly the thought had never occurred to her father.

She really must get Lord Bennington into the bushes.

"Lord Bennington, perhaps we could be of some assistance here. If we were to join Miss Peterson—and Mr. Parker-Roth if he has found her—for a stroll, the lady's presence in the garden would be completely unexceptional, wouldn't you say?"

Bennington's brows contracted. "I—"

"That's a splendid idea." Lord Frampton's relief was palpable.

"I don't know. I—"

"Lord Bennington, you are too modest." Felicity laid her hand on the viscount's sleeve.

"I am?"

Both peers gaped at her. She smiled back.

"Indeed you are. Don't you agree, Lord Frampton, that Lord Bennington's consequence would most assuredly keep Miss Peterson from disgrace?"

Lord Frampton blinked. "What? Oh! Oh, yes. Definitely." He turned to Bennington. "If you will only lend your support, my lord, I'm certain disaster will be averted."

"Well . . ."

Felicity would swear Bennington puffed out his chest. She tugged on his arm. "Come, Lord Bennington. We should not delay."

"No, definitely not!" Frampton moved, blocking the door to the ballroom. "Please don't waste another instant."

Felicity felt the moment Lord Bennington gave in. The arm under her hand relaxed. "Oh, very well. I guess I can't turn my back on a young woman who could use my help."

"Exactly." Felicity started toward the stairs, keeping her hand firmly on Bennington's arm. "If you'll excuse us, Lord Frampton?"

"Of course."

"The girl deserves whatever she gets," Bennington muttered as they descended. "She is definitely no better regarded than she should be."

"Hmm." Felicity stroked Bennington's forearm. This mix of excitement and . . . affection was quite overwhelming. "She should be better—much better."

"What?" He looked at her hand on his arm, then up to her face. The poor man was so puzzled. She could hardly wait to enlighten him. "What do you mean?"

"I mean"—they passed beyond the reach of the ballroom light into deep shadows—"that I would be very much worth the trouble if you were to come with me into the bushes." She trailed her fingers up his arm to his biceps.

He sucked in his breath as she let her other hand graze the front of his pantaloons. "Someone will see us."

"I don't think so." She knew Easthaven's garden intimately—she had been intimate with enough men in it. For the first time that thought was distasteful. Well, if she were successful with her plan, she would no longer be entertaining anyone but Bennington. She smiled.

She'd been steering the viscount toward her favorite spot from the moment they'd left the stairs. It wasn't far. "I think we can find a nice dark location where we can have a moment of privacy—several moments. As many moments as we need."

Here it was. Thankfully Miss Peterson had not found it before them. She stepped through a break in some dense bushes into a small clearing around a sturdy tree. The bushes served as an admirable screen and the tree—well, occasionally one needed the support its trunk provided.

"Shouldn't we be looking for Miss Peterson? We told Frampton we'd come to her aid."

Felicity smiled and reached for the fall of his pantaloons. "I think Miss Peterson can fend for herself. Didn't you say she deserves whatever she gets?" She grinned. "I suspect she wants to get Mr. Parker-Roth. Just as I want to get you."

"Uh, but—ack!"

Mmm. The man was already large.

"Shh, Lord Bennington." She opened a button. "Sound travels at night, you know."

"Uh." He was panting. He lowered his voice as she lowered his fall. "Wh-what are you doing?"

"I thought that was obvious. I'm making myself well worth your trouble." She smiled. "I find myself unable to resist you."

Oddly, it was true.

"Me?" Bennington almost squeaked. It was clear no one had seduced him before. The warmth in her chest grew. She was quite hot, really.

Bennington was flushed as well. "I, ah, oh."

He fell free in her hand. She'd never handled an organ so impressive. She cradled it in her fingers, and felt it grow more impressive still. She eagerly looked forward to a closer inspection, but first . . .

She ran her tongue over her lips. "Kiss me," she whispered. "Please."

The man didn't need a second invitation. His lovely, thick, wet lips covered hers and his tongue plunged between her teeth.

Mmm. Delicious.

"Are you bored, Lord Bennington?"

"God, no. Never." He explored her ear with his

tongue. "Call me Bennie, sweetings. Bennington is so formal."

She shivered. "Mmm, Bennie, that feels *so* good." When would he attend to her breasts? She arched a bit to encourage him.

He was most perceptive. His hands slid down and lifted her free of her corset. He bent his head and sucked.

Ah. She was hot and getting hotter. It was a very good thing the tree trunk was handy. She let go of him and leaned back against it. Her knees were threatening to give out.

She closed her eyes to better concentrate. It had been so long, she'd forgotten how good a man's touch felt. She'd forgotten how the place between her legs throbbed. She was so swollen, so achy, so wet. She needed—desperately needed—Bennington to attend to a very specific part of her anatomy. Immediately. Sooner than immediately, if possible.

Bennie knew. Thank God he wasn't a dolt. She felt him lift her skirts, felt his warm breath on her thighs. She arched toward him. His tongue. She needed his tongue. Please, God, just the slightest flick of his tongue. Just the tip, right *there*.

She was going to scream.

Lud! Bennie had a lovely, lovely mouth. And a *very* skilled tongue. He was taking her to release so quickly. She was almost there. She—

She had the oddest feeling she was being watched.

She opened her eyes—and looked directly into Lady Dunlee's disapproving face.

Chapter 11

She was letting her emotions run away with her. She should stop and confront Mr. Parker-Roth. Hadn't she decided just this evening to take charge of her life?

Her feet kept flying over the grass.

She would take charge tomorrow, in a more public location, far, far away from the man currently pursuing her.

She dodged around a shadowy shrub.

Why *was* he pursuing her? Couldn't he take the hint that she did not want his company?

A vine grabbed at her hair. She ducked and tripped over a root, almost falling full length into an ungainly rhododendron. Her skirts tangled around her legs and something hard poked into the sole of her foot. Her silly little dancing slippers had not been designed for any activity more strenuous than a lively reel. They had certainly not been meant to be taken on a mad dash through the shrubbery.

She panted, heart pounding, and pushed her hair out of her face. How close was he? Was it possible he wasn't following her at all? Perhaps he'd realized the impropriety of haring off after her into the bushes.

After all, the man did not seem overly fond of scandal. Perhaps—surely—he'd reconsidered.

"Miss Peterson?"

"Ulp—" She pressed her lips tightly together, but it was too late. The sound had already escaped. Damn. She couldn't see him yet, but he wasn't far away. Her name hadn't been much more than a whisper, yet she had heard it clearly.

She had to hide. Where? The infernal garden was not half so dark as it had seemed from the terrace. She needed someplace darker, someplace sheltered. Some snug little hidey hole where, with a bit of luck, she could secrete herself and watch Mr. Parker-Roth walk right past. Then she'd be able to return to the ballroom by herself.

A stray beam of moonlight illuminated a streak of mud on her dress.

It would take more than luck for her to reenter Lady Easthaven's ballroom. It would take a miracle. How could she get Emma's attention to let her know she wished to return home? Would she be required to lurk in the bushes until her sister noticed her absence and sent out a search party?

She repressed a groan. She couldn't worry about that now—she had more pressing concerns. She heard the scrape of a pebble. Definitely more pressing.

She raised her skirts higher and ran. Another branch pulled at her hair, sending it tumbling over her shoulders. She would not be surprised if she were adorned with more than one stray leaf. She rounded a substantial yew—and knew hope.

Easthaven must have decided to experiment with the picturesque style of garden design, because the vegetation here was extremely wild. She had never been especially enamored of overgrown plantings, but if the excessive leafage screened her from Parks tonight, she might become a devotee.

She spotted a small forest of pine trees clustered together to shield the garden from the back alley. Perfect! She'd squeeze her way past the feathery branches to the stone wall. No one would find her there. She could watch Parks go by and then—

"Eek!"

A large, bare, male hand closed around her upper arm.

"Going somewhere, Miss Peterson?" Mr. Parker-Roth's voice held a distinct edge—and blast it all, the man wasn't even breathing hard.

"Uh . . ." *She* certainly was breathless. She swallowed, staring at his large male fingers. They were so dark against her pale skin. He had spent too many hours working in the sun among his plants.

He pulled, turning her. She took a sustaining breath. God willing, she'd manage more than a squeak when she spoke. She forced her lips into a smile.

"Mr. Parker-Roth. Fancy meeting you here."

Heavens, did he growl? His face was expressionless, but a muscle jumped in his cheek. His eyes narrowed slightly.

She wanted to look away. Instead she raised her chin and stared back.

A peculiar heat coiled deep in her middle. Odd. The evening had turned unseasonably warm. She needed a fan—not that she could use it with his hand holding her hostage.

"A man might wonder, Miss Peterson, what you are looking for in this darkened garden."

"Really? I thought that would be obvious. Solitude, Mr. Parker-Roth. I am seeking solitude."

His fingers tightened and she drew in a sharp breath.

"You are hurting me, sir."

"My apologies." He loosened his hold. "I find your answer somewhat disingenuous, Miss Peterson. You left the ballroom in Lord Frampton's company. Rather odd behavior, wouldn't you say, for someone wishing to be alone?"

Exceedingly odd behavior, but she certainly was not going to admit that. "The man is not with me now, is he?"

"Only because he refused your invitation to scandal." Parks took a deep breath as if he were struggling to control his temper.

"Balderdash. He merely did not care to take a turn in the garden." She forced her smile wider. "And my desire for solitude struck me rather suddenly. It came on when I saw you approaching in the ballroom and intensified when you stepped onto the terrace."

Did she actually hear his teeth grind? Impossible! Still, his nostrils flared and his jaw looked as if it had been carved from marble. His eyes narrowed to slits.

This might be the first time she'd encountered someone literally speechless with anger.

Perhaps she *had* pushed him more than was wise. She wet her lips. Yes, circumspection might have been the better course, but he wouldn't harm her, would he?

If he decided to turn nasty, there was little she could do. She certainly couldn't free herself from his grasp—he was much too strong. And she was too far from the ballroom to call for help. She—

No. She was letting her imagination run wild now. Mr. Parker-Roth was a gentleman. Of course he would not harm her.

Just as Lord Bennington was a gentleman . . .

But Lord Bennington had been amorous. Mr. Parker-Roth was merely murderous.

"Miss Peterson—"

"Mr. Parker-Roth, do not say another word. Please. Just return to the ballroom. I shall be fine by myself."

His grip tightened again, but he relaxed his fingers the moment she inhaled.

Why should he be agitated at all? It was not as if she had accepted his offer of marriage. What she did or didn't do was no concern of his. He was being completely unreasonable.

Unfortunately her heart was being unreasonable as well. It was pounding so hard, she had trouble breathing. She felt slightly ill. Her stomach was . . . shivering and her cheeks were hot. She was fevered, that was it. Hot and . . . throbbing. Damp in the most embarrassing place . . .

"I will not leave you alone. It is not proper."

He was glaring at her.

Damn it, why was he reprimanding her? He was behaving like a colossal prig. Apparently, he had never committed the slightest transgression. He must be unbearable to live with.

"Unhand me, sir, and I will do you the favor of leaving *you* alone."

"I would like nothing better, but I am a gentleman. I cannot leave a lady—a woman—alone in the dark."

What did he mean by calling her a woman in that tone of voice? "You are insulting, sirrah!"

"You are incorrigible, madam."

"I am not! How can you say so?"

"How can I not say so? Have you not made a habit of frequenting the darker corners of the *ton*'s vegetation with a variety of men? One would think, if you were an intelligent woman, you would have learned your lesson after your encounter with Bennington."

She had a sudden desire to see the red prints of her

fingers on his face. Unfortunately, his reflexes were excellent. He grabbed her hand before she'd fully raised it.

She pulled back, but his hold was like iron. She could kick him in the shins, but her foot throbbed even as she thought of it. Her dancing slippers had already proven how flimsy they were—she'd only bruise her toes further.

She contented herself with the fiercest glare she could manage. "At the risk of repeating myself, Mr. Parker-Roth—*go away!*"

"And at the risk of repeating myself, Miss Peterson, no. I am not leaving you alone in this garden."

She really, really would like to kick him.

"Sir, you are not my keeper—"

"Bloody hell, woman." Mr. Parker-Roth transferred his grip to her shoulders—he looked as though he would have preferred to put his hands around her neck. "Someone needs to be your damn keeper and I don't see a blasted queue forming for that honor."

"I do not need a kee—mphft."

The annoying man had covered her mouth with his own.

The woman was driving him mad—stark, raving mad. Did she think she could hide from him in the vegetation? She was beyond bird-witted if that were the case. Her light blue gown and pale skin—an inordinate amount of pale skin—were laughably easy to see in the dark.

Best let her get farther into Easthaven's plantings. He had a few choice words to say to her that could best be communicated without an audience. He did not care to entertain any idiot of the *ton* who happened to stroll onto Easthaven's terrace.

He stepped from the grass to the garden path. Even if he were blind, he'd be able to follow Miss Peterson. She was crashing through the shrubbery like a frightened deer. What did she think he would do to her?

Some entrancing possibilities popped into his head.

Damn! Heat flooded his face and, um, another part of his anatomy.

Bloody hell! He was not some unlicked cub, at the mercy of his urges. He was a mature—an *experienced*—man. He had a mistress, for God's sake. Such salacious thoughts had no business intruding on his consideration of Miss Peterson—and they certainly had no business affecting him in such a . . . prominent way. The girl was a well-bred, well-connected virgin.

He paused. *Was* she a virgin?

He clenched his teeth. Of *course* she was. What was he thinking? He repressed an odd thrill of, of . . . something . . . that thudded in his chest. He should not be considering Miss Peterson's state of virginity.

Another odd sensation assailed him, though this time it did not target his chest. He adjusted the fall of his pantaloons. He was feeling very out of sorts. Perhaps the lobster patties had not agreed with him, or he'd had a bit of bad fish.

Miss Peterson's behavior in Lady Palmerson's parlor gave evidence of her innocence. She'd struggled to keep that damn shawl covering her—No, he would not think about her lovely, white—

Well, she was admittedly less innocent now than she'd been before she'd entered that parlor, and if she didn't stop frequenting dark corners, she'd be much, much less innocent shortly. There was a reason young women were cautioned to avoid the shrubbery. Men could—

The shocking image of what a man . . . what *this* man could do with Miss Peterson in the shrubbery sent a jolt of molten lust directly to the part of him most eager to misbehave.

Damn, damn, *damn*. He needed to get his thoughts under control.

All right, perhaps it wasn't his thoughts that most needed control.

Miss Peterson was safe from him. He had offered her his name and she had declined. That was the end of it. She did not want him, and he had asked merely for convention's sake. He had no interest in her at all.

His lack of interest chose that moment to increase the intensity of its throbbing disinterest, forcing him to bend over slightly.

He avoided a boring, nondescript shrub. No matter what he thought, it must be clear to anyone with half a brain that Miss Peterson was in desperate need of close supervision. Why wasn't Lady Knightsdale keeping her sister out of the bushes?

He ducked under a low hanging vine. Easthaven's gardeners needed to do some judicial pruning. It was one thing to cultivate a wild look, quite another to risk hanging one's visitors.

Well, if Lady Knightsdale would not do the job, he would see that Miss Peterson understood the appropriate behavior for an unwed young woman. Hell, if she were his sister—

His stomach twisted. She was *not* his sister. He definitely did not have brotherly feelings for the woman. The very thought was obscene.

Still, if Jane had—well, Jane *had*, but only with Lord Motton.

Perhaps he *should* demonstrate exactly what could happen to a young lady alone in the dark with a man.

He paused. He needed a nice, cold fountain. Icy cold. Freezing. A dunk in very, very cold water would certainly help his concentration.

What he really needed was to get back to the Priory. The noxious London air had infected his brain.

All right, they were far enough from the ballroom now. He would stop Miss Peterson and give her the sharp edge of his tongue—

God! The ache turned into a stabbing pain. He bent over, bracing his hands on his knees. Where was a nice icy fountain when you needed one?

No tongues. Best leave tongues out of consideration entirely. Scold her. That was what he would do. She would feel his anger. Anger. That was all she would feel.

Truly, if he didn't drag his mother home from London soon, he'd be moving into Bedlam.

"Miss Peterson?" He whispered in case someone else was out in the garden. He knew she wasn't far away.

"Ulp."

The small sound was cut off abruptly. There was a pause, and then he heard the sound of more furious running.

Was the woman completely crazy?

He followed her. The foliage grew more dense and bushy. Either Easthaven had chosen to attempt a picturesque landscape or he should fire his gardeners.

There she was, standing by some pine trees. Was she thinking of hiding? Ridiculous. He stepped forward and wrapped his fingers around her upper arm. Her flesh was incredibly soft.

"Eek!" She jerked and stared at his fingers. Was she afraid to meet his eyes? Was she afraid of *him*? He did not care for that thought. Why would she fear him? Had he ever used her poorly?

Well, perhaps in Lady Palmerson's parlor, but she had not been complaining—not at all. She'd been a very active participant in those activities.

"Going somewhere, Miss Peterson?" Even he heard the odd anger in his voice.

"Uh . . ." She kept staring at his fingers. They were large and dark against her skin. He turned her.

"Mr. Parker-Roth." Her voice was breathless. "Fancy meeting you here."

Surely she was not going to act as though she'd just been out for a leisurely stroll? Her hair had tumbled over her shoulders and down her back and was sporting more than one leaf. Her bosom was rising and falling rapidly. She was panting, for God's sake.

He was panting.

"A man might wonder, Miss Peterson, what you are looking for in this darkened garden."

A man might wonder many things. He drew in a deep breath and smelled pine needles and woman. Miss Peterson. Meg.

He wondered if he'd imagined how soft her breasts were, how wonderful her skin tasted, how quickly he could get her out of her ball gown.

No, no, of course he didn't wonder that.

She was saying something about wanting solitude. Solitude? Right. That was just what she needed. What he needed. Time alone to get his raging lust under control. He could never reenter the ballroom in his current state of . . . excitement.

"You are hurting me, sir."

Damn. "My apologies." He loosened his hold. He was going to give her his tongue. No! No tongues. He was going to jump down her throat—no, no. He was going to ring a peal over her. That was it. No tongues, no throats.

The tip of her tongue peeked out to moisten her lips. She swallowed, her delicate throat flexing, arching. He would love to taste those lips again; to run his tongue from the sensitive point under her ear down her throat to the pulse he knew was beating—

A scold. She deserved a scold.

"I find your answer somewhat disingenuous, Miss Peterson." God, did he really sound like an old prig with a poker up his arse? "You left the ballroom in Lord Frampton's company. Rather odd behavior, wouldn't you say, for someone wishing to be alone?"

Even in the dim light of the garden, he saw her flush. The dark color swept up her throat to her cheeks. Did it move down as well? If he lowered her bodice, if he freed her from her corset, would he see her breasts pinken? Her belly, her sweet—

Well, his skin was certainly changing color. He didn't need to look to know that. He could feel the heat, the swollen—

"The man is not with me now, is he?"

Good thing. He wasn't certain he could behave in a civilized manner if Frampton were present. He feared he'd darken the poor man's daylights for him.

"Only because he refused your invitation to scandal." Frampton had behaved like a gentleman.

"Balderdash. He merely did not care to take a turn in the garden. And my desire for solitude struck me rather suddenly. It came on when I saw you approaching in the ballroom and intensified when you stepped onto the terrace."

God give him patience. He was going to wipe that smirk off her face if it were the last thing he did. How dare she act as if he were the one behaving unreasonably?

She was in need of a lesson and he was just the man to give it to her.

"Miss Peterson—"

"Mr. Parker-Roth, do not say another word. Please. Just return to the ballroom. I shall be fine by myself."

Fine by herself?

He heard her sharp intake and relaxed his fingers again.

Fine by herself? The woman was mad. She was the one who belonged in Bedlam.

"I will not leave you alone. It is not proper."

Her eyes flashed. "Unhand me, sir, and I will do you the favor of leaving *you* alone."

"I would like nothing better, but I am a gentleman." And a liar. No, he *did* want to leave her, but he also wanted to wrap his arms around her, back her up against a tree, and—

He was losing his mind.

"I cannot leave a lady—a woman—alone in the dark."

"You are insulting, sirrah!"

Perhaps he had put the wrong emphasis on a word. Who the hell knew? Didn't the girl comprehend that it was a miracle he was actually forming coherent sentences?

"You are incorrigible, madam."

"I am not! How can you say so?"

"How can I not say so? Have you not made a habit of frequenting the darker corners of the *ton*'s vegetation with a variety of men? One would think, if you were an intelligent woman, you would have learned your lesson after your encounter with Bennington."

That got to her. He grabbed her hand before it connected with his face. Did she think to frighten him with that glare?

"At the risk of repeating myself, Mr. Parker-Roth—
go away!"

"And at the risk of repeating myself, Miss Peterson,
no. I am not leaving you alone in this garden."

"Sir, you are not my keeper—"

He swore his head was going to explode. He had
never been so angry—he actually saw red.

"Bloody hell, woman." He grabbed her shoulders.
They felt so delicate under his hands. He could break
her as if she were a porcelain doll. Had she no sense at
all? "Someone needs to be your damn keeper and I
don't see a blasted queue forming for that honor."

Miss Peterson raised her chin. There wasn't a hint
of fear or caution in her eyes. By God, she *did* belong
in Bedlam.

"I do not need a kee—"

He had heard enough. His mouth came down on
hers without conscious thought. Let her taste the
danger she flirted with.

Taste. Mmm. Yes. She tasted hot and sweet. He licked
the line between her lips—they softened, opened. He
slipped inside. Her weight sagged against him.

This was much better than arguing.

He stroked the dark, wet wonder of her mouth. God,
it was so good—as good as he'd dreamed since that
bloody evening in Lady Palmerson's parlor. Better.

Well, not quite. In his dreams, Miss Peterson was
naked, gloriously, splendidly, completely naked.

Another jolt of lust targeted his groin. He *was* going
to explode.

He slid his hands down her back, past her hard corset
to the lovely soft expanse of her bottom. He traced its
contours, cupped it, pressed it closer to his ache.

Was he scandalizing her? Frightening her? He didn't
want to—

She made an odd little noise in the back of her throat and wiggled closer. Another movement like that and he was going to disgrace himself.

The most recalcitrant part of him throbbed in anticipation at the thought. He sent it a stern reprimand and flexed his hips back slightly as he kissed her jaw. Her breathy pants and little moans filled his ears. She smelled of roses and need.

Good God. Her hands slid down *his* back, under his coat tails, to his posterior. The minx! She was tugging on him, trying to pull him back against her.

She was in serious need of a thorough lesson, and he was going to—

Damn.

"John—"

"Shh!" He covered her lips with his fingers. Yes, he was right. It was a wonder he'd heard anything over the blood roaring in his ears, but he had. Someone was approaching.

A meeting would be most inadvisable. Miss Peterson looked delightfully wanton and he . . . well, his pantaloons were much too fitted to disguise his current sentiments.

He tugged her farther into the pine trees.

They reached the stone wall separating Easthaven's garden from the alley before Meg had completely recovered. Really, if Parks hadn't wrapped his arm around her waist and supported her, she would have melted into a puddle on the ground. He was almost carrying her.

"John—"

This time she didn't need his muffling fingers. She heard a woman's voice clearly.

"Confess—you enjoyed it."

Oh, lud! It was Lady Dunlee.

She swallowed a groan and put her head on Mr. Parker-Roth's chest. His hand came up to tangle in her hair—hair that was shockingly tumbled over her shoulders and back.

His fingers comfortingly massaged her scalp.

She really was ruined this time. Once was bad enough, but to be found in the bushes twice with Mr. Parker-Roth? Lady Dunlee could dine out on this tale for the rest of the Season—if not the next Season and the next.

A man snorted. "I will not. I don't see why you must keep dragging me into the shrubbery, Clarissa. We have a perfectly good bed at home."

Bed? Clarissa? That was Lady Dunlee's Christian name and the man speaking sounded like Lord Dunlee, but . . .

Bed?!

Were they going to sleep in the shrubbery? They couldn't . . . surely they were far too old to use a bed for anything other than slumber.

Meg peered out through the pine needles.

"I can't help it, Edgar. You know how these spells come on me. I get so hot—flushed and damp. I can't stand being in the stuffy, close air of the ballroom. And then, well, sometimes I get . . ."

The woman giggled!

"Sometimes I really can't wait. And you weren't protesting very vehemently a few moments ago, my lord."

Lord Dunlee cleared his throat. "Well, no. Always ready to be of service, of course, my dear. It just seems at our age . . . my rheumatism . . . well, a bed is vastly more comfortable, don't you agree?"

"Sometimes. And sometimes a quick . . . encounter . . .

on a secluded garden bench is exactly what I need for my comfort."

"I'd say so. You were like a wild animal, my dear. I hope I have not lost any buttons."

"If you have, we'll just have new ones sewn on."

"But I have to reenter the ballroom."

"Then I'd best check to see all is in order, hadn't I?"

Lud, surely Lady Dunlee wasn't going to . . . ? She was! She put her hand on Lord Dunlee's . . .

Meg buried her face in Mr. Parker-Roth's cravat. Were they going to resume whatever activity they'd been engaged in?

Thankfully not.

"Clarissa, you must give me time to recover."

"Oh, pooh. Very well." Lady Dunlee emitted a short, disgruntled-sounding sigh. "You used to be able to perform more than once in an evening."

"I used to be many years younger."

Lady Dunlee laughed. "True—as was I. And I must say whatever you lack in quantity, you more than make up for in quality." She made a funny little purring sound.

Meg covered her ears with her hands, but she couldn't completely block out the conversation.

"I can't wait for the next time."

"The next time will occur in our bedchamber, madam. Now straighten your gown and behave yourself."

"Must I?"

Yes. Meg squeezed her eyes tightly shut and stuck her fingers in her ears. Please, behave. Go back to the ballroom.

How could she ever look at Lady Dunlee again without seeing—hearing—this scene?

"They've left."

Meg lifted her face from Mr. Parker-Roth's cravat. He had a distinctly bemused expression in his eyes.

"What were they—"

He covered her lips with his fingers again. "Sound travels at night."

Her stomach twisted. "They must have heard us, then."

Mr. Parker-Roth rolled his eyes and pulled her toward the back wall. "I believe they were too involved in their own activities to be eavesdropping. However, that is not the case now."

Meg followed behind him. Fortunately there was a narrow path by the wall so they weren't forced to battle the vegetation. "What are you doing?"

"Looking for the back gate. I don't believe you will be reentering the ballroom."

Meg pushed her hair off her face. No, she would definitely not be gracing Lady Easthaven's ballroom again tonight.

"I'll—"

The man stopped so suddenly, she bumped into him. "What is it?"

"You don't want to know."

"Yes, I do." She hated to be patronized. She ducked under his arm—and stopped.

Thankfully, she was still hidden by the overgrown pine trees. Through their branches, she saw Lord and Lady Dunlee on the other side of a small clearing. They were frowning at Lady Felicity. Lady Felicity was . . . well . . . she was leaning against a tree. She had a very odd expression, and her dress was . . . was . . .

"Is there someone under Lady Felicity's dress?"

"What . . . ?"

Mr. Parker-Roth put his hand over her mouth once more. Really, the man was becoming extremely annoying. Still, she was appreciative of his action this time. She might otherwise have brought unwelcome attention to their presence.

"Lady Felicity," Lady Dunlee said, "just whom might you be entertaining down there?"

Chapter 12

"What was he doing?" Meg had been trying to puzzle out the answer to that question ever since she'd seen Lord Bennington emerge from under Lady Felicity's skirts in Easthaven's garden two days earlier. "He's not a physician." She frowned, replaying the scene in her mind for the hundredth time. "Though Lady Felicity did look very odd. Do you suppose she was in pain?"

"She was not in pain."

Mr. Parker-Roth sounded distinctly testy. Meg glanced over at him. His ears looked distinctly red, as well. Was he embarrassed? Why?

He did not meet her gaze, but lengthened his stride so they were almost galloping across the lawn at the Duke of Hartford's estate on the Thames.

"Will you slow down? We are not in a footrace, are we?"

"No, of course not."

If anything, the man increased his pace. Meg put out her hand and caught his arm.

"What is the matter?"

"Nothing is the matter."

She blew out a short, annoyed breath. "I am not a complete ninnyhammer. *Something* is the matter."

Mr. Parker-Roth stopped and looked at her. "Why didn't you ask your sister about the scene in the garden?"

Meg felt her cheeks flush. She avoided Parks's eyes. "I don't know. It was too hard to describe, I suppose. Too odd. I mean, who would believe a grown man would be under a woman's skirts in the garden outside a ball? It is . . . absurd."

"Exactly. Just put it out of your mind."

She couldn't do that, either. She'd tried. There was something about the tableau that would not let it be forgotten.

"Lord Bennington and Lady Felicity are engaged now."

Parks snorted and resumed his breakneck pace down the hill toward the group of people playing bowls.

"I would hope so."

"Why?"

He stopped again. "Miss Peterson, please. You may not understand exactly what Lord Bennington was up to, but you certainly understand he should not have been involved in any activity requiring a visit beneath a lady's skirt."

"Of course, but—"

"*And* he was discovered by Lady Dunlee."

Meg snorted herself this time. "Lady Dunlee is not one to preach propriety after what she was doing in the garden." She paused. What *had* Lady Dunlee been doing?

"Lord and Lady Dunlee are married. What they do between themselves cannot be construed as scandalous."

"*I* was scandalized." She didn't need to know the specifics to know something shocking had occurred.

"You are a virgin. You don't count."

"What do you mean, I don't count?" She grabbed his

arm again. She might not be experienced, but still . . .
"Weren't you scandalized?"

Mr. Parker-Roth flushed. "I might have been surprised, yes. I hadn't considered . . . one doesn't usually consider . . ." He shrugged. "But scandalized? No.
As I say, they are married. A certain degree of . . .
intimacy . . . is to be expected in marriage as a matter
of course."

Meg shook his arm. "But in the *bushes?* Lady *Dunlee?*"

Parks shrugged and started walking again. She fell
into step beside him. Lord and Lady Dunlee were old.
Who would have thought old people could still engage
in activities requiring screening by bushes?

She should have thought it. Lady Dunlee was quite
possibly younger than Papa and Harriet, and they were
certainly very . . . ardent. Of course, they had only been
married a few years, but still, if marital enthusiasm were
limited by age . . .

No, it wasn't Lady Dunlee's age that made the incident in Easthaven's shrubbery so shocking, it was her
role as society's arbiter of decorum. She'd shamed Lord
Bennington into a marriage proposal minutes after
she'd been . . . well, she'd been doing *something* that
involved a secluded garden bench and potentially missing pantaloon buttons. For her to then act outraged at
what Lady Felicity and Lord Bennington had been
doing—

What *had* they been doing?

"I do wish you would explain the situation to me."

Parks almost broke into a run. "I am not explaining
anything to you. It would be most inappropriate. Ask
your sister if you are so curious."

"Has anyone told you that you are a shocking prig?"

He glared at her. "If you don't care for my company,

please seek a more congenial companion. I don't believe I've been forcing you to stay by my side."

"I was just trying to be polite."

"That's a first." He muttered the words, but she still heard him quite clearly.

She should take his hint and leave him alone. She certainly had not intended to seek him out. She'd been extremely annoyed with the man and had planned to ignore him thoroughly. But she couldn't. When she'd seen him arrive with his mother and Miss Witherspoon, she'd been drawn to him like a moth to flame. And then Mrs. Parker-Roth had suggested he take her for a stroll. She'd known he hadn't wanted to do so, but she hadn't refused when he'd offered.

Well, she'd had a question to ask him, which he'd now made abundantly clear he had no intention of answering, ever.

He was outpacing her again. Surely a man with even a modicum of manners would match his step to hers? She hurried to catch up.

No, not a moth to flame. The analogy was more a fly to dung. A maggot to rotting meat.

She could not ask Emma what Lord Bennington had been doing under Lady Felicity's skirts. For one thing, Emma was not very pleased with her at the moment. The *ton*'s attention had been on the delightful scandal of the viscount and the disreputable earl's daughter, but Emma's eyes had focused on Meg's muddied gown and tumbled hair. She had whisked her out the back gate before she had even approached the ballroom and had rung a peal over her the entire carriage ride back to Knightsdale House.

No, she was definitely not going to ask her sister anything about scandalous behavior.

* * *

"Your son does not look very interested in my sister."
Emma leaned forward in her chair on the terrace and
frowned as she watched Mr. Parker-Roth stride across
the lawn below her. Meg had to almost run to keep up.

"I would say he's very interested." Mrs. Parker-Roth,
ensconced in the chair next to her, sounded almost
smug. "Exceedingly. I've never seen him take such an
interest in a female before."

The woman must be addled in the head. If Mr.
Parker-Roth was showing interest in Meg, Emma would
hate to see what his disinterest looked like. "How can
you say—oh!"

Lord Henry had found a dead fly and was preparing
to pop it into his mouth. Emma dove for his chubby
little hand.

"No, Henry. Dirty!"

She wrested the disgusting item out of his fingers. He
howled for a moment and then crawled off in search of
another revolting morsel.

"Henry!"

He giggled and crawled faster. Emma lunged and
grabbed him around his waist. He tried to wiggle free.

"No you don't, you little monkey."

She plopped him down to stand at her knees. He
blinked up at her and then squealed with glee, the two
small teeth in his bottom gum glistening like tiny
pearls. He grabbed her skirts, balancing on his fat
little legs.

"It might have been more relaxing if the duchess had
not made this a family party," Mrs. Parker-Roth said,
laughing.

"Definitely. Dealing with Henry is like wrestling a
greased pig—not that I've ever wrestled one, of course."

"Of course."

Emma frowned. Why did she feel so overwhelmed with Henry? He let himself down and crawled over to investigate an ornamental frog. "Charlie wasn't this active."

"Charlie is your oldest. Henry watches him and tries to do what he does."

"But they are two years apart. There is no possible way Henry can match Charlie's actions."

"Tell Henry that."

Henry had lost interest in the stone frog and was busily pulling flowers out of a planter.

"Henry!"

He grinned and crawled back toward them.

"Stephen is two years younger than John, and he was always trying to do whatever John did. Thankfully John was rather cautious or Stephen would have had many more bruises—and I would have had many more gray hairs."

"And yet you had six children." Emma handed Henry a biscuit.

Mrs. Parker-Roth chuckled. "Well, I wasn't thinking of tending the babies when I was making them. My husband is very . . . persuasive."

"Ah." Emma glanced at Mrs. Parker-Roth. The woman had an odd, dreamy expression.

Lud! Mrs. Parker-Roth must be close to Papa's age. Of course Papa had married Harriet only a few years ago and Charles thought they still—

A knot of panic twisted Emma's stomach. Surely the woman would not share any details of . . . ?

No, she could not consider it. A change of subject was in order—or a return to the original subject.

"Why do you think your son is interested in my sister?" Emma asked. "He was almost running away from her a moment ago."

Mrs. Parker-Roth grinned. "I know. He had a very hunted expression on his face, did he not?"

"He did. And men do not like to be hunted—at least, Charles did not. That's why he married me—to avoid being fox to all the matrimonial hounds after he inherited the title."

The other woman laughed. "You don't really believe that, do you?"

"Of course. He said—"

"Oh, pooh." Mrs. Parker-Roth flicked her fingers at her. "That may have been what he *said*. That may even have been what he believed at one point. Men do so hate to expose their feelings. Much easier to say—and think—they are marrying for convenience rather than love. But do not fool yourself. The marquis is madly in love with you."

"He cares for me, certainly." Emma handed Henry another biscuit. A good bit of the first had found its way onto his clothes and into his hair.

Did Charles love her? She thought so—until she came to London.

It was not as bad as she had feared before her marriage. He did not just come down to Knightsdale to get her with child. He stayed in the country as much as he could, but he had to go to Town to take his seat in the House of Lords. He wanted her to come with him, but she hated London. She much preferred Kent where the air was clean and society was so much more comfortable. And it was better for the boys and for Isabelle and Claire to be in the country.

But Charles was a man with healthy appetites. Had he visited the many London brothels or taken a mistress? She refused to ask. He was as attentive as she could wish when she was with him. What he did when she wasn't . . . well, what she didn't know wouldn't hurt her.

The women in London were so lovely, and she was so short and ordinary and . . . somewhat stout might be the most charitable adjective . . . from bearing her two babies. She sighed.

"I assure you, I cannot compete with the London ladies."

"You do not need to. *You* are the marchioness, not they."

Emma shrugged and watched Henry finish his last crumb of biscuit. The servants had brought a jug of water. She would clean him off with her handkerchief.

Mrs. Parker-Roth touched her knee. "Emma, you must not sell yourself short."

"How can I not?" She bit her lip. She would *not* cry.

She had not meant to say it, but she was so weary of pretending to fit in with the *haut ton*. She did not. No matter how hard she tried, she felt out of place, like a . . . a pig in a parlor.

Mrs. Parker-Roth frowned at her. "Emma, people take us at our own valuation, you know. If you think yourself unworthy, society—particularly the nasty gabble grinders—will agree with you. But if you act as if you belong—which you most certainly do—they will accept you. You are the Marchioness of Knightsdale, for goodness sake."

Emma shrugged and dipped her handkerchief in the water jug. "Come here, you messy little creature." She grabbed Henry, glad her voice hadn't broken. "I just wish Charles had really chosen me—not just settled for me."

Lud, where had *that* come from? She bent her head closer to Henry's, blinking away sudden tears to concentrate on cleaning the wet paste of biscuit and baby spit from his face.

Mrs. Parker-Roth clicked her tongue. "Emma, the

marquis can never prove his love beyond all doubt. No one can. You have to trust him. Has he given you reason to doubt him?"

"No, of course not." She balled up the messy handkerchief and stuffed it in her reticule. How had this conversation become focused on her anyway? She pinned a smile to her lips and looked at Mrs. Parker-Roth. "You still haven't told me why you think your son is interested in my sister."

The older woman frowned, her eyes searching Emma's face, but Emma would not let herself look away. Finally Mrs. Parker-Roth smiled slightly.

"That's simple. If he were not, he would not be attending these social events."

Emma frowned. "But he needs to escort you."

Mrs. Parker-Roth snorted. "Believe me, Johnny is not that dutiful a son. This is not our first visit to London, remember. I come up every few months for art supplies—and to try to find him a wife. He knows my motives. He has become very adroit at avoiding society gatherings—but this time he is indeed accompanying me, albeit complaining vociferously at every opportunity." She smiled. "The only reason I can fathom for his change in behavior is the presence of your sister."

"But he looks as if he is trying to avoid her."

"If he really wanted to avoid her, he would do so." Mrs. Parker-Roth chuckled. "It is quite amusing to watch him. After his unfortunate experience with Lady Grace, he convinced himself he would never marry. But now he is attracted to your sister. He is having a terrible struggle with himself." She grinned broadly. "I am delighted."

"You are?" How could a mother enjoy watching her son struggle? Emma picked Henry up and hugged him.

His warm weight felt so good. She could not imagine him as a grown man, his soft cheeks scratchy with stubble, his plump arms hard and muscled.

Henry squirmed. She put him down and he crawled off toward the edge of the terrace. She caught him when he reached the balustrade. She did not need him getting his head stuck.

The duchess was walking by on the lawn below, talking to her husband, Baron Tynweith. The duke was asleep on the baron's shoulder, his fingers in his mouth.

Mrs. Parker-Roth joined her by the balustrade.

"What do you think of our hostess?" The duchess seemed like a safe topic, and Emma *was* curious. "My husband said she used to be called the Marble Queen—and then the Marble Duchess—but she doesn't strike me as cold."

"That's because she's changed. This second marriage has been very good for her."

"She barely waited a year to remarry. People say . . ." Emma lowered her voice. "People say the baby is Tynweith's."

"I imagine that's true. The man certainly dotes on the child as if he were his own son."

Emma blinked. The older woman did not seem shocked in the slightest. "Hasn't the alternate heir complained?"

"Oh, Claxton has been complaining since the old duke married. There isn't much he can do, however. Hartford died *in flagrante delicto* nine months before the duchess's baby was born. Only a fool would try to prove the child isn't legitimate—and Claxton is not that big a fool."

Henry chose that moment to make a rude noise with his mouth—a trick Charlie had taught him.

"Shh, Henry."

He did not listen. Emma sighed. Henry *never* listened.

"You said the duke died, um, well . . ." Charles had said the man had more than eighty years in his dish. "Surely you don't mean . . . he wasn't . . . was he?"

"Indeed he was. As to whether he was coming or going, I can't say, but it was clear he had been engaged in the proper activity to result in an interesting event nine months hence."

"Oh." Emma swallowed. Some things were best left unimagined.

"And it helps that Charlotte is so much pleasanter now. Tynweith, too. He'd turned into a complete recluse—when he wasn't hosting disreputable parties at his estate, that is."

Emma flushed. "Meg was at one of Lord Tynweith's parties—the one where Hartford died. It's where she met your son."

Mrs. Parker-Roth chuckled. "That was one of Tynweith's moderately acceptable gatherings. Lady Dunlee was there with her husband and daughter—and, as you say, Johnny was there as well. *He* certainly was not looking for scandal." Mrs. Parker-Roth sighed. "I imagine he went to view the topiary."

"Oh. Well, but still, if I had known . . ." Emma ran a hand over Henry's smooth head. He was sucking on his fist, getting hungry most likely. All he needed was to be fed and washed and hugged. So simple.

"Do not apologize. I'm very happy your sister was there. If she hadn't been, Johnny might never have met her." Mrs. Parker-Roth smiled broadly. "When he got home, I could tell something of interest had occurred."

"Really? Did he mention Meg?"

"Oh, no. Johnny is very taciturn, especially concerning his feelings. He just seemed less . . . content. More restless, short tempered . . . surly, even. And he spent even more time with his plants."

Henry let himself down, crawled over to Mrs. Parker-Roth, and tried to pull up on her skirts.

"Henry!"

"Oh, it is quite all right. I love babies. I can hardly wait for my daughter to present me with my first grandchild." Mrs. Parker-Roth offered Henry her fingers. "Here, my lord, let me help you."

Henry looked up to see who belonged to this strange voice. He wobbled for a second and then sat down with a thump. His lower lip jutted out, and he clearly considered crying, but turned and started crawling away instead. Emma caught him just as she saw Isabelle approaching.

"Isabelle, will you take charge of Henry, please?"

"Of course. Come here, Henry." Isabelle scooped the baby up and sat him on her hip. "Do you want to go see the ducks?"

Henry grinned and clapped his hands.

"Be sure to keep him away from the water, Isabelle."

"Don't worry, I will."

Isabelle sounded so confident, but did she have any real understanding of the danger? It took only an instant for tragedy to strike. "Look for Charles, Isabelle. He's probably down by the pond with Charlie."

Isabelle just waved.

"They'll be fine," Mrs. Parker-Roth said.

"But . . ." Emma let out a short breath. "I worry."

"Of course you do. You're a mother." Mrs. Parker-Roth laughed. "Let's go down to see these ducks. That way you can also see what a splendid job Isabelle does—and if something goes wrong, you'll be on hand to fix it."

They descended the stairs and started over the lawn.

"Does mothering ever get easier?"

"Not really." Mrs. Parker-Roth smiled. "When children are small, you try to keep them safe from all the dangers around them—like duck ponds. If they stumble into one, you can rush and pull them out. But when they are older, you have to stand back and watch them wade into life's duck ponds if they want. You can't do a thing to prevent them—except advise them not to do it, but most times they won't listen."

"*Why* won't they listen?"

Mrs. Parker-Roth laughed. "Because they are young and they think they know everything." She smiled. "I wager you wouldn't have followed your mother's counsel either, had she lived to provide it."

"No, how can you say so?" Emma stopped and frowned at the older woman.

"Because that's the way of all children, Emma." Mrs. Parker-Roth linked arms with her, putting her head close to hers and resuming their walk. "But if we are discreet—and a little bit cunning—we can influence them very nicely." She grinned. "Now, how shall we influence my stubborn son and your charming sister to see reason and make a match of it?"

Chapter 13

Viscount Manders let out a hearty belch, quite impressive for such a small person. He grinned as a trail of milk dribbled down his chin.

"Good boy," Lizzie said, wiping him off and kissing him before offering him her other breast. He made little grunting, snuffling sounds and then was quiet, the tiny fingers of one hand spread out against Lizzie's celestial blue gown.

Could she ask Lizzie about the odd scene with Bennington and Felicity? Meg shifted in her chair. She and Lizzie—and Lord Manders—were seated under an oak tree quite a distance from the rowdy group playing bowls.

Would Lizzie know the answer? She *was* a married woman—but what did the activity in the garden have to do with marriage, besides the fact that the viscount was now engaged to Lady Felicity? Surely Robbie hadn't— no, she could not contemplate the thought.

She was not a complete innocent. In her many hours spent outside observing plants, she'd happened on a few animals engaged in the act of procreation. She had a general idea of the mechanics of the deed—or at least, she'd thought she had. A hot flush heated her cheeks.

None of the creatures she'd seen in the fields and farms of Kent had engaged in any of the activities Mr. Parker-Roth had initiated. The animals had not even faced each other during the encounter. Really, the whole thing had looked rather embarrassing and uncomfortable—not that she had looked carefully, of course. Once she'd ascertained what they were about, she'd averted her gaze. She knew the rules of proper behavior, even if she chose to break them on occasion.

Frankly, the only reason she'd been able to discern for enduring such indignities was to have a baby—and even that was a mixed blessing. Emma had been terribly uncomfortable when she'd been in the family way. She'd been tired and ill in the beginning, and tired and cranky at the end. She hadn't been able to eat or breathe or see her feet. Lizzie had managed a little better, but she and Robbie had been frantic when her pains began, afraid she'd die in childbed like her mother.

And then, of course, there was all the work and worry of actually tending an infant.

No, after hearing Emma and Lizzie discuss their ordeals—suitably edited for her poor, unwed ears—and watching them go days without sleep with fussy babies, she wasn't terribly eager to take her turn. But if she wanted her own home, she'd have to marry, and men wanted children—or at least they wanted to engage in the activity that resulted in children. Not that they had to do the work of bearing and birthing their progeny. Of course not. If they did, well, she'd wager there'd be significantly fewer children in the world.

Still, the things Parks had done to her had certainly

been . . . intriguing. She fanned herself with her hand. Perhaps there *was* something pleasant about procreation.

Lizzie coaxed another burp from Lord Manders.

What had Lord Bennington been doing with Lady Felicity? Parks seemed to know all about it, but he'd never ventured under *her* skirts, though his attentions had caused a very odd reaction in—

She fanned herself harder. Surely Bennington hadn't been investigating *that* part of Felicity's anatomy?

"Why are you so flushed, Meg?"

"I'm not flushed."

Lizzie snorted and returned her attention to Lord Manders.

Lady Felicity must have been so embarrassed. She hadn't looked embarrassed, though. She'd looked almost triumphant once Lord Bennington had finally emerged from whatever activity had occupied him under her skirts.

"You're such a lovey boy, aren't you, Bobby-wobby?" Lizzie was nuzzling Lord Manders' neck. The viscount giggled. "Such a smart widdle baby."

Meg kept herself from rolling her eyes . . . barely. What was it about babies that turned sensible adults into idiots?

"So, when are you going to marry Parks?"

"What?" Her jaw dropped. She snapped it shut. Where had that come from? "I told you I'd declined his offer."

"I know you did. Robbie and I couldn't believe it." Lizzie settled Viscount Manders in her lap. He sucked his thumb and stared at Meg. "Surely you've changed your mind?"

"I have not. Mr. Parker-Roth no more wants to marry me than he wants to marry Lady Beatrice."

Lizzie laughed. "Oh, I'm certain he wants to marry you more than Lady Bea."

Meg suddenly understood the expression "gnashing one's teeth." "You know what I mean."

"Do I? Tell me why Parks was in Easthaven's garden with you, then."

"How do you know he was?"

Lizzie gave her an expressive look. "Emma told me, of course. And if she hadn't, I would have heard it from Robbie—Charles told him."

Meg wished her friends and relatives were a great deal less busy about her business. "We were not discussing matrimony."

"No? What *were* you discussing?"

Meg flushed. "We weren't discussing anything."

Lizzie merely looked at her and raised an eyebrow. Meg felt her face burn even redder. Botheration.

"The fact remains that Mr. Parker-Roth came to my aid when Lord Bennington was accosting me. He should not be punished for doing a good deed."

Lizzie rubbed Lord Manders's head. "Well, of course not. There's no punishment involved. He's obviously madly in love with you."

Parks in love with her? "You're the one who's mad. Mr. Parker-Roth views me as a source of aggravation and annoyance, nothing more."

"Right. That's why he was sitting in Lady Palmerson's hideous red chair with you half naked on his lap."

"Uhh." Put that way, it did sound . . . odd. "Mr. Parker-Roth was merely . . . he was just . . . that is . . ." Lizzie looked highly skeptical. Meg addressed Lord Manders instead. "I'd just had an upsetting experience with Lord Bennington. Mr. Parker-Roth was comforting me."

Lizzie snorted. "With your gown down around your waist and your br—"

"Don't say it."

"—*breasts* completely exposed?"

"Ohh." She was going to die of mortification here at the Duke of Hartford's estate. Meg dropped her face into her hands.

"I don't know what you are so upset about," Lizzie said. "You were quite taken with Parks at Tynweith's house party last year."

Meg raised her head. Why deny it? "That was last year. The man didn't make the slightest effort to seek my company again until he found me with Bennington. I obviously failed to make much of an impression on him."

"I don't know about that. He looked rather impressed in Lady Palmerson's parlor."

"Urgh." Meg dropped her head back into her hands.

"Didn't you tell me when I was in a similar position that some men are afraid of matrimony, but settle down nicely once the knot is tied—like a horse being broken to bridle?"

"I am certain I was wrong. Mr. Parker-Roth is nothing like a horse. He is more like a mule—stubborn, headstrong, completely infuriating."

"Ah, I see. Then he is a simple creature merrily eating, sleeping, and fornicating?"

"*Must* you throw my words back at me?"

Lizzie laughed. "It *is* amusing."

Lord Manders grunted and squirmed.

"Oh, dear. I think Bobby is going to need a change in a moment."

"I see." There were some things Meg did not care to see if she could avoid them. She stood quickly. "I believe I'll go watch the bowlers."

"Coward." Lizzie grew serious. "Just don't be a coward about the important things, Meg. I think Parks is perfect for you."

Meg shook her head. "Oh, really? Tell him that."

Lizzie didn't smile in reply. "I don't think I need to tell him. Remember, Meg, Robbie didn't want to offer for me, either. If Lord Andrew hadn't attacked me and forced the issue, I might still be unwed—and Bobby would not be here."

Lizzie hugged her baby. Meg frowned. The situations were not similar at all. "Robbie's loved you for years."

"*I* didn't know that."

"You would have if you'd opened your eyes."

"And perhaps you need to open *your* eyes, Meg."

"Balderdash. I—"

Lord Manders grunted once more and something other than his eyes opened.

Meg backed away. "I'll see you later after you, um"— she gestured toward the viscount's posterior—"tidy up."

"You're sure you wouldn't like to practice changing a baby?"

Meg just waved and kept walking.

"Well done, Parks."

Westbrooke clapped him on the back. Parks grinned. It had been an inspired bowl if he said so himself. He'd sent Bennington's ball spinning off to the right, far beyond hope of scoring, and guaranteed his team the win. He bent to pick up his coat.

"I don't believe you've made a friend, however." Lord Frampton, his other teammate, nodded at Bennington. The viscount was definitely glaring at him. If looks could kill, Parks would be taking his last breath.

He shrugged and turned away. "Bennington and I have an unpleasant history."

"Because you came between him and Miss Peterson?"

"Good God, no." Parks stared at Frampton. The man looked sincere. He was not being malicious—just stupid. "Where did you get that notion? Miss Peterson has absolutely nothing to do with it."

"No?" Frampton raised his eyebrows. "There were rumors Bennington was interested in her for her connections. Oldston told me he overheard the viscount talking at White's about some expedition he needed funds for—a trip to South America or Africa or some outlandish location—and that he might take a stroll in the garden with Miss Peterson. Sample the wares, he said, to see if he could bear to make her an offer. Said he probably would, though. That he could bed any goose if she laid a big enough golden egg, and anyway, there were plenty of whores to warm a man's bed if a wife proved too chilly."

"Bloody hell!"

Westbrooke laid a hand on Parks's arm. "You might want to keep your voice down to a low roar. You're distressing the ladies."

"What?" He looked in the direction the earl indicated. A gaggle of silly debutantes scowled at him and scurried away. Good. Fewer ninnyhammers for his mother to push toward him. He turned back to Frampton. The man was looking mulish.

"It's common knowledge Miss Peterson has been entertaining in the bushes."

Apparently the baron had the intelligence of a mule as well. "Miss Peterson has *not* been entertaining anyone in the bushes."

"Oh? She tried to drag me off into the shrubbery at Easthaven's just the other night, if you'll remember."

Parks took a deep breath and forced his hands to open out of the fists they'd formed. Starting a mill on the Duke of Hartford's lawn with the majority of the *ton* as witness would not be a good idea. His intentions must have been clear on his face, however, because the baron stepped back.

He would not shout. He took another, deeper breath and let the red haze of fury dissipate somewhat. "I hope you have not been spreading that tale, Frampton. I assure you sincerely—it would be a very serious error to do so."

Frampton had a death wish, it was the only explanation. The man blinked at him, then opened his asinine mouth. "Ah, yes, I see. I thought . . . well, pardon me for saying so, but the chitter-chatter had you declining to offer for the girl after you were found in rather compromising circumstances."

He felt Westbrooke's hand on his arm again. He shrugged it off. He was not going to kill Frampton . . . today. When they weren't standing in front of so many interested witnesses, however . . . well, the thought was extremely appealing.

"Do you seriously think the Marquis of Knightsdale would have let me *not* offer for his sister-in-law if I had compromised her?"

Ah, a new concept found its way into the ass's brain box. Frampton scratched his head. "No, I don't suppose he would." He nodded. "So you have a private understanding?"

"I am not at liberty to say." He certainly wasn't going to tell this idiot Miss Peterson had refused him.

"But why keep it secret? You must know the girl is subject to all kinds of unpleasant speculation."

"You've just illustrated that fact."

Frampton flushed. "Well, yes, my apologies. I didn't completely understand the situation."

"Damn right." The situation was a bloody mess.

"Are you fellows going to bowl or not?" Lord Pontly asked.

"We're done," Westbrooke said. "Feel free to take our place."

They stepped away from the competition. Unfortunately, Frampton was like a dog with a bone—he would not let the subject go.

"So why do you say it is not Miss Peterson who comes between you and Bennington? Stands to reason it would be. He wants her; you have her."

Sudden lust kicked Parks in the . . . He sent a stern reprimand to his most unruly organ. He did not "have" Miss Peterson nor was he going to unless she changed her mind.

His body begged to differ. Begged and—

He looked to Westbrooke for assistance. The damn earl was grinning at him like a bedlamite. Obviously, there would be no aid from that quarter.

"Because," he said, "—not that it is any of your concern, of course—Bennington has hated me for years. Long before either of us knew Miss Peterson graced the world."

"Why?"

God give him patience. Did he quash the man for being a busybody or just answer his question?

Westbrooke finally found his tongue—regrettably.

"Plants, Frampton, if you can believe it." The earl snickered. "Bennington hates Parks for his plants."

Frampton's lower jaw dropped, causing him to bear a striking resemblance to a codfish ready for gutting. "Why would anyone be at daggers drawn over greenery?"

Parks sighed. He was all too familiar with this reaction.

"Because Bennington fancies himself in competition with me. He is jealous of my extensive gardens and greenhouses, especially my collection of exotic specimens. That is why he wants money—to search for new plant species."

Frampton continued to gape at him for another few seconds.

"Bloody hell," he said, finally. "I never would have guessed."

Parks did not care for the man's tone. There was something about it . . . He did not think they were discussing Bennington's horticultural ambitions any longer. "What wouldn't you have guessed?"

Frampton flushed. "Oh, nothing. Just surprised, that's all." He cleared his throat. "I'm sure flowers and weeds and what have you can be fascinating to a, um, certain kind of fellow."

Was the man insinuating . . . ? No. He couldn't be that much of a dunderhead.

"Surely you've heard of Humphry Repton, John Claudius Loudon, Sir Joseph Banks—"

"Parks!" Westbrooke was laughing again. The man spent far too much time grinning. "You're wasting your breath. Frampton doesn't read anything that doesn't discuss horses or hunting, do you, Frampton?"

"Of course not. Should I?"

"Exactly." Westbrooke nodded. "See anything at Tatt's recently, Frampton?"

"Actually, yes. I have my eye on an excellent bit of blood . . ."

Frampton droned on about some horse he'd seen at Tattersall's. It was probably a bone-setter of the worst sort—the man was a notoriously poor judge of horseflesh. No matter. Frampton could recite the collected works of Shakespeare for all Parks cared, just as long as he stopped talking about Miss Peterson. He let Frampton and Westbrooke walk ahead.

Miss Peterson. Damn and blast. To think Bennington was bandying about her name at White's . . . the cad. He should have hit the bloody cur's head instead of his wood just now. No, he'd rather have his guts for garters—literally. He'd stab his stomach with a blunt knife and carve him open slowly—

"Mr. Parker-Roth, a word, if I may."

The Marquis of Knightsdale stood by his side, his face like stone. He'd been a cavalry officer—a major—on the Peninsula before his brother died and he inherited the title, and he looked ready to do battle now.

His stern façade was marred by one detail. He was holding a child—a boy barely out of babyhood—with the same curly brown hair and clear blue eyes as his own. Obviously his son, the Earl of Northfield. The earl stared at Parks, and then laid his head on his father's shoulder.

"Papa, I'm *hun*gry."

"How can you be hungry, Charlie? You've been eating all day."

"But I *am* hungry." The earl widened his eyes and turned down the corners of his mouth so he looked completely pitiful.

The marquis sighed and reached into his pocket, pulling out what appeared to be a partially eaten macaroon adorned with bits of lint.

"Here you go, then. Aren't you glad I saved this for you? You wanted to throw it out, remember."

The earl nodded, taking the biscuit and picking off the worst of the fuzz, before popping it into his mouth.

"Parker-Roth?" The marquis gestured with the hand that wasn't holding his son.

"Of course." Parks matched steps with the marquis as they walked away from the crowd. He should be nervous—Knightsdale obviously did not want to talk of the weather—but he wasn't. He glanced again at the earl. The child gave him a wide, crumb-filled grin.

God.

He looked away. What was the matter with him? He felt . . . Well, something about Knightsdale and his son made him think having progeny would be a good thing.

He was losing his mind. He didn't want children. They were noisy, dirty, destructive nuisances. He'd grown up in a family of six, hadn't he? It had been chaos. It still *was* chaos when his two youngest sisters set to hair pulling. Most of the time he was forced to arbitrate their disputes himself. His parents . . . Well, he'd made the mistake once of seeking them out in his mother's studio when the girls were fighting. Good God, he was never doing *that* again. He still couldn't bear to think—

No, no children. He just wanted to be left in peace to work in his garden.

"I've been meaning to speak to you about my wife's sister, sir. The marchioness is concerned—as am I—that there has been no announcement."

They stopped at a shallow ornamental pool. Parks had been slightly surprised he hadn't heard from the marquis earlier—in the form of an invitation for pistols for two, breakfast for one. Dueling was illegal, but the man had been a cavalry officer . . .

"Look, Papa. Ducks!"

"I see, Charlie." The marquis put his son down. "Why don't you watch them while I talk to Mr. Parker-Roth?"

The earl nodded. "May I feed the ducks, Papa?"

"I'm afraid I don't have any bread, Charlie. We'll go get some after I finish this conversation."

The earl's lower lip stuck out and he looked as if he were considering throwing a tantrum, but changed his mind when two more ducks landed on the water. He ran over to look at them—and they swam to the opposite side of the pool.

"Just don't fall in, Charlie."

"I won't, Papa."

The marquis turned back to Parks. "So, Mr. Parker-Roth, about my sister-in-law?"

"Surely Miss Peterson informed you that I offered and she declined?"

"Yes, after the incident in Lady Palmerson's parlor. Given what I saw . . . well, I don't suppose you need me to describe the scene that greeted the marchioness and me when we entered that room."

"No. No, that isn't necessary." Knightsdale could only recount what he'd seen—Miss Peterson, half naked, sitting on Parks's lap. Parks remembered *every* detail. God, remembered? They haunted his dreams—the weight of her soft bottom on his thighs, the silkiness of her skin, the light scent of roses that grew as she warmed under his hands, her sweet responsiveness—

Devil take it! His breeches were becoming distinctly uncomfortable. He looked away. The earl was laughing, chasing the ducks from one side of the pool to the other.

"What do you expect me to do? As I say, Miss Peterson declined my offer. A woman in this day and age cannot be forced to the altar."

Knightsdale frowned. "No, of course not. I would never force Meg to wed." He blew out a short, forceful breath, and ran his hands through his closely cropped hair. "It's just that, well, the situation is becoming complicated. You must know people are gossiping. Meg's reputation hangs by a thread. I am quite certain if I were not the Marquis of Knightsdale, the *ton* would have turned its collective back on her already."

Damn right they would have. The shallow-minded, nasty gabble grinders were definitely whispering about Miss Peterson—Easthaven's ball had proven that.

The earl was beginning to lean over the edge of the pool to reach the ducks. Should he mention it to the marquis?

"It would be one thing if Meg had taken a dislike to you, but that isn't the case."

"What?" His gaze snapped back to Knightsdale. The man looked serious. "Why do you think that?"

Knightsdale lifted an eyebrow. "Emma told me about Meg's disappearance into Easthaven's garden and the state of her attire afterwards."

"She had been walking through the vegetation."

"With you in pursuit."

"I—" It had not been pursuit, exactly. "I just felt it was unwise for Miss Peterson to be alone in a dark garden. She might have found herself the recipient of unwanted male attentions."

Knightsdale snorted. "Well, she certainly found herself the recipient of male attentions."

Damn and blast. Parks looked away. Zeus, he hoped his face wasn't as red as it felt.

"Thank God Bennington created such a scene that Emma was able to whisk Meg away without drawing undo comment on her untidy appearance."

Parks grunted in assent.

"At least you don't deny that you were responsible for her dishabille."

He forced himself to look Knightsdale in the eye. "What do you want me to do? I will offer again, but I think Miss Peterson will only reject me again."

"That's what I don't understand. Meg is not stupid—

or reckless, even though recent evidence seems to be to the contrary. She obviously hasn't taken a dislike to you or she wouldn't keep disappearing into the shrubbery with you. I think she wishes to marry and set up her own household. So why does she keep turning you down?"

A question he had asked himself countless times, particularly in the middle of the night when his dreams had woken him hot and hard. "I really can't say."

"Perhaps you need to be more persuasive."

Parks frowned. "I don't see how I can be more persuasive."

"Papa!"

"In a minute, Charlie." Knightsdale was actually flushing. "The situation cannot stay as it is. In the normal course of events there would be plenty of time for extended wooing, but this is not the normal course of events. You need to focus on the goal here, Parker-Roth. Meg has no choice but to marry you. You need to persuade her to see reason."

Parks almost laughed. Get Miss Peterson to see reason? "That is not so easily done, my lord. Miss Peterson has a mind of her own."

Knightsdale rolled his eyes. "Don't I know it."

"Papa!"

"Yes, yes. I'll be right with you, Charlie." Knightsdale clasped his hands behind his back and turned even redder. "The thing is . . . well . . . that is. Oh, blast." He leaned forward. "Meg is obviously mad for you, man. You need to take action—get her emotions to storm her damn brain."

Parks stared at the marquis. Surely the man . . . he couldn't be suggesting . . . did he want him to seduce Miss Peterson?

"Pa—"

There was a loud splash. The marquis whirled around as the ducks fled quacking across the pool.

"Charlie!"

The Earl of Northfield stood waist deep in water.

"Sorry, Papa."

Chapter 14

Mr. Parker-Roth sent Lord Bennington's ball spinning off across the lawn. Meg clasped her hands tightly to keep from clapping. She did not want to bring attention to herself—and she definitely didn't want Mr. Parker-Roth to know she was watching.

Not that he would notice if she did make noise. She'd chosen this location carefully—a good distance from the rest of the spectators and shaded by a sturdy oak. With luck, no one would notice her. She snorted. She was quite tired of being noticed. Lady Dunlee and the other old tabbies had spent the afternoon turning their noses up at her as if she were sour milk.

She could tell the world a thing or two about Lady Dunlee . . . She blew out a short breath. Parks was right—what one did with one's husband couldn't be so very scandalous, even though one should restrict such activities—whatever they were—to the privacy of the marital bedchamber.

She watched Robbie congratulate Mr. Parker-Roth. Parks grinned. Even from here, she could see his even white teeth.

Had she ever seen him smile like that?

Had she ever seen him smile? She must have, if not this Season then last year at Lord Tynweith's house party. Hmm. Yes. He'd joked with Robbie. He hadn't grinned, though, not like this.

If only she were closer.

Ridiculous. He'd not have smiled if she'd been nearby. He was too serious, at least around her. Tense and annoyed. As if she were one more unpleasant chore to be dealt with, one more responsibility.

Could she have gotten him to grin last year? She had thought he favored her company, but it must have been the plants that had sparked his enthusiasm. She'd been the only one in attendance who'd been willing to discuss horticultural issues. If Lady Beatrice had been interested in landscape gardening or plant cultivation, he would have been just as happy to wander in the foliage with her.

She'd wanted to flirt with him, but she hadn't known how.

He bent to get the coat he'd removed to bowl. He was not as tall as Robbie, but he was broader. His shoulders were—

She was not going to drool over his shoulders, for goodness sake. He could keep his broad shoulders to himself. Really, the man was incredibly annoying. Why wouldn't he simply explain what Lord Bennington had been doing in Lord Easthaven's garden? He obviously knew. He could satisfy her curiosity with just a few simple words. He was certainly nimble enough with his tongue when the occasion warranted.

Very nimble. Mmm. None of the other gentlemen who had escorted her into the shrubbery had used their tongues in such a commanding fashion. She had felt . . . filled. In an odd way, complete. And very, very . . . um . . . odd.

If anyone had described the action before she'd experienced it, she would have thought the notion completely revolting. To have another person's *tongue* in one's mouth? Disgusting! But it had not been revolting at all. Even now, standing on the lawn in the daylight at an event attended by most of the *ton*, she felt the thrilling heat of him—the strength of his arms, the hardness of his chest, the soft yet firm touch of his lips, the wet thrusting of his tongue . . .

She shivered, wrapping her arms around her waist. Lud! She was damp and throbbing down there again. What did it mean?

Parks could probably provide the answer to that question as well.

"Miss Peterson?"

"Eep!" She whirled about. A giant female was standing not three feet from her.

"Pardon me. Did I startle you?"

No, I always scream and jump when approached. Meg swallowed that retort.

"No, of course not."

The woman raised an eyebrow.

All right, so she was lying. So what? People who ask stupid questions should expect stupid answers. Why was the woman bothering her, anyway? Couldn't she discern Meg preferred to be alone? One did not go off to a secluded corner at a social gathering if one wanted company.

Her conscience—why was it her conscience always had Emma's voice?—urged her to make polite conversation. She told her conscience to take a damper. She didn't feel at all polite. In fact, she felt aggressively impolite.

She crossed her arms and stared at the woman.

The woman glared back at her. Wonderful.

Who *was* she? She was close to Parks's height and extremely . . . well, buxom. She had lovely porcelain skin, copper-colored hair, full lips, a blunt nose, and green eyes. Not classically beautiful, but definitely striking. They had not been introduced—Meg would remember if they had. There were just not that many females so large, for one thing. But she had seen her before. . . .

At the Palmerson ball—that was it. She'd been with a very tall man. Meg hadn't given her much thought—she'd been too focused on luring Lord Bennington into the shrubbery. Had she seen her at the Easthaven ball also? That evening was a blur of embarrassment, but now that she considered the question . . . yes, she had seen the woman coming in from the garden, again with the tall man. He must be her husband. At least no one had started gossiping about *her* excursion into the greenery.

Why was she seeking Meg out?

The woman was in no hurry to state her business. Really, the silence was growing ridiculous. They were like two dogs fighting over a bone—but over what bone were they fighting?

"Did you approach me for some particular reason, Miss . . . ?"

"Lady Dawson." The woman said each word separately, as if her name should be significant. She raised both her eyebrows.

Meg raised hers right back. Did *Lady* Dawson think she'd swoon with delight, a mere "miss" meeting so august a personage? Probably. Since coming to London, she'd had the misfortune to meet many people who thought their titles granted them godhood.

She wasn't an American like the Duchess of Alvord. She did not think the only title a man should have was "mister," but she did believe nobility of character outweighed nobility of rank.

"Surely you've heard of me?" Lady Dawson said.

"I'm afraid I haven't." Meg tried to emulate Lady Easthaven who'd been the picture of condescension when she'd greeted Meg at her ball. She permitted herself a small smile and shrug. "We must travel in different circles. My sister is the Marchioness of Knightsdale, you know, and my good friend is the Countess of Westbrooke." There. She could be disdainful, too.

Lady Dawson's eyebrows snapped down in a deep frown. So, she didn't care for a dose of her own medicine, did she?

"I know your connections. Your father is a vicar, is he not?"

"He is." She would not stoop so low as to point out Papa was the son of an earl. Granted, the fourth son of an earl, but still connected to the peerage. But perhaps Lady Dawson already knew Papa's pedigree. Had the woman been researching her background? Not that it would take much effort to uncover the information, but still it was extremely odd. Why would she be interested?

Lady Dawson was nodding. "And this is only your second Season, isn't it?"

"Yes."

"Yet you are well past the age when a girl usually enters society."

Was the woman saying she was *old*? Lud! That was the outside of enough.

"Lady Dawson, I don't mean to be rude"—*at least no ruder than you*—"but do you have a point?"

"I do, in fact." The woman straightened to her full height.

Meg straightened too, raising her chin and looking Lady Dawson in the eye. She would not be intimidated.

"Miss Peterson, you are obviously not aware of my friendship with Mr. Parker-Roth."

A hollowness opened in the pit of Meg's stomach.

"Why should I be aware of it?" She cleared her throat, willing her voice to remain steady. "Mr. Parker-Roth is merely a passing acquaintance."

There went Lady Dawson's eyebrows again.

"Really? That is not what the tittle-tattle says."

"Lady Dawson, certainly you don't listen to gossip?"

"I would say this is more than gossip, miss. How can you be surprised? You've been luring men into the shrubbery all Season." Lady Dawson shook her head. "It's a wonder you are still accepted by polite society. If your brother-in-law were not the Marquis of Knightsdale, I sincerely doubt that you would be."

Meg doubted it, too, and after the disparaging looks she'd been receiving at this gathering, she'd dispute how accepted she really was. She cleared her throat again and hoped her face wasn't as red as it felt. "I do have an avid interest in horticulture and botany, you know."

Lady Dawson snorted. "Botany?" She said the word as if it tasted of vinegar. "I'll wager you were studying biology, not botany, in the bushes."

Meg knew she was red now. The woman was incredibly insulting. Who gave her the right to castigate her?

"Lady Dawson—"

"Miss Peterson, listen to me. I cannot sit idly by while you toy with Mr. Parker-Roth's affections."

Meg did laugh then. "Put your mind at rest. Mr. Parker-Roth's affections are not engaged. He has much the same sentiments toward me as you apparently do."

Lady Dawson paused with her mouth open.

"He does?"

"Yes."

She tapped her finger against her lips. "No, I think you are mistaken."

Was the woman a fugitive from Bedlam? "I am not mistaken."

"I grant you, it is hard to discern his feelings. That is my fault, I'm afraid."

"Your fault? What do you mean?"

"You really have not heard the story?"

"No." Meg was not at all certain she wanted to hear it.

"I would have thought someone would have told you, as you are virtually betrothed to John."

"What?!" Virtually betrothed to Parks? What was the woman thinking? And . . . John? Lady Dawson called Parks by his Christian name? Just how closely associated were they?

Did she really want to know?

"I am not now nor do I anticipate ever being betrothed to Mr. Parker-Roth. Listen carefully as I am growing very tired of saying this: the gentleman has absolutely no interest in wedding me."

"I think you are wrong."

Meg experienced a strong urge to grab her hair—hers or Lady Dawson's—by its roots and pull. "What do you mean, you think I am wrong?"

"I've been watching John. He watches you."

"Ridiculous." The woman *was* a refugee from Bedlam.

"No, it's true. I noticed it at the Easthaven ball. The moment John entered the ballroom, he looked for you."

"You are mistaken." If Parks *had* looked for her it was only to make note of where she was so he could avoid her.

"I am not mistaken. You don't understand. I feel . . .

guilty about John. I worry about him. Are you certain you've never heard the story?"

Meg considered screaming. "Yes, I am certain I have not heard the story. Why don't you tell me it?"

"You're quite sure John has never mentioned me?"

"Lady Dawson, I have been trying to explain. Mr. Parker-Roth and I do not converse." The man is too busy doing other things with his tongue to have a conversation.

Meg pressed her lips together. She hadn't said that last bit aloud, had she? Apparently not. Lady Dawson had not run screaming with her hands over her ears or collapsed into a massive fit of the vapors. Instead the woman sighed.

"I suppose I shouldn't be surprised. The memory may still be too painful for him."

Meg lost her patience. "What memory, Lady Dawson?"

The other woman looked away. "I . . . that is . . . well . . ." She bit her lip. "It is rather difficult to discuss."

On second thought, perhaps it would be better if she did not hear this story. Something painful involving Lady Dawson and "John" was probably best left unmentioned. "Don't feel you need to—"

"No, I do. I owe it to John." Lady Dawson took a deep breath and looked directly at Meg. "You see, I left him at the altar."

Meg felt as if someone had kicked her in the stomach. "You what?"

"I left John at the altar four years ago." Lady Dawson glanced away. "It was not well done of me."

Meg's breath hadn't come back and now her heart was pounding as if she had just run a mile.

Parks had been engaged to Lady Dawson. He had almost married her.

He had loved her.

Did he love her still? Was *that* why he had sworn off marriage?

She forced herself to breathe.

She had to think. Unfortunately her brain was not functioning.

Lady Dawson was standing right next to her, noting her reaction. She clasped her hands tightly. She could not let the woman know she was upset.

She was *not* upset. Why should she be upset? The world had not ended. She was still standing under an oak tree on the Duke of Hartford's estate. Ladies were still strolling along the lawn; gentlemen still playing bowls; children still running, babies crying. Life had not changed one iota simply because she now knew . . . because Lady Dawson had just told her . . .

Because it was clear Mr. Parker-Roth did not love her.

Of *course* he did not love her. Why would he? Or perhaps more to the point, why would she think he would? He had not made the slightest effort to contact her after he'd left Lord Tynweith's estate last year. He had not sought her out when he returned to London this Season. Their only connection was due to his misfortune of being in the wrong place at the wrong time. He had offered for her, yes, but his offer had been compelled by circumstances. Well, perhaps it had also been compelled by Emma and Charles, but the point was the same. Love had nothing—*nothing*—to say to the matter.

Why was she even considering the issue? She had already refused him. And in any event, *she* did not love *him*.

Right.

She was a terrible liar.

To be fair, she hadn't realized the extent of her feelings—her *folly*—until just now.

She cleared her throat. Conversation. She had to speak of something before Lady Dawson discerned the depth of her foolishness.

"So you left Mr. Parker-Roth at the altar? You walked away—"

"No." Lady Dawson looked down at her hands. "I never came."

This was worse than she thought. "You never came to the church at all?"

Lady Dawson nodded.

"But surely you told him beforehand? You didn't let him face his family, his friends, all the guests thinking you were coming?" Had the man literally been left standing at the front of the church, and then, when it became painfully apparent his bride was indeed not going to appear, forced to face all the questions, the pity, the whispering?

And now she was subjecting him to more tittle-tattle. No wonder he was short-tempered. He must hate her. Certainly he would not wish to face another wedding no matter how much Emma and Charles pushed him.

"It was despicable of me, I know, but I misunderstood . . ." Lady Dawson was saying. "I thought my father—" She shook her head, then leaned forward and jabbed her finger at Meg. "The point is, Miss Peterson, I will not let John be hurt again, so if you have any intentions of playing fast and loose with his affections, I suggest you reconsider."

Meg did not care for Lady Dawson's tone. Why was the woman taking her to task? *She* had not left Mr. Parker-Roth standing in the church without a bride.

"Lady Dawson, believe me, I do not have Mr. Parker-Roth's affections in my control."

"As I've said, I am not so certain I believe that is true."

"Well, believe it."

They were back to snarling over the same bone—not that either could lay claim to it.

Lady Dawson blinked first. She stepped back.

"I will be watching you, Miss Peterson. You may have lofty connections, but I, too, can bring influence to bear. My husband is a baron and my father is the Earl of Standen. More importantly, I have been out in society more years than you. I know which ears to whisper in to speed a story through the *ton*. I can ruin you, Miss Peterson, and I will if you injure John in any way. Do not doubt it."

Lady Dawson turned on her heel and strode back to the rest of the party. Meg didn't even watch her go. She was too angry.

The woman was insufferable. To assume she would toy with Parks's affections . . . to assume she had any hope of influencing those affections . . .

Damn and blast! She needed an entirely new vocabulary to express her feelings on the subject.

"Miss Peterson, how delightful to see you again." Miss Witherspoon was dressed in a puce sari today with two yellow plumes in her hair. She smiled as she piled her plate high with lobster patties. As she grabbed the last one, she glanced at Meg. She paused, the food suspended in air, and then sighed and released her prize. "Do try the lobster patties before they are all gone."

"Do you recommend them?" Meg glanced around. Except for Miss Witherspoon and herself, the refreshment room was deserted.

"Yes, indeed. They are among the best I have sampled, and believe me, I am quite the connoisseur."

"I see." Meg looked back at the table. She stared at the lone lump of lobster. Normally she liked the dish, but she was still too upset from her encounter with Lady Dawson to contemplate putting anything in her stomach. "Unfortunately, I find I am not hungry."

"What a shame." Miss Witherspoon scooped the remaining patty back up almost before Meg stopped talking. "Perhaps you would prefer some stewed eels?"

"No." Stewed eels did not tempt her even in the best of circumstances.

Miss Witherspoon added a helping of eels to her plate. "I cannot imagine why you sought out the refreshments if you were not hungry, Miss Peterson."

"Um." There was no plausible explanation. She'd just needed to get as far from Lady Dawson and the bowling green as she could. And as far from Parks as possible. Lud! In trying to elude Lady Dawson, she'd almost stumbled onto him talking with Charles by an ornamental pool.

Perhaps a glass of lemonade would help calm her nerves.

"These social gatherings are a trifle flat, don't you agree?" Miss Witherspoon completed her selections with a spoonful of marrow pudding. "The level of conversation is severely lacking."

"Um." The lemonade wasn't helping. A woman started to enter the room, looked at Miss Witherspoon, and turned, managing to retreat without getting more than half of her body over the threshold.

"Please, sit with me." Miss Witherspoon grabbed Meg's elbow and directed her to a table by a window. "I've been meaning to talk with you."

"You have?" Parks couldn't be hungry, could he? She

looked out the window. She had a good view of the lawn. She should be able to see him coming and flee in time.

"Yes, indeed. I just received a letter from my friend Prudence. We are leaving for South America in two weeks' time. We will sail up the Amazon and explore the jungle. I thought of you immediately. You must join us."

Meg stopped staring out the window to stare at Miss Witherspoon. The woman popped a forkful of stewed eels in her mouth and smiled.

"Oh, I . . ." The Amazon! It was botanical heaven. She'd never dared dream she could visit the Amazon. The wealth, the variety of vegetation . . . She was sure to discover new species of any number of plants.

So why did she not feel more excited? Worse, why did a certain gentleman's face keep intruding on her thoughts? She most definitely did not want to think about Parks.

"I don't know if—"

"Nonsense." Miss Witherspoon speared some more stewed eels. "Be decisive, Miss Peterson. You are twenty-one years old, are you not?"

"Yes, but Emma—"

"Bah! Your sister must cut the leading strings sometime. You are a grown woman. You need to make your own way in the world." Miss Witherspoon leaned closer, stewed eels dangling on the fork between them. "Mark my words, Miss Peterson. If you don't choose your own course, your sister and my friend Cecilia will chart it for you—straight into Pinky's bed."

Meg swallowed. The thought of making her way to Mr. Parker-Roth's bed caused a number of disturbing changes in her physiology, changes that were becoming all too commonplace. She told her traitorous body to stop humming in anticipation. The man was either pining for Lady Dawson or determined never to wed—or both.

"What do you say, Miss Peterson? Will you join us? It is time for you to seek some adventure in your life."

"Yes, yes, you're right. I just don't . . . it is all rather sudden. I will have to think about it."

"Well, don't think too long. Opportunity knocks but once and all that. You need to be ready to open the door."

"Um." The door that immediately sprung to mind was the door to Mr. Parker-Roth's bedchamber.

She was in a sorry state indeed when "adventure" made her think more of bodies than botany. "I will definitely give it serious consideration."

"Felicity, this is not the appropriate place for such activities. Someone might come upon us at any moment."

"Bennie, you worry too much. Concentrate on the matter at hand." Felicity stroked the matter in her hand and the viscount drew in a sharp breath.

"Felicity!" His voice was an urgent whisper; his head turned right and left; his eyes scanned the area; but his . . . well, he did not step back out of reach. "We are in plain sight."

"Only to someone coming from the house. Anyone approaching from the bowling green or the river needs to walk around this splendid hedge before he or she catches sight of us." She unbuttoned the fall on his pantaloons. "There are very few people at the house."

He grabbed her wrist. "There are *some* people at the house."

She laughed and employed her other hand. It was

such fun teasing him. She had never flirted with anyone so staid.

She had never flirted in quite this way. She had teased before and tempted, but not . . . played this way. She had never focused much on the person attached to the organ. She had thought one male interchangeable with any other. She grinned at Lord Bennington.

She had been mistaken. Bennie was quite unique.

"I will keep a sharp look-out." She ran her fingers up his growing length. He was a splendidly robust man. She could hardly wait to enjoy his full . . . attention.

She frowned. Frankly, she could not wait at all. Father's financial situation was worsening rapidly. It was possible Bennington would jilt her if he learned the full extent of the earl's liabilities before parson's mousetrap snapped shut. It would be a scandal, but most of society would forgive him easily. She was only evil Lord Needham's daughter, after all.

A silly pain settled around the area of her heart. *Would* Bennie jilt her if he knew she was on the verge of poverty? Probably. She had no indication that more than lust was involved, at least on his part. But then men were so often driven by lust.

No, she definitely needed a wedding ring on her finger before word of her father's pecuniary disaster flooded the *ton*. The problem was Lord Bennington wanted a large wedding to suit his sense of importance, which was very large indeed.

She hoped lust would persuade consequence that a special license and a hurried exchange of vows was the best plan.

She moved her fingers and felt him leap in her hand. He was breathing quite heavily and had shifted his grip to her shoulders. Should she employ her mouth as well?

No. She heard the crunch of shoes on loose stone. Their little interlude was over for now. She patted him as she withdrew her hand. She smiled at his low growl.

"My lord, we have company."

It took a moment for rationality to return to his eyes. He muttered a curse and jumped back.

Perhaps she wouldn't have much longer to wait for that wedding ring.

Damn. Parks stopped on the stone walk. For an instant he thought about ducking down a side path, but it was too late. She'd seen him. It would look exceedingly odd now if he changed directions.

"Miss Peterson. Are you enjoying the day?"

She didn't look as if she were enjoying anything. She looked . . . well, it was a little difficult to describe how she looked. There had been a flash of what could have been pleasure—he thought her eyes had brightened and her lips turned up—but the expression had vanished so quickly, he wouldn't swear he'd seen it at all. Now her face was bright red and she was frowning at him.

Knightsdale had said she was mad for him. The marquis was the one who was mad. Miss Peterson looked simply angry.

"What are you doing here?"

He felt his eyebrows shoot up. So angry she'd forgotten her manners or even her wit. She must have realized her tone was less than polite because she looked away, crossing her arms under her breasts.

Her very nice breasts. He remembered in exquisite detail how they felt and tasted.

Could he seduce her?

No, of course not. What was the matter with him? She

was a gently bred young lady—who apparently hated him. The sister-in-law of a marquis—a marquis who had tacitly invited him to have his wicked way with her. Were hatred and love so different? Where there was one passion, couldn't the other follow?

Damn and blast. He *was* losing his mind. He did not want to marry anyone, let alone Miss Peterson. He wanted to get the bloody hell out of London and back to the Priory where he could think clearly. He'd go to the Horticultural Society meeting this week and then he would drag his mother home. His plants had been without him too long as it was.

"I am aimlessly ambling around this bloody *blasted* estate until I can persuade my mother and Miss Witherspoon to depart. What are you doing?"

"The same." She smiled slightly when she said it. "Well, the aimlessly ambling part. I have nothing to say about your mother's and Miss Witherspoon's departure."

It was better for his peace of mind when she was scowling.

"Shall we amble aimlessly together?" He offered her his arm. She smiled again—almost shyly—and took it.

Damn it all to hell. He should not be feeling a thrill at the touch of Miss Peterson's gloved fingers on his arm. It was Knightsdale's fault for putting thoughts of seduction in his head. He was only male, after all—and the most male part of him was exceedingly thrilled at Miss Peterson's proximity.

Vegetation. He would study the vegetation. Concentrate on botany, not biology. Flower beds not . . .

The ambient vegetation was damn dull.

They strolled in silence down the walkway. The top of Miss Peterson's head came just to his chin. Was she still smiling? Her bonnet hid her expression completely.

What if he stopped and kissed her? Would she slap him soundly?

One would hope. Perhaps some sense could then find its way through the lust-filled fog of his brain.

"Oh!" Miss Peterson stopped abruptly.

What could be—oh, indeed. Lord Bennington and Lady Felicity stood not twenty yards ahead of them. Even at this distance he could see the man's fall was unbuttoned, for God's sake. Was it too much to hope that Miss Peterson hadn't noticed? They would nod politely and he would steer her to safety.

"Miss Peterson, how lovely to see you." Lady Felicity smiled and stepped forward, fortunately blocking their view of Lord Bennington. The man took the opportunity to put his person to rights.

But why had Lady Felicity stopped them? Surely it would have better suited her purposes to have them pass by? If he were any judge, Lord Bennington would have been very much happier. The man looked pained. Hell, given his obvious state of . . . enthusiasm . . . when they'd come upon him, the viscount *was* pained. He did not like Bennington at all, but any man had to feel some sympathy for the fellow's predicament.

Miss Peterson had removed her hand from his arm as if burned. "Lady Felicity." She cleared her throat. "Lord Bennington."

Bennington cleared his own throat and nodded at them. "Miss Peterson. Parker-Roth." He did not meet their eyes.

Lady Felicity laughed. "We've been enjoying ourselves, haven't we, Bennie?"

Bennie's eyes bulged. At least those were the only organs bulging at the moment. What was Felicity about? It was one thing to make conversation; quite another to recount her detour down the primrose path.

"Isn't it delightful to stroll in the gardens? To admire the way . . . things . . . grow? How a sensitive plant can swell to quite a stalk—"

"Speaking of bio-*botany*—" If Bennington wasn't going to stop Felicity—and since the man was staring slack-jawed at her, odds were good he wasn't—Parks would. "Are you going to the Horticultural Society meeting this week, Bennington?"

For once Bennington looked delighted to have him speak. "Yes. Rathbone is discussing the expedition to the Amazon, isn't he?"

"Yes, I—"

"The Amazon?" Miss Peterson put her hand back on his arm. "You will be discussing the Amazon?"

"At the Horticultural Society meeting this week, yes." Why was Miss Peterson so excited?

"I must go."

It was his turn to stare slack-jawed.

"Miss Peterson, please." Bennington chuckled. "That's rich. You at the Horticultural Society meeting."

She snatched her hand back to put it on her hip. "What is so amusing about my wishing to attend this meeting?"

"Miss Peterson, surely you know the Society is only open to men?" Parks frowned. This was Miss Peterson's second Season. She must know everything there was to know about the Horticultural Society, given her enthusiasm for all things botanical.

"Of course I know that, but this is different. I have a very special interest in the Amazon."

"I imagine Parks or I can lend you a book, if you like, Miss Peterson." Bennington had recovered his habitual tone of condescension. "I know I have some basic texts that should suit your understanding."

Evidently the slack-jawed phenomenon was contagious. Miss Peterson now gaped at Lord Bennington. But only for a moment. Her jaw snapped shut and her eyes narrowed.

"I don't believe Miss Peterson cares for your offer, Bennie," Lady Felicity said.

An understatement. Parks could almost hear Meg's teeth grind. Surely the woman wouldn't physically attack the viscount? He should deflect her attention.

"Why are you so interested in the Amazon, Miss Peterson?"

"Because I may be accompanying Miss Witherspoon on an expedition to that location."

The slack-jawed phenomenon was definitely contagious. "You're joking."

She turned her glare from Bennington to him. "I am not."

"But that's"—he saw her gaze sharpen, but the words were out before he could stop them—"ridiculous."

If looks could kill, he'd be dead already.

Chapter 15

Lend her a book would they? Meg glared at the innocent novels that adorned the shelves. A basic text that would suit her understanding? She bared her teeth at *The Mysteries of Udolpho*. It was a very good thing the beef-witted coxcombs weren't present or she'd be sorely tempted to improve *their* understanding by walloping them in the brain box. There were plenty of suitable weapons at hand. Miss Austen's *Sense and Sensibility* might do. Or *Pride and Prejudice*. Actually, the heavier the tome, the more efficacious its application.

"I agree *The Castle of Otranto* is not great literature, Miss Peterson, but it hardly merits such displeasure."

"What?" Meg turned. Miss Witherspoon stood next to her. She was wearing a conventional dress today, a garish combination of pea green and puce. She and Lady Beatrice must patronize the same dressmaker.

Miss Witherspoon raised her lorgnette and surveyed the selection of reading material. "You were growling."

Growling? It made her sound like a dog. "I was not."

"Indeed you were." Miss Witherspoon transferred her attention briefly to Meg. "I heard you. Fortunately, it was a low growl, so I believe you did not attract any attention."

Meg glanced around. A man sat by the fireplace, reading a newspaper. Two young women walked past, whispering and giggling. No one was staring at her. She turned back to Miss Witherspoon.

"I was not growling at a book."

Miss Witherspoon gave her an intense look. "So you do not deny that you were growling?"

"Botheration! I wasn't—"

"Shh." The woman put a gloved finger to her lips. "Not so loud."

Meg glanced around again. Still no one appeared to take special note of her.

"If you don't mind my saying so, Miss Peterson, you seem a trifle testy."

Meg sighed. Why deny it? "All right, I am a little on edge."

Miss Witherspoon made a tsking sound and touched her lightly on her arm. "I hope it doesn't have anything to do with Pinky—or, I should say, Mr. Parker-Roth?"

"Of course not." Meg turned back to examine the literary offerings again. They might as well have been written in Russian. She could not focus on the titles.

"Well, that's good at least. No point in letting a man cut up your peace."

No, no point at all. Perhaps if she repeated that twenty times a day, she would believe it.

Miss Witherspoon dropped her lorgnette so it bounced against her ample bosom. "So, have you considered further about the Amazon expedition? I don't mean to press you, but time is running short."

Amazon. That was the seed of her discontent.

"Miss Witherspoon, did you know a Mr. Rathbone is addressing the Horticultural Society meeting this week?"

"*Sir* Rathbone. No, I didn't know."

"He's speaking about his trip to the Amazon." Why wasn't the woman more excited? "I thought it would be very educational. I had hoped to attend."

Miss Witherspoon snorted. "You can hope to attend as much as Rathbone can hope to get the money to sail across the ocean."

"You mean he hasn't already gone to South America?"

"Rathbone? No. He hasn't a feather to fly with. Still looking for someone to sport the ready cash so he can outfit an expedition, I imagine."

"Oh." Now that she thought about it, Bennington hadn't said the Amazon expedition was completed. "Why can't he join your group?"

"Too stubborn. Needs to be in charge—which he wouldn't be if he joined us. Diego, our leader, knows better than to let Rathbone hold the reins. Still, the man *is* very knowledgeable. It would be worth hearing him speak, if you could bear all his prattle and self-aggrandizement."

"So you recommend I attend?"

Miss Witherspoon employed her lorgnette again. "You do know that women are not permitted at Horticultural Society meetings, do you not, Miss Peterson?"

Meg shrugged impatiently. "Surely they would make an exception in this case."

Miss Witherspoon snorted again. "Gravity is more likely to make an exception should you trip leaving this building. No, Miss Peterson, trust me. The Horticultural Society will not make any exceptions."

"That is ridiculous."

"As are many activities involving large groups of men, but there you are. I'm afraid there is nothing to be done about it."

Meg frowned. She wanted to hear Rathbone speak and perhaps ask a question or two. Books were all well and good, but sometimes there was no substitute for actually speaking with a knowledgeable human being. And if a certain cabbage-headed nodcock happened to hear her and realize she was not an uninformed ninny-hammer, so much the better.

"You are certain not one woman has ever attended a Horticultural Society meeting?"

"Well . . ." A corner of Miss Witherspoon's mouth tilted up and she leaned closer. "Perhaps one."

So there *was* hope. "Who was it?"

"My friend, Prudence Doddington-Prinz." Miss Witherspoon glanced around and then lowered her voice to a whisper. "It was just after Wedgwood formed the Society—around 1804, if I remember correctly. Prudence was as determined as you to go—she is an avid botanist and gardener—so she hounded Wedgwood and some of the other men every chance she got, but they remained adamant. No women." Miss Witherspoon smiled. "Finally, Prudence took matters into her own hands. She went—dressed as a man."

"She did?" Meg felt a frisson of shock. "And no one suspected?"

"No one. In fact, Prudence attended the meetings all that year. She only stopped, she said, because she got tired of hearing all those puffed up cocks crowing and strutting about."

"I still cannot imagine how a woman could pass herself off as a man."

Miss Witherspoon shrugged. "I am sure I could not do so. I am too short and too, well, generously endowed. But Prudence is more like you—thin and boyish. Without many curves. I imagine it wasn't too difficult for her."

Meg straightened. Mr. Parker-Roth had appeared to

enjoy her meager curves in Lady Palmerson's parlor. And the other men she'd lured into the bushes . . .

She couldn't be certain what the other men thought. Except for Lord Bennington, they'd all been quite willing to leave the shrubbery when she'd suggested they return to whatever social event was in progress. Bennington had clearly been more attracted by her connections than her charms. But Mr. Parker-Roth—

Mr. Parker-Roth had been completely immune to her charms from the moment they'd met at Lord Tynweith's house party until he'd been forced to play knight-errant and rescue her from the viscount. She should face facts. His actions in Lady Palmerson's parlor had been nothing more than an attempt to make the best of a bad bargain. And the interlude in Easthaven's garden? The same. He must know Emma and Charles—even his own mother—thought they should wed. He certainly didn't act as if he *enjoyed* his encounters with her.

"Miss Witherspoon, I have decided. I will definitely be accompanying you to the Amazon."

"Are ye sure this won't get me in trouble, miss?"

"Don't worry, Annie. No one will know you helped me."

Meg stared at the clothes laid out on her bed while Annie, one of the younger chambermaids, fidgeted by the door. It was just luck she'd overheard the girl talking about her brother who was a footman in Lord Frampton's London house. It had taken a little persuasion, but now she had a complete outfit of male attire. She hoped it fit. If it didn't, she was out of luck. The Horticultural Society meeting was tonight.

One thing was clear—she would not be wearing a

corset. How was she to keep her meager curves in check?

"Did you bring an extra cravat, Annie?"

"Yes, miss."

"Good." There was no point in delaying. "Help me off with my clothes, will you?"

She'd told Emma and Charles she wasn't feeling well—which was true. Her stomach was a leaden knot in her middle. Could she really pass for a man? If she were discovered—

No, she would not consider that possibility.

She shed her dress, corset, and shift, and pulled on the male drawers and pantaloons. It felt very odd having fabric between her legs and hugging her thighs. She took an exploratory step. She liked the freedom of movement male apparel gave her.

She glanced in the mirror. Oh, dear God—her hips and thighs! She had never seen them so exposed. They had never *been* so exposed, except when she slipped in and out of her bath. And now she was going to walk out onto the streets of London like this?

She really was going to be sick.

She swallowed her nerves and studied her reflection more closely. Her hips did not look like any man's she'd ever seen. Annie's brother's coat had better hide them well. And her small charms bounced quite alarmingly.

"Time for the cravat."

Annie wrapped the cravat round Meg's chest three times, pulling the cloth tight after each circuit, but not so tight that it restricted her breathing. She pinned it there and then wound the remaining cloth around Meg's body to her waist, helping to further muffle her shape.

Meg pulled on the shirt and waistcoat and studied

the effect in the mirror. Not bad. She was ready for the other cravat.

"Can you tie a Mathematical, Annie?"

"Yes, miss, I think I can, but . . ." Annie chewed her lip.

"But what?"

"Your hair, miss."

"My hair?" It was a mess, spread out over her shoulders. She'd braid it and pin it up under—oh. "I don't suppose men would be wearing hats at the Horticultural Society meeting, would they?"

"Not likely, miss."

Meg stared at the long, light brown waves. She liked her hair. It was one of her better features.

It would have to go.

She sniffed. There was no point in crying. It was only hair. Surely it would be vastly more convenient to have it short in the Amazon. And she was definitely sailing with Miss Witherspoon and her friend. Mrs. Parker-Roth had told Emma who had told her that Parks was planning on returning to his estate at the end of the week.

"How are you with a scissors, Annie?"

It took some trial and error—mostly error—but Annie finally managed to craft a hair style that did not look like it had been created by a drunken monkey. The right side was a bit longer than the left, and a few tufts stuck out at odd angles, but it would do. No one would be studying her coiffure, after all.

Annie finished by helping her with her cravat and coat. Finally, Meg took the high-crowned beaver and placed it on her head.

"What do you think, Annie? Will I pass?"

"I dunno." Annie tilted her head and stared while

Meg turned slowly, holding her arms out. "I guess ye will."

Meg looked in the mirror once more. The pantaloons were a bit tight, but that couldn't be helped. The coat hid her hips from the back, and the waistcoat and cravat masked her chest. She looked odd, but not particularly feminine. She shrugged.

"People see what they expect to see, Annie, and none of the gentlemen at the meeting this evening will expect to see a woman in men's clothing. I'll be fine—but to be safe, I'll try to stay in the shadows and not call attention to myself."

"That would be good, miss, but what will ye do if yer discovered?"

She really would throw up.

No, an intrepid world traveler would not let minor dangers keep her from her goals.

"I will not be discovered, Annie. Now see if the corridor is clear, and I'll make my way down the servants' stairs."

"How can you leave London now, Johnny?"

Parks struggled for patience. Mother had been dancing around this topic ever since Hartford's fete. When he'd announced his plans on the carriage ride home, she'd held her peace, though he'd seen she'd had to bite her tongue to do so. The next day, she'd started to mention the subject, but stopped herself—six times. Then the hinting began. Now she was reduced to a full frontal assault, all finesse discarded.

"I've been away from the Priory too long, Mother, much longer than I intended."

"Oh, pish. You work too hard. You need to take time for some amusement."

He took a deep breath. He would not shout. "I do not find the *ton*'s antics amusing." Another breath. Speak calmly, rationally. "You know I was expecting a large plant shipment from Stephen when we left. I need to get back."

"But I haven't had time to purchase my brushes and paints."

He counted to ten, teeth gritted. "You have had more than enough time to purchase a bloody *blasted* lifetime supply of brushes and paints." All right, not so calm or rational.

His mother looked at him, her eyes large and sad, her mouth turned down.

She'd had at least thirty years to perfect that expression. Longer if she'd used it on his father—or on *her* father.

"Mother, you know I am right."

She sighed and turned away. "I just want you to be happy, Johnny."

Was there a catch in her voice? He almost snorted. That was why she'd moved so he couldn't see her face. She could manage to sound like she was crying, but she'd never mastered the trick of actually producing tears on demand. Well, he was having none of it.

"I'll be happy when we get back to the Priory."

She looked over her shoulder at him. As he'd suspected, her eyes were dry. "But what about Miss Peterson?"

"What about her?"

"You compromised her."

"I also offered for her and was rejected. My duty to Miss Peterson has been discharged."

Mother frowned. "But don't you . . . I mean, I know you . . ." She waved her hand vaguely in the air. "You know."

"I don't know what the hel—" Another deep breath.

This was his mother he was speaking to. "I really don't know what you are talking about."

Mother faced him directly then, real worry and concern filling her eyes. He closed his own. God, this was the worst.

"Johnny, you love her. You can't let her go."

Why did he have to have this conversation? Why couldn't he be like other men who had mothers who minded their own damn business—or at least had the sense to keep their thoughts to themselves?

"My feelings—or lack thereof—concerning Miss Peterson are immaterial, Mother. She leaves in two weeks for South America. She is joining Miss Witherspoon and her friend on their Amazon expedition."

"No!"

Mother looked shocked. She looked the way he'd felt when Miss Peterson had so blithely informed him of her plans to put thousands of miles between them. He'd made his decision to go home as soon as the words had left her lips.

God! He was an idiot. Hadn't he learned after Grace? He was not going to pine after another woman. Not that he had ever pined for Grace, of course. But he was done with thinking about the creatures. He would go home and have some nice, mindless bed play with Cat.

"Yes indeed, Mother. So you see, there is no need for me to remain in London. I suggest you purchase your supplies today as we are leaving after the Horticultural Society meeting."

"I'm leaving for the Continent tonight."

"You can't." Felicity glared at her father. They were standing in what had once been the library. The shelves were empty; the desk, the chairs, and all the furniture were gone, sold to stave off her father's creditors. Rectangles of faded wallpaper testified to where paintings had once hung.

The earl shrugged. "No choice. Can't escape the duns any longer. If I don't get out now, it'll be debtors' prison for certain."

"And what's to become of me?"

Her father shrugged, evading her eyes.

She wanted to scream, but screaming would serve no purpose. "If you bolt now, Bennington will surely cry off."

"You're betrothed. The man can't cry off."

"Do you think he'll marry me when your name is on everyone's lips? It was bad enough when you were just a brothel keeper, but wealth forgives many sins. To be a penniless brothel keeper . . . Bennington will drop me like I'm week-old fish and no one will fault him for it."

She bit her lip. She would not cry.

Her father shoved his hands in his pockets and hunched his shoulders. "It can't be that bad—"

"It *is* that bad—or will be if you brush and lope. You can't leave."

"I *have* to. My ship sails at dawn."

"All right." She was not going to have all her plans come to naught at this point. "That gives you about ten hours. Figure out a solution. I want to be a viscountess before the *ton* knows I'm a pauper."

"I can't—"

"You *can*. For once you can damn well do something to take care of your daughter, you bastard." She would not scream. God damn it, she would not cry. She would not scratch his bloody, lying eyes out.

He straightened. "I'll see what I can do."

* * *

"Charles . . ." Emma put down *Pride and Prejudice*. She must have read the same sentence twenty times. She just could not concentrate. She kept hearing Mrs. Parker-Roth's voice in her head.

She studied her husband. He was sitting across from her in a big upholstered chair. Candlelight played over his curly brown hair, grown a little long now, and the broad planes of his face. She still got a fluttery feeling in her stomach whenever she looked at him, even though they were now an old married couple of four years and two sons.

When they were home at Knightsdale, this was her favorite time of day—well, second favorite. She flushed, thinking of her favorite time. The babies were tucked into bed, the house was quiet. It was just the two of them.

Did Charles love her? He liked her well enough, she knew that. He was comfortable with her—and willing enough to come to her bed. But did he *love* her?

"Charles."

"Hmm?" The man didn't even look up from his book.

"Charles, do you ever wish you'd married someone else, someone more at ease in London?"

"Of course not." He turned a page.

He was engrossed in his book, at least. She should just let him be. But when would she get another opportunity like this? Meg was usually with them.

Perhaps it was providential that her sister wasn't feeling well and had retired to her room early.

"Do you ever . . . well, do you ever get lonely here in London by yourself?"

He finally looked up. "Of course I do, Emma. I miss you and the children, but I know you prefer the country."

"But do you ever . . . I mean, most men do, of course,

but . . ." She studied his face. He looked politely puzzled.

Her courage deserted her.

"Never mind." She waved at the book open on his lap. "I'm sorry I bothered you. Please, go back to your reading."

He looked at her a moment more and then *did* go back to his book. Well, she had told him to, hadn't she? She picked up *Pride and Prejudice* again.

It could have been written in Greek. She shifted in her chair. She just needed to concentrate. She had enjoyed Miss Austen's *Sense and Sensibility*. She'd been meaning to read this book for the longest time.

She sighed, crossing her ankles and adjusting her skirt.

"What is it, Emma?"

She looked up. Charles was frowning, leaning toward her, his book closed, his finger marking his place.

"What is what?"

"You've been huffing and sighing and squirming in your chair all evening. What is the matter?"

"Nothing."

"Emma . . ."

Courage. There was no time like the present. If she let this opportunity go by . . .

But what if he told her he *did* visit brothels—or keep a mistress—when she was in Kent?

Better to learn the truth than live in ignorance.

"When I'm at Knightsdale . . . well, it would be completely understandable if you . . . if, um . . ." She took a deep breath and straightened in her chair. "I know men have certain needs and you, especially, have, well . . . are very . . ." She blew out her breath. She could not say it.

"Emma, you aren't suggesting I'm not faithful to my marriage vows, are you?" Charles looked very stern, his brows pulled into a deep furrow. She flushed.

"N-no." She bit her lip. She should not lie. "Well, perhaps. I mean, not that anyone would fault you. We spend long months apart—"

"So you've been taking lovers while I'm in London?" *Pride and Prejudice* hit the floor as Emma surged to her feet. "I have not! Of course I haven't. I love you. I would never—"

Charles had risen, too. He put his finger to her lips. "I would never, either, Emma. I love you—only you. I miss you when we are apart." A corner of his mouth turned up in a half smile. "God, do I miss you. And yes, I'd love to have you in bed beside me—I'd love to be inside you—but I want *you*, Emma, not just a woman, not just a female body. How can you think otherwise?"

"I—" She studied his cravat. He put his finger under her chin and turned her face up to his. His eyes searched hers and she felt her face redden.

"Have I ever given you reason to doubt my word, Emma?"

"Of course not. It's just—" She cleared her throat. "It's just that I know you only married me to get a mother for the girls and to avoid the Marriage Mart—"

"Emma! If I've given you that impression—" He shook his head. "Do you truly believe that?"

"I . . . I don't know. When we are home in Kent, I don't. But when I come to London and see all the worldly, beautiful women and see how the *ton* behaves, I think I must be a fool to expect you not to take advantage of . . . of all that." She swallowed. "Especially since I am such a boring little country mouse."

He dropped his hands to her shoulders and shook her gently. "You are not a boring little country mouse, Emma. You are a strong, brave woman who has a heart far bigger than most of the lovely London ladies you seem to envy. Do you think I only see the surface of people? I know what matters more than a pretty face and an alluring body is what is inside here"—he touched her lightly on her forehead—"and here"—he placed his hand on her breast, over her heart.

"Oh, Charles." She buried her face in his chest, hugging him tightly. She felt like crying. She felt as if her heart would burst, it was so full of love.

He bent his head to whisper in her ear. "Of course, I also love your luscious surface. I love your mouth"—he kissed the sensitive point behind her ear—"and your breasts"—he moved down to the base of her throat—"and your lovely, lovely thighs." He trailed kisses from her jaw to her mouth, hovering just over her lips. "I love tasting you"—he brushed her lips—"and sliding deep into your sweet warmth."

She was panting. Heat pooled in her womb and she throbbed with need. She wanted him inside her now. She wanted his love and his seed.

"Shall I see if the library's lock works," Charles asked, "or shall we just risk scandalizing the servants?"

Chapter 16

"I think I've made a mess of things, David."

Lord Dawson sighed and closed his book. "Grace, if I had a shilling for every time you said that, I'd be a rich man."

"You *are* a rich man."

"I'd be a richer man. So what is the problem now?"

"I spoke to Miss Peterson when we were at the Duke of Hartford's estate."

"Ah. And it was not a good conversation?"

"No, it was not." Grace dropped her head into her hands and moaned. "*When* will I learn to hold my tongue?"

"I am not holding my breath in anticipation."

Grace looked up and glared at him. "*Very* funny."

"Well, you do have a propensity for putting your lovely foot in your mouth, my dear. What exactly did you do this time?"

"I threatened the woman with social ruin if she hurt John's feelings."

David slowly nodded his head. "I am sure she received that well." He grinned. "I believe I advised you to stay out of Parker-Roth's business, did I not?"

"Oh, do not say you told me so. Nothing terrible has happened yet—except Miss Peterson seems to have taken a healthy dislike of me."

"I am not surprised. How would you have felt—how *did* you feel—when people advised you on your behavior with regard to me?"

Grace bared her teeth. "I should have listened to them. They obviously had my best interests at heart."

"Liar."

She stuck out her tongue and then dropped her head back into her hands. "I worry about John. It's not surprising. We've been friends since we were children. I feel responsible for his unmarried state. I—"

"Grace, you give yourself too much credit."

"What?" Her head snapped up and fire shot from her eyes. It was a good thing he was not easily intimidated. "You know he was terribly wounded when I stood him up on his—our—wedding day."

David sighed. They had been over this many times before. Would Grace ever forgive herself? Perhaps only once Parks wed.

He fervently hoped the man tied the knot with Miss Peterson.

"Parker-Roth is a grown man, Grace. I'm not saying he wasn't . . . upset when you failed to show up at the church. I'm certain he was embarrassed and angry and, yes, hurt." He permitted himself a slow smile. "And he would have been even more . . . mmm . . . upset had he known exactly what you were doing when you were supposed to be saying your vows to him."

"David!"

"But he is in charge of his own life, completely capable of making his own decisions. I am certain he would not want your pity. In fact, I wager he'd be horrified if he knew you were agonizing over his fate like this."

"But—"

"Leave it be, Grace. Let him find happiness with Miss Peterson or let him tell her to go to the devil . . . but let him do it by himself, without your interference. Trust me, he truly would not welcome it. No man would."

"How do you know that?"

"Because, my love, I am a man myself, and if that fact has slipped your mind, I would be happy to refresh your memory."

Grace opened her mouth as if to argue, but stopped. Her lips slid into a half smile. "Perhaps I do need a reminder."

He put his book on the table. "Here or in our room?"

She looked around the library. "Here." She grinned. "And in our room." She got up and wrapped her arms around his neck. "My memory is truly deplorable. It needs frequent . . . um . . . prodding."

"Then I am just the man to assist you. Indeed, it would be my pleasure." He brought her hips snugly against the part of him most eager to prod her . . . memory. "My very great pleasure."

Meg let out a long breath as the hackney drove off. The first part of her adventure had been completed successfully. The hackney driver had not suspected she was a female—or if he had, he hadn't said anything.

Could he have guessed? Surely not. She'd kept her face down and her hat tilted to block as much light from her countenance as possible. She'd lowered her voice and spoken gruffly and quietly . . . He wouldn't have allowed her in his coach if he'd suspected, would he? Or would he have been happy of the fare, no matter how odd or scandalous the passenger?

It didn't matter. He was gone now into the mass of

London humanity. He did not know her name. She would never see him again . . .

Lud! She hadn't thought. How was she going to get home?

She straightened and tugged on her waistcoat. She would worry about that later. Now she had many other hurdles to jump, such as how she was going to pass as a man in the much brighter light indoors—or how she was going to get indoors in the first place. Did one just knock or was there some ritual she didn't know? Her ignorance would betray her before she'd even crossed the threshold.

Sweat trickled down between her shoulder blades. Perhaps she should give up now. But she still had the problem of how to get home.

She couldn't give up. She just needed to make her feet climb two shallow stairs. She would grab the knocker—it was in the shape of a pineapple, quite unalarming—and give it a hearty rap. The butler or footman would answer and—

She'd be discovered.

She closed her eyes and took a deep breath. And another. And another . . .

She couldn't do it.

She heard a group of gentlemen approaching and stepped quickly into the shadows. Lud! She recognized them—Lord Easthaven, Lord Palmerson, the Earl of Tattingdon. Lord Smithson, leaning heavily on his cane, brought up the rear.

This was her opportunity. The gentlemen were all old enough and exalted enough that they could not have the slightest inkling such a lowly individual as a Miss Peterson existed. Lord Smithson was more than a little deaf and his vision was very weak. Perfect. She stepped in behind them, entered the foyer, and reluctantly handed her hat to a footman.

Lord Smithson was having trouble negotiating the stairs to the next floor. Without thinking, she reached out to help him. When they got to the top, he stopped her.

"My thanks, young—" He squinted at her. "Do I know you?"

"Y-yes." This was it. She was going to be discovered in this house full of men. She would be ruined beyond imagination. She drew in a breath to begin begging everyone's pardon.

"No, don't tell me." Lord Smithson's voice was almost loud enough to wake the dead—Meg fervently wished she were among that number—but fortunately his companions, apparently assuming he was in good hands with her, had gone on ahead. "Have to test my memory, don't you know. Exercise it, just like I exercise my legs, so it stays in fine fettle."

Lord Smithson peered into her face. How she kept from expiring right there was more than she could fathom.

"You look familiar."

Oh, dear God.

"Young 'un. Barely shaving."

She could only nod. Her heart was pounding so violently she could barely hear his words, loud as they were.

"I have it!" Lord Smithson pounded his cane on the tile floor.

Her heart stopped.

"You're one of the Devonshire Beldons, ain't you?"

"Uh." What could she say? "I, um—"

Lord Smithson frowned. "Have a touch of the grippe, Beldon? Your voice sounds mighty odd."

She was a coward. She nodded. "A touch," she whispered. She coughed weakly and, she hoped, pitifully.

Lord Smithson grunted. "Best get some hot punch for that. Come along."

He led her into a large drawing room. The low drone of male voices was untempered by any lighter feminine notes.

"Here you go, Beldon. This will cure you of anything that ails you." Lord Smithson sloshed a glass full of punch and handed it to Meg.

"My thanks." She took a sip—and almost spat it over Lord Smithson's shirt front. This tasted like no punch she'd ever had before.

Lord Smithson took a long swallow from his glass and wiped his mouth on his sleeve. "Finish it all, my boy, and you'll feel like a new man."

Meg smiled and pretended to take another sip. If she finished all this, she would definitely feel different. It must be more than half alcohol.

"Palmerson, have you met young Beldon here?"

Perhaps a fortifying sip would be a good idea. Meg gulped down a mouthful and started coughing.

"Beldon's got a touch of the grippe, don't you know," Lord Smithson said.

"Sorry to hear that."

Meg nodded and focused on Lord Palmerson's shoes.

"I say, Smithson, do you know where they've hidden the chamber pot?"

"It's usually in this cupboard."

"Ah, good. Been at White's drinking all evening, you know."

Lud! Meg glanced up. Lord Palmerson had one hand on a cupboard door and the other on the fall of his pantaloons.

"Excuse me." She turned and fled.

She found a seat on the other side of the room by a healthy potted palm and a large table. Two narrow little chairs, obviously added to accommodate the antici- pated crowd, were perfectly situated in a back corner by a closed door that might provide a means of escape if she had need of one. As an added bonus, there were no chamber pot-harboring cupboards in sight.

"If you could all take a seat, we are ready to begin."

She claimed her chair and deposited her glass on the table. Any more of that punch and she'd be in serious trouble. She was feeling a trifle lightheaded as it was.

Botheration. A pillar obstructed her view of the short, rat-like man who must be Sir Rathbone. Should she change places? The chair next to hers offered a better view and more screening from the palm, but if she moved, someone might take her current seat. She most definitely did not want company.

She stayed put. One or two gentlemen glanced at the empty chair, but since they would have had to climb over her to reach it and there were still other, more comfortable alternatives, they passed her by.

Finally everyone was settled. She waited a few more minutes and then moved. Now she could see the speaker and still hide under the screening foliage. She expelled a sigh of relief. So far, so good.

She had congratulated herself prematurely.

She heard the creak of a hinge, felt a puff of air, and then saw a strong, pantaloon-encased thigh slide into the seat she had just vacated. She couldn't help herself. She glanced over quickly to see who it was.

Mr. Parker-Roth nodded at her. He froze mid-nod and frowned, a puzzled look in his eyes.

Horror held her motionless for a moment and then she snapped her eyes back to her hands. What was she going to do? He was blocking her exit. She could try upending the palm to escape that way, but it was a very healthy, heavy specimen. Could she—

A large male hand wrapped itself around her wrist.

"What the *hell* do you think you're doing?"

Felicity waited in the shadows. Her father had proven useless once again, but at least she'd wrested the traveling carriage and enough money to pay the coachman from him before he'd fled for the Continent. With even a modicum of luck, she'd be free of him for years. He could charm his way into a rich woman's bed or set up a host of brothels in Paris or Vienna or Constantinople— she didn't care as long as he stayed far from London.

There—Bennie had emerged from his townhouse. God, her heart leapt just to see him. How ridiculous— but true. She wanted him. If she knew what love felt like, she might even say she loved him.

He walked toward his carriage.

"My lord!" She ran to intercept him.

He whirled to face her. "Lady Felicity! What are you doing here? Is everything all right?"

She allowed a few tears to leak from her eyes—not enough to turn them or her nose an unsightly red, but enough to elicit pity. "No." She managed a sob. "Oh, Lord Bennington, everything is definitely *not* all right."

She pressed her lips tightly together. If she weren't careful, she *would* turn into a watering pot.

Bennington gestured for his footman to hold his carriage. "What's amiss?"

"It's my father." She grabbed his arm and shook it slightly. "Bennie, he is so upset, he is beside himself." All true. She had never seen the earl in such a state.

He'd never been so certain he'd be hauled off to debtors' prison. She leaned closer. "I'm afraid . . ."

Bennington frowned. "Surely he would not harm you?"

She shrugged. Hadn't he already harmed her by gambling away all his money? "I . . . I . . ." She let more tears flow. Bennington took her arm and led her a few steps away from his servants.

"Don't worry, Felicity, all will be well. I'm off to the Horticultural Society meeting now—"

He was going to go natter on about plants when she was so distressed? That would never do. What if someone at the meeting had heard about the earl? She wanted him on the road to Gretna Green now before any gossip about her father reached him. She grabbed his arm again.

"Bennie, please don't leave me." She gestured toward her carriage. "I've managed to steal away. I was hoping you would take me to Scotland. Once we are wed—once I'm your viscountess—I'll be safe. My father won't be able to touch me." She leaned farther into him and tried to look totally adoring. Fortunately they were by a streetlight and her face was well illuminated. "I'm depending on you, Bennie."

Bennington looked torn. "I was looking forward to this meeting, Felicity."

Was he as dense as the cliffs of Dover? Surely he wouldn't rather sit in a roomful of men and talk about vegetation when he could ride in a dark coach with her? She ran her hand over his waistcoat.

"I know, Bennie, but I'm afraid. If we delay, I don't know what will happen."

"Well . . ."

"Please?" She slid her hand lower, stopping at his waist. "I know I'm asking a lot, but I'll"—She let her fingers stray lower. Did she see a sign of interest outlined in kerseymere?—"make it up to you. I'm sure you'll enjoy the trip north almost as much as your meeting." Her fingers ventured lower still. Yes, he was definitely interested—and growing more interested by the moment. As was she. She was having difficulty standing. All she could think of was getting him alone in the coach, finally peeling off his layers of clothing, touching him—all of him . . .

"Well . . ."

She pressed her body against his. "I *need* you, Bennie. In every way."

"Uh . . ."

She wrapped her arms around his waist and whispered in his ear. "I don't want to be alone. I need you to hold me . . . all night long."

"Ah." She had his full attention now. "But we aren't married."

She was almost panting. "We will be. What difference does a few days make one way or the other?"

He stared at her and then nodded. "Yes . . . um . . . indeed. Very true. Makes no difference at all." His hands touched her hips briefly and then dropped back to his sides. "Just let me pack a few things."

Each minute they delayed increased the odds that some breath of scandal would reach his ears—but more, each minute meant yet another minute until she could tear off his waistcoat and shirt and pantaloons and . . .

"I can't wait, Bennie. I've brought a few necessities for you." She moved her hands under his coat and down to his buttocks. "You won't need much. I've got the traveling carriage. Let's just go. Please?"

He stared at her mouth. She ran her tongue slowly over her lower lip.

"Milord? What would ye want me to do with yer coach? The horses are gettin' restless."

"Take them back to the stables, William," Bennington called over his shoulder. He kept his eyes on Felicity. "And tell Ferguson and Mrs. Ferguson I'll be away for a few days."

"Yes, milord."

Felicity smiled as she heard Bennington's coach move off. "Shall we go, my lord?" She touched the hard ridge in the front of his pantaloons. "I really can't wait to get started."

"Mmm. Neither can I, my love. Neither can I."

Parks was late. He leapt down from his carriage.

"Come back at midnight, Ned."

"Yes, sir."

He hurried into the building as Ned pulled the carriage away. Damn and blast. He hated being late. He would have been on time—he would have been early—if he hadn't wasted precious minutes talking to Mother about Miss Peterson. Now the Horticultural Society meeting was already underway. He'd missed the opportunity to converse before the program began. There'd be no chance for rational conversation until Rathbone finished droning on about the damn Amazon.

He handed the footman his hat.

"Upstairs—"

"Yes, thank you. I know the way."

He took the stairs two at a time. It really was not fair. The one thing that made these trips to London bearable was the opportunity to discuss botanical issues with fellow horticultural enthusiasts. Now he'd have to sneak in and grab a chair in the back.

And why the *hell* did the topic have to be the

Amazon? When he thought about Miss Peterson sailing off to South America, he wanted to hit something. Or strangle someone—preferably Miss Peterson.

She could not seriously be considering traveling with Miss Witherspoon and Miss Witherspoon's odd companion, could she? Surely Knightsdale would put his foot down, or if he did not have authority over her, then her father would object. Her sister. *Someone* must talk sense to the woman.

The main door was closed, so he slipped through the red drawing room to the other entrance. As he expected, Rathbone had already begun his boring presentation. He scanned the crowd. All the usual attendees were present—Smithson, Palmerson, Easthaven. Perhaps after the meeting he'd have a word with Easthaven concerning the state of his garden. The picturesque was all well and good, but portions of the earl's plantings were veering out of control.

The plantings were not the only things veering out of control in that garden. He felt an uncomfortable heat move up his neck to his ears as he remembered how little control he'd exhibited there. He obviously would not be discussing *that* topic with Easthaven.

He glanced around the room again. Someone was missing. Who was it? Not Eldridge or Tundrow or—

Bennington. That's who it was. Odd. Bennington always came and always, without fail, sat directly in front of the speaker. He'd probably done the same at Eton, trying to be the teacher's favorite. What could possibly have kept the viscount away? *He* didn't have a mother yammering at him to wed. Well, he'd already addressed that issue—the man was engaged.

He shrugged. Bennington's vagaries were not his concern.

There was an empty seat by a young man with the

worst haircut he'd ever seen. It looked like the fellow had cut it himself—with his eyes closed. He slid into the seat and glanced over. Did he know the boy?

The profile was vaguely familiar. Actually, it was more than vaguely familiar. It was as if he were viewing something he'd seen many times, but some crucial detail was missing. What?

The boy looked up. How old was he? His face was so smooth, it couldn't have felt the scrape of a razor yet. And he looked so . . . stricken. Surely the boy wasn't afraid of him?

The eyes. He had seen those eyes before. Warm brown, the color of rich loam with flecks of green. He'd seen them flash with spirit . . .

Good God! It couldn't be—

It was. It bloody hell *was* Miss Peterson. She looked down at her hands—now the profile was so clear. Miss Peterson had chopped off her hair, donned pantaloons—

Pantaloons. The woman was wearing pantaloons. Her thighs were exposed for the world to see. He could see them quite clearly. Well, not quite as clearly as he would like, since they were covered in kerseymere . . .

He grabbed her wrist.

"What the *hell* do you think you're doing?"

Miss Peterson made a little squeaking sound and kept her head down.

He glanced around quickly. No one was looking at them; everyone was watching Rathbone, listening to him drone on. Thank God they were at the back of the room. He leaned over to whisper in her ear.

"We are leaving now. Do you understand?"

She nodded.

He let go of her wrist—and his fingers brushed kerseymere. He froze. He was touching her leg. If he dropped his hand an inch—less—he'd have his palm on her thigh. He could trace its length all the way to . . .

He snatched his hand back, dropping it in his own lap so it covered . . . anything that needed covering.

This was ridiculous. He must get his unruly thoughts under control.

He glanced at her legs again. Control might be out of the question.

Damn. He fisted his hands so they couldn't find their way back to her delectable person. She had taken a horrendous risk tonight. Fear—and on its heels, anger—flooded his gut. Someone should teach Miss Peterson a thorough lesson.

At this particular moment, he felt like the most qualified man to do so.

She was going to be sick. Her heart was lodged in her throat. She couldn't breathe.

Meg stared at Mr. Parker-Roth's hand encircling her wrist. It was so much larger than hers. So much stronger. There was no possible way she could break his hold.

If she wanted to.

She clenched her teeth. Of course she wanted to. She wanted him to go away, to permit her to die of embarrassment in peace—alone.

"We are leaving now. Do you understand?"

She nodded, and he finally released her. His fingers paused, hovering over her leg.

She closed her eyes. He must be looking at her thigh.

She really would die of embarrassment. If only the palm tree were larger. If only she were already in the jungles of the Amazon. If only the ground would open up and swallow her.

She wished to be anywhere but here, sitting next to

Mr. Parker-Roth, having him stare in shock at her scandalously pantaloon-clad thigh.

If he'd ever had an ounce of respect for her, the slightest glimmer of positive regard, it must be gone now. No respectable man could think kindly of a hoyden who dressed in men's clothing and attended a male gathering, Miss Witherspoon's friend notwithstanding. Well, Miss Witherspoon's friend had not had the ignominy of being caught.

Mr. Parker-Roth was saying something. She swallowed to clear the roaring from her ears.

"What?"

"I said, you leave first. Wait outside the chamber door. I'll come along shortly. If anyone notices us, they'll think you are unwell and I've gone to assist you."

She certainly felt unwell. "I'll have to push past you."

He grinned at her. He bore a marked resemblance to a wolf anticipating his dinner. Not that she'd ever seen a wolf, of course, but there was something distinctly feral in Mr. Parker-Roth's expression. His eyes were . . . hot.

"That's quite all right." He looked around the room, and then back at her. "Now go."

She stood. There really was very little room to get by. Couldn't the man move to let her out? She looked at him. He flashed that particularly unsettling grin back at her and gestured with his head for her to continue.

Well, the sooner she was out of here the better. She started to squeeze past him, stumbled on his foot, and bumped her discarded punch glass.

"Ulp!" She reached for the glass in a vain attempt to save it. Instead, she knocked it over as she felt a hand run up her leg under her coattails. A large male hand.

Heat flooded her belly. She felt branded, though there was no pain—unless one counted the throbbing ache in a very embarrassing location. She watched a trail of punch flow from her spilled glass across the table top toward Mr. Wicklow's elbow.

She hoped she wasn't panting.

The hand continued across her derriere. If her poor brain weren't so overheated, she'd muster the intelligence to scream.

No, men didn't scream, did they? She should hit him.

She bit her lip to keep from moaning. He was tracing the outline of the kerseymere now, coming perilously close to the throbbing, aching . . .

She wanted him to touch her there. She dropped her head, overcome by mortification and need.

Mortification won. The trail of punch must have finally reached Mr. Wicklow's elbow. His arm jerked off the table and he leapt out of his seat.

"What the—" He glared at her. "This is my best coat, you bloody bastard."

The hands on her derriere were pushing her now. She didn't need any encouragement. Mr. Wicklow looked ready to darken her daylights.

"So sorry." She clapped her hand over her mouth. She did feel ill. Everyone was staring at her.

Mr. Wicklow stepped back quickly. "Good God, man, don't shoot the cat here. Go on." He flapped his hands at her as if she were a stray dog. "Go."

She needed no more urging. She turned and fled.

Chapter 17

There was no point in waiting to leave now. Miss Peterson had caused such a scene, he might as well complete it by departing immediately.

He nodded at Wicklow, shrugged as if to say *Young cubs, can't hold their alcohol, can they?* and headed for the door.

To be fair, the scene had not been solely Miss Peterson's fault. No, to be honest, it had hardly been her fault at all. If he'd kept his hands to himself, she would have slipped out quietly. But zounds, how could he have helped himself? Her sweet arse was right there in front of him, begging to be touched.

Mmm. He paused with his hand on the doorknob. If only it hadn't been covered in kerseymere. If only he'd had his hands on her soft, naked flesh. He could imagine exactly . . .

Bloody *hell.* It wouldn't take anyone's imagination to discern where his thoughts had traveled. One look at the bulge in his pantaloons would reveal all. And since all the men in the room thought Miss Peterson was a boy, he'd find himself a social outcast in short order.

Damn. At least the woman must realize now the

danger she courted by parading about in men's clothing. Not that he should be entertaining salacious
thoughts about a gently bred young woman of course,
but, damn it, a man had his limits. He was only male—
more obviously male than usual at the moment, devil
take it.

Apparently—*very* apparently—he had more pressing
needs than he knew. He shook his head. His odd state
must be due to the Sodom and Gomorrah atmosphere
of London. He didn't usually have trouble controlling
his urges. Hell, he didn't usually have any urges to control. His weekly visits to Cat dealt with that issue quite ad-
equately.

He flushed. The last time he'd been in her bed, he'd
caught himself contemplating a new fertilizer mix
almost before the deed was done.

He blew out a short breath. He just needed to get
back to the Priory and his gardens. Tomorrow morning
he'd shake London's dust from his boots and life would
return to normal.

She took a deep breath the moment she closed the
door behind her. She had to think.

She couldn't wait for Parks to take his time exiting
the room. She had to leave immediately. What if Mr.
Wicklow came after her to demand satisfaction for ruining his coat? Or, or what if some lord felt the need of
a chamber pot—there was a cupboard just to her right
that might contain such a receptacle.

Or what if Mr. Parker-Roth wanted to touch her
again?

Lud!

She covered her face with her hands as a wave of
mortification crashed over her. He knew who she was.

He had seen her in pantaloons and he *knew*. He'd had his hands on—

Ohh.

She felt ill. Heat burned her face and . . . other places.

What had he meant by it? He'd obviously been angry. She'd expected him to read her a scold at his first opportunity. She had most definitely not expected him to . . . she could never have imagined he would . . .

She had to get away. She glanced over her shoulder. The door was still closed, but it was unlikely to stay closed long.

Where were the stairs? She'd not come in this way. The room was very large, with red curtains and big gilt frames holding dark pictures of men in helmets and togas. Somewhere there must be a—

"Eep!" There was movement on the other side of the room. Who was it? She couldn't see—the light was too dim. Someone was trying to save a few pence by limiting the number of candles. It was definitely a gentleman, though. One would have thought he'd have made his presence known when she'd entered, but he seemed as taken aback as she.

"Good evening, sir. Could you point me toward the stairs?" She cleared her throat. The man didn't say a word. "It is rather urgent. I must leave immediately." Lud! She heard the door hinge squeak. "Please, I beg of you—"

A male hand closed around her arm. She screamed.

"Good God, woman, do you want to bring the entire Horticultural Society running in here? Keep your voice down."

She pulled back. Why wasn't the other man coming to her aid? Was he afraid of Mr. Parker-Roth? Surely after her scream, he could not think she welcomed this contact?

"Unhand me, sir." She gestured toward the other man. "You can see we are not alone."

"What?" Parks looked across the room. "What are you talking about?"

"The other gentleman." She called to her potential rescuer. "Sir, please, I am in need of your assistance."

Mr. Parker-Roth snorted. "There's no one else here."

"What? But I distinctly saw—"

"You distinctly saw your own reflection. Come on."

"What? How can you say—oh." He was right. She looked at her "savior." He was standing next to Mr. Parker-Roth, with Parks's hand wrapped around his arm. "I didn't realize. It is so dark in here."

He grunted. "It's not going to be dark enough to hide the fact you're a female when Rathbone stops yammering and all those men spill out into this room."

Truthfully, she wasn't eager for that to happen either, but Parks was not giving her sufficient credit. "I did make it here without being discovered, you know."

His fingers tightened on her arm. "*That*'s a miracle. What did you do, come in with a blind man?"

She bit her lip. "Lord Smithson introduced me. He thought I was one of the Devonshire Beldons."

"Good God."

Mr. Parker-Roth escorted her out of the room and down a very short hall. When they reached the stairs, he released her.

"We're going to collect our hats and leave. Don't say a word to anyone."

"But—"

"Not a word. Trust me, you sound nothing like a man."

She shrugged. She had no desire to waste time arguing. The sooner she left this place, the happier she would be.

Mr. Parker-Roth proved extremely efficient. They stepped onto the street in moments without eliciting any noticeable reactions from the servants.

"Shall I call for your carriage, sir?" one of the footmen asked.

"No, thank you. We shall walk." Parks strode up the street in the direction of Knightsdale House. Meg hurried after him.

"Why aren't we taking your carriage?" She lowered her voice, stepping closer to Parks as a trio of drunken lords stumbled by.

"Ned went home. I told him not to come back till midnight."

She heard a retching noise and then a splash behind them.

"Then what about a hackney? It's rather a long walk, isn't it?"

There was enough light to see his glare clearly. "I find I need the exercise. I am slightly agitated by the night's events."

"Oh."

"Oh, indeed." He kept walking.

She tried to match his steps. It was easier walking in pantaloons than skirts—she could definitely get used to that—but the shoes she'd borrowed didn't fit well enough for an extended perambulation. She'd have blisters in the morning. And her legs weren't long enough to keep up without almost running. She was getting breathless.

Why was he so upset anyway? He wasn't her father. He had no responsibility for her. What she did had absolutely nothing to do with him.

"I don't know why you are so peevish. I'm not the

first woman to attend the Horticultural Society meetings in male attire, you know."

That got him to pause. "What *are* you talking about?"

His tone was not encouraging. It was somewhere between incredulous and vicious.

She stiffened her spine. She would not let herself be intimidated. The man was much too overbearing for his own good. "Miss Witherspoon told me her friend came for an entire year and no one was the wiser."

He snorted. "You don't mean Prudence Doddington-Prinz, do you?"

"Yes, I do."

"Good God." He resumed walking. She had to skip to keep up. They were now passing a long line of carriages waiting for Lord Fonsby's ball to end. The baron's townhouse, still a few houses ahead of them, glowed with the light of hundreds of candles. The sounds of music and voices drifted out the open windows. A few of the coachmen, loitering by the carriages, glanced at Meg—at least she felt they were looking at her. Were they suspicious? She tried to use Parks as a shield.

"What do you mean? What is the matter with Miss Doddington-Prinz?"

"Have you ever seen her?"

"Well, no. But what does that have to say to the matter?"

He glared at her again. "Miss Peterson, believe me—"

"Shh!" Meg looked significantly at the coachmen. Had they heard him call her "Miss"?

Mr. Parker-Roth seemed not to notice.

"It is no surprise at all that Prudence Doddington-Prinz passed as a man for a year. The woman is tall and square with no curves to speak of. She has more hair on her upper lip than I do."

"Oh." Were more of the coachmen stopping their

own conversations to listen to theirs? "*Please* lower your voice, sir."

Mr. Parker-Roth might have been deaf for all the attention he paid her. He stopped. She looked around. Lud! Was he blind also? Not only did a host of coachmen have their ears cocked in their direction, but they were now standing directly in front of Lord Fonsby's townhouse, illuminated for all the world to see. She took his arm and tried to pull him a few steps farther along into the shadows. She felt as if she were trying to tow the Tower of London up the Thames.

"Do you want to know the *real* reason I did not call a hackney?"

Why was he so agitated? Perhaps if she agreed with him, he would calm down.

"Yes, certainly. I'd love to know exactly that. Please tell me, but first let us step along to a more private location. In case you haven't noticed, we are being observed." She tugged on him again. If they could just get past Lord Fonsby's house. It was not far.

It was too far. He shook her off. "A more private location? Ha!"

There was no denying it—every coachman on the street had found a reason to congregate just ten feet from them. Perhaps she should simply remove Mr. Parker-Roth's cravat and gag him with it.

"Sir, I'm certain you will regret this."

"Yes, I'll regret this. I do regret this, but I can't help myself. You torture me; you defy every convention. You go out into the shrubbery with other men; you plan to sail off to the jungles of the Amazon with no more thought than you might give a trip to Hyde Park." He grabbed her shoulders and shook her. "Do you know how I felt when I saw you at the meeting tonight? When you waved your kerseymere-clad arse in my face?"

She felt her jaw fall open at his vulgarity. She was shocked . . . but the odd warmth that was becoming all too familiar coiled low in her stomach, too.

She looked away—and saw that she was not the only one shocked by Mr. Parker-Roth's words. The coachmen were gaping, too. If they leaned any closer to glean every detail of this spectacle, they'd fall over. But there was no need for them to strain. Mr. Parker-Roth was speaking loudly enough for the entire neighborhood to hear.

"And now you suggest a more *private* location?" He gave her another shake. "Be careful what you wish for." He squeezed her shoulders and bit out each word. "I did not call a hackney because I did not trust myself in a darkened carriage with you."

The coachman directly behind Mr. Parker-Roth gasped. Surely that was not Lord Dunlee's livery the man was wearing?

"Sir, are you foxed?" Meg hissed. "Lower your voice."

"No, damn it, I am not foxed. I am mad. Completely and utterly insane. A candidate for Bedlam." He finally lowered his voice—and his head. His lips brushed hers. "I have lost my mind." She felt the words as much as heard them. "You have stolen it. Like an invasive vine, you have choked all the sense out of me."

She wasn't certain she cared for that simile, but she was given no opportunity to argue. His mouth covered hers.

The man *was* insane, and she had caught his insanity. At the warm—no, the hot—touch of his lips on hers, she forgot where she was. She forgot half the coachmen in London were staring at them. She forgot she was in pantaloons, coat, and cravat on a London street in front of a townhouse that would at any moment disgorge scores of the *haut ton.* She forgot everything, lost as she was in the hot, wet wonder of his mouth.

She welcomed the sweep of his tongue over hers. She delighted in how it filled her, possessed her. She clung to him and opened her mouth wider, letting him take what he wanted. What she wanted.

She traced his tongue with hers and he growled deep in his throat. His hands slid down her back. She frowned. Her breasts ached for his touch, but they were flattened under layers of cloth. He could not reach them. She whimpered and pressed closer.

Ah. There *were* some advantages to male attire. She rubbed against the interesting bulge she'd discovered. His hands reached her bottom—

"Good God!"

That sounded like Lord Dunlee's voice.

John's mouth left hers. One arm came up around her waist to pull her tightly against him; one hand flew up to press her face against his shoulder. She felt shielded. Protected.

She did not fight him. If Lord Dunlee was here, Lady Dunlee could not be far behind.

"Good evening, Lord Dunlee," John said. He cleared his throat. "Lady Dunlee."

Meg tried to bury into his shoulder.

"Why, Mr. Parker-Roth." Lady Dunlee's strident voice carried to the farthest reaches of the *ton.* "I never imagined you favored . . . I would never have guessed your preferences turned to . . ." She coughed. "I suppose this explains why you aren't married."

"You have to marry him now, Meg." Charles rubbed his forehead. They were seated in Charles's study—well, Meg was seated. Charles and Emma stood, looming over her. "Sodomy is . . . well, the man's reputation is completely ruined."

"But he wasn't . . . I mean, I'm a woman."

"But no one who witnessed the event knows that," Charles said. "Parker-Roth protected your identity at considerable cost to himself."

"There are horrid caricatures of him up in all the print shops." Emma looked pointedly at Meg's head. "Which you would know if you could go about in society."

Meg resisted the urge to put her hands to her shorn hair. She hadn't left Knightsdale House since Mr. Parker-Roth had brought her home. Fortunately, Lizzie and Robbie had been attending Lord Fonsby's affair and had hurried them into their carriage before the situation could get more out of hand than it already was.

"They won't prosecute him, will they?" If Parks were brought to stand trial for such an offense . . . it didn't bear thinking of. "Lizzie's cousin Richard was never charged, and he definitely . . . well, everyone knew he and his valet were . . ." Meg didn't know the details of such relationships, but it was no secret Richard Runyon had engaged in one.

"But Richard didn't advertise his proclivities on a London street in plain view of half the *ton*." Charles sighed. "And since he also frequented London's brothels, both fashionable and not, there was some doubt as to his habits. Parker-Roth, on the other hand, has been more discreet in his activities. However, that means society has to guess what his preferences are, and the *ton* always prefers to assume the most salacious possibilities."

"There is no need to assume anything after the exhibition in front of Lord Fonsby's townhouse. If Lizzie's description is even half accurate, the man was practically making love to Meg on the street." Emma crossed her arms and glared at Meg. "What in God's name were you thinking, Meg?"

"Um."

"Your sister has a point, Meg. Your behavior has been less than exemplary."

"Less than exemplary?" Emma's voice rose. "Call it what it is, Charles. Meg has been behaving like a common harlot."

Meg swallowed. She felt as if she'd been kicked in the stomach, but Emma was right. Her behavior had been shocking. Completely scandalous. She closed her eyes briefly, remembering the hideous moment when she'd been pulled out of her madness by the sound of Lord Dunlee's voice.

"Don't you think you are overstating the case slightly, Emma?"

"I am not. What else do you call it, when a woman engages in such . . . pursuits . . . on a London street?"

Charles blew out a long breath. "Well . . ." He looked at Meg. She looked down at her slippers.

"Even if you'd been dressed in your finest gown, Meg," he said, "you'd still be compelled to marry Parker-Roth. You see that, don't you? This is at least the second time you've been observed in close embrace with the fellow."

Emma threw up her hands. "I don't understand what the problem is. You obviously don't find the man repulsive. I cannot understand why you are resisting, unless—" Her tone sharpened. "Have you been behaving this way with other men?"

"No!" Meg looked up, horrified. "How can you say so?"

"Because you've been disappearing into the shrubbery all Season. Even I will not assume you were only examining the foliage."

Meg flushed. "Well, I was not . . . um . . . doing what I was doing with Mr. Parker-Roth."

"Thank God for that!"

"Why *are* you resisting, Meg?" Charles asked. "I know Parker-Roth offered at the Palmerson ball. And, as Emma says, you obviously have some feelings for him."

"Feelings," Emma said, "that should only be expressed *after* you have received Mr. Parker-Roth's wedding ring, miss."

Charles and Emma stared down at her. What was she to answer? She didn't understand it herself.

"I don't believe Mr. Parker-Roth wants to marry me."

Emma snorted. "He clearly wants to do *something* with you—and he can only honorably engage in that activity after he puts a ring on your finger."

Meg flushed. "You don't understand. He really doesn't want to have anything to do with me. It's just that . . . well, I annoy him."

"That's one way to describe it."

"Emma . . ."

"Charles, the girl is being foolish beyond permission. If she can't see the man is beside himself with lus-love, she is blinder than I am." Emma flourished her spectacles.

Charles laughed. "Well, perhaps Parker-Roth is just as blind as you are—not that I expect you to compare spectacles, of course—because I suspect he doesn't recognize his own emotions. I don't know why." He shook his head. "I just about gave him *carte-blanche* to seduce Meg."

"You didn't!"

"Charles!"

For once Meg felt Emma was in complete accord with her. They both gaped at Lord Knightsdale.

He shrugged, though his cheeks were markedly

redder than normal. "It seemed clear to me the two of them were attracted to each other. I just encouraged Parker-Roth to move things along. I was tired of worrying—and having you worry, Emma—about the situation. I can't say I'm impressed with his response."

"I can't *imagine* you would do such a thing," Emma said.

Meg could not find the words to express her horror. Charles had actually told Mr. Parker-Roth to . . . ? How mortifying. But even more mortifying was the fact the man hadn't acted on Charles's invitation. If she'd ever needed proof Parks did not wish to marry her, she had just had it handed to her on a silver platter.

"If he would just stop concerning himself with my activities, I would not be in this predicament."

Emma glared at her again. "If you would just stop kissing him, you would not be in this predicament."

"He kissed me first."

"Ladies, please, you are becoming ridiculous. It makes no difference. Parker-Roth has already gotten the special license. He and Meg will be married tomorrow morning."

"What!" Meg leapt up. She was getting married tomorrow? "When were you going to tell me this?"

"Now." Charles grinned. "I saw no point in taking your fire any sooner than I had to."

"I do think Mr. Parker-Roth should propose to Meg." Emma looked at Meg and raised her eyebrows. "Again."

"Why should he?" Charles said. "Neither of them has any choice in the matter."

"I do have a choice." Meg scowled. Granted, she had behaved badly. She had made some poor choices. But she was not a child. She could make her own decisions. "I could leave England."

"Leave England?" Emma acted as if she'd suggested jumping naked off London Bridge.

"Yes. I hadn't told you yet, but Miss Witherspoon invited me to accompany her and her friend to the Amazon. It would be a wonderful opportunity to—"

"Are you mad?" Emma clasped her hands tightly together. Meg was certain her sister would rather have wrapped them around her neck. "You can't go to the Amazon. And even if by some odd stroke of fate you could, you could not go with those women."

"What do you mean, 'those women'?"

"Let's just say Agatha Witherspoon and Prudence Doddington-Prinz are extremely—*extremely*—close."

"Oh."

"Ladies." Charles held up his hands. "This is all beside the point. It is Parker-Roth, not Meg, who needs extricating from this scandal and he cannot simply flee. He has an estate to manage."

Emma nodded. "And leaving the country wouldn't solve his problems in any event. A scandal of this nature will reflect on his entire family. Perhaps his parents and his married sister can weather the storm, but his brothers and his other sisters will not be so fortunate. Certainly it will ruin the younger ones' matrimonial prospects."

"It won't." Meg felt ill. Emma must be overstating the case.

"It will, and it will make it impossible for Mr. Parker-Roth ever to marry." Emma put a hand on Meg's arm. "This is not a small scandal, Meg. It is on everyone's lips now—*everyone*'s. It will not be forgotten. Even I know the *ton* has a very long memory."

"Especially for something of this nature," Charles said. "Parker-Roth was not merely caught with someone's wife. In the eyes of society, he's a sodomite. Men as well as women will avoid him."

"No."

"Yes, Meg. Think about it. He was clearly seen passionately kissing what looked to be another man by twenty or thirty people. What *is* society to think?"

Meg covered her face with her hands.

"The only solution to his problem is for him to marry immediately, and you are the logical choice. I'd say you were honor bound to wed him."

Charles was right. She couldn't let Parks face this alone. Meg dropped her hands and looked up.

"All right," she said. "I will do it. I will marry Mr. Parker-Roth."

Damn, damn, damn.

He hated being coerced, but even he recognized he had no choice in this matter. If he didn't wed Miss Peterson, he and his family would be shunned. Hell, it had started already. The parade of footmen sent to withdraw invitations had filled the Pulteney's lobby the morning after his ill-timed embrace of Miss Peterson.

He was getting an excellent notion of how a leper must feel. When he ventured out of the hotel, people not only gave him the cut direct, they crossed the street to avoid him. He'd been told he was no longer welcome at White's, and even the Horticultural Society had sent a letter withdrawing his membership. No one in London wanted anything to do with him.

Except for a few. He flushed and turned to look out the coach window, hoping his mother would not notice his heightened color.

Who would have guessed Lord Easthaven had such unusual predilections? He'd crossed paths with the earl after he'd been turned away from White's. He'd been so happy to have someone speak to him that he hadn't given much thought to stepping into that alley with the man. He understood Easthaven might not wish to be seen with him, but when the earl had put his hand on his arm and explained exactly why that section of his garden was so overgrown, he'd made a hasty excuse and bolted for the thoroughfare.

It was a hard call which was worse—that experience or his encounter later that day. He'd been sitting on a bench in an out-of-the-way part of Hyde Park, contemplating the bleakness of his existence, when a servant had approached and gestured to him. He'd recognized the silver and green livery as Baron Cinter's, so he'd followed the man to a leafy glade. Lady Cinter was there waiting for him. He'd greeted her cautiously, but she'd had no designs on his virtue. She'd merely wished to watch him engage in carnal play al fresco with the footman.

He closed his eyes. The servant had dropped his breeches in record time, a tactical error. Parks hadn't waited to explain the misunderstanding—he'd left at a run. The man gave chase, but fell, tripped up by his own clothing.

No, he had no alternative to marriage.

"I'm so sorry your wedding has to be under such unpleasant circumstances," his mother said. They were on their way to Knightsdale House so he could tie the knot and end the storm of gossip.

He shrugged. "You should be happy. You've accomplished your goal. Are you going to turn your attention to Stephen now and get him a leg-shackle?"

Pain flashed over her face. He wished he could take the words back, but he was too angry to apologize.

"Johnny, you know I only want you to be happy."

He nodded and looked out the window again. He did know it, but that didn't help him feel better about his predicament. And yes, he realized his troubles were largely his own fault. If he hadn't succumbed to his urges and kissed Miss Peterson, he'd be traveling home to the Priory now instead of to Knightsdale House. But Miss Peterson was equally to blame. If she'd been a proper female, if she'd stayed out of the bushes, if she'd stayed in her skirts, he also wouldn't be heading toward this meeting. He had only been chivalrous. He had only tried to save her from her own folly.

All right, so the folly wasn't only hers. Kissing her in front of Fonsby's townhouse had been the height of lunacy. He'd experienced an atypical loss of control . . .

Bloody hell. Losing control was all too typical around Miss Margaret Peterson.

"We're here." Mother turned and hugged him. He patted her shoulder weakly.

"I think you can be happy with Miss Peterson, Johnny, if you will only try."

He nodded. What did she expect him to say? She knew he did not want to step into parson's mousetrap, and yet that was what he was going to do within the hour.

Bloody hell.

He helped his mother down from the coach. The carriage he'd hired for Miss Witherspoon was just pulling up. He'd not trusted himself to ride with the woman who'd been, in effect, the author of this farce. If she hadn't suggested Miss Peterson travel with her to the Amazon, if she hadn't told her about Miss Doddington-Prinz's bizarre masquerade—

To put it nicely, he was not feeling charitable toward the woman at the moment.

"I wish your father and the rest of the family were

here," Mother said as they waited for the Knightsdale butler to open the door. "But you and the marquis are quite right. The sooner you wed Miss Peterson and the notice appears in the papers, the better."

He grunted. He was beyond coherent speech. He wasn't certain which emotion was strongest—anger, dread . . . or, yes, lust.

He decided anger was most likely to get him safely through the next hour.

Chapter 18

"I need to speak with you, Meg."

"Hmm?" Meg looked out on the square. Was that Mr. Parker-Roth's coach pulling up? Her stomach clenched into a tight knot and she felt a wave of heat sweep up her neck. She bit her lip. She both longed to see him and dreaded it. What was the matter with her?

The footman was opening the door and letting down the steps—

"Meg!"

"What?" She pulled her attention away from the window. Emma stood just inside her bedroom door, dressed for the wedding but holding Henry—a very, very quiet Henry.

"Oh, dear." Meg hurried over and put her hand on Henry's forehead. He didn't move, just kept his head on Emma's shoulder and sucked his fingers. He was burning up. "Henry's sick now, too?"

Emma nodded and kissed Henry's sweat-dampened hair. "I meant to come talk to you last night, but Charlie was still throwing up, and Henry started this morning. At least Charlie seems through the worst of it. He's in the nursery with Nanny, sleeping."

"Poor Charlie." Meg rubbed Henry's cheek and he smiled weakly. "Poor Henry." She looked at Emma. Her sister's eyes were bloodshot, and lines creased her forehead. "Poor Emma."

Emma smiled slightly. "I hate it when the boys are sick. I worry so."

"Of course you do. You love them."

Emma pressed another kiss to Henry's head. "I love you, too, Meg."

Meg flushed again. It really was overly warm in the room. "I know." She looked away, cleared her throat. "I'm sorry I gave you such cause to worry, Emma. I never meant for you to drag the boys and Isabelle and Claire to London."

"I know." Emma sighed. "And I'm sorry you have to wed in this helter-skelter fashion, but it can't be helped. If you could have moved about in society yesterday and today"—she looked pointedly at Meg's hair. Emma's abigail had trimmed and shaped it, but there was no escaping the fact that it was woefully short—"you'd have seen how awful it is. People are saying terrible things about Mr. Parker-Roth."

Meg closed her eyes. Another wave of heat surged through her, and tears gathered behind her lids. It wouldn't do to start crying now and go down to her wedding with a dripping nose and blotchy face. "I'm sorry Mr. Parker-Roth is compelled to marry me to extricate himself from the mess I created."

Emma snorted. "Well, that is one thing you *don't* have to regret. The man is obviously besotted. I don't know why he didn't persuade you to have him sooner." She frowned. "Unless . . . have you taken a dislike to him, Meg? Is that the problem? Charles and I didn't think it was, but . . ." She sighed. "I'm very sorry if that's the case, because there's really nothing to be done now."

Meg put her hands on her heated cheeks. "No, I haven't taken a dislike to him, precisely. I just . . ." She shrugged. Her head was beginning to ache. "It's too hard to explain."

Henry fussed a little and Emma rubbed his back, rocking from side to side. "Shh, baby. Shh."

Would she have her own baby to comfort this time next year—hers and Parks's?

Her stomach twisted. She couldn't think about that now.

"Is it time to go down?" Suddenly, she just wanted to get it over with.

"Yes, but first we need to have a little talk."

"We do?" What could Emma wish to discuss now? They'd already had a little talk. Parks was downstairs waiting.

"Yes. As I said, I'd meant to come last night, but Charlie was sick."

"I see." Meg waited. Emma kept patting Henry. She made no move to break the silence. Perhaps her sister needed some encouragement. "So, what did you wish to say?"

Emma flushed. "It's a matter of some delicacy."

"It is?" What could she be getting at? "I don't underst—oh."

Emma's color deepened. "Yes—oh. I . . . well . . ." She cleared her throat. "Perhaps the best way to proceed is simply to ask if you have any questions about . . . about marriage and what happens"—Emma pointed with her chin at Meg's bed—"you know."

She didn't know. She was terribly curious—and terribly embarrassed. Ridiculous! This was no time to be missish. Women *should* discuss such things—an unmarried woman such as herself should know exactly what to expect when she climbed into her marriage bed. Unmarried men certainly knew—most had already experienced the . . . event. Parks certainly had no questions.

Her stomach twisted. He was waiting for her downstairs.

She wet her lips. She would ask now. Just a moment of courage, a few words, and she would know.

How could she ask? She had a rudimentary understanding of the procreative procedure from stumbling upon various animals engaged in the act. To think Emma and Charles had actually performed that bizarre exercise . . . yet Emma was holding the irrefutable evidence that they had.

"Are you certain you don't have any questions?"

She would know all too well what was involved by this time tomorrow.

Panic closed her throat. She swallowed.

"Well, if you are quite sure you have no questions." Emma sounded relieved. She turned to go. "I'll see you downstairs. I just have to put Henry in the nursery."

Meg found her voice. "Does it, um, well . . . does it hurt?"

Her sister paused, her hand on the doorknob. She flushed again, but she answered. "Perhaps a little the first time, but even then, most of it is quite . . . pleasant. I hope . . . I mean . . . I'm certain Mr. Parker-Roth will be an attentive husband. He is very good to his mother, after all."

Somehow that thought was not reassuring.

Emma turned to look directly at Meg. "And you did not appear to be complaining in Lady Palmerson's parlor or in front of Lord Fonsby's townhouse." She smiled. "I would guess you have nothing to worry about."

Someone knocked on the door. "My lady, my lord asks you and Miss Peterson to come down to the blue drawing room. Mr. Parker-Roth and his mother have arrived."

"Thank you, Albert. We'll be right there." Emma looked back at Meg. "You go along. Tell Charles I'm putting Henry in the nursery, will you?"

"All right."

"Don't sound so nervous. Everything will be fine."

Easy for Emma to say—she wasn't minutes from wedding a virtual stranger. It would help if her head wasn't pounding so much. She rubbed her forehead. Her stomach was still clenched into a tight knot as well. She felt ill.

She took a few deep breaths. She needed to get her nerves under control. She'd managed to create enough of a scandal without throwing up on her bridegroom.

Meg made her way slowly down the stairs, holding tightly to the banister. This was not how she'd imagined her wedding—not that she'd spent much time imagining it. She'd assumed it would be just like Emma's—in the parish church she'd known all her life with Papa officiating. Instead she was marrying in London, in her brother-in-law's drawing room, in haste, in scandal.

"Meg!" Lizzie stood at the bottom of the stairs, smiling up at her. "You look beautiful."

Lizzie was being kind. She knew what she looked like—she'd seen herself in the mirror. Her skin was colorless; she had dark circles under her eyes. She looked dreadful.

"I wish Papa were here."

Lizzie hugged her. "Charles sent his fastest carriage. Your father might still arrive in time."

She sniffed. Tears were pooling in her eyes again. She wasn't usually such a watering pot. "I wish we could w-wait."

Lizzie hugged her again. "You have to be on the road within the hour so you can get to the inn before sunset."

Meg nodded. She knew that. They had all decided, given the nature of the scandal, that it would be best for her and Parks to leave London immediately. She'd agreed. The thought of being newly married and having to face Lady Dunlee and the other gossips made her stomach churn even more.

Adjusting to married life would be difficult enough—she didn't need the *ton* observing her every breath.

Emma clattered down the stairs behind her.

"How's Henry?"

"Sleeping." Emma smiled. "Good morning, Lizzie. I'm sorry I'm late. Charlie and Henry have been sick."

Lizzie frowned. "Nothing serious, I hope?"

"No. Charlie is already on the mend, but Henry just got sick this morning." Emma pushed a stray lock of hair off her forehead and turned to Meg. "Are you ready?"

She tried to speak, but her voice had deserted her. She nodded. She was as ready as she would ever be.

She followed Lizzie and Emma into the blue drawing room. Charles was there with Robbie as were the Duke and Duchess of Alvord, Mrs. Parker-Roth, Miss Witherspoon, and Isabelle and Claire.

Mr. Parker-Roth was glaring at the minister. She walked toward him, and his attention dropped to her attire. She'd had no time to get a suitable wedding dress, so she was wearing the ball gown she'd worn at Easthaven's party. Obviously it was not one of his favorites for his scowl, already quite pronounced, grew darker.

Lovely, she thought as she greeted the minister. What else can go wrong?

* * *

Parks was not usually given to fits of temper, but today was an exception. He would dearly love to hit something.

The minister, standing next to him, cleared his throat. Perhaps *he* would be a good target. The man had been trying to make conversation with him since he'd arrived—the sanctimonious little twiddlepoop. Couldn't he see Parks was not in the mood for bibble-babble?

At least no one was blaming *him* for this disaster, though perhaps anger and condemnation would be better than the embarrassment and pity he was currently being met with. Lord Knightsdale and Westbrooke were far too understanding. Yes, Miss Peterson should not have been traipsing around London in men's clothing, but he should not have kissed her, especially in such a shockingly public location. And it had not been a little buss upon the cheek. He'd had his tongue halfway down her throat and his hands all over her arse. Really, he had earned a little condemnation.

He closed his eyes, remembering all too clearly the feel of her—both the wet warmth of her mouth and the soft curves of her bottom. Heat flooded him, causing a particular appendage to swell to an all-too-obvious size. Damn. Anger was definitely the safest emotion to get him through this day.

"Here is your bride." Reverend Twiddlepoop touched him on the arm . . . and then ran his palm down his sleeve.

What the hell? He jerked his arm away.

"When you are back in London, come see me." The damn minister kept his voice low so no one could overhear. "I know many discreet men with similar interests."

He was definitely going to hit something. Someone. Now.

"You mistake the matter, sirrah!" The words came out in a hiss.

Reverend Bugger stepped back. "My pardon. I assumed . . ."

His jaw was clenched too tightly to reply, but the minister appeared to get his message nonetheless. He would love to see Reverend Abomination's damn body on the floor of the drawing room; unfortunately, a dead clergyman would be unable to perform the ceremony. And the ladies would not care to witness his temper applied to this miserable—

He forced himself to turn away. Miss Peterson was approaching. Unless he missed his guess, she was wearing the same gown she'd worn at Easthaven's ball. Easthaven who had tried to lure him into his bloody overgrown bushes. London was crawling with sodomites.

But he was not one of them. He let his gaze travel slowly over Miss Peterson's hips and waist, her lovely breasts and shoulders and neck. The jolt of lust he felt was reassuring. The world had not really gone mad. He was a man, with proper male thoughts. Well, not *proper*, precisely . . . natural. He had a very natural, male reaction to an attractive female body. His malest organ was quite healthy, strong and thick and ready to be about its business—

Anger. That was the emotion he needed today.

He focused on Miss Peterson's face. Here she was not looking well. She was too pale, and she had dark circles under her eyes. She looked tired and tense.

This could not have been the wedding she'd hoped for.

Well, it was her own fault. If she hadn't behaved like such a hoyden, she wouldn't be facing a hurried wedding. *He* wouldn't be facing it. His name wouldn't be whispered about in every London drawing room, gossiped about over every tea cup—even every brandy glass. He wouldn't be blackballed from White's, barred from the Horticultural Society.

He wouldn't have Reverend Atrocity brushing up against his breeches. He glared at the man again while the minister mumbled some pious platitudes to Miss Peterson. Talk about whited sepulchers! This perverted parson took the prize.

The worst part of this social disaster, though, was its effect on his mother. Many of the *ton* had given her the cut direct, though she'd said that was better than the snide comments others had felt compelled to share with her.

Rage boiled up in him with the memory. He glanced over to where his mother stood talking to Lady Knightsdale. She caught him looking at her and beamed back at him.

Perhaps she saw her social standing as a minor loss if it brought her a bigger prize—his marriage.

Knightsdale came over then. "Shall we begin?"

Miss Peterson's head came up. "Couldn't we wait a moment or two more? I'm so hoping Papa might arrive."

Her voice was strained. Instinctively, Parks took her hand in his, and she smiled fleetingly up at him. He squeezed her fingers. "I don't mind waiting," he said.

Knightsdale sighed. "We agreed you should leave London today. If you don't—"

"Are we in time?"

Miss Peterson whirled around. "Papa!"

She ran to the door and threw her arms around a thin, scholarly-looking man standing next to a short, gray-haired woman. The man hugged her back.

Parks looked at Reverend Sodom and bared his teeth in an expression that might resemble a smile but most certainly wasn't. "I guess we won't be needing your services—*any* of your services—after all."

"I'm glad—"

"—to leave." His voice must have risen in volume, because he felt Knightsdale's hand on his shoulder. Thank God, *he* didn't try to stroke him.

"But—"

"Thank you, Reverend Phillips," Knightsdale said, "but I do believe you can safely leave now. As you can see, Miss Peterson would much rather her father officiate." He smiled. "Of course you will be compensated for your time."

"Well." The man cleared his throat. "If you are quite certain—"

"Quite." Parks must have sounded rather menacing since both Knightsdale and the minister gave him a startled look.

"That's decided then." The marquis took the minister's arm. "If you'll just come this way, Reverend Phillips, we'll get everything settled in a trice and you can be on your way."

"What was that about?" Westbrooke came up to stand beside Parks. They watched Knightsdale usher Reverend Phillips out of the room.

"You don't want to know."

"All right. I hope you don't have an aversion to all men of the cloth, though."

"Why?"

"Because of your soon-to-be father-in-law, of course." Westbrooke nodded to someone behind Parks. "Reverend Peterson, so good to see you again."

Good God. Parks turned slowly to face Miss Peterson's father. His mouth felt dry as dust. The man must hate him. He didn't look angry, though. Perhaps Miss Peterson had explained—but how could she explain anything so bizarre?

"Papa, this is Mr. Parker-Roth, my . . . my . . ." Miss Peterson smiled slightly and shrugged.

"Good morning, sir." Parks extended his hand. Reverend Peterson took it. That was a relief—at least he wasn't going to cut him. Surely he knew he was not . . . he did not . . . that he was a normal male. "I'm sorry about the unusual circumstances. Has your daughter explained . . . ?" If Miss Peterson hadn't clarified matters, Parks was certain he could not.

"Not completely. Let me introduce my wife."

Mrs. Peterson smiled and offered Parks her hand. He didn't see any anger in her warm, brown eyes either. Caution, yes, but no condemnation.

"My pleasure, Mrs. Peterson."

"I am happy to finally meet you, Mr. Parker-Roth."

Finally? What did she mean by that?

"I am sorry . . ." Parks tried again, but stopped. What could he say?

Reverend Peterson shook his head. "Do not apologize. Meg is a grown woman. She is quite capable of making her own decisions." He smiled. "You have the support of the duke, the marquis, and the earl—and, more importantly, their wives. I am not too worried about Meg's future." He opened his prayer book and adjusted his spectacles. "Now, I understand there's need for haste." He smiled again. "Though not, I'm happy to say, for the usual reason."

Parks felt a damned blush heat his ears. He glanced at Miss Peterson. Her color, too, was heightened.

"Shall we begin?" her father said.

She was married. Her head throbbed; her stomach twisted. She was married, permanently bound to this unsmiling man at her side. Had she just made the biggest mistake of her life?

Her father kissed her. "You know you can always come home if you need to."

"Uh, yes, Papa."

He turned to Parks. "And you know I will kill you if you make her unhappy."

Parks nodded. Meg gaped. Scholarly Papa threatening violence? He must have been reading the *Iliad* before he left home.

"Don't worry." Lizzie hugged her while Robbie shook Parks's hand. "Everything will be fine."

"How can you say that?"

"Because I know you. You are very sensible—and Robbie says Parks is a good man. You just have some rocky ground to get over first, just as I did."

"But that was different."

"Only because it was me and not you." Lizzie hugged her again. "Don't worry. I know you'll be happy."

She wished she shared Lizzie's optimism, but she'd already found one error in Lizzie's thinking—she felt anything but sensible.

Emma grabbed her next. "Oh, Meg," she sobbed. "I'll miss you."

"I'll only be in Devon." Emma's hold was almost strangling her. "I'm not going to the Amazon, remember."

"Thank God for that." Emma smiled. "I hope we'll be coming to the christening of your first child next year this time."

"Uh." Babies? They did often follow after marriage. She slanted a glance at Parks. He was talking to Miss Witherspoon. Well, to be more precise, Miss Witherspoon was talking to him. He looked as stiff and unyielding as a fireplace poker. He did not look as if he ever wanted to have babies.

"Welcome to our family, dear." Mrs. Parker-Roth smiled widely and hugged her. "I'm *so* happy you wed Johnny." She sighed and shook her head. "I've been worried about him, you know. He's too serious—I'm afraid he's forgotten how to laugh." She leaned closer. "And I don't believe he's ever gotten over Grace jilting him. It is past time for him to get on with his life."

Meg smiled as brightly as she could. Splendid. She really hadn't needed to be reminded that her new husband was pining for another woman.

Charles's butler appeared at the door. "The wedding breakfast is ready, my lord."

"Thank you, Blake." Charles addressed the room. "We would be delighted if you would all join us for a brief celebration before the newlyweds depart."

Lud! Meg's stomach clenched again. She was leaving within the hour, traveling all the way to Devon with this solemn man at her side. The Amazon might be considerably farther, but it suddenly seemed much less frightening.

"If you are not happy, Meg"—Charles had come to stand beside her—"you know you have only to send word and we will have you back home in an instant."

Her head was throbbing again. She looked up at Emma's husband. Poor man, to have married into the uncomfortable role of being her brother-in-law. "I'm sorry to be such a bother—"

"You are *not* a bother, Meg. Emma and I and the children care for you deeply. We want only what is best for you."

She sniffed. "I know."

Charles turned to glare at Parks. "Be certain you make my sister-in-law happy, sir." He was not smiling, and his voice had a distinct edge. "Or I shall happily kill you myself if my father-in-law does not."

Parks did not smile either. "I will do my best, Knightsdale."

"See that you do. You owe Meg some degree of gratitude, you know. She could have refused to marry you, leaving you in a very uncomfortable position."

"I am completely aware of my debt to Miss—to my wife."

They looked like two dogs, snarling at each other. Thankfully, everyone else had left the room.

"Please, Charles, don't be ridiculous. Of course I married Mr. Parker-Roth. The situation was all my fault—"

"It was *not* all your fault." Now Parks was glaring at her! What was the matter with the man? She knew her responsibility all too clearly.

"I don't believe you came to my bedchamber and forced me to don men's clothing, did you?"

"No." The man sounded as if he were speaking through clenched teeth. "And I don't believe you forced me to kiss you in front of Lord Fonsby's townhouse just as the evening's entertainment was ending."

Her temperature, which had been fluctuating wildly all morning, shot up again. "No, but . . ."

Parks nodded. "No. The answer is no, you did not. As Knightsdale says, the fault is mine. I am completely in your debt."

"I really don't think . . ." This was all too confusing. She knew she was to blame—he was just being chivalrous. Yet he genuinely seemed to believe he was culpable. She didn't want a husband who resented her for ruining his life, but neither did she want one whose main emotion was grudging gratitude.

It made no difference what she wanted—she now had a husband, resentful, grateful, or furious.

She rubbed her forehead. It would be much easier to think if her head didn't hurt so much.

"Come." He took her arm. Charles had left at the beginning of their argument—if it was an argument. "We'll have something to eat and be on our way."

Her stomach tightened further into a hard knot. Eating did not sound like an inspired notion.

He was married. The deed was done. He was committed.

He sat by Miss Peterson—he couldn't keep calling her that—at the wedding breakfast.

At least Knightsdale hadn't flattened him. Actually, it had been a relief to see some anger. He would be furious if any man treated his sisters the way he had treated Miss—Meg. He *had* been furious on Jane's behalf last year, but that had all turned out well. Perhaps. He smiled slightly. Lord Motton had better get home before his heir was born or Jane might sell the baby to the highest bidder—or just the first bidder. Hell, she might give the child away.

Meg was pushing the paper thin slices of ham around her plate.

"Aren't you hungry?"

"No." She pressed her lips together. "I don't feel quite the thing."

She *was* pale—actually a little green.

"Would you prefer to leave now?"

She nodded. "If you—and your mother and Miss Witherspoon—don't mind."

"Of course not. Mother and Miss Witherspoon are traveling in a separate carriage in any event, so you and

I can leave whenever it suits you. Are your bags ready? Do you have anything left to pack?"

She pressed her lips together again and shook her head. He stood.

"If you will excuse us, Mis—my wife would like to leave."

"What, before the toasts?" Westbrooke grinned. "I have an excellent one prepared especially for you, Parks."

That was definitely a treat to be missed. He took Meg's arm and helped her to stand. "So sorry. We really must get on the road."

"I've already had Meg's luggage loaded onto the carriage, Parker-Roth." Knightsdale grinned. "And I've sent the announcement off to all the papers."

"My thanks." Parks looked at Meg as she hugged her father, her step-mother, her sister, Knightsdale's nieces, and Lady Westbrooke goodbye. Her color was definitely not good. Perhaps once she was in the quiet of the carriage, she would improve.

"Take care of my daughter, sir."

He took Reverend Peterson's hand. "I will try my best."

"That's all we can ask." Reverend Peterson smiled. "Meg does have a mind of her own, you know."

That was an understatement. "I've noticed."

Reverend Peterson laughed.

All the ladies were crying as Parks led his wife down the front stairs to the waiting coach.

"Be sure to write, Meg," Lady Knightsdale said.

"Often," Lady Westbrooke said.

Miss Peterson—Meg—just waved and let him help her into the carriage. Once he saw she was settled, he knocked on the roof, and Ned gave the horses their office to start. The carriage pulled away.

They were alone.

Miss Peterson stared at her hands clasped tightly in her lap. He shifted in his seat. It was going to be a very long trip to the Priory, but at least there was one subject he could address immediately.

"You know, I cannot keep calling you Miss Peterson."

She nodded.

"Should I call you Margaret? Or would you prefer Meg? I noticed your family calls you Meg." He was chattering. He stopped.

"M-Meg is fine."

Well, at least she'd said something.

"And you must call me John."

She nodded. "J-John . . ."

"Yes?" Her voice was so low and strained.

"John, I think . . . I'm . . ." She swallowed. "I'm g-going to be sic—"

Unfortunately he had not packed a chamber pot. He offered her the only receptacle he could think of—his best high-crowned beaver. He snatched it off his head and handed it to her just in time to spare the carriage floor.

Chapter 19

"Welcome to the Priory, Miss—um . . ." Mr. Park—*John's* father grinned. "Well, you're Mrs. Parker-Roth now, but that's going to get dashed confusing—and as you'll soon learn, this house is confusing enough. What do you want me to call you?"

"Everyone calls me Meg, sir." She felt as if she were looking at *her* Mr. Parker-Roth, just thirty years older. Except for the eye color—this man had blue eyes while his son had green—the gray hair, and the lines around the eyes and mouth, the two men could have been twins.

Physically twins. Their temperaments appeared to be as different as night and day. She glanced around the small, cramped office. She could not picture her Mr. Parker-Roth in such a disordered environment. Books were shoved every which way on the shelves and stacked in piles on the floor. Some—victims of gravity or an incautious foot—cascaded under chairs. Papers littered every horizontal surface, and she feared she saw a corner of toast peeking out from a mound of used blotting paper.

Her eyes came back to her host. He wore a dark,

loose garment that might once have been blue, but was now mostly gray with an ancient ink stain on the breast. His fingers, long and well-manicured, were also ink stained, much like Papa's.

"What should I call you?"

He shrugged. "Whatever you like. John calls me Father; the rest call me Da"—he grinned again, his eyes behind his spectacles crinkling with amusement—"when they aren't calling me something worse."

"I see." He was much too informal to fit "Father." It would have to be "Da." "I suppose I'll—"

"Damn and blast!" A very pregnant woman shoved open the door. She stopped abruptly on the threshold. "Oh, sorry." She grinned. "You must be John's new wife."

"Yes. I'm Meg Pe—" No, she wasn't Meg Peterson any longer. She repressed a sigh. This would take some getting used to. "I'm Meg."

The woman stuck out her hand and Meg grasped it. "I'm John's sister, Jane." She patted her belly. "The married one."

"The very short-tempered one," Mr. Parker-Roth said.

Jane laughed and pushed a pile of papers off a chair so she could sit.

"You'd be short-tempered, too, Da, if you looked like a snake that's swallowed a goat."

"I would be more than short-tempered. I would be dumbfounded—and that doesn't begin to describe what your mother's reaction would be."

Jane snorted. "Very funny." She turned to Meg. "Men! Trust me, if *they* were the ones condemned to carry babies in their bellies for nine months"—she shifted in the chair—"most of the time on their bladders, they'd keep their breeches buttoned."

Mr. Parker-Roth held up an ink-stained hand. "Jane, please, let's not send Meg screaming from the house yet."

Jane shrugged. "She's married, isn't she?"

"Barely."

"That's right." Jane grinned at Meg. "Shot the cat, didn't you? And now John's upstairs puking his guts out, and Mama and Agatha have collapsed in their beds." She frowned. "I'd better not get sick. To be retching and breeding at this stage would be beyond terrible."

"Yes. I hope you don't fall ill." Meg looked at Mr. Parker-Roth. "I am very sorry. My nephews were sick when I left. I must have gotten it from them."

He chuckled. "Puked in John's hat, MacGill said."

Would she ever recover from the embarrassment? "There was nothing else at hand." She swallowed. "Your son was quite the gentleman."

Jane hooted. "I wager he was. Lord, I'd love to have seen John holding a hatful of vomit."

"It was not amusing."

"No, I suppose not." Jane was still grinning. "John must really be in love."

Meg did not have the courage to tell them the real story. Perhaps when . . . John . . . had recovered, he would tell his family the particulars of their marriage. Or Mrs. Parker-Roth would tell her husband. There had not been time for that. They'd arrived not even half an hour ago. John had bolted for his room; his mother and Miss Witherspoon, still slightly green around the gills, had tottered off to lie down and recoup their strength. At least the women were almost recovered from the malady.

The bemused butler had led Meg here.

"Did you have a reason for bursting in, Jane?"

Jane shrugged again. "Not really."

"Just wanted to deliver your daily tirade on Motton's absence?"

"Right." She looked at Meg. "Viscount Motton is my husband—my *missing* husband. He is off attending his dying aunt in Dorset."

"The aunt who cannot die quickly enough for Jane's tastes."

"I am not so unfeeling." Jane frowned. "However, she will die whether he is there or not."

"Just as this baby will be born whether he is here or not."

"But it is *his* baby! This"—she touched her stomach—"is at least partly his fault. If I have to be here, he should, too."

Mr. Parker-Roth rolled his eyes. "We can hope Motton's aunt is thoughtful enough to expire promptly. Meanwhile, do you suppose you could show Meg up to the yellow bedroom? I'm sure Claybourne has already had her things taken up."

"All right. It's better than sitting here moaning."

"Definitely, especially as I would like to return to my sonnet." Mr. Parker-Roth smiled at Meg. "Don't let Jane alarm you. Her bark is definitely worse than her bite."

Jane heaved herself out of her chair. "Unless your name is Viscount Motton."

Meg followed Jane out of the room. They started up the stairs, but Jane had to stop every few feet and rest.

"Are you all right?"

"Yes, I'm fine."

Meg put her hand on Jane's arm. "Certainly someone else could show me to my room."

"No, no, Da is right. It's better for me to be doing something other than moping around." She smiled, though Meg thought her effort was slightly strained. "And Da really did want to get back to his poetry. I assume John has told you all about our odd family?"

A reasonable assumption, if theirs had been a normal courtship. "No, not really."

Jane grabbed her side.

"Are you *sure* you're all right?"

"Yes, it's just a stitch. I've been getting them for the last few days. There's just not enough room inside me for this baby anymore." She held onto the banister and breathed deeply.

"When is the baby due?"

"Not for another month—and first babies always come late." She took another breath and let it out slowly. "That's better." She continued up the stairs. "So John didn't tell you about our family?"

"No."

She smiled down at Meg from two steps above. "A whirlwind courtship? Never thought John was so impassioned!"

Meg smiled weakly. "It's, um, a little complicated."

Jane looked as if she might press the issue, but apparently thought better of it. She turned back to climb another step.

"About our family—I prefer to think of us as adventurous or eccentric rather than odd. The one who's odd, really, is John. To use a horticultural simile, John is like a topiary . . . pig in the middle of a forest. We think he's a changeling."

John, a topiary pig? How absurd! "What do you mean?"

"Haven't you noticed? He is so very orderly and proper." Jane grinned, one eyebrow flying up to meet her hairline. "Or maybe he hasn't been so very proper with you?"

Meg flushed. She was not going to discuss John's impropriety with his sister. "And the rest of you are not proper? Your mother seems perfectly unexceptional."

"She can behave in company—well, we all can—but

she's an artist." Jane laughed. "Wait until you see her studio before you decide how proper she is. Da is a poet—you saw how properly he dresses. Mama makes him clean up for company, but no matter what he puts on, it still looks . . . not improper so much as disheveled. John is never disheveled." She waggled her eyebrows. "Is he?"

Meg ignored her. "John is the oldest?"

"Yes. Stephen's next—he's two years younger than John. He roams the world, collecting plants for John and doing Lord knows what else. I think he's a pirate. I'm twenty-five"—she patted her belly—"and I *had* to get married. Nicholas, who's at Oxford when he isn't being sent down for some prank, is twenty-one. Juliana's sixteen and a scientist—she's often blowing up things. And Lucy is fourteen and wishes to write the sequel to Mary Wollstonecraft's *A Vindication of the Rights of Woman.*"

They finally reached the top of the stairs. Jane turned right, and Meg followed her down a long corridor hung with unpleasantly graphic hunting paintings.

"Ugly, aren't they? Mama has to avert her eyes, but Da thinks they're funny. One of his ancestors must have been an avid huntsman—or just an atrocious judge of art."

Meg averted her eyes as well. "Will I meet Juliana and Lucy tonight?"

"Oh, no. They've been sent off to visit Aunt Reliham. Mama felt their presence would be too upsetting to someone in my delicate condition."

"I see."

"Eventually you will. Here's your room."

They had almost reached the end of the corridor. There was one more door beyond the one they'd stopped at.

"And that is . . . ?" Meg was almost certain she knew the answer, but she wished to hear her suspicions confirmed.

"John's room, of course." Jane grinned. "Don't worry—there's a connecting door. You'll be able to—oh."

Jane bent over, leaning against the wall next to an unfortunate depiction of a dead fox. "Ohh . . . I-I think . . . I think perhaps f-first babies do not always come l-late."

Death would be welcome.

Parks curled into a ball on his bed. Thank God the Priory had not been another hundred yards down the road. He would never have made it.

"Are ye gonna let me help ye out of yer clothes now?"

He grunted. Was Mac crazy? Even opening his eyes was too much movement.

"Ye'll be more comfortable in yer nightclothes."

"Shut up. Go away."

"All right. I've brought ye a nice clean bowl in case ye need it."

God, surely there was nothing left in his aching gut! He opened one eye and found a large ceramic bowl in front of his nose. It was close enough he could identify the decorative figures as painted blue pigs without his spectacles.

He closed his eye and grunted again.

"I'll be back later." Mac draped a blanket over him. "Maybe ye'll sleep a bit and be in a better temper then."

He heard Mac's footsteps cross the floor, and the door open and shut.

He let out a shuddering breath. He was alone at last, free to suffer without an audience. If Meg's and the other ladies' experience of the disease was any guide, he need only endure another twelve hours of intense discomfort before he began to recover. He put his cheek against the cool ceramic bowl and waited for time to pass.

He must have dozed because he startled when he heard footsteps again. His stomach twisted.

If he lay very still perhaps he would not be sick again.

"Go away, Mac. You can strip me bare if you want, but not now."

"I'm not Mac," a female voice said. "Would you like me to get him?"

"What?" He sat up quickly—a very big mistake. Fortunately the bowl was still at hand. He emptied what little remained in his stomach and then heaved helplessly for a few more minutes.

"I'm so sorry," Meg said.

She stood by his bed—by his heaving, weak body. Why in God's name didn't she have the decency to leave?

He flopped back on his pillows, and she picked up the bowl full of vomit and took it away.

He was going to die of embarrassment before he died of this bloody illness. He closed his eyes. God, let him die now.

God wasn't listening. He heard Meg's footsteps returning.

"I'm so sorry I've made you ill."

"It's not your fault." Perhaps if he kept his eyes closed she would leave.

"Yes, it is."

He heard the sound of chair legs sliding over the carpet. He sighed and opened his eyes. Clearly, she was not leaving anytime soon.

She handed him a clean bowl. "And I ruined your good hat, too."

He took the bowl from her and put it on the bed within reach. "Don't give it another thought."

Meg plucked at her skirt. "If I had not gone to the Horticultural Society meeting, you would not have been obliged to wed me."

How many times were they going to have this conversation?

"Stop blaming yourself. As I have already told you, our marriage is not your fault." Nor, obviously, was it her wish. Did she want a title that much? Her only chance now was if he died young.

His stomach clenched and he moved the basin closer. The way he felt at the moment, he'd happily oblige her.

"That is very kind of you to say, but, well . . ."

His glare must have impressed her, because she stopped and shrugged. "I didn't come here to argue with you. Your mother sent me to tell you Jane has had a son."

"Really?" He inched up on his pillow. "That was fast." He must have slept longer than he'd thought. Mac had pulled the curtains before he'd left, so he had no idea what time it was. "She and the baby are well?"

Meg grinned. "Very well. And it was not so fast. After talking to Jane's maid, your mother thinks Jane has been in labor for the last few days. Still, hard labor *was* quick, and the best news is Lord Motton arrived at the same time as the midwife, a good twenty minutes before his son was born."

"That's fortunate. Jane might have castra—cared if he'd missed the event."

Meg grinned. "He seems—they both seem—very happy."

Something besides nausea stabbed at his gut.

What was the matter with him? Well, he knew what

was the matter—this mawkishness must be related to
his illness. He'd never felt this—God!—weepy over a
baby's birth before. He certainly remembered Lucy's
and Juliana's babyhoods well enough to know infants
were noisy, messy, inconvenient creatures.

He shifted on the pillows as his gut clenched again.

Westbrooke seemed uncommonly fond of his child.

Of course he was. The man needed an heir and had
been uncertain as to his abilities in that department.
He must be very relieved to have the job done.

He didn't have those concerns. And to be truthful,
doing anything more strenuous than breathing at the
moment was out of the question.

"You shouldn't be trying to sleep in all your clothes.
Shall I help you—"

"No!"

She looked offended at his vehemence. Was she
crazy? He was not going to let her strip him when he
still felt like he might puke at any moment.

She flushed. "We are married. Wives are supposed to
care for their husbands."

"Thank you for the offer, but I would prefer you send
MacGill in to help me."

She stood up. "Very well. If that is what you would
prefer."

"Yes. Definitely."

He heaved a sigh of relief when the door closed
behind her.

"Jane and the baby are doing well, Cecilia?"

"Splendidly. Jane was very brave, John." Mrs. Parker-
Roth poured some water into the wash basin and chuckled. "Well, perhaps it was more that she was desperate

not to be pregnant any longer. I'm just happy I made it home before the baby was born."

Her husband snorted. "I'm certain Jane would have managed well enough without you."

"No doubt, but a mother belongs at her daughter's side during such a time." She splashed water on her face. To think she might have stayed in London and missed the birth of her first grandchild! Thank God for the scandal and the hurried wedding. Still, she'd been certain she'd had another couple weeks. "I think Jane must have miscalculated."

"I think Jane must have anticipated her vows."

"Of course she did. They *were* caught in a very compromising situation. Still, I admit to being a little surprised. I didn't think Edmund would have . . . I mean, he's not the kind of man to . . ." She shrugged. "Well, that's neither here nor there. Everything turned out for the best."

John grunted. "At least Motton got here in time. Claybourne told me he arrived with the midwife."

"Yes, indeed. Jane was delighted to see him. She spent every breath she could spare cursing him. Quite took her mind off her worries."

"Then it's a good thing she didn't have a knife at hand. The man might have found himself separated from his testicles. Jane has not been a very pleasant companion these last few weeks."

"Poor thing. I'm sure she was most uncomfortable."

"She was not the only one."

"John, you need to have some sympathy."

"I *had* some sympathy. It left about a week ago."

Cecilia paused in washing her face. John's voice was decidedly testy. She smiled. She knew exactly what he needed. She was too excited to sleep anyway.

"How did Motton hold up to her abuse?"

"Well enough," she said. "He seemed not to take offense. He knows her—and I think he knows how hard his absence has been for her." She dried her face.

"Jane had best watch that her waspish tongue doesn't send him into some other, more congenial bed."

"My, you *are* in a bad mood this evening."

"I'm not."

"You are." She picked up her brush. For a poet, he was not being terribly eloquent. No matter. She would shortly give him plenty of opportunity to show how nimble his tongue was.

She shivered in anticipation. She had missed him, too.

"I assume Motton's aunt finally cocked up her toes?"

She laughed. "No. Edmund said she had a miraculous recovery. She'll probably stage another deathbed scene when she gets lonely again. He did promise to bring the baby by so she could see him—that's what made her perk up." She pulled her brush through her hair. Perhaps she would not do a hundred strokes tonight. A different part of her body longed for a different kind of stroking. She would just get the worst of the tangles out. "Oh, John, the baby is so precious. Can you believe he has a thick head of brown curls? He must get that from Edmund's side."

"Didn't ours have hair?"

"Of course not! Don't you remember? They were all so bald, we couldn't tell what color their hair was until they were a year old."

How could the man not remember? Well, it *was* many years ago. Lucy, the baby, was already fourteen. Where did the time go? She looked at herself in the mirror. There were definitely more wrinkles around her eyes and lips; more gray in her hair. And now there was a grandbaby. One . . . maybe more . . .

"What do you think of your new daughter-in-law?"

"She seems nice enough. She didn't get the best introduction to the Priory, though. Claybourne dumped her in my office when you all deserted her. And then Jane came in to complain, in excruciating detail, about the woes of pregnancy."

"I am sorry about that. I should have stayed with Meg, but I felt so dreadful. I do hope Pinky is on the mend."

"You know John doesn't like to be called Pinky, Cecilia."

"Johnny, then."

"And *Johnny* is over thirty. He's well past needing a mother."

"Everyone—every *man*—needs a mother, at least until he is married." She put down her brush. Meg and Johnny were married, but there was still something keeping them apart. What? Why had Johnny fought the match so hard? Any clod pole could see they were meant for each other—any clod pole besides her son, apparently.

He wasn't really still wearing the willow for Lady Grace Dawson, was he? Had he sworn off all women because he'd been left at the altar? Surely not. Yes, it had been a very unpleasant experience, but it had happened years ago. It was in the past. He needed to look to the future.

She turned to face her husband. He was propped up in bed, reading a book—more poetry, no doubt.

She loved looking at him, as her many paintings attested. Agatha was correct in that regard. She *had* fallen in love with a pair of broad shoulders—and with the man who came with those shoulders. He understood her as no one else did, and he'd given her six children whom she loved beyond life. How could she have chosen art over marriage?

And she had her art, just not in the single-minded way she would have if she'd done what Agatha had advised.

Was Johnny choosing work over love—was that the problem? He was safely married now, but he was stubborn enough to deny he felt anything more than lust for his wife—if he would even admit to that emotion. She sighed. She almost wished a fire would sweep through his blasted gardens and greenhouses, so he would pull his head out of the compost long enough to see the world around him.

"What's the matter?"

"I think we need to come up with a plan to bring Johnny and Meg together."

"They *are* together, Cecilia. They are married. How much more together can they be?"

"Well, yes, they've said their vows, but they aren't *together*, if you know what I mean."

John pushed his spectacles up his nose. "No, I don't know what you mean."

"Don't be such a nodcock. I'm quite sure they haven't consummated the marriage."

"Well, why didn't you just say so instead of beating around the bush? You've been in London too long. You've picked up their mealy-mouthed ways."

She wouldn't call Lady Dunlee mealy-mouthed, but it was true she'd been in London too long. She wet her lips. She was so glad John eschewed nightshirts, preferring to sleep in the buff. The glow of candlelight on his skin—on the strong column of his neck, the sweeping line of his shoulders, the thick graying hair curling across his chest—demanded that she paint him . . . after she did other things, of course.

She loved his body. She'd loved it when they were newly married, and she loved it now when he'd passed his sixtieth birthday.

"Not everyone ignores the proprieties like Jane and Edmund," he said. "And it's a little difficult to be busy between the sheets if you're busy puking your guts up. I'm sure they'll get around to attending to matters once they are both healthy."

"I don't know. Johnny can be very . . . pigheaded."

"Not *that* pigheaded. He is a man, Cecilia. Leave him alone and he'll do his duty."

"And what is Meg to be doing while she's waiting for Johnny's animal instincts to get the better of him?"

"Just that—waiting."

"Pshaw! Meg has a very strong personality. I doubt she'll be willing to sit around netting or embroidering handkerchiefs while the idiot boy makes up his mind to be a husband."

John shrugged. "If she's so bloody strong-willed, she can seduce him. I assume the door between their rooms works in both directions."

"Seduce him? Are you—" Wait, why *couldn't* Meg seduce Johnny? It was not the way most virgins climbed into their marriage beds—and she did indeed think Meg was a virgin, no matter what the London gabble grinders whispered—but that was not to say it wouldn't work perfectly well. Of course it would. As John had said, Johnny *was* a man. He might not be a rake, but he knew how the relevant organ operated. He did have a mistress in the village.

Cecilia frowned. "Do you suppose you should have a word with Mrs. Haddon?"

"Definitely not." John scowled at her. "You are not supposed to know of her existence."

"Of course I know of her existence. I make it a point to know everything I can about my children."

He snorted and turned back to his poetry. "Stop meddling, Cecilia."

"Hmm." She smiled slightly. Perhaps the mistress was not an issue. She must remember the way Johnny had watched Meg in the London ballrooms. He just needed a little encouragement. A little privacy. A little seduction.

She could teach Meg a thing or two about seduction. She loosened her dressing gown and let it slide off her shoulders. "Perhaps you are right. Having Meg seduce Johnny might work."

"Of course it will—" John sat up, closing his book with a snap. "*What* do you have on?"

"Just a little something I found in London." A very little something. The sheer scraps of willow green barely covered her crucial parts. She spread out her bare arms and turned, feeling the silky cloth slide over her breasts and flutter around her thighs. "Do you like it?"

"It is indecent."

"Of course it is—but do you like it?" She made certain she had the fire behind her.

John growled and pulled the bedcovers back.

"Come here and I'll show you just how much I like it."

Chapter 20

"What a beautiful baby." Lady Felicity—Lady Bennington, now—cooed at the Honorable Winthrop Jonathan Smyth, Lord Motton's new son and heir. The Honorable Winthrop Jonathan Smyth, reclining in his mother's arms, yawned.

"He's a good baby," Jane said. "He sleeps most of the night already."

Meg repressed a smile. Jane, who had been complaining vociferously about entertaining "that leg of mutton dressed as lamb," was now beaming at Felicity as if she were her new best friend. And Felicity did seem genuinely taken with the baby.

"You are so fortunate to be delivered of such a healthy boy," Felicity said. "I'm hopeful of presenting my husband with an heir as soon as may be." She giggled. "Bennie is certainly very eager to be a papa—and very conscientious in his efforts to realize that goal."

Meg dropped her gaze quickly to her hands, folded in her lap. To think of Lord Bennington's slug-like lips in close proximity to her person—ick! She was certainly glad she did not have to suffer that man's attentions.

She did not have to suffer any man's attentions. It

had been three weeks since her marriage and still the door between her room and John's remained closed.

She shifted in her chair. It made perfect sense, really. Things had been very unsettled. She had been sick—it had taken her a while to recover completely from the revolting illness she'd caught from Charlie—and then John had been sick as well. Jane had had her baby. There'd been estate business for John to deal with—his father delegated to him the running of the Priory. A new shipment of exotic plants had arrived while John was in London, so he'd spent a lot of time in his greenhouses cataloguing and coddling his new acquisitions.

She would have liked to have helped him with that at least. She might not be as knowledgeable as he, but she was far from a total ignoramus. But he hadn't asked for her assistance. In fact, she'd gotten the very clear impression he wanted her to stay as far from him and his plants as possible.

She sighed. The situation could not continue as it was. She had to talk to him. She would . . . soon.

Felicity leaned over and touched her knee. "Sighing over your husband?"

"Uh . . ." Meg looked to Jane for help, but her sister-in-law was concentrating on nursing her son. Her lips were pressed tightly together, her jaw clenched. She obviously wished to let loose her normal string of curses when the baby latched on to her breast, but refused to do so in Felicity's presence.

Mrs. Parker-Roth had assured Jane her nipples would toughen up any day and then breastfeeding would cease to be such torture. Jane was not mollified. She was not a terribly patient woman.

Felicity was sighing herself. "I find I like married life much more than I could ever have imagined." She shook her head as if in wonderment. "Bennie may seem dull as ditchwater on the surface, but he's not. Well, I suppose someone else might find him so, but I don't." She grinned. "And he's surprisingly satisfying in bed. Of course, it helps that he has an impressive coc—"

"Yes, well, indeed, I'm glad you are so happy." Surely the woman was not going to discuss what went on behind the closed door of her bedchamber?

Felicity frowned. "You sound like a virgin."

"Don't be ridiculous. I've been married three weeks."

"You *are* a virgin, aren't you?"

Wild horses would not draw *that* truth from her lips. "Do you miss London?"

"Of course not." Felicity rolled her eyes. "You had your own scandal brewing, so I'm sure you didn't pay attention to the tittle-tattle about my father. He fled England under a cloud of debt. I won't be returning to any London ballrooms until I've presented Bennie with his heir."

"I see."

The worst of Jane's torture must be over. She was smiling now and running her fingers through the baby's thick brown curls, but she still wasn't attending to the conversation.

"Let me give you some advice," Felicity said, leaning close. "Technically, I was a virgin on my wedding night—well, my wedding trip—but I've had extensive experience with men. They are simple creatures. Unless Parker-Roth is . . . odd, he just needs a little encouragement to do his duty."

"Encouragement?" Meg had once counseled Lizzie on how to bring Robbie up to scratch. She'd spent hours and hours observing the social interactions of men and women. She'd thought herself an expert, but she was not. Being a participant was vastly different from being an observer.

"Yes. It is not terribly subtle, but I guarantee it will do the trick." Felicity grinned. "Just show up naked in the man's bed."

"No hard feelings, are there, Parker-Roth?"

Bennington stood on the other side of the study. He could not have put more distance between them had he tried—and he had tried. The moment his foot had crossed the threshold, he'd moved as far from Parks as he could, which suited Parks perfectly. With any luck, Felicity would get tired of admiring Jane's baby soon and take her husband home.

"Hard feelings?" Of course there were hard feelings. Bennington hated him—and he'd have to admit, he didn't care much for Bennington. Though besides the fact the man was avoiding him, the viscount seemed surprisingly mellow. Marriage must agree with him.

He wished he could say the same for himself.

He smiled and clasped his hands tightly behind his back.

"Why would I harbor any hard feelings?"

Bennington raised his eyebrows. "If I hadn't been out in Palmerson's garden with Miss Peterson—I mean, your wife now, of course—you would not have found yourself compelled to offer for her."

"Are you suggesting I was forced into marriage?" He had been, but he did not care for Bennington saying so.

Bennington blinked. "It's not precisely a secret, though now that I consider the matter, the events at the Palmerson ball are not those mentioned when your nuptials are whispered about. Lord Peter scribbled something about you kissing Fonsby—"

"Good God, are you mad?! I bloody well did *not* kiss

Lord Fonsby! The thought is revolting. Repugnant. Loathsome." The English language did not contain a word strong enough to describe the horror that mental image evoked.

"I didn't think you had—Lord Peter has a terrible scrawl. But I'd say something unusual happened. Tundrow, whose hand is quite legible, wrote to say you'd been tossed out of the Horticultural Society." Bennington couldn't suppress his grin, though he did try. "Sorry to hear it."

Right. "It was only a misunderstanding. I'm quite confident I can have my membership reinstated should I choose to do so."

"Oh? Might you choose not to?"

Parks shrugged. The thought of going back to London was more unpleasant than ever, but in a few months his mother was certain to want to see her artist friends again. And his . . . wife . . . might want to go, as well. He should make the effort to establish her in society, especially since their marriage had been—was still, apparently—such an *on-dit*.

"I suppose I might—when I get around to it, of course."

"Of course."

Bennington smiled briefly, then turned to examine the bookshelves. Parks examined the carpet.

What was he going to do about his wife? The door between their rooms might as well be nailed shut.

She had not wanted to marry him. She'd wanted a title to match the title her sister had captured. Any woman would. She'd just been unlucky that Lady Dunlee had stumbled upon her with *him* in Palmerson's garden. If he'd left her to her own devices, she might be a viscountess now. And though dressing as a man and attending the Horticultural Society meeting had been beyond shocking, she would have escaped unnoticed if he hadn't chosen to maul her in front of half the *ton*.

It was really his fault she was condemned to be merely Mrs. Parker-Roth instead of Lady Somebody.

Claybourne stuck his head into the study. "My lord, Lady Bennington is ready to depart."

"Ah! Thank you, Claybourne." Bennington bolted for the door. "Glad we spent this time together, Parker-Roth. Cleared the air, heh?"

"Well—"

He was left addressing only the air.

Did Bennington really believe he would attack him with amorous designs? Unbelievable—though apparently most of London believed it.

He needed to have things out with Meg . . . but not quite yet.

He slipped out the side door and headed for the main greenhouse.

It really didn't matter that Meg had had her heart set on a title. She was married to him now. And he was married to her. They had no choice—they must just make the best of it.

It was his duty to take the first step. He had only to open the damn door between their rooms—Mac had threatened to open it for him any time this past week.

He didn't want to do it.

What *was* the matter with him?

It wasn't that he didn't want Meg. God, he needed to drug himself with brandy to fall asleep, and even then he woke hard as a poker in the middle of the night. His dreams were . . .

He wouldn't think about his dreams.

He couldn't even visit Cat for relief. Not only would it be a betrayal of his marriage vows, but she'd already found his replacement. He'd stopped by her cottage to give her her congé and a diamond necklace he'd bought in London to assuage her exacerbated sensibilities, and discovered she was planning to marry the blacksmith.

Did no one care for *him*?

He stepped into the greenhouse and took a deep breath of the warm, moist air, full of the calming scent of dirt and growing things—only he didn't feel calmed today.

"What the hell are ye doing here, Johnny?" Thomas MacGill frowned at him from the potting table.

"It's my greenhouse, Thomas. I think I'm entitled to be here if I wish."

MacGill grunted and went back to repotting a fuchsia plant.

Parks looked around. He had work to do, lots of work . . . he just couldn't decide what to do first.

"How are the new plants coming?"

"Fine." MacGill sent him a disparaging look. "Better than yer new wife is, according to William."

"Thomas!" Not for the first time Parks considered the disadvantages of having his valet's twin as his head gardener. "My wife is neither yours nor your brother's concern."

"But she *is* yer concern, Johnny."

"Thomas . . ." He also wished he'd had the foresight to hire proper English servants and not these upstart Scots who did not know their place.

"She was in here the other day."

"She was?" He should take Meg for a tour of his gardens. She would enjoy it. "Well, that's not surprising. Meg is very knowledgeable about plants, as I'm sure you discovered."

MacGill nodded. "Aye, I did that. And I discovered something else."

Why did he have a bad feeling about this? MacGill looked far too serious—very much the dour Scot. "What was that?"

"Yer wife's not happy, Johnny."

Parks felt like he'd been punched in the gut. "Now, Thomas—"

MacGill glowered at him. "Don't 'Thomas' me, Johnny. It's been three weeks since yer wedding. Ye need to be fertilizing something besides yer rose beds."

"Meg, may I speak with you?"

"Of course, Mrs., um . . ."

"Call me mother, dear." Mrs. Parker-Roth patted Meg on the arm. "I do think of you as one of my daughters, you know."

"Oh. Um. All right. M-mother."

"Let's go down to my studio. We can have a comfortable coze there without fear of being interrupted."

An interruption might be a good thing, depending on the conversational topic, but Meg went along without protest.

Mrs. Parker-Roth's studio was in a cottage orné on the other side of an ornamental lake.

"John—my husband, John, that is, not *your* husband—often comes here to concentrate on his sonnets," Mrs. Parker-Roth said as they approached the building. It was larger than Papa's vicarage. "He says the walk clears his head—and makes everyone else consider carefully whether they really need his attention. When the children were young, they'd run to him to settle their fights. When they reached the lake, though, they'd get distracted. The girls stopped to gather wildflowers; the boys, to skip stones. It saved John a lot of interruptions."

Mrs. Parker-Roth took a large key from her pocket and unlocked the door. "I like it because I can leave my paintings out and know they will not be disturbed." She grinned. "And, frankly, Johnny thinks many of my paintings are not appropriate for the children." She laughed. "Well, for anyone, really. Johnny is so easily embarrassed."

Meg followed Mrs. Parker-Roth into the darkened entry. The smells of paper, ink, paint, and turpentine enveloped her.

"Over here is my husband's study—you can see it's much larger than the one in the house."

It was indeed much larger—and just as messy.

"And here is my studio."

Meg looked into a large, airy room filled with sunlight. Canvases lined the walls.

"Would you like to see what I'm currently working on?"

"Yes, please." Why did John's mother have that glint of mischief in her eyes?

Mrs. Parker-Roth threw off the sheet that was draped over a large painting in the middle of the room. Meg stared at the image of a naked man reclining on a chaise-longue, legs carelessly bent to display his . . . well, fortunately that part of his anatomy was only sketched in broad outlines. Meg's attention traveled to the man's face.

Good God. She squeezed her eyes shut. It couldn't be. She cracked an eye open. It was.

Her father-in-law gazed back at her, a very sultry expression on his face.

Her mother-in-law giggled. "I've been trying to finish this painting for weeks, but, well, I, um"—thankfully she covered the canvas again, unfortunately she gestured toward the red and gold upholstered piece of furniture against the wall—"get distracted."

Meg took the long way back to the main house—the very long way. She was in no hurry to be among people. She listened to the roar of breaking waves and smelled salt in the air. She climbed a hill and gazed out over the sea. Storm clouds hung heavy in the sky; the water was gray and turbulent. Just like her thoughts.

What was she going to do about her marriage?

Her mother-in-law told her to seduce John, but could her opinion really be trusted? She had naked paintings of—Meg shook her head in a vain attempt to dislodge the image.

Felicity had said essentially the same thing, but Felicity was hardly a pattern card of respectability.

What did Meg know of seduction anyway? It was ridiculous. John would laugh himself senseless should she be foolish enough to attempt it.

Yet they had been married three weeks, and there had not been even a whisper of seduction from John. Of course, he'd been sick at first, too sick to do anything involving a bed besides sleep. And then he'd been busy with his plants and estate business. She had been busy as well, helping Jane and Mrs. Parker-Roth with the new baby. There hadn't been much time . . .

There had been three weeks.

She bit her lip. She'd hardly seen John since they'd arrived at the Priory; they'd exchanged a handful of words—and nothing else.

To be brutally honest, he was avoiding her.

The wind tried to rip her bonnet from her head; she untied its strings and let the cool air rush over her heated face, drying her tears.

She should be happy. She had acres of land to explore and a dizzying wealth of plants to examine.

She wasn't happy. The sad—the alarming—truth was, for the first time in her memory, she truly did not care what grew under her feet.

She was interested in babies. In Jane's tiny son. In having a child of her own.

Surely John would get around to doing his duty eventually. She need only be patient.

Or would he? He didn't need an heir. He hadn't married her because he wanted to, but to avoid a horrific scandal—a scandal she had caused. He must hate her.

And then there was Lady Grace Dawson. Mrs. Parker-Roth assured her John no longer pined for his former betrothed. That his primary feeling was—had always been—embarrassment. That he had never loved the woman.

How did Mrs. Parker-Roth know? She'd admitted John had not told her. She'd merely cited mother's intuition.

But then why had John never married until now, when he was forced to do so?

She wiped her eyes. What was the matter with her? Love had not been part of her plans. She'd wanted a home of her own, which she now had. She'd been willing to have a child, but not anxious to do so.

Now she *was* anxious.

She started walking again, the motion helping marshal her thoughts.

Surely John must understand Lady Dawson was beyond his reach. She was married, happily by all accounts. His love was destined to be unrequited.

And love wasn't necessary to accomplish the procreative procedure anyway. He'd been able to manage the deed with his mistress; surely he could accomplish it with her. Really, it would be vastly more convenient for him. Instead of going into the village, perhaps in the rain and cold, he need only step through a door into her room. Or she would step into his room. He would not have to leave the comfort of his own home.

With luck, he wouldn't have to exert himself too many times before her goal was accomplished.

It was a simple plan. What could he object to?

Unless he hated her for trapping him into marriage. Lack of love should not be an issue, but hate? That might indeed be a problem.

She turned away from the sea and shoved her bonnet back on. The indecision and uncertainty had gone on long enough. She would approach John tonight. She would ask him for a child.

If she didn't puke first.

"Are ye ever gonna visit yer wife's bed, Johnny?"

"MacGill!" Bloody hell. First his head gardener, now his valet. He should get rid of them both. "My marriage is none of your affair."

"Of course it is. Ye've been fashing about it ever since ye got home."

"I have not."

MacGill just lifted an eyebrow, damn him.

"I have been sick."

"Johnny, ye've been well fer at least two weeks—and ye were not that sick to begin with."

"Not that sick? I felt like I was dying."

MacGill snorted. "Aye, I'm sure ye did—fer a day or two. Yer appetite"—MacGill waggled his eyebrows—"is fine now, isn't it?"

He chose to ignore his valet's insinuation. "No, actually. I've not been very hungry at all."

"Because ye've been tying yer stomach in knots over yer marriage—or non-marriage. Ye've got to bed the lass, Johnny."

Bed Meg? Part of him leapt at the thought.

But how was he going to accomplish that feat? Just knock on her door and present himself? He should have done that two weeks—or more—ago. It was rather late now. He would feel like a fool.

"Hand me a new cravat, will you? I've ruined this one."

MacGill gave him more linen. "Go to her tonight, Johnny. There's no point in putting it off any longer."

Damn. He'd ruined another cravat.

"I don't . . . the thing is . . . well, as you know, the circumstances of our marriage were rather . . . unusual."

"What difference does that make? Ye're wed now, aren't ye?"

"Yes, but—"

"No buts, Johnny. Ye're bound by yer vows—both of ye."

MacGill was right—neither of them had a choice any longer. If Meg would have preferred to have married a title, well, it was unfortunate, but she would have to resign herself to her situation.

"It's only gentlemanly to visit her bed, ye know. Ye can visit yer mistress—"

"No, I can't. I would not dishonor my vows—and even if I would, she is marrying the blacksmith."

"Is she?" MacGill grinned. "Ye do know she was seeing him on the side?"

"I didn't know." He'd suspected he wasn't Cat's only customer. It stood to reason, since he'd visited her so infrequently, that she wouldn't be lying in bed waiting for him. Well, the lying in bed—yes; the waiting—no.

The blacksmith was welcome to her.

"As I was saying, it's only gentlemanly ye visit yer

wife's bed. She has needs, too, which she can satisfy only with ye."

"Needs?"

"Aye."

"What kind of needs?"

"Ack, Johnny, surely ye know women crave men just as men crave women?"

They did?

"I hadn't really thought about it." Was *that* why Meg had been luring men into the shrubbery? She certainly had been exceedingly passionate in *his* arms.

"Well, think on it. The poor lassie is likely half out of her mind with lust."

A jolt of lust—no, shock, definitely shock—shot through him to lodge in his most sensitive organ.

"MacGill! Meg is a gently bred young woman."

"She's a woman, Johnny, gently bred or no. I've seen the way she looks at ye. She's burning, man. Burning for ye."

Parks snorted. Damn, but he had been more than halfway to believing the Scottish bastard. He had *wanted* to believe him.

"Nice try, MacGill, but you got a little too dramatic at the end there. Next time stop before you get so carried away."

MacGill laughed. "I almost had ye though, didn't I?"

Parks was not going to answer that question. "Help me into my coat. It's time to go down to dinner."

MacGill held up his dark blue coat. "I wasn't completely joking, Johnny. Ye need to do something about yer marriage."

"I know." He slipped the coat on and straightened his cuffs. "I will attend to it."

"Tonight, Johnny. That's another thing I wasna

joking about. I've seen yer wife watching ye. She wants—she needs—ye in her bed."

If only MacGill were right. *Could* he be?

No. He must be mistaken.

MacGill was not usually mistaken about anything.

Well, there was only one way to find out. He would visit Meg's bed tonight. Then he would know.

A mix of dread and anticipation twisted his gut.

He went downstairs to try to consume some dinner.

Chapter 21

That had been the most uncomfortable dinner of her life.

Meg dropped her head into her hands and swallowed a groan. Thank God she was finally safe in her bedchamber. She should lock the door and never come out.

Every time she'd looked at her father-in-law, she'd seen the partially finished painting in Mrs. Parker-Roth's studio—and the red and gold chaise-longue nearby. If she averted her eyes to her mother-in-law, she found herself wondering how such an ordinary looking matron could engage in such wild—

No. She pulled on her hair and squeezed her eyes tightly shut in an attempt to expunge the thought.

And then there was John. Mrs. Parker-Roth had seated them together, of course. Well, that was to be expected. Lord Motton had eaten upstairs with Jane and the baby, so there were only Mr. and Mrs. Parker-Roth, John, and herself at table. And Miss Witherspoon. Thank God for Miss Witherspoon. The woman had prosed on and on about her trip to the Amazon. Meg had hung on every word.

All right, she had *pretended* to hang on every word. She had really been thinking about how to raise the question of children with her husband.

She had not come up with an answer. In fact, she had been so despairing of ever mentioning the topic that she'd considered—just for a moment, of course—running off to the Amazon with Miss Witherspoon.

She was still despairing.

She got up from her dressing table to examine her figure in the cheval glass. Mrs. Parker-Roth's maid—at some point she should acquire a maid of her own, she supposed—had helped her into her nightclothes—her very virginal nightclothes. The gown was white flannel and buttoned up to her chin.

It was not at all the thing to wear to a seduction.

She needed something very different, something that would make John mindless with lust. She wanted him to forget all his reservations and just do . . . it.

Surely once he'd done it the first time, he wouldn't be so shy about doing it again.

Unless he found the activity unpleasant.

She let out a long breath. *Would* he find it unpleasant? She couldn't say, obviously. She might well be clumsy and inept. It would be no surprise if she were— she had no experience. But she was a quick learner. If John were disappointed, he need only tell her what she must do differently. And if he wouldn't tell her, she must ask.

Though now that she considered the issue, he had not appeared bored or dissatisfied in Lady Palmerson's parlor or Lord Easthaven's garden—or on the street in front of Lord Fonsby's townhouse. Surely the activities he'd engaged in at those locations must be related to the procreative act.

Enough. Worrying about it served no purpose. She could only do her best.

She turned away from the looking glass to the wardrobe and pulled open a drawer. Her first step on her path to seduction must be to shed this voluminous gown. Fortunately, Emma had given her something more appropriate as a wedding gift.

She opened a small, insubstantial package. This nightgown was white also, but the similarity ended there. She held it up and blushed. It could not be as scandalous as it looked.

She very much feared it was. She pulled off her flannel nightgown and slipped the new gown over her head. The silky fabric slid over her body, caressing her skin. She went back to examine the effect in the looking glass.

Yes, indeed, it was very, very scandalous. Two thin straps attached to a tiny bodice that barely skimmed the tops of her breasts. The skirt flowed over her hips and around her legs—and was slit up to her thigh on one side. The fabric itself was almost transparent, revealing far more than it hid.

She could not walk into John's room like this. She grabbed a heavy woolen dressing gown, yanking it on before opening the connecting door.

Mr. MacGill spilled his cup of tea onto his lap. He leapt out of his chair.

"Oh dear. Are you all right?" Meg rushed forward.

"Yes, yes." The man mopped his pantaloons with a towel he'd grabbed from the washstand. "Don't fash yerself. The tea had cooled. No damage done." He paused with the towel pressed to his knee, looked up, and grinned. "And is there a reason ye're here, lassie?"

Meg flushed. "No. Well, that is, I was looking for my husband."

Mr. MacGill's grin widened. "I'm verra happy to hear it. Why don't ye wait for him? I'm sure he'll be along shortly. Or I could fetch him—"

"No!" She most certainly didn't want John dragged away from whatever he was doing. "No, thank you. Please don't do that. There's no hurry. I can wait." She glanced back at her room. She didn't want to sit here making small talk with John's valet. "I'll just go back—"

"Ah, don't do that. I'm sure Johnny would want ye to wait here. Please, make yerself comfortable. If ye're tired, ye can stretch out on the bed." Mr. MacGill looked as if he were hiding a smirk. "I was just going anyway."

"Well, if you're sure?"

"Lass, I was never surer of a thing in my life."

Mr. MacGill bowed and headed, whistling, for the door.

John hid in his study. His mother was trying to get his father to discuss his marital duty with him. Fortunately, Father was resisting.

He poured a glass of brandy, listening to the rain pelt the windows. The storm had come up after dinner. It would be good for the new plantings—the weather had been too dry recently.

The door opened and his father stuck his head in.

John put down his glass. "You aren't going to talk to me about what I think you are, are you?"

Father looked over his shoulder, nodded to someone in the hall, and slipped inside the room, shutting the door firmly behind him. "Pour me some brandy, Johnny."

"All right, but I won't listen to a lecture."

His father settled into the seat closest to the fire—
and farthest from the door.

"I suspect your mother has her ear to the keyhole."

"I suspect she does, too." John handed his father his
brandy, and then went over and opened the door. His
mother fell into the room.

"Wouldn't you be more comfortable sitting in here,
Mother?"

"Oh, no. I was just going up to bed."

John raised an eyebrow. His study was not on
Mother's way to her room—nor was hanging at key-
holes a normal pre-bedtime activity. "You're certain you
wouldn't like to join us?"

"Yes." She sent Father a very glaring look. "You must
have all sorts of male things to discuss. I would be very
much in the way."

Well, he certainly had no desire for her company. His
father had the good sense not to carp at him, but his
mother did not. "Good night, then."

Mother smiled at him. "Good night, Johnny. Don't
let your father keep you down here too long. Meg has
already gone up to bed, you know."

He didn't know. He nodded to his mother and then
watched her walk down the corridor to the stairs. He
turned back to the study. Father was pouring more
brandy.

"That was quick."

"Nerves." Father took another gulp. "She'll ask me
what happened when I get upstairs."

"Tell her you told me to do my duty and I said that I
would."

Father smiled broadly. "I will—and will you?"

"Will I what?"

"Do your duty?"

"Father! That is none of your business." John eyed

the brandy decanter, but resisted its lure for the moment. "You can't even complain you need me to carry on the line. You don't have a title and you do have two other sons. The Parker-Roth name is certain to survive another generation."

Father shrugged. "I know. It's just, well, the way things are now . . . it's not natural. You are wed and not wed. It disturbs your mother, and so it disturbs me."

"My marriage happened under unusual circumstances."

"Perhaps, but it *did* happen. Or, part of it happened. The consummation is still waiting."

"Father, please!"

"I imagine you know all about the mechanics, Johnny. You do—or did—have a mistress, but if you have questions—"

"I do not have any bloody questions." So his father—and of course his mother, damn it—knew about Cat. He should move to America. Maybe then he would have some privacy, though he wouldn't be surprised if Mother had spies in the New World, too.

"Didn't see how you could have." His father took another swallow of brandy. "We just want you to be happy, you know."

John sighed. It wasn't his father's fault things were in such a damnable coil. "I know. Rest assured that I am perfectly capable of doing my duty. I promise I shall resolve the issue shortly."

"Tonight?"

"Father!"

"Sorry. You know how your mother is when she gets the bit between her teeth."

"This is not her bit, for God's sake." He took a deep breath. "You can reassure Mother that I will—in my own time—attend to matters."

His father grunted. "Just don't make 'your own time' too long. I can stave her off for a day or two, but you know she'll start to meddle again if she thinks you still haven't—"

"Yes! Yes, I know." Mother wouldn't actually lock him naked in Meg's room until he displayed the blood-stained sheet—at least, he hoped she wouldn't—but she'd do just about anything else to see that matters were resolved to her satisfaction.

Father nodded and put down his half-empty brandy glass. "Very well. I'm for bed, then. I can tell your mother with a clear conscience that I did my best."

"Indeed you can."

John let out a long pent-up breath as soon as the door closed behind his father. First the MacGill brothers, now his parents. He would have no peace until he settled things with Meg.

He poured himself some more brandy and sprawled into the chair his father had vacated. It was not as if he were being forced to do something against his will. He had decided before dinner that he would seek Meg out tonight. It was, indeed, past time to resolve the issue.

What the hell was he going to say?

He took a large mouthful of brandy, holding it on his tongue, letting the fumes warm his mouth.

In a perfect world, he would have already wooed Meg in small stages. A drive in the park; a waltz; an accidental touch; a stolen kiss. In a perfect world, she would have chosen him, not been forced by scandal to save him from his social suicide.

In a perfect world, he would not have to negotiate his way into his wife's bed.

He swallowed the brandy in one gulp, almost enjoying the pain as it burned its way down his throat.

In *her* perfect world, he would have a title.

Did he really want to slide between the sheets of a woman who had been literally beating the bushes for a peer? Who had taken *Bennington* out into the shrubbery?

The rest of his body assured him he did.

Damn.

Well, there was no doubt he was physically attracted to the girl—he'd mauled her every time he'd gotten a moment alone with her. He closed his eyes briefly. And not so alone, as Lord Fonsby's many guests could attest.

Still, he couldn't spend his life in bed with her, could he?

He frowned down at the organ that had answered an enthusiastic 'yes.'

He dropped his head back against the chair and stared up at the shadows the fire threw on the ceiling.

It wasn't just her body he craved. She had a sharp mind. He'd noted it last year at Tynweith's house party. He didn't usually discuss serious topics like horticulture and gardening with females, so it had been very . . . stimulating to match wits with her over his favorite hobbies. And she certainly had plenty of integrity and courage. He smiled, remembering how she'd faced down her family—and his mother—in Lady Palmerson's parlor. Nor had she cowered before all the society gossips.

Of course she *had* engaged in a number of harebrained, beef-witted, cabbage-headed activities. Why she'd thought donning male attire and attending the Horticultural Society meeting was a good notion was beyond his comprehension. Displaying her legs for all the world to see . . .

Mmm. He took another sip of brandy and closed his eyes. He wouldn't mind seeing those lovely legs again. What would they look like naked? How would they feel wrapped around his?

He ached for her—and not just the obvious part of him ached. His mind, his heart ached, too. He wanted a companion, a lover, a friend. He wanted Meg.

He put his glass down and let himself out of his study. He must remember Meg's behavior was impossible to predict. Who would have thought a gently-bred miss would be dragging men into the shrubbery or parading down London's streets in pantaloons? She might tell him in no uncertain terms she wanted nothing to do with him.

What would he do then?

Yet she had married him. She was intelligent. She must see she was out of options—the time for compromise had come.

He climbed the stairs. Would she be asleep already? Should he wake her or wait until tomorrow night?

No, Father was right—he had to resolve matters sooner rather than later. Jane and Edmund would be leaving as soon as Jane and the baby could travel. Then Mother would have nothing to distract her from his business. She would be relentless.

He stopped in the corridor outside Meg's door. He should go to her through his room, but he did not care to encounter MacGill's knowing smirk. He glanced both ways. There was no one to see him.

He slipped through the door. The sitting room was dark, but the fire gave enough light for him to navigate without tripping or knocking anything over. It was so quiet. She must be asleep.

The door to her bedchamber was open. He paused to listen.

It was *too* quiet. He should hear something—the rustling of bedclothes, soft breathing . . . something. It was as still as death.

Good God! Certainly nothing dire had occurred?

He grabbed a candlestick, lit it in the fire, and held it high. Shadows whirled around the room. He stepped close to the bed, pushed aside the curtains.

The bed was empty, the coverlet smooth and undisturbed.

Where the bloody hell was his wife?

The door from her room banged open. Meg jumped, clutching Repton's *Sketches and Hints on Landscape Gardening* to her breast.

"What are you doing here?" John sounded extremely annoyed. This was obviously not the time to ask him if he might be willing to provide her with children.

"Er . . . I couldn't sleep. I was looking at your books. I hope you don't mind?"

He frowned and glanced around the room. "Where's MacGill?"

"He, um, left when I arrived. He didn't say where he was going." Hopefully the light was too dim for John to notice her heightened color. MacGill had realized why she'd come in here; why couldn't John? She put the Repton book carefully back on the shelf. Perhaps he did realize, and just didn't want her here.

He grunted and clasped his hands behind his back.

She could offer to leave, but if she did, she might never again find the courage to open the connecting door. She *had* to persevere.

She had to find an excuse to remove her dressing gown.

"Is it hot in here?"

John blinked. "I don't believe so. Are you warm?"

"Yes." It was a lie for a good cause. "I am."

"I see." He frowned. He appeared to be searching for

words. Was he trying to find a polite way to ask her to go back to her room?

She couldn't leave until she had at least *tried* to seduce him. But she couldn't take her dressing gown off with him staring at her like that. It was too embarrassing.

She needed a distraction. If she could get him to turn away, she could do it.

"Do you think I might have a small glass of brandy?"

"Brandy?"

"Yes." She nodded for emphasis. "I see you have a decanter on the table over there."

John glanced over his shoulder. "Oh. Yes. Certainly."

She slipped out of the dressing gown the moment his back was turned—and shivered. John was correct—it was not overly warm in the room, and now she was as good as naked. Her nipples pebbled into hard buds.

Perhaps he wouldn't notice.

How could he not? They were practically sticking through the gossamer fabric.

Should she put the dressing gown back on?

No. She kicked it off to the side and stepped closer to the fire, resisting the urge to wrap her arms around herself. This was her golden opportunity. She could not squander it for a few minutes of warmth.

John finished pouring the brandy and turned, glass in hand. "Here you—" His eyes found her by the fire.

"Good God."

His mouth fell open as the glass full of brandy splashed to the floor.

Chapter 22

He had died and gone to heaven.

Meg stood in front of the fire, dressed in . . . well, almost nothing. Her shoulders and arms were completely bare, and a thin white gown clung to her breasts and hips like spider webs at sunrise. The firelight behind her illuminated all that the pantaloons had only outlined—the delicate line of her calves, the curve of her knees, the sweep of her thighs, the shadowy curls at—

He reminded himself to breathe.

"Oh, dear. Look what you've done."

"Huh?" She was hurrying toward him. Zeus, there was a slit in the gown's skirt. Her leg from thigh to ankle flashed at him as she walked, teasing, taunting . . .

He opened his arms. He had to hold her. He had to feel her against him. He had to—

She crouched down to examine the rug.

"Do you have a towel to mop the carpet with?"

"A towel?" He moistened his lips. The back of her neck, the curve of her back, the shadowy cleft between her buttocks—all beautiful.

"Yes. The stain is spreading."

"The stain?"

She frowned up at him. "From the spilled brandy."

"Oh." From this angle, he could see her breasts quite clearly. Well, not as clearly as he'd like. He would like them both naked in front of him, close enough to kiss, to lick . . .

If she moved her face forward half a foot, her lovely mouth would be just the right height to—

"What is the matter with you? Why are you just standing there?" She looked down again and picked up the empty brandy glass. "Perhaps you should ring for MacGill."

"No." She was right, though. He couldn't just stand there, dumb with lust. He reached for her. "MacGill would be very much in the way."

She felt his hands on her shoulders—his gloveless, large hands spread over her bare shoulders. His strong, thick fingers, warm and dry, smoothed her skin. The slight friction started a throbbing low in her belly. Her nipples tightened, though not with cold this time.

She shivered.

"Meg." His voice was deeper than usual.

She was afraid to look up. She stared at the spreading damp stain. The carpet was not the only thing growing damper.

His hands slid over her shoulders to her throat. He cupped her chin, tilting her face so she had to meet his gaze.

"Why did you come to my room tonight?"

"Um." She tried to look away, but he wouldn't let her.

"Why did you come to my room?"

She was panting. He was breathing a bit heavily, too. It was time for courage. She stood up; put her hands on his waistcoat.

"To seduce you." She cleared her throat. "To ask you to give me children."

"Ah." He closed his eyes for a moment. When he opened them again, they held a mix of heat and hesitancy. "And you won't mind that your children will lack a title?"

She heard the whisper of pain in the words.

"Of course not. Why would I want a title?"

"All women do."

"Not this woman." She reached up to touch his jaw, and he turned his head to kiss her palm. She smiled. Mmm. Courage. She would give him the gift of her heart. Perhaps knowing she loved him would salve the wound Grace had inflicted. "I've wanted you—I've loved you—since I met you at Lord Tynweith's house party."

He shrugged off her touch, turned away. "No."

"Yes." She wrapped her arms around his waist and rubbed her cheek against his back. He had far too many clothes on. "No one has ever understood my passion for plants. I've always been the vicar's odd daughter, the poor little girl whose mother died when she was just a baby, the sad romp whose father should have reined her in and taught her the proper way to go on, the blue stocking who drones on and on about vegetation." Her voice broke. Why was she crying? None of this bothered her. She'd grown used to it.

John turned back and pulled her close, pressing her face against his chest, tangling his hand in her hair, cradling her head. It felt so good.

"You understood. I could talk to you—really talk to you. And then, after Robbie and Lizzie wed, you went away. It was clear you did not feel what I felt."

He brushed his lips over her temple. "I hate London. And I was afraid. I'd told myself for years I would never marry, and then I met you." He sighed. "Well, I am not very flexible. Ask Mother. She'll tell you once I have a notion in my head, it takes nothing less than a miracle to dislodge it." He raised her face from his chest. "And you, my love, are a miracle."

His lips touched hers gently. She opened for him, relaxing against his body. His tongue stroked slowly into her. It was not a kiss of passion so much as . . . connectedness.

Oh, and passion, too. Her nipples peaked, her breasts ached. Need curled low in her belly, and an emptiness only he could fill grew in her.

"Shall we go to bed?" he whispered.

"Yes, please."

Need such as he had never known surged in him. Meg wanted him. *Him.*

She loved him.

It was beyond comprehension. His mind couldn't grasp it, but his heart could. For once, he let that organ guide him. He took her hand and led her to his bed. He stopped her when she started to climb in.

"Wait." He went down on one knee before her. "I never properly proposed to you, Meg."

She tugged back a little on her hand, but he didn't let her go. "It was an odd situation."

"Yes, it was." He kissed her palm. "So I will ask you properly now. Will you marry me, Miss Margaret Peterson?"

She laughed uncertainly. "Silly. I already have." She blushed. "Do get up."

He didn't move. Instead, he kissed each of her fingers, lingering over her wedding ring. "Will you wed me, truly? Will you be my wife and have my children? Will you love me now and forever?"

She bit her lip. "Yes. Yes, of course I will."

Joy began to bubble up inside him. "And I will love you. In London I gave you my ring. Tonight I shall give you my body."

Meg inhaled sharply. "And . . . and I will give you mine."

He grinned. "Splendid." He had chosen this position, before her on his knee, because it was traditional, but he discovered it also gave him a wonderful view and excellent access to her scantily clad, lovely, seductive body. He reached for her ankles and slid his hands slowly up her legs, over her soft skin, taking the gauzy scrap of fabric she was wearing with him. Up her calves, past her knees to her beautiful thighs.

She was panting now and moaning just a little, her hands on his shoulders, her fingers clutching him each time *his* hands moved higher.

He stopped at her waist. Her lovely private curls were displayed for his inspection.

"John . . ."

Did she sound embarrassed? She tugged on him, as if to lift him from his contemplation.

He kissed the crease where her right leg joined her body.

"John!"

He treated her left side to the same attention.

"John, this is . . . I'm certain you should not be . . ."

Her curls tickled his nose. He loved the heat of her and the slightly musky smell of this secret place.

He had never done this before. He had never wanted to make love to Cat. He'd just wanted release—his release—as quickly as possible.

He was in no hurry now. He wanted to explore, to enjoy. To play.

Had he ever played? Certainly not since he'd grown from boyhood. Certainly not with a woman.

He wanted to give Meg pleasure. Oh, he wanted his pleasure, too. Anticipation of that pleasure hummed throughout his body. He smiled and slipped his tongue into Meg's curls, into the dark, moist—wet—place hidden there. He found the tiny nub—

Her hips jerked, and she squeaked.

"What are you . . . eep!" She pulled on his hair.

He licked her again. She tried to twist away from him, but he held her hips still.

"What are you doing?! I'm sure you should stop that." She pulled on his hair again. "It is most unseemly."

He looked up past her lovely, heaving breasts with their tightly budded nipples outlined against the transparent fabric to her flushed face. "Do you like it?"

"I . . . I am sure I should not."

"But *do* you?"

"Y-yes. I mean, it feels very *odd*." She squeaked again as he licked her one more time.

He gave that part of her a parting kiss and moved upward, kissing her belly, her navel, her waist, her ribs. He pulled the nightgown completely off then, freeing his hands to cup her lovely breasts while his mouth and tongue explored her nipples.

"John. Oh. John." She pushed at him, breaking his concentration finally. "John!"

He drew back. She was flushed and panting, but she had a very determined look in her eyes. Certainly she was enjoying his touch? "What is the matter?"

"You—you still have your clothes on." She took a deep breath, causing her breasts to move delightfully. "You should remove them."

"I should?"

"Yes." She cleared her throat. "I want you . . . naked." She swallowed. "Completely naked."

"Ah." He grinned. So she *did* like what he was doing. "What a wonderful suggestion." He pulled back the bedclothes and lifted her to sit on the mattress. He kissed each breast once more and then stepped back. "I will be happy to accommodate you."

She was going mad. Need was eating her up so all that was left was an aching, throbbing emptiness.

"Hurry up."

He chuckled. "So impatient."

Slowly—too slowly—he unwound his cravat and un-buttoned his waistcoat. He draped them carefully over a chair. Then, *finally*, he grabbed the hem of his shirt and pulled it over his head.

"Oh. Oh, my."

"Like what you see?"

"Yes. Very much." He was beautiful. His arms curved with muscle; his shoulders stretched broad and straight. Short, brown hair covered his chest, trailing over his flat stomach to his pantaloons. She leaned forward to touch his stomach. He was like warm marble.

"Take off the rest of your clothes."

"Yes, ma'am."

He stripped his pantaloons and drawers off quickly and straightened. She sucked in her breath.

The male organ was very odd-looking indeed. John's was startlingly large.

If she understood the process correctly, that very large appendage needed to fit inside . . . She winced.

She could see why the procedure might hurt the first time. Or every time.

Well, she had never been missish, and now was defi-nitely not the moment to start. Emma and Lizzie had lived through the experience—Emma had even said it was pleasant. And John must have accomplished the deed numerous times without killing any women. The human race would not survive if the various procreative pieces did not fit together.

Now that she considered it, babies traversed the same passage, and they were much larger than this organ. Somehow the relevant portion of her anatomy must expand appropriately.

It felt as if it were expanding now.

She glanced up at him. He was watching her intently.

"May I touch?"

His throat moved as he swallowed. "Please," he croaked.

She ran her finger up his length, then took him gently in her hand. This part of him was hard, too—and silky and warm.

Yes, she felt very expansive.

He had licked her. Could she . . . ?

"Meg!"

She could.

"Meg, love, please, that's enough." He sounded desperate. He put his hands on her head and gently moved her back.

"Don't you like it?"

He shuddered. "I love it, but if you don't stop now, things will be over before they begin."

"I don't underst—"

He stopped her argument with his mouth. And his tongue. He pulled her off the bed and pressed her body to his.

Mmm. He felt as good as he looked. She rubbed against his chest and the large organ now cradled against her belly. She ran her hands over his muscled back down to his buttocks.

His hands were not idle either. They slid down to her hips, traced the curves there, and then traveled back to her breasts.

Oh, yes. She felt extremely expansive. And damp. There was no question in her mind—she could definitely accommodate his splendid organ without any difficulty whatsoever. She was anxious to try. Extremely anxious.

He lifted her onto the bed again and joined her on the mattress. His mouth moved from her throat to her breasts. He kissed their tops, their sides . . . and then moved down to her ribs.

She wanted to scream. Her breasts felt so swollen, her nipples hard little nubs crying for the moist touch of his mouth. Surely he knew she wanted him to . . . kiss her there.

She squirmed. He was licking the bottom of her ribcage. That was all very well, but that was not the spot—the spots—most aching for his touch.

Ah, he got the hint. His tongue flicked over one hard nub while his thumb attended to the other.

She almost flew off the bed.

"Do you like that, Meg?"

"Uh." She was beyond coherence. She arched again, encouraging him to explore further. He laughed and suckled her.

This was wonderful—much, much better than any of their other encounters. Naked and horizontal—in a lovely bed behind a lovely closed door—with a wedding ring and the blessings of their families . . .

Yes, this was a wonderful improvement.

But now the spot between her legs was throbbing. She needed him there, too. Immediately. She twisted her hips.

Magic. His lips left her breasts and moved in exactly the direction she wished.

Oh, lud! His mouth had felt heavenly before, but

now the wet rasp of his tongue—just a single stroke—caused her to sit bolt upright.

"John!"

He grinned at her from his position between her legs.

"Are you all right, Meg? You look very flushed. Perhaps you would prefer I stop?"

"No!" She panted. "Don't you dare stop!"

He swept his tongue over her again, and she sucked in her breath.

"But I thought you wanted children?"

"Huh?"

"Children, Meg. A son or a daughter. Not because we have to, but because we want to."

His mouth was on hers now, and his weight was bearing her back against the bed. "Would that be all right with you?"

"Uh." She felt his organ touch her aching, wet place. It just brushed against her, teasing her. "Yes, yes. Please. Now."

He smiled against her lips. "My pleasure."

He came into her, then, slowly filling her emptiness. Too slowly. She pulled on his hips, bringing him closer, feeling a slight burning deep inside, a momentary pain, and then just pleasure.

He was heavy and warm on her. Hot. She reveled in his heat, in the fullness he gave her . . . and then he moved. Out and in again. She was caught between the wall of his chest and the bed, impaled on him, surrounded by him.

It was beyond wonderful, but she needed something more. Each stroke of his body wound her tighter and tighter. The tension was unbearable. She—

"Ohh."

Wave after wave of feeling crashed through her, flooding her with exquisite sensation, and then, in the peace after the storm, she felt a different flooding deep inside her, the warm pulse of John's seed.

She smiled and hugged him as he collapsed onto her.

He felt wonderful. He'd never thought the act of joining could be so . . . overwhelming.

He wanted to stay exactly where he was, but he must be crushing Meg. He lifted himself off and out of her body, then stretched out on the bed beside her. He leaned up on his elbow so he could watch her. Her eyes were still closed; her mouth had the barest curve of a smile.

"Did I hurt you?"

She shook her head without opening her eyes. "Not really."

He put his hand on her breast and she made a small, almost purring noise. "Was it what you expected?"

She turned her face, then, to look at him. "Oh, no, I could never have expected that."

"And it was . . . ?"

She laughed. "Fishing for compliments? I will give them freely. It was wonderful." She rolled to her side and ran her hand up his arm. "I loved it. I want to do it again, very soon." She waggled her eyebrows. "Many times."

Happiness swelled to fill his chest. He had never felt this carefree before.

"I see you are insatiable. That's a very good attribute in a wife."

She grinned. "I want to make you forget Grace."

He brushed a kiss on the top of her head. "Grace? Who is Grace?"

"So I've already pushed your former love from your mind?" Meg smiled, but her eyes were serious. "I hope you do not forget me so easily."

"I could never forget you, Meg." He traced the line

of her eyebrows. He wanted her—needed her—to understand. "I did not love Grace, not in the way I love you. I liked her"—he smiled slightly—"but I liked her land more. She had a splendid spot for a rose garden." His smile broadened. The hurt and embarrassment of that day had faded over the years, but now, in this bed, they truly vanished. Sunlight had lit the persistent shadow. He felt almost giddy. He leaned over and kissed Meg's nose, wrapping his arms around her and settling her against his chest.

Meg cuddled close. "She hurt you."

"Not really. I was embarrassed more than hurt."

"But you swore off marriage."

He cupped one of her breasts in his hand and grinned when he heard her sharp intake of breath. "I was obviously misguided." He flicked her nipple with his thumb and she wrapped her leg over his, pressing against his thigh. "And most importantly, I hadn't met you."

She made a fussy little exhalation. "You met me last year, but you didn't seem terribly impressed."

He ran his hand down to her hip. "I never said I wasn't an idiot, but if I had thought about it"—he kissed her forehead and slipped his forefinger into her hot, wet center—"I would have thought I had no chance with you."

Her eyes were slightly glazed. He moved his finger and she bit her lip.

"Why—" She sucked in her breath sharply as he moved again. "Why do you say that?"

"You wanted a title, didn't you?"

"No—stop that, I can't think."

He withdrew his finger, laying it just outside her entrance. She squirmed a little and then sighed.

"Why would I want a title?"

"All women want titles."

She snorted. "As I said before, not this woman."

He almost believed her. "But then why did you take all those titled men into the bushes?"

"Were they titled?" Meg started moving her hand in a very interesting direction. "I didn't notice." She kissed his chest. "If I couldn't marry you, I didn't much care whom I married."

He caught her fingers before they reached their destination. "But why Bennington? The man's a sap."

"Well, yes, but he *does* have a very extensive plant collection."

"Not as extensive as mine."

She grinned. "I know."

He sat up and stared at her. "You married me for my *plants?*"

She tried not to laugh, but John looked so offended. Surely he knew she was joking? She took immediate advantage of the fact he'd let go of her hand to slide it the rest of the way down his body. "Well, I wasn't aware of the other wonderful thing you could grow."

The thing in question was growing very nicely indeed. She stroked it again, and it swelled and stiffened further.

John's voice shook. "You are a minx of the worst sort, madam. I can see I will have to teach you proper behavior." He sucked in his breath when she used her mouth in place of her hand. "But some other time. A little . . . ah! A little . . . yes! A little improper . . . Oh, God . . . behavior can be . . . Don't stop . . . very *proper!*"

The last word came out in a shout. John flipped her onto her back and thrust into her so deeply she'd swear he touched her womb. She came apart—and a second later, so did he.

She sighed with pleasure. It truly didn't matter if he

owned a hundred acres of exotic plants or one sad ficus, the love he'd sown in her heart flourished past all her imaginings. She tightened her arms . . . and another part of her body . . . to hold him close while she whispered in his ear.

"You know, John, for once we are in complete agreement."

Don't miss this delightful peek
at Sally MacKenzie's THE NAKED BARON,
coming in 2009 . . .

Lady Grace Belmont grabbed the door handle and held on as if her life depended on it.

Damnation, her life *did* depend on it. If she got out of this carriage and went into the Duke of Alvord's brightly lit townhouse—

She shuddered. It didn't bear thinking of. All those eyes, staring at the Amazon from Devon . . .

She tightened her grip, bracing her foot against the inside of the coach. Her very large foot. She glared at the offending body part, clad demurely in white satin. *Why* had the blasted shoemaker felt compelled to share with her the fact that he'd just finished a pair of men's pumps smaller than these slippers? As if she'd needed the reminder that her form was most definitely not ladylike.

Sykes, the butler-cum-footman, frowned and tugged on the door again, but she was prepared. It didn't move an inch. In a moment he'd look up and see her through the window—and have yet another odd tale of Lady Oxbury's niece to spread through the servants' quarters. She leaned back into the carriage's shadowy interior—and felt a small hand push firmly between her shoulder blades.

"What are you doing, Grace?" There was a distinct edge to Aunt Katherine's whisper. "Let Sykes open the door."

"No." Sykes pulled again and Grace's arms jerked forward. She narrowed her eyes and yanked back, putting her considerable weight into the effort. Sykes wasn't going to win this battle.

"Ow!" Two hands shoved her this time, hard enough to push her away. "Stop! You're crushing me."

"Sorry, Aunt Katherine." She looked over her shoulder. Her aunt was glaring at her like a wet cat.

Who would think such a tiny woman could be so strong? Blast it all, who would think a woman who looked as fragile as the finest porcelain would have a niece who was such a . . . a . . . She grimaced. Such a female Gargantua. A damned Brobdingnagian. If they entered the ballroom together, the assembled *ton* would stare just as the tradesmen had these last few days.

Her grip on the door handle tightened.

"Grace, I don't understand why you are behaving this way. It is certainly no surprise that you find yourself arrived at a society ball. We've seen more than enough mantua makers, milliners, and merchants of every stripe since we arrived in London. I think I've been pricked by more pins in the last week than I have in my entire life."

"I know." Grace turned back to give her complete attention to the door. "But I've just discovered that knowing about a ball and actually stepping into the ballroom are two vastly different things. Rather like being told stewed eels are nasty and then tasting them yourself."

"I like stewed eels."

"Then you may have my portion whenever I have the ill luck to find the dish in front of me. And you may also go to this ball without me. I'll be delighted to let Sykes open the door if you are the only one who goes through it."

"Ridiculous. This is your come-out, Grace."

"I'd rather stay in." *Why* did she have to be so large? Her mama had been normal-sized. She'd barely reached Papa's shoulder, if the painting in the family gallery was to be believed. Grace, on the other hand, could examine the top of the earl's balding pate by glancing *down*.

No, Papa had been right. Blunt, but right when he'd expressed his . . . opinion to Aunt Katherine back in Devon.

She remembered every single word. Adams, the Standen butler, had told her Aunt Katherine had arrived, so she'd come down from inventorying the linen to greet her. She'd known why her aunt was there. She'd planned to tell her going up to Town was impossible. She had too much to do at Standen.

She'd been just outside the closed drawing room door when her father had started bellowing . . .

"My God, woman, are you insane? Grace will be a laughing stock if you drag her to Town!"

"But, William—" Aunt Katherine's voice had been considerably softer.

"'But William,' my arse. There's no need to waste the time putting the girl on the marriage mart. Got a neighbor who's agreed to take her off my hands." Papa'd snorted. "Has his eye on a corner of my property which he says is just perfect for some damn flower or other." He'd laughed and she'd heard him open a decanter—probably the brandy. "And this saves him the bother of trotting up to Town, doing the pretty. The man hates London. Don't blame him."

"Still—"

"Good God, let it go, Katherine. Grace likes Parker-Roth well enough, and she's not stupid. She knows his is the best—he'd snorted again—most likely the *only* offer she'll get."

She'd seen red then. Her own father thought so little of her? It was not a great surprise, but still . . . She'd show him. She *would* go to London.

She glared at the coach door handle. Damn, blasted temper! She was too often ruled by it. Well, now she was paying for her fit of pique. Papa was right. This trip to Town had been a huge mistake. Even if she were the proper size, she was much too old for a debutante. She definitely should have stayed home. She did like Mr. Parker-Roth—John. They'd been friends since childhood. She liked his family; she'd be close to Papa—

Well, maybe being close to Papa wouldn't be so wonderful. Still, going husband hunting in London was the height of idiocy. The *height*—ah, indeed.

"Grace, you are being foolish beyond permission." Aunt Katherine gave her another determined shove. "And if you aren't careful, you'll go flying out of this carriage when Sykes finally opens the door."

She snorted. That would be an entertaining spectacle for the duke's guests—Lady Grace Belmont, daughter of the Earl of Standen and niece of the Dowager Countess of Oxbury, landing in an ignominious heap—a very large ignominious heap—on the public pavement.

It was a risk she was willing to take. She most definitely did not wish to grace His Grace's ballroom.

She was larger than Sykes—she should be stronger.

And the fact that she was more than forty years his junior didn't hurt.

"I am not getting out. Tell the coachman to take us—me—home, please."

"I most certainly will not. I did not go toe to toe with your father down in Devon nor did I do battle with the Weasel—I mean, the new Lord Oxbury—for the keys to Oxbury House just to have you cry craven and cower in your bedchamber all Season."

Grace glared over her shoulder at her aunt. "I will not be cowering in my bedchamber."

"Then where will you be cowering?"

Grace blew out a short, impatient breath, causing the tendrils that had worked themselves free of her coiffure to float briefly in front of her eyes. She shook her head. She had been mad to listen to Katherine—mad, mad, *mad*.

Sykes pulled on the door again. She jerked it back again. She watched him frown and scratch his head under his wig.

"I will not be cowering at all, Aunt Katherine. I merely have decided, on further reflection, that appearing at balls and other such social events would be a mistake. I'm sure I would not fit in—"

Katherine wormed her way around to face her. "Not fit in? Why would you not fit in? You are not some upstart mushroom. You're the daughter of the Earl of Standen. You should have taken your place in society years ago."

"Exactly. I am too old now—"

"Too *old*?!" Katherine's hands rose as if to wrap themselves around Grace's neck. "If *you* are too old at twenty-five, what, pray, am I, with forty years in my dish?"

"That's different. I only meant I am too old to make my bows. You have already been about in society—"

"Twenty-three years ago, and then for a mere two months. I hardly believe that qualifies me—ah, Sykes."

"Da—" Grace bit her lip before the curse completely escaped her tongue. Devil take it! She'd let herself be distracted. She'd loosened her grip for just a moment, and the bloody man had taken advantage.

Sykes glanced at her, raising one bushy, white eyebrow. The insufferable servant knew exactly whom he'd been wrestling with. She glowered at him. He bowed and turned to Aunt Katherine.

"I am so sorry, my lady. I can't imagine"—his eyes drifted back toward Grace—"what could be the matter with the door latch. I will have someone look at it the moment we return."

"Don't bother, Sykes. I believe it was merely a temporary problem." Aunt Katherine also looked at Grace. "Just let down the steps. We are holding up the other carriages."

"Very well, my lady."

Bloody hell! The creak of the coach's stairs unfolding must sound just like the French guillotine's blade dropping to sever some poor soul's head from his neck. Her palms were suddenly so wet, they dampened her gloves. She swallowed and drew back. "You first, Aunt Katherine."

"Nonsense." Aunt Katherine glared at her. "Don't think I'm not fully aware of what you're up to, miss. I wasn't born yesterday. If I get out first, you'll slam the door behind me. I believe we've created enough of a spectacle this evening."

"But—"

Sykes extended his hand. Grace looked at it as if it were a poisonous snake.

"Go, Grace."

Aunt Katherine's tone was short and sharp. She must have run out of patience—and she wasn't the only one.

"Hurry on, man," the coachman behind them called out. "I can't keep the horses standing much longer." As if to punctuate this point, one of his grays sidestepped, jingling its harness.

"Lady Grace?" Sykes raised his hand a little higher. She glanced at his face. Perfectly expressionless, except for the eyebrows which jumped impatiently toward his wig.

"Grace . . ." Aunt Katherine sounded as if she were considering shoving her out the door, perhaps with her delicate foot applied to Grace's not-so-delicate derriere.

Grace sighed. Clearly, she had no choice. She was condemned to brave the duke's ballroom.

She took Sykes's hand and left the safety of the carriage.

Thank God! Kate had thought Grace was never going to get out. She followed her niece down the stairs, pausing when her foot reached the pavement. She looked up at the Duke of Alvord's London townhouse.

Lud! It was just as she remembered it, glowing with the light of hundreds of candles. Magical. How could Grace not be enchanted?

Grace did not look the least bit enchanted. She was standing by the green iron fence, arms crossed, scowling at the receiving line. It was so long it had spilled out the front door.

Oh, dear. Apparently the servants' gossip was correct. All the *ton* wanted to see the American female who was living under Alvord's roof—and see whether Alvord's unpleasant cousin would create a delicious scene. That had been one advantage of hiding away in the country. The local gossips were not as vicious as their London counterparts.

Well, there was no point in standing here on the walk like blocks.

"We shall not be late, Mr. Sykes."

Why was the man grinning at her? And he had a distinctly cat-in-the-cream-pot look. Her stomach tightened.

What did he know that she didn't?

"What is it?"

"Oh, nothing, my lady." His grin widened. "I'm just thinking the evening might hold a surprise or two."

A surprise? She did not like surprises.

Perhaps she should have followed Grace's lead and stayed in the carriage. Her stomach tightened further until it was a rock-hard knot.

Dear God! Sykes couldn't mean . . . No, of course not. Yet the gleam in his eyes was most pronounced.

He couldn't mean that Mr. Alexander Wilton would be in attendance?

No. She was letting her imagination run away with her. Alex never came to Town. She knew—she'd been reading the London gossip columns for years. And William would not have let her bring his daughter to London if there was the slightest chance they might encounter a Wilton. He hated that family with a passion that hadn't dimmed in twenty-three—no, thirty-one—years.

Sykes put up the stairs. "You know," he said quietly, so quietly she had to strain to hear, "Lord Oxbury—your dear departed husband, not the current bast—" He coughed. "Well, the old lord wouldn't want you to mourn him too long. He'd want you to find happiness."

"Uh—" Her eyes must be starting from her head. Why was Sykes bringing up *this* topic?

"He knew he was too old for you."

"Oh, no. I mean, I don't, um—" Had Oxbury confided in Sykes? Well, they *were* of an age, and she'd always wondered if their connection was closer than master and servant.

"He would never want you to spend the rest of your life alone."

"No, uh, of course, um, that is, I hadn't thought—"

But she *had* thought. She looked away. Surely the light was too uncertain for Sykes or Grace to notice her flushed cheeks?

She hadn't . . . she had barely admitted it to herself, but she had thought . . . only in a general way, of course . . . that while Grace was looking for a husband, she might also take a glance around the *ton's* ball-rooms. Oh, not for another husband necessarily—though Oxbury's heir was certain to make living in the Dower House miserable—but, well, she *was* a widow, and widows were allowed—almost expected to take—certain . . . liberties.

She'd admit she'd had Marie lace her stays a little tighter than usual—a little tighter than comfortable. Stupid! She'd wanted to look young again, slim and virginal and seventeen. Impossible. Worse, futile. Marie could tighten her stays until the strings broke, she'd still have a deep crease between her brows, lines at the corner of her eyes, threads of gray in her hair . . .

Forty. She was forty years old. Too old for—

Just too old.

Well, this was most certainly not a conversation to be having on the public walk in front of the Duke of Alvord's townhouse with half the gossiping *ton* milling about—and half their coachmen loudly urging Sykes to *get the bloody move on, mate.*

"We won't be late," she repeated, firmly.

Sykes winked, then clambered up next to the coachman. "Right. Have a pleasant evening, my lady."

"Sykes!"

The man just waved as the horses moved off.

"What was that about?" Grace had walked over to stand next to her. At least the odd scene with Sykes had taken her out of her sulks for the moment.

Kate shrugged. "I don't know. One of Sykes's odd starts, I suppose."

"Sykes has odd starts?"

"Well, not that I'd noticed, but being in London can do strange things to a person." It was certainly doing strange things to her. She was actually considering . . . well, *something*.

"Yes." Grace was nodding. "Very strange things. I think we should go home immediately."

"Nonsense. We can't go home—you saw Sykes just left with the carriage." Lud! People were starting to stare at them. "You were eager enough to enjoy the Season before we came."

Grace's brows snapped down. "I was never eager. I was angry. I came to spite my father." She looked back at the receiving line. "But he was right. I *will* be a laughing stock."

"You will not. And don't frown, you'll give yourself wrinkles."

Grace, ignoring her advice as usual, scowled at her. "How can you know the *ton* won't laugh me out of that ballroom?"

Kate took as deep a breath as her too-tight stays would allow. Patience. She must strive for patience. It was nerves that were making Grace so tetchy.

"I can't know the idiots won't laugh, but I do know they won't chase you from the room. You must simply look down your nose at them. You are an earl's daughter, after all. Show some backbone."

Her tone was sharper than she'd intended, but Grace

was not the only one on pins and needles this evening. Why had Sykes mentioned surprises?

A slight breeze brushed her cheek. The noise of the street—the creak and jingle of harnesses, the rattle of wheels on cobbles, the shouts of the coachmen—competed with the drone of conversation that drifted from the receiving line and out of the open windows.

She'd stood here twenty-three years ago, eager for excitement and surprises. Only seventeen, in her first—and last—London Season, she'd had her head full of silly dreams of handsome men and stolen kisses. Of love and marriage. Of happily ever after.

Of fairy tales! At least Grace stood in no danger of falling prey to such airy dreams.

"Come on, Grace," she said. "We need to join the receiving line."

Grace made an odd noise, a cross between a snort and a gag. "Join that revolting collection of fops and toadies?"

"Shh!" What was the matter with the girl? Did she *want* to marry that boring neighbor William had picked for her? "You'll meet scores of eligible young men tonight. Aren't you the least bit—?"

"*Look* at me, Aunt Kate."

"I *have* been looking at you." She tilted her head back to look again. Grace's copper-colored hair was gathered high on her head, a few tendrils escaping to frame her face. She was beautiful—except for the frown marring her forehead and turning her full lips down at the corners. "You know, some small semblance of conviviality would not go amiss."

"Aunt Katherine, I could smile until my face cracked, it would make no difference. No one would notice. No one would *see*. In case you haven't made note of it, I tower over everyone."

"Surely not everyone, Grace. There are tall gentlemen among the *ton*." Alex's face flashed into her memory, but she banished it immediately. "There's sure to be some here tonight."

"Aunt Katherine, this is not the first ball I've attended. We do have some society in Devon. I know how the women will whisper and the men will stare."

"No, they won't."

"Yes, they will. They *are*."

"What?"

Grace looked significantly toward the receiving line. A fop in a hideous canary waistcoat had his quizzing glass to his eye and was directing it at Grace's—

"Oh!"

Kate stepped briskly in front of her niece. Let the mutton-headed nodcock inspect her glaring countenance instead.

"Stupid coxcomb! Just ignore him, Grace."

"But Aunt Katherine—" Grace sighed. Aunt Katherine didn't understand. How could she? She was small and delicate. She'd never had to listen to women gasp and giggle when she entered a room. She'd never seen men's eyes widen—and then widen more as they focused on the most prominent part of her anatomy.

Height was not her only notable attribute.

Thank heavens she'd been able to convince the mantua maker to fashion a high neck on most of her gowns. It had been a challenge. For some reason the woman—and even Aunt Katherine—had had the ridiculous notion that displaying her . . . charms for all the world to see was a good idea. Had they never observed how gentlemen behaved? If she wanted any hope of conducting a rational conversation with a member of the opposite sex, she needed to cover her two most prominent distractions.

She had not won the battle entirely. Three of her ball gowns had scandalously low necks, but she was confident that the problem could be remedied by the judicious use of fichus.

"Come, Grace." Aunt Katherine linked her arm through hers. "You'll have a splendid time once we are finally inside. London is as different from Devon as chalk from cheese."

Doubtful, but there was little point in arguing the matter. No point, actually—as Aunt Katherine had pointed out, the carriage had left. She was stuck here. She could while away the hours amidst the potted palms and chaperones considering how best to persuade Aunt Katherine to let her forgo the Season's myriad social entertainments. She would much rather spend her limited time in Town viewing the sights. This might be—most likely was—her last opportunity to see London. When she wed John, she must be governed by his wishes, and he wished never to stir from Devon and his bloody beautiful gardens.

They joined the receiving line behind a small blonde woman who looked to be close to Grace's own age and two older females.

"The rumors are ridiculous, Charlotte." The shorter of the two older females—the one with the sharp, beak-like nose—sniffed, causing her remarkable nostrils to flare. "Alvord won't marry the American."

The blonde shrugged. "Really, Mother, I didn't think he would."

"I don't know." The other woman was almost as tall as Grace, but thin and bony. "She *is* the Earl of Westbrooke's cousin."

The blonde and her mother stared at the third woman.

"Don't be ridiculous, Huffy." The mother's nostrils

Sally MacKenzie

curled up as if she smelled something particularly offensive. "She's the daughter of Westbrooke's black sheep uncle and some Scottish merchant's spawn. Compared to Rothingham's lineage and my own—well, there is no comparison, is there? Alvord would have to be a complete flat to choose that . . . *mushroom* over Charlotte."

"Well, yes, I see your point—"

"Of course you do. It is as obvious as the nose on my face."

Lud, the woman hadn't actually said that, had she? Grace turned her startled laugh into a cough immediately, but it was too late. She'd caught the woman's attention. Hard little eyes glared up at her.

"Have we met, Miss . . . ?"

"*Lady* Grace Belmont," Aunt Katherine said, stepping closer and glaring back at the woman, "the Earl of Standen's daughter. And I am her aunt, Lady Oxbury."

"Hmm." The nostrils flared. "Lady Oxbury. So it's been a year already since Oxbury died?"

Aunt Katherine could look rather impressively haughty herself. "Indeed. I put off my widow's weeds two months ago." She raised an eyebrow. "I'm sorry, I don't believe I heard your name, Mrs. . . . ?"

Huffy drew in a sharp breath.

The nostrils flared again. "Of course, it has been *so* long since you've graced the *ton* with your presence, we can't expect you to be *au courant*, can we? How many years *has* it been, Lady Oxbury?"

"A few."

The woman smirked. "*Quite* a few." She raised her massive nose higher. "I am the Duchess of Rothingham." She nodded at the blonde. "This is my daughter, Lady Charlotte." Lady Charlotte yawned and played with her fan. "And my friend, Lady Huffington."

Lady Huffington nodded slightly, puffing out her scrawny chest as though she were especially proud to be called the duchess's friend.

The duchess raised her eyebrows and twitched her nostrils at Aunt Katherine. "What, may I ask, brings you to Town, Lady Oxbury?" Her smirk grew. "Husband hunting, perhaps?" She made an odd sound, something between a hiccup and a throat clearing that might have been meant as a giggle. "I've heard the new earl is not so delighted to have inherited his cousin's relict along with the title."

Bloody hell! The woman might be a duchess, but that gave her no right to be insulting.

"Now—ouch!" Aunt Katherine had trod on her foot! Grace turned to glare at her aunt, but Aunt Katherine ignored her.

"I'm here to chaperone my niece, of course, Your Grace."

Surely Aunt Katherine wasn't trying to turn the harpy up sweet, was she? She wouldn't sink that low!

Apparently she would.

"This is Lady Grace's first Season." Aunt Katherine actually smiled at the despicable duchess.

Grace clenched her teeth, clasped her hands, and counted to ten. Lady Charlotte snorted along with her mother. Well, really, Grace couldn't blame them. She *was* ridiculously old for a debutante.

"How"—the duchess glanced at Lady Huffington and raised her eyebrows to her damn turban—"nice."

Lady Huffington snickered.

Grace counted to twenty.

The line advanced, and the duchess's august party stepped through the front door, thankfully turning their elegantly attired backs on them.

Grace bent to her aunt and hissed, "I can't believe you didn't kick that old harridan in the shins."

"Grace!" Aunt Katherine sent a furtive glance at the duchess's back. "Shh! We don't want to annoy the duchess."

"*You* may not. I don't give a flying fig whether I annoy her or not."

"Well, you should. You don't want to make such a powerful enemy."

"That's ridiculous."

"It is *not* ridiculous."

The gentleman and lady behind them paused their conversation to look at them. Aunt Katherine took Grace's arm and urged her forward.

"London is not Standen, Grace. Everyone knows you in the country; your reputation and your father's title protect you from malicious gossip. But here in Town . . . Well, the duchess could ruin your Season before you step into Alvord's ballroom."

"Gammon! I don't believe a word of it."

"Believe it." Aunt Katherine's mouth formed a thin, straight line.

"But they are just in front of us. They can't—"

"They *can.*" Aunt Katherine's mouth twisted. "Gossip runs like fire through straw in London."

Her voice held a distinctively bitter note. Had she been scorched by the *ton's* tittle-tattle? How could she have been? As the duchess had said, it had been years since Aunt Katherine had been in London. Was that why she had stayed away, because of some ancient *on dit*?

Impossible. Aunt Katherine was the pattern card of composure and restraint. Even when she'd been arguing with Papa at Standen, trying to persuade him to allow this trip, she hadn't raised her voice. No, surely

Aunt Katherine had never done a scandalous thing in her life.

They stepped into the entry hall then and Grace's mouth dropped open. She snapped it closed when she felt Aunt Katherine's surreptitious tug on her arm.

She was not completely green. Papa was an earl, after all; Standen was a large, stately pile. She had been to a number of balls and parties, but nothing compared to this.

The broad marble staircase, sweeping up from the wide entry with its black and white patterned floor, was crowded with men in precisely fitted black coats and snowy white cravats and women in debutante white or gowns of brilliant colors, their heads adorned with turbans or flowers or ostrich feathers, their necks dripping with jewels. And the noise! The sound of so many conversations reverberated, becoming a roar. It was hard to imagine how anyone could understand a word.

She and Aunt Katherine made their way slowly up the stairs—Grace looked back to see that people were still coming in the door—and down the receiving line. The duke was young—not yet thirty at a guess—and tall, taller than she, as was the Earl of Westbrooke. Even the American girl, the earl's cousin, Miss Sarah Hamilton, was roughly Grace's height, though of a slighter build.

"See," Aunt Katherine said as soon as they'd stepped through the wide double doors into the ballroom, "you did not tower over the duke or the earl or even Miss Hamilton. You have been in such a pucker over nothing."

"Hmm." Could it be that she wouldn't stand out here as she did at home? She looked out over the crowded ballroom and felt a small frisson, a slight shiver of excitement. Perhaps this trip to Town would not be a complete disaster. Perhaps Papa was wrong. "I might have overreacted slightly."

"Might have?" Aunt Katherine shook her head. "There's no 'might' about it. I thought you were not going to leave the carriage."

"Well—"

"And now look." Katherine made a small, graceful gesture encompassing the ballroom. "You have all of society at your feet."

"Until we descend these stairs and join the crush."

Katherine grinned. "True. So take a moment before we do"—they stepped aside to let another couple, just free of the receiving line, pass down the steps to the ballroom—"to look. I see a number of tall gentlemen— and I daresay they see you."

"Ack."

Katherine actually giggled. "Shall we make our way to that poor man over by the ficus? Or the one by the windows? Or perhaps the two gentlemen by the . . . by the—oh, dear God." Aunt Katherine turned as white as a sheet; she put her hand on Grace's arm as if to steady herself.

"What is it?"

Grace turned to see what—or who—had so disturbed Aunt Katherine. She saw two gentlemen, partially hidden by a clump of potted palms. Aunt Katherine was focused on a tall, pleasant-looking man, with dark hair, graying slightly at the temples. A distinguished looking gentleman, not alarming in the slightest. What could be the matter with Aunt—

Her gaze traveled to the other man.

Oh, my.

The second man was even taller than his companion and roughly ten years younger. His black coat stretched tightly across impossibly broad shoulders. His hair, dark blond and slightly longer than fashionable, waved back from his broad forehead. He had deep-set eyes, high cheekbones, a straight nose, firm mouth . . . and was that a cleft in his chin?

He was staring at her. A very odd feeling began low in her belly. Lower even. A heat and a heaviness. A dampness.

She flushed. Could he tell?

Aunt Katherine's fingers dug into her arm. "I . . . I . . . I need to go to the ladies' retiring room," she said. "Now!" Retiring—no, retreating—sounded like an excellent notion.

ABOUT THE AUTHOR

A native of Washington, D.C., Sally MacKenzie still lives in suburban Maryland with her transplanted upstate New Yorker husband. She's written federal regulations, school newsletters, auction programs, class plays, and swim-league guidance, but it wasn't until the first of her four sons headed off to college that she tried her hand at romance. She can be reached by email at writesally@comcast.net or by snail mail at P. O. Box 2453, Kensington, MD 20891. Please visit her home in cyberspace at www.sallymackenzie.net.

Discover the Romances of
Hannah Howell